FALLING FOR
Nashville

JANE RHYAN

Edition I, published July 2018
Edition II, published November 2021

ISBN: 978 0 6453545 08

Typesetting, Formatting, Proofreading & Cover Design by
Little Lace Proofreading & Design
www.littlelace.com.au

TRIGGER WARNING

This book contains scenes and storylines that involve cheating or possible cheating.
If this is not your thing, read on at your own risk!

For Jirrico

Chapter One

• DARCY •

Packing the last of my boxes, I look around the empty living room. The bare off-white walls, free of my favourite artworks and photos; the little dents in the carpet where items of furniture once stood. I created so many great memories in this apartment, and I'm sad to be leaving it behind, but I just can't stay here anymore. The good memories have been overshadowed by the bad and it's time to move on and make a fresh start. New city; new job; new friends; new life.

As I load the last box into my hatchback, I look back towards the apartment, convincing myself I'm doing the right thing. It's time to do something for myself. I slide my key into an envelope and drop it into the mailbox as my landlord requested, and jump behind the wheel.

The drive to Summerlake from Blackborough will take me a little over six hours and I'm looking forward to hitting the open road and turning the radio up.

After a few hours of car karaoke, I decide to stretch my legs. I pull into the main street of Northwell and make my way to the local bakery. Sitting on the verandah eating my lunch, I watch the world stroll by. The bakery is certainly the place to be at this hour, with a constant flow of customers lining up out the door. After a quick bathroom break, I head back to my hatchback destined for Summerlake.

This time, I complete the drive in silence, with only my thoughts to keep me company. I'm starting to get excited—thinking about the new job I'm starting in just over a week. I've been employed as Great Scott Design's newest Graphic Designer. It's been over a month since I left my previous design job, so I'm looking forward to getting back into work and being creative again. I'm also excited about working with my new boss, Jesse Scott. I've heard lots of good things about him, and know he is very respected. Although I was only interviewed via video conference, I certainly get the feeling that he'll be easy to talk to and great to work with.

He's still only young, probably only a few years older than my twenty-six. He wears his sandy blond hair short at the back, but longer on top. He takes pride in his appearance—I can tell that just from our brief meeting. He is extremely easy on the eye too. I know he'll have no lack of female attention.

As I near Summerlake, I program the address of the real estate agent's office into my GPS, and head in that direction to collect my new house keys. The apartment I'm renting is already furnished with the basics, and the removalist company I've hired to transport the rest of my belongings, is due to arrive later this afternoon.

With my new keys in hand, I pull into my new driveway and park under the carport in the spot closest to my apartment. The agent informed me that I'm sharing the driveway and carport with my neighbor, who lives in a smaller apartment behind mine. We also share an outdoor living area and back garden. I make a mental note to go out back and introduce myself once I'm settled in.

Later that afternoon, the removalist's bring in the last of my boxes and leave me to the unpacking. I actually enjoy this part—finding new places for all my things, and turning my apartment into a home. I have a reasonably sized modern kitchen, overlooking a large open plan living area. A large LCD TV hangs on the furthest wall, which I can see easily from my kitchen. Between that, sits a large comfy chocolate suede couch, complete with matching throw cushions and a large wooden dining table that seats six.

Past the kitchen, I follow a small hallway that leads to a laundry, guest bathroom, guest bedroom and master suite complete with ensuite. I have all I need. I decide to set up the main living area first, and then make my way back to complete the bedrooms after that. Boxes surround me. The task seems daunting and I decide I need sustenance if I'm going to make any dent in the unpacking tonight. First, I'll have to find my local supermarket to buy some basics and something for dinner.

I grab my keys, jump in my car and head down the road in search of a supermarket. My street is gorgeous and leafy, with beautiful Jacaranda trees on either side forming a glorious canopy over the road. When the breeze blows it creates a stunning shower of purple trumpet-shaped flowers.

I locate a supermarket just two minutes down the road—the perfect distance to walk if I want to. I head in and grab the essentials—milk, coffee, sugar, bread and a frozen pizza for dinner; not something I would normally eat, but I want something super quick and easy tonight.

Rather than head straight back home, I decide to go for a little drive around the neighborhood to see what I have close by. I need to locate a gym, as I haven't been in a few months, and I'm feeling incredibly out of shape. I'm normally very dedicated to my workouts, but with everything that's happened in the last few months, I've become slack and let myself go a little. I'm petite, but I can certainly pack a punch. It's important to me to stay fit, toned and healthy and I decide I'll head out for a run tonight before bed—like I used to. Running before bed always helps me fall asleep, something I've really struggled to do in recent months.

On my drive, I locate lots of interesting looking little stores that I plan on visiting in the near future. I also locate a library, which is an important find, as I love nothing more than to curl up on the couch with a good book after my evening run.

Heading back onto Emerald Avenue, I turn into my driveway and cut the engine, then grab my bags of groceries from the back seat. As

I step out of my car, I hear the rough rumbling of an engine and turn to see a black motorcycle pull into the drive. It roars to a stop next to me as I shut my car door.

The rider is clad in black boots, faded blue denim jeans and a black leather jacket. He's wearing a shiny deep red helmet with the visor down. Even sitting on his bike, I can tell he's tall and well built. He has a definite air of confidence about him though. I give him a friendly smile as he swings his leg over the bike, and he returns a polite nod without removing his helmet. He *is* tall, around 6" 3', at a guess. He casually strolls off toward the apartment behind mine while fiddling with his helmet. He's intriguing, but considering he's now unlocking his front door, I decide the introductions will have to wait until tomorrow. My neighbor enters his apartment still wearing his helmet, without even a backwards glance.

I enter my apartment with groceries in hand and set them on the kitchen bench. I place the milk in the fridge and turn on my oven to heat the pizza, then place the last few remaining items in the large walk-in pantry. While waiting for the pizza to cook, I start on one of the many boxes waiting for me in the living area. The first box I open contains most of my books, so I push it carefully towards the large wooden bookshelf that's leaning against the side wall. I love to read, so my collection of novels is varied and extensive. My friends back in Blackborough never needed to visit a bookstore or library when in search of a good read, they always knew where to come instead. I unload book after book onto the rows of shelves until my first box is empty.

Taking in the smell of my cooking pizza, I head over to the oven and pull it out to check if it's ready. With the crust just starting to burn, I turn off the thermostat and place the round pizza tray I found earlier, onto the metal dish drainer next to the sink. Realizing I have absolutely nothing to slice the pizza with, I rummage around in a few boxes marked *kitchen* until I find some utensils. I cut a few slices using a large butcher's knife, sit on one of the breakfast bar stools and proceed to eat straight from the tray. *Classy all the way!*

Re-thinking my unpacking strategy, I decide to hit the kitchen boxes next. It's near impossible to do much without them sorted. Once I've made significant progress, I decide to head to my bedroom to find my workout gear. I really want to get that run in before bed. It's a mild, beautiful night, so I unpack my black full-length yoga pants and a hot pink fitted tank. I lace up my runners and head to the living room to find my house key, phone and AirPods. I shove the AirPods into my ears and make my way out the door. Once outside, I complete a few stretches before heading off down the driveway. I notice the motorcycle is still there, so I turn and see that the rider's apartment light is on. I think about going back and knocking on his door, but decide against it and instead continue up the driveway and turn onto the footpath.

Heading up my street, the breeze is cool but refreshing as I watch Jacaranda flowers fall from the trees in a purple shower around me. I pick up the pace with music pounding in my ears. I love upbeat, motivating tracks to keep me focused, and I spend the next hour tuning out the world and concentrating on my breathing. As I continue to run, I start to feel a little disorientated. I stand on the corner of two streets that look very similar to mine with my hands on my hips catching my breath, looking in both directions trying to decide which way to go.

As I look around in the darkness, I start to worry a little as a few cars pass by, wondering which direction is home. I make a decision to go left, when I hear a familiar beefy rumble coming up behind me. As I turn around, I see that same deep red helmet atop black leather pulling up beside me.

"You look lost," comes a sexy deep voice with an American accent.

"No, I'm fine thanks," I respond politely.

"Which way are you headed?"

I turn and point to my left.

"If you're heading home, I think you'll want to go the other way," he replies with a chuckle.

I look back towards the way he's directing as I feel a blush come over me.

"Oh, okay thanks," I reply, feeling stupid.

"Hop on, I'll give you a ride. You look exhausted."

"No seriously, I'm fine. I'm happy to run home. Thanks for your help though, I appreciate it."

"I insist. It's dark, and I wouldn't feel right leaving you here by yourself when you're obviously not really sure where you are."

"Um, I'm not sure. I've never ridden on a bike before. Do you have another helmet?"

"I don't, but you can wear mine, and I'll take it slow. We're not that far from home, and we won't be travelling on any main roads. Hop on."

He removes this helmet and extends it towards me with a raised eyebrow. I worry my bottom lip, trying to decide whether or not to take it, but conclude that he seems harmless.

I nervously look around and quickly hop on the back of his bike. I look for something to grab onto behind me, but come up empty.

"What do I hold onto?" I ask.

He turns around with a smile in his eyes and says, "me."

He has the most beautiful chocolate brown eyes I have ever seen— deep and full of warmth. I could get used to looking into those eyes.

"Oh, um … okay." I sound like a stuttering fool.

"Just wrap your arms around my waist and hold on tight."

I do as he says, and nervously clasp my hands around his middle. Even through his leather jacket, I can feel the hard ridges of his abdomen. He's all muscle.

"Ready?" he calls back.

"Yep, I think so."

"Great. I'm Travis Gardel, by the way."

"Darcy Hastings," I reply.

"Nice to meet you, Darcy Hastings."

He turns back around with a nod, and puts the bike into gear. I hold on for dear life as we take off at a ridiculous speed, and I feel him chuckle beneath my arms. *Smart ass!*

Chapter Two

• TRAVIS •

Darcy Hastings. It's a pretty name and it suits her.

I feel her arms tighten around me as I pull out fast into the street, and I have a little chuckle. Poor thing must be terrified—I should have some fun with her!

I race down the road, much faster than I should, and she grips me so tight I think she might crack a rib. We're only a few streets away from home, but I decide to weave around a few extra back roads just to make the trip last longer. I can feel her thighs squeezing me tight as she holds on for dear life. As one hand makes its way up my body and clutches on to my chest, I feel my heartbeat going a million miles an hour. I pray she can't feel it through my leather jacket. It's been a while since I've had a woman wrapped around me like this. The last woman I had on my bike was Laila, but I don't want to think about her now. I'm enjoying my time with Darcy too much.

As I slowly pull into our driveway, I've barely come to a stop when Darcy jumps off the bike.

"Oh my god. You said you'd take it easy, you maniac!" she screeches as she whacks me on the arm.

"I did," I laugh mischievously. "Are you okay?"

"Yeah, I'm fine," she recovers quickly. "Just a little shaky from the ordeal you just put me through."

I chuckle again and she gives me another swat across the arm.

"Do you take pleasure in torturing women on that bike of yours?"

"Not usually, but you have to admit, that was kind of fun."

"Fun! It was terrifying. I honestly thought I was going to die tonight."

"Not a chance," I say, "I'll look after you."

She looks at me with unconvinced narrowed eyes.

"Thank you for the ride home. I suppose I was a little lost."

"No worries at all Darcy, any time. It does take a little while to get used to the streets around here—they all look the same."

"Can I offer you a coffee or something?" she asks, while looking at the ground.

In her mid-twenties, with big blue eyes, long wavy chocolate-brown hair that's pulled into a ponytail, and a petite figure, with curves in all the right places—there is no way I'm going to knock back an offer to get to know this girl. I know I shouldn't, considering I'm not staying in the country for very long, but there's just something about her that calls to me. She's mesmerizing—enchanting even. *How corny is that!*

"I don't have much yet," she adds, "but I do have coffee."

"I'd love a coffee," I reply.

She smiles nervously and leads me through the front door into her apartment.

Chapter Three

• DARCY •

I can't believe that I just asked a complete stranger into my apartment for coffee. *What am I thinking?* I'm thinking—this guy is completely hot, and I should never let him out of my sight! If his gorgeous southern accent isn't enough, I now have to contend with his beautiful face. He is honestly perfect.

He has that rugged look going on, with amazing tanned skin. His face is square with a jawline that looks like it's been chiseled from granite, and he has this gorgeous dimple in his right cheek, that I just want to dip my tongue into. His eyes are a stunning warm chocolate brown, set under manicured brows. Travis obviously takes pride in his appearance.

As I head to the kitchen to make the coffee, I notice him removing his leather jacket. *Oh Lord have mercy!* He's wearing a tight white t-shirt with faded blue denim jeans, and a belt with a thick silver rectangular buckle—very cowboy-like. His t-shirt showcases every defined muscle across his chest, abdomen and broad shoulders, it's true perfection. As he turns around to place his jacket over the back of the couch, I get a view of his back—and what a back it is! I swear I'm about to combust at the sight of him!

I gather myself, and ask how he takes his coffee.

"Cream with one sugar, thanks," he replies.

"Um, does that mean milk? I'm not really up with the American lingo."

"Yes, milk is perfect, thank you," he chuckles.

I walk around the kitchen bench towards the couch he's sitting on, hand him his mug and take a seat at the opposite end.

"Tell me about yourself," he says after taking a sip.

"There's not much to say really, I'm pretty boring."

"I highly doubt that. Why the move? Are you from Summerlake?"

I shift nervously, not really wanting to divulge my life's story to this stranger just yet.

"No, I moved here from Blackborough. I just wanted a fresh start."

His eyebrows rise as he considers what I said, and if I'm honest, he suddenly looks rather uncomfortable.

"What about you," I ask.

"I'm originally from Memphis, Tennessee, but have been living in Nashville for the past twelve years. I moved there when I was twenty-one."

I quickly do the math in my head, which puts him at thirty-three. Seven years older than me—I can work with that. *I think you're getting ahead of yourself, Darcy!*

"What did you do in Nashville?" I ask him.

"I'm a musician."

This time it's me with the raised eyebrows.

"Wow, that's hot!" I say, before my brain has time to catch up to my mouth.

He looks surprised, and totally pleased with himself, as he chuckles quietly.

"Oh, I mean, umm, I'm sorry, I mean that's really interesting. What sort of musician?" *Nice Darcy, real nice. I must be beet red right now!*

"I dabble with a bit of everything, but I mainly sing and don't go anywhere without a guitar."

"Country music?" I ask.

"Of course, is there anything else?"

"Obviously not," I grin.

"What do you do for work," he asks me.

I explain how I'm about to start work at a well-respected design agency as a graphic designer, which I'm really excited about. I talk about my new boss, Jesse who seems lovely, and how I'm looking forward to making some new friends.

"Have you moved here permanently," I ask him, "or are you heading back to the States?"

"I'm here for the time being. I'm taking some time off, and don't have any set plans as to when I'll go home, but I am gigging a bit at a local bar while I'm here. You should come and hear me play sometime."

"I'd love to," I say genuinely. "When's your next gig?"

"Tomorrow night at a bar called, *The Den*."

"I'll be there," I smile.

We continue talking for another fifteen minutes, before the topic of family comes up—my sore point.

"Tell me about your family," Travis says.

"I don't have any family," I reply quickly.

"None at all?" He looks shocked.

"None I want to talk about."

"That's cool, I can appreciate that. We don't have to talk about anything you're not comfortable with, but know I'm here if you ever change your mind."

"Thanks, I appreciate that—although we have only just met each other."

"I know, but I have a good feeling we're going to become great friends."

"Is that so."

"It is," he smiles with a nod.

I give him a huge grin—I think he's absolutely right.

"What about your family then," I ask him. "Am I allowed to ask you that question considering I didn't tell you about mine?"

"Of course! I have a great family. Big and super loud, but they're all amazing and I love them to death."

I smile happily at him. I can see in his face just how much he loves them. His eyes absolutely light up.

"Obviously there's my mom and dad, but I also have three brothers and one sister. I'm the baby of the family."

"Five kids? Wow!"

"Yep, life is always busy in our family home, especially on holidays. Are you ready for the barrage of names?"

"Yep, hit me with them."

"Okay, well, my eldest brother is Leo and he's married to Ava. They have three kids—Rupert, Ivy, and Holly. Then there's my brother, Kelly, who's married to Jade. They have two girls—Sophie and Charli. Next is my third brother Wren and his wife, Drew. They have one daughter Evie. My sister Quinn and her husband, Ryan, have two girls—Everly and Haven. Then there's me, the runt of the family."

"Wow, if you're the runt, I'd love to see the others!"

He lets out a hearty chuckle.

"Maybe you will someday."

"Do they all live in Nashville or are they still in Memphis?"

"Actually, once I moved to Nashville, they all gradually followed a few years later. Although I'm the runt, it seems I'm the favourite."

He smiles a cheeky grin, and I can't help but give him a smile in return.

"So, you've never married?" I ask him hopefully.

He immediately looks at the floor and takes a deep breath.

"Umm, actually, I am married," he says rubbing the back of his neck and keeping his eyes on the carpet.

My heart drops so quickly, I feel like I'm going to be sick. This is not what I wanted to hear.

"Oh, I just noticed that you weren't wearing a wedding ring," I say apologetically.

"No, it's a perfectly reasonable thing to assume. My wife, Laila and I, are actually going through a divorce right now. That's kind of the main reason I moved over here—to get away from it all for a while."

"I'm really sorry. Is it amicable?"

"No, unfortunately. I found out Laila had been having an affair with my best friend for the good part of a year. We had a prenup, but now she's not happy with the terms and is dragging things through the courts trying to get more money out of me. The prenup had a fidelity clause, which means she'll lose out pretty badly financially, so she's fighting that now, saying I can't prove she cheated. Walking in on him and her in our bed was all the proof I needed," he says sadly. "It's become pretty messy, but my lawyer is dealing with all that now. I just wanted time away from the whole horrible mess."

"I'm so sorry you're going through that," I sniffle as a few sneaky tears roll down my cheeks. I brush them aside quickly, hoping he hasn't noticed. He must think I'm some kind of crazy woman crying over him like this. *If he only knew.* He doesn't need my burden on top of his own horrible story.

"It's okay, I'm okay. Are you alright?"

"Yeah, I'm fine," I say, quickly jumping up from the couch. "Did you want a refill," I ask him.

"No, I'm fine thanks. I should probably be heading off anyway and leave you to your night."

"Okay, no worries," I say as I head to the kitchen with our mugs.

He stands and collects his jacket from the back of the couch, before making his way to the door. I follow him to unlock it and hold it open for him.

"Thanks so much for this," he says. "It was really nice talking to you. Hopefully, we can do it again sometime soon."

"I'd love that," I say.

He reaches out to shake my hand and I put mine in his, but he pulls me forward instead, and places a kiss on my cheek that lingers just a second or two longer than I would normally expect, and I feel a bolt of electricity zap through my body. Wow! If that's how I respond to a kiss on the cheek, I can only imagine what his lips would feel like on mine. *Stop thinking like that! The poor man is going through a divorce!*

"I'll see you around," he says.

I give him a polite nod and watch as he makes his way around to his apartment. I close my door and flop on the couch, feeling completely exhausted. *Oh boy, I'm in trouble.*

Chapter Four

• TRAVIS •

As I throw myself on my couch following my coffee and chat with Darcy, I can't help but think how much I enjoyed talking with her—although her emotional reaction to the news of my divorce was a little unexpected. There's obviously more to her story than she was willing to share with me at this stage, which is fine.

Without thinking, I invited her to hear me play at the bar tomorrow night. I really want her there, but it could make things a little tricky if I want to keep my true identity a secret. Changing my surname while I'm in Australia, was the only way I could keep that part of me hidden a little, although I have had people recognize me now and then. So far, I've managed to brush them off that I just look like Nashville country music star, Travis Danvers. It does get a bit harder when I'm actually performing at the bar though. My fans are used to the big stage shows and my enormous backing band, whereas here, it's just me and my guitar. I've actually really enjoyed going back to my roots for a bit, and Australia doesn't have anywhere near the fan base that the States does. It's such a novelty to be able to walk down the street without being ambushed and followed by the paparazzi. I'm really enjoying being 'Travis Gardel'.

Before I head to bed for the night, I decide that I really need to check in with my manager. Picking up my phone, I dial home.

"Travis! Do you know what time it is? Whatcha been up to man?"

"Hey Brant, sorry I wasn't thinking about the time. What is it there, like 4.30am?"

"Yeah, around there. You're lucky I'm still out at a launch party, and coherent enough to even speak to you."

"Geez, I don't miss those all-nighters. How are ya?" I ask.

"Can't complain. You comin' home yet, or what?"

"Haha, yeah not yet mate. I'm really enjoying the time off. I may never come home."

"Don't even joke about something like that. It's boring around here without you to stir things up."

"I'm sure you're enjoying the break too."

"Yeah, well I'll be much happier when things go back to the way they used to be," Brant says.

"Yeah, I know buddy. I need more time here though. I want to make sure everything has blown over before I head back to Nashville."

"Yeah, I get it, but don't stay away too long."

"I probably need at least another few months, mate. I've only been here seven weeks. Do you think you can handle things till then?"

"Yeah, we'll make it work. It's been crazy in the lead up to Lacey Wilde's signing, so that's keeping me busy."

"Good. How's she going?"

"Yeah, doing good. A little overwhelmed by it all I think, but she's taking it all in her stride. I think she'll be great. Good for the label to have some new blood."

"Good to hear. Look, I'll let you get back to it. I'm about to head to bed, but I'll chat again soon. Say hi to all the crew for me."

"Will do mate. Take care."

"You too, bye."

⌘

The following morning, I hop on my bike and head to the gym. I pull into the parking lot and grab my bag off the back of the bike. Pulling out my swipe card, I let myself in and make my way to the change rooms. I quickly change into my workout gear and place my bag in a locker. Heading out onto the floor, I notice a few of the regulars, plus a host of new faces too. I make my way to the treadmills first for a warmup jog. Most are in use, so I start toward one that's between two young women near the end of the row.

The woman on my left is running flat out with headphones in her ears and totally focused, completely unaware of anything around her. The woman on my right is quite the opposite. She's jogging leisurely and looking all around the floor. As I catch her eye, she gives me a huge grin and flicks her long blond ponytail over her shoulder. I climb onto the treadmill and start it up at walking pace, gradually increasing speed until I'm at a steady jog. Blondie next to me, sees this as her cue to start up a conversation—the one thing I hate when working out.

"Hi, I haven't seen you here before. I'm April," she says in her over-bubbly, high-pitched voice.

"Travis," I nod politely.

"Hi Travis. Is this your first time here? I love this gym, I'm here most mornings but I've never seen you before, and trust me, I would remember you. You obviously work out somewhere regularly, with arms like that."

Is she gonna take a breath! She eyes my biceps up and down and gives me another grin while batting her eyelashes at me. *Oh boy!*

"I really love a man who knows how to look after himself and makes the time to keep his body in peak condition."

Why did I forget my headphones, today of all days! I just smile politely and turn up the speed a bit, hoping she takes the hint. She doesn't. She babbles on and on about who knows what, and I just try to tune her out without appearing rude. Every now and then, I look in her direction and give her a smile, but each time I do, she gets all giggly and tries to touch my arms. *Seriously, who does that when someone's on a treadmill!*

After about twenty minutes, I give up and move over to the rowing machines. Unfortunately, Blondie follows, continuing on with her mindless babble and blatant ogling. This time, I completely tune her out—she doesn't pause to take a breath to let me fit a word in anyway. After about ten minutes of this, I get up and wipe down the machine with my towel and look around for where I can head next where it'll be difficult for her to follow. I decide on the free weights, as it's more of a male dominated area, and perhaps, she might find someone else to latch onto.

Of course, she follows but at least she doesn't focus all her attention on me. Instead, she chooses to flit amongst all the guys in the area, parading herself. Most seemed pissed that she's getting in the way and interrupting their workouts, although one dorky looking guy is doing all the peacocking he can to get her attention. Unfortunately, it doesn't work, and she comes back to hover around me again.

Deciding to quit early, I look in her direction and give another polite smile.

"Nice to meet you, I might see you back here again some time."

"Oh, you're heading off?"

"Yeah, I need to get going."

"Oh, well can I give you my number? I'd love to have coffee or something with you sometime."

She bats her eyelashes at me and holds onto my forearm with a pleading look in her eyes.

"I'm actually seeing someone, so that wouldn't be appropriate," I lie while I brush her arm from mine.

"Oh, I don't mind," she says with a smile that I'm sure she thinks is sexy.

"Well, I do."

I quickly head to the change rooms to take a shower, and once I'm dressed, I peer out the door to see if the coast is clear. I notice Blondie back in the free weights area talking to a big bulky guy covered in tatts, so I make my way out quickly without a backward glance.

As I walk to my bike, I remind myself to get here a bit earlier next time—and not to forget my headphones—that is a mistake I will not make again!

———◦◦◦———

Setting up for my gig at *The Den*, all I can think about is Darcy, hoping she'll turn up. She wasn't home earlier when I popped over to give her the details of my gig, so I'd slipped a note under her door. Hopefully, she's since been home and seen it.

My set is starting in fifteen minutes, and I'm so distracted looking around for Darcy, that I can hardly concentrate on getting ready. My backup singer, Ella, can't seem to hold my attention for more than a few seconds, and I'm sure she's starting to get really annoyed with me—particularly as she's a little nervous about a new song we're performing tonight.

After I went to bed last night, I could not get Darcy off my mind, so I got up and started strumming on my guitar, and before I knew it, I had a new song. Considering Darcy had inspired it, I thought tonight would be the perfect night to debut it. Ella loves the song but is not a fan of singing something new with only five minutes notice. We'd run through it together a few times to give her an idea of the melody, and being the professional that she is, she picked it up with ease, but I can tell she still isn't very happy with me.

Dead on nine o'clock, Frank the bar manager, gives me his usual nod to tell me I'm up. I take one more look around the bar hoping to see a familiar beautiful chocolate-brown-haired girl with blue eyes, but I'm disappointed when I can't spot her. I step onto the stage, introduce Ella and myself as usual, and we start our set. We play two songs, and between the second and third, Ella pulls me aside as I grab a drink, asking if everything is all right. I apologize for being a little distracted but promise to get my head in the game. She gives me a knowing look and turns back to her microphone.

Our third song is a soft ballad, and I finally feel myself relaxing into my normal rhythm. Singing about broken hearts and lost love, I shut my eyes and let the song take over, really feeling like myself again for the first time tonight. As the song comes to an end, I look up over the large crowd to acknowledge their applause, and my breath is literally knocked from my lungs—because she's here—sitting by herself a few tables back from the stage.

She. Is. Beautiful! Her long hair is down and falls around her shoulders in soft waves. Her black fitted halter-neck dress, skims across every one of her perfect curves, and how she manages to stand in the killer fire engine red heels she has on her feet, I will never know. She looks very different from the casual Darcy I met yesterday. She's a knockout!

She catches my eye, and I give her a quick smile and a wink. She offers a warm smile back, and I'm rewarded with a gorgeous blush. Turning to Ella, I whisper that I want to sing the new track. She nods, and I start on the guitar.

"This is for Darcy," I say into the mic.

I look up and catch Darcy with her mouth open and her face the color of her shoes. I give her another smile before I start singing. Every now and then when I look up, I notice Darcy sipping her drink, with a gorgeous grin plastered across her pretty face. Her eyes are fixed on me, and my heart is pounding in my chest, and I'm certain everyone in the bar can hear every beat. As the song finishes, the bar erupts and I notice Darcy stand and applaud along with them, with a shy look and a shake of her head. She's special, this girl. I just know it.

After two more songs, I announce that we're taking a short break. I let Ella know I'll be back soon, as I place my guitar on its stand.

"Darcy, hey?" she asks in an inquisitive tone.

"My new neighbor," I inform her.

"Aha," she smiles and turns to head off stage.

I jump down and head in Darcy's direction, but before I make it to her table, a familiar looking blond jumps in front of me and grabs both my arms. Pulling me in, she kisses both my cheeks and rubs her hands up and down my biceps like she's trying to warm me up or something.

"Travis," she yelps. "April, from the gym this morning. How are you, sweety? I can't believe I ran into you here of all places, and you're a singer! I love a man who can sing. You really are the whole package, aren't you?"

"April, hi, nice to see you again," I lie as convincingly as possible. "I'm actually here with someone, so I really should get back to her. I might see you around sometime."

I make to move around her, but she grabs my arms even tighter and pouts her lips at me.

"What about that coffee, another time then?" she asks.

"I don't think my girl would really appreciate that," I reply.

I remove April's hands from my biceps and say goodbye, before I head towards Darcy's table.

She looks up and catches my eye, and I flash her my brightest smile.

"You made it," I say enthusiastically.

"Wouldn't have missed it," she says. "Sorry I was late though."

"No worries at all. We have another set to play in about fifteen minutes."

"You're really good," she says.

Now it's my turn to blush a little.

"Thanks," I smile while looking down at the table. I never get shy around girls. *What on earth is going on with me?*

"I can't believe you dedicated a song to me. It was beautiful," she says.

"Thanks. I actually wrote it last night after we talked."

"Are you serious! I thought it sounded a little specific to what we'd talked about. You are seriously talented, Travis."

"Stop … you're going to give me a big head in a minute."

She giggles and continues to sip her glass of wine.

"How often do you sing here," she asks.

"I usually do about four nights a week. Just depends on what I have going on, or if the bar has any special events on."

"I'll have to come back again."

"Yeah?" I ask in excitement.

"Absolutely. Your voice is amazing. I could listen to you all night."

I cannot wipe the grin from my goofy face. I could fall hard for this girl, and that would be a bad thing considering I can't stay in the country for more than a few more months. Besides, I'm not even certain that she is into me. She certainly doesn't seem to mind me, so that's a good sign I suppose.

"Who's your friend over there?" she asks, looking in the direction of April, who looks thoroughly pissed off.

"Oh, her name's April. I met her at the gym this morning. She can't seem to take a hint though. I have no idea how she knew I'd be here. I'm sure it's not a coincidence. I told her you're my girl, just to get her hands off my arms. I hope you don't mind?" I look at her a little embarrassed.

She looks at me and giggles.

"Apparently, I'm the whole package," I shrug.

"Is that right?" she asks with a raised brow.

"That's what she tells me. What can I say?" I reply with a chuckle.

Darcy laughs along with me, just before she looks over my shoulder with a slight frown.

"She's heading this way," she says. "Play along."

What? Play along. Okay!

The next thing I know, Darcy slides over onto my lap and wraps one arm around my neck, while running the other hand down my chest. She then leans in to whisper something in my ear.

"I hope this is okay, and I'm not making you too uncomfortable? I think it's working though, because your friend looks absolutely filthy."

I have to use everything within me to hold myself together.

"No, it's totally fine. Whatever you have to do," I smile. "Just don't let her get at me again."

Out the corner of my eye, I can see April slowly approach from the side, and as Darcy said, she doesn't look happy. Before I know what's happening, Darcy leans in and plants her soft lips right over mine.

I'm in so much shock, that I'm sure my heart just stopped beating. When she moves the hand that was on my chest up to cup my face, I think my heart is going to give up altogether. *This girl has guts, and boy can she kiss!* All too soon, she pulls away with a beautiful radiant smile. She jumps from my lap, so I can stand up, and then wraps her arms around my waist and looks up into my face.

"You better get back up there, Trav," she says with another chaste kiss to my mouth. "All your adoring fans are waiting."

No one calls me Trav. Not even Laila called me Trav. I love the way it sounds coming from her. *I honestly think I just fell in love.* I look at Darcy in absolute wonder, then turn to head back to the stage, when the cheeky minx gives me a little slap on the ass. I turn back to her in shock, and she just giggles at me and sits back down.

As I get to the stage, Ella corners me.

"You never told me you were seeing this new neighbor of yours."

"I'm not actually. She really is just my neighbor. She was just playing the part of my girlfriend to get rid of a crazy stalker woman."

"Geez, if that's playing a part, you're in trouble, my friend."

"Tell me about it. I think I'm in love," I smile, looking over at Darcy.

Ella laughs as she heads to her mic, and I pick up my guitar ready to commence our next set.

"Hey y'all, glad you could stick around. I'm Travis Gardel, and this song is called *Crossroads*."

I start strumming my guitar as the crowd starts to join in around me. Throughout my set, I look over at Darcy more often than I should—I'm sure by now she's thinking I'm some sort of creeper. After a few songs, I look up and notice that April is talking to Darcy. She still doesn't look happy, but Darcy can't seem to wipe the smile from her face. *I'd love to know what they're talking about.*

All I can think about is finishing my set, so I can get back to Darcy. Perhaps I can offer her a ride home again. Have her wrap her arms around me again. Yeah, that's a plan, although she probably drove herself here. Damn!

Finally, our set comes to an end, and the bar erupts with cheers and whistles and the crowd swamps me as I try to climb down from the stage. Everyone wants selfies and I try my best to smile, but all I can think about is getting to Darcy. Eventually, the crowd clears a little, and I spot her still sitting at her table, with April lingering nearby.

As I get closer, Darcy stands and calls out to me.

"Hey baby, you were so good!" she says. She pulls me into her arms and plants another soft kiss on my lips. *There is no way I can let this girl get away.*

As she steps back, I give her a huge grin.

"You're really enjoying this, aren't you," I say.

"I am actually," she giggles. "That April woman is a nasty piece of work. She's not going to give up you know. She's determined to have you."

"She can be as determined as she likes, it's not going to happen."

"She even had the nerve to ask me what you're like in the bedroom—can you believe that!"

"You're kidding! What did you tell her?"

"That you're mind-blowing!" she says with a raised brow and a smirk.

"Mind-blowing, huh?"

"Yep, that seemed to knock the wind out of her sails a bit, although now that I think about it, she'll probably want you even more now."

I laugh at how much Darcy seems to be enjoying this game.

Chapter Five

• DARCY •

When I arrived at *The Den* earlier, I was shocked to see the crowd that had formed around the stage Travis was performing on. It was just him on his guitar and a female backing singer, singing a beautiful country ballad. Travis had his eyes closed, so hadn't noticed me yet. The women around the front of the stage, were swooning and trying to touch his legs.

He totally has the cowboy look going on—black boots, faded blue denim jeans, a belt with a big silver buckle, a tight-fitting black t-shirt that shows every defined muscle on his perfect chest, and a black cowboy hat. He is totally sexy, and every woman in the bar thinks exactly the same thing. I keep my eyes on the stage and drink him in, while he still had his eyes closed.

As the song finishes, the crowd goes nuts, and Travis looks up and thanks them. As he looks over the audience, he catches my eye and gives me a little smile and a wink. I smile back, but instantly feel myself blush. *Damn, I hate the effect he has on me!* He turns to his backup singer and says a few words, and she nods her approval. I take a sip of wine and wait for the next song to start.

"This is for Darcy," he says into the microphone.

What! I feel my mouth fall open and can do nothing to close it.

He sings about two friends, and how good it is at the beginning when you're getting to know each other over coffee. There are mentions of rides on the back of a motorcycle, new starts, families and generally lots of the things we had spoken about last night. I'm gob smacked!

As the song comes to an end, the crowd goes crazy again, and I stand to give my applause. Travis looks at me and I give him a shy smile while shaking my head.

Once he's finished his set, I can't help but let my true self, and my playfulness, come out. Helping him keep that April woman away was so much fun!

"Did you drive here," Travis asks looking at my glass of wine.

"No, I thought I might have a few drinks so I got a cab."

He nods.

"Do you usually hang around for a while after your gigs?" I ask.

"Not normally. I'm not much of a fan of desperate drunk women trying to grope me from all directions," he smiles.

"No?"

"No," he replies firmly.

"You could have your pick of any woman in this bar," I say looking around.

"I'll admit, I used to love this. Having all these women throwing themselves at me, but it gets old pretty quickly. I'm not like that anymore. I know what I want and it's not that."

"What *do* you want then?" I ask.

"Someone to love. Someone who loves me. Someone to spend my life with," he shrugs. "Honestly, since I left Laila, I've been pretty lonely. I've got great friends and an amazing family but it's not the same, you know?"

I nod. Yep, I did know.

"I want to go to sleep with someone I love wrapped in my arms, and I want to wake up with her too. I want someone to treasure, to adore, to spoil. All that mushy stuff."

He looks at me with an embarrassed smile.

"Do you think that sounds pathetic?"

"Not at all," I say honestly. "I think that sounds perfect."

With that, he stands abruptly and hits his palms on the table.

"Well then, I think it's time to head home," he says.

"I'll just call a cab," I reply smiling.

"No, you won't, I'll give you a ride."

"No really, I'm fine. Besides, there's no way you could carry me plus your guitar and cowboy hat on the back of your death trap."

"Death trap!" he replies in mock offence. "I'll have you know; I've not died once while riding my bike."

"That's really good to know," I laugh. "But last time I rode with you, I literally saw my life flash before my eyes."

"I promise to take it easy this time, and I bought a spare helmet with me just in case. You'll be safe with me."

"What about your hat and guitar?"

"I leave them both here, locked in the storeroom. I have another guitar at home I practice on," he says.

I look at him with narrowed eyes.

"I promise to take it slow," he implores.

I sigh. "Okay."

"Great, let's go."

He grabs my hand and I feel a shiver run right through my body.

"Hey, shouldn't you say goodbye to your girlfriend," I tease.

"Nope, you can say goodbye if you want to though."

I turn back to where April has been standing and watching us. She has that bitter scowl still plastered across her face, so I give her a huge smile and a cheeky wave. I then turn back around, but not before I reacquaint my hand with Travis' sexy, firm ass. Her eyes narrow and I hear Travis gasp. I laugh out loud as I pull him toward the door.

"I can't believe you just did that," he says with a giant grin. "You're a cheeky brat, aren't you?"

"I'm sorry. I just wanted to give April something to remember me by. I hope you don't think I'm like one of those women trying to feel you up."

"I think you did more than feel me up tonight, don't you?" he says with a smirk.

I drop my head, suddenly feeling very awkward.

"I was joking! I'm sorry," he laughs. "I didn't mean to make you feel bad. I honestly had a blast with you tonight. I can't believe how gutsy you are. It totally made my night a whole lot easier. You'll have to come along to all my gigs from now on to protect me from the poachers."

I look up at him and smile.

"Well, maybe. You obviously have no idea how to fight them off yourself," I reply.

With that, he laughs and lifts me onto the back of his bike.

Chapter Six

• TRAVIS •

I can't believe how much fun I've had with Darcy tonight. She's so playful and gutsy, especially when April is around. Perhaps she's a possessive type when it comes to relationships. I kind of hope so, I like it when a woman protects what's hers.

I'm the same when it comes to relationships—overprotective. Perhaps that's why Laila wandered. She'd never mentioned or indicated that she felt suffocated by me, but I know I was probably too possessive. Maybe that's why it hurt so much when I found out she'd been with Sam for so long. All my overprotecting had been for nothing. It had been going on under my nose for nearly a year.

Now I have Darcy on the back of my bike again, with her arms wrapped around my torso, and it feels amazing. I can imagine myself being very protective of her; she's a special woman, and I want to be able to protect her, to tell everyone that she's mine, and I'm hers. But I'm getting ahead of myself. I have no idea if she's interested in me, and even if she is, would it be fair to pursue something with her, when I'm moving back to Nashville soon?

I should just let her be and enjoy getting to know her as a friend—but I don't know if I can do that. She's captured me in such a short space of time. The feeling both thrilling and terrifying all at once. I want her in my arms. I had a taste at the bar tonight and now I'm hungry for more.

As we ride home in the darkness, I feel her face pressed against my back. When we stop at some traffic lights, I turn around and ask her if she's okay. She nods and gives me a tight squeeze.

When we pull into the driveway, I jump off the bike and then lift Darcy off. I help her with her helmet before I remove mine.

"Thanks so much for inviting me out tonight, I had so much fun," she says.

"No, thank you. I probably would have been eaten alive tonight if it wasn't for you."

"Yeah, that's true," she giggles. "Aussie girls obviously love the sexy American cowboy thing."

"Sexy American cowboy, hey," I laugh.

She looks away embarrassed.

"Coffee?" she asks quickly.

"Love one," I respond with a grin.

Darcy leads me inside, and I notice all the boxes are gone.

"Wow, you've been busy today," I say.

"Yep, I locked myself away all day and only stepped out quickly to grab some groceries. I hate being unorganized and not knowing where things are."

She heads for the kitchen to put the kettle on.

"Cream and one sugar?" she asks with a grin.

I smile. "Yes, thank you."

"So, did you like the music tonight?" I ask.

"Are you kidding? Like would be a massive understatement. You are seriously talented, Travis. I've never been into country music much, but you converted me tonight. I could listen to only your voice for the rest of my life and be completely happy—and I love music!"

"Wow, that's quite the compliment," I reply feeling a little chuffed.

"It's truly warranted. You're amazing."

"Thank you," I smile.

Darcy brings our coffees over to the couch and we sit in the same spots we did the night before.

"So, when do you start your new job?" I ask.

"Tomorrow actually. I'm starting to get a little nervous.

"I'm sure you'll be great. What's your boss like?"

"He seems great. His name is Jesse Scott. He's young, probably only a few years older than me. I've only met him via video conference, as that's how I was interviewed, but he seems easy to talk to and very friendly—very easy on the eye too," she smirks.

"Oh, I see how it is," I force a smile.

"No, I would never go there again. Mixing business with pleasure is a bad idea."

"Again?" I ask.

She looks at the floor with a frown, obviously realizing her mistake.

"Yeah," she looks up at me sadly, "I've mixed the two before and it didn't end well."

I watch her with concern, waiting to see if she'll give me any more. I don't want to press her on something if she's not ready to share. She fidgets with her fingers around her coffee mug and lets out a soft sigh.

"I met my last boyfriend, Adam, at work," she says. "We worked in the same office, both as designers. It wasn't long before we moved in together. You'd think that working together so closely, and then also living together would get to be too much, but it worked for us—or so I thought. We'd been together for four years when I started to notice that he was going out for lunch a lot. He usually just ate lunch at his desk, but he suddenly seemed to have a lot of business lunches off-site. I questioned him about it, but of course, got the brush off, and he was always able to show me which client he was meeting with. One day, I had an afternoon conference that I was attending. I'd planned to change outfits, but realized that I'd left everything home that morning. So, before my conference, I ran home to change. I wasn't expecting to walk in on Adam in bed with my sister."

"Oh God, Darcy, I'm so sorry," I say with my head in my hands.

"Apparently, it had been going on almost daily, for two years. Even my parents knew about it and didn't seem to have a problem with it.

They figured that since he was cheating, it meant there must have been a problem in our relationship—that I obviously wasn't satisfying him—and I should be happy for my sister. Can you believe that?"

I'm sitting here in shock, shaking my head. How could anyone do that to this beautiful woman? Who in their right mind would give her up?

"Needless to say, that day I lost nearly everything in my life—my boyfriend, my parents, my sister, most of my friends and my job. I couldn't go back to work after that. There was no way I could work alongside him anymore. Anyway, he's now shacked up with my sister and all my stuff. That's why I moved into a fully furnished place—he moved out while I was out for the day, and they took all our furniture. I didn't bother to fight it; I just didn't want to see either of them again."

"Geez, Darcy, that's just messed up. I don't know what to say," I reply honestly.

She smiles sweetly at me.

"I'm so sorry I just unloaded all that on you when you've gone through a very similar situation yourself recently."

"Don't be, I'm so glad you told me. I can tell that was hard for you to do. I completely understand, although you've lost a hell of a lot more than I have. I realize now why you said you have no family. Shit, that's screwed up."

"It's not a situation I ever thought I'd find myself in at twenty-six years of age."

"No, I guess not."

"Anyway, I'm looking forward to a fresh start tomorrow."

"I hope you get absolutely everything you're after, Darcy."

"Thank you," she says. "You're really easy to talk to."

"I'm glad. You can talk to me anytime. I'll give you my cell number and you can call it whenever; day or night and I'll be here in an instant."

She gives me a soft smile.

"You're sweet."

"I try," I grin.

"Are you planning on writing any songs tonight?" she asks shyly.

I laugh. "No, not tonight. I actually really need to do some laundry, I haven't done any in about a week, so I'll need to go and sort that, so I can head to the laundromat first thing in the morning."

"Oh, you don't have a machine at your place?"

"No, my place is much smaller than yours. I don't have a laundry room."

"Don't waste your time and money at a laundromat. You're more than welcome to use my laundry whenever you need," she says.

"No, honestly. The laundromat is fine, I wouldn't feel comfortable imposing on you like that."

"I'd actually appreciate the company. Besides, laundromats are the most boring places on earth! Plus, I always keep the coffee stocked and you're welcome to help yourself to it any time."

"Seriously, who offers that to a stranger?"

"I don't know," she chuckles, "I just feel like I can trust you."

"You absolutely can. I mean that, Darcy. You can trust me. Us southerners were brought up to be gentlemen."

"I can see that," she says with a soft smile.

"Well, it's getting pretty late—I should leave you to it, especially considering you have a new job to start tomorrow."

"Yeah, of course. Thank you again for tonight, I had a great time—not just at the bar, but thanks also for listening to my sorry story."

"You're more than welcome, any time—remember you have my number."

"Thank you."

Darcy leads the way to the front door and unlocks it.

"I'll see you later then," I say with a gentle smile.

Darcy leans up on the tips of her toes, puts her hands on my shoulders, and kisses me softly on the cheek.

"Bye, Trav," she says.

'Trav' … what are you doing to me, Darcy Hastings?

Chapter Seven

• DARCY •

As I walk into the building of Great Scott Design, I look around at the modern, airy office space. It's funky and quirky with neutral décor, but with bursts of color here and there. You can tell it's a very creative space. I make my way to the reception desk, introduce myself, and ask to see Jesse Scott, my new boss.

The receptionist is friendly and tells me her name is Winnie, before buzzing Mr Scott.

"I've been looking forward to meeting you, Darcy," says Winnie. "We're a bit over-run with men here, so it'll be nice to have another female around the place. We'll have to have lunch sometime once you're settled in, so we can get to know each other."

"I'd love that, thank you so much," I reply.

Just then, Mr Scott walks around the corner. He's dressed in a perfectly tailored charcoal suit, white dress shirt, and charcoal pinstripe tie. He's much taller than I was expecting and even better looking in person than he appeared over my laptop screen.

"Darcy! So nice to finally meet you in person," he says.

"You too, Mr Scott. I'm really excited about the opportunity."

"Please call me Jesse, we're pretty casual around here."

I give him a nod and soft smile.

"How about I show you to your office first, and we can talk there."

My own office, wow!

"Sounds great, thanks."

Jesse leads me to my new office, which happens to be right next door to his. He has a large corner office with glass walls, except for the wall separating ours. Mine is similar but smaller, and it's further along the corridor. There are only two other offices like mine; the rest of the staff share a large communal area with modern cubicles. It's not what I was expecting at all. I was sure I'd be in one of those cubicles.

Once I've dropped my bag at my new desk, Jesse takes me next door to meet my other office neighbor. Ben is another young guy, not much older than me, with a mop of dark wavy hair and a friendly face. He is very energetic and quickly jumps up to shake my hand.

"Nice to meet you, Darcy. I look forward to working with you."

"Thanks, Ben, you too," I smile.

Next door to Ben is Dexter. He looks quite a bit younger than me, and has a definite surfer look about him, with longish blond hair and a killer tan.

"Great to meet you, Darcy. Where are you from?"

"I've just moved here from Blackborough," I say.

"Oh yeah, not much surf in Blackborough," he replies.

"Nope," I giggle. "Not much at all."

"You ever been surfing before?" he asks.

"No, I can't say that I have."

"Well, now you're here, I'll have to take you away surfing for the weekend sometime. A lot of us here go away now and then."

"Sounds like a lot of fun, thanks," I say.

"Shall we meet the rest of the team?" Jesse asks me.

"Please," I reply.

"Nice to meet you, Dexter."

"Dex," he responds.

"Nice to meet you, *Dex*," I smile.

Wow, I have never met a friendlier bunch of people—especially all together in the one workplace. With his hand on the small of my back, Jesse leads me out into the communal area with all the cubicles. As we come to the center of the room, Jesse suddenly lets out an ear-piercing whistle, and everyone stops and looks in our direction.

"Holy cow," I say with a laugh and a hand clutched to my thumping heart.

"Sorry," he chuckles. "I should have warned you I was going to do that."

"All good," I smile. "I'll just put my heart back in my chest now."

"Everyone, I'd like you to meet our newest Senior Graphic Designer, Darcy Hastings. She's just moved here from Blackborough, so make her feel welcome. I'll send her around to meet you all throughout the day, before I get her started on some real work. Alright, back to work, slackers," he says.

He turns and directs me back to my office. As we enter, I go to sit on one of the chairs opposite the desk.

"Hey, your chair is on the other side," he says.

"Oh, you sure?" I ask.

"Of course, it's your desk."

I move around to sit in my new chair, and Jesse takes the seat I had just vacated.

"Thanks for all the introductions," I say. "Everyone seems incredibly friendly and happy to be working here."

"We're a really great team," he says. "We try to keep things fun, casual and friendly, which improves productivity and makes everyone want to put in their best. We're actually all under thirty, so we love socializing together on weekends, or after work at the pub on the corner or a local bar. You don't have to join us, but you're always more than welcome."

"It sounds amazing," I say. "The only person I know in Summerlake is my new neighbor, so it will be a great way to meet people."

"You don't have a boyfriend, husband, partner?" he asks.

"Nope, just me," I reply with a smile.

"Great, I think you'll fit in perfectly around here. Most of us are single too, there are only a few of the cubies who are attached."

"Cubies?" I ask with a puzzled expression.

"Oh, staff that work in the cubicles. Just a pet name we call them."

"Oh okay, I'll have to remember that."

"Well, I have to head off shortly for a client meeting, so I'll let you settle in for a bit. You can boot up your laptop, and I'm sure there'll already be emails to go through. As soon as you feel comfortable, make your way out to the cubies one-by-one, and they'll introduce themselves. They're all great people, so I don't think you'll have any issues. I'll be back just before one o'clock, and I'll take you out to lunch so we can get to know each other better; that's if you don't have any other plans?"

"No, I'm all good. That sounds great, thank you so much."

"Great, I'll leave you to it then. Oh, I forgot to mention, the break room is at the end of the corridor next to Dex's office. Help yourself to tea, coffee, biscuits, whatever you can find in there—it's for all staff, so make yourself at home. I'll catch you later."

"Thanks, Jesse."

He gives me a huge smile and heads out the door toward his office. I lean back in my chair and sit for a few minutes just taking everything in. Everyone seems amazing so far. What a great place to work! I decide to boot up my laptop and have a look through my emails. I soon find out that most are either junk or jokes sent between staff. There is one from Jesse to all staff, giving details of where drinks will be held tonight. He encourages everyone to be there, considering it's my first day, and he wants to make sure I feel welcome and part of the team. I'm surprised to see that the suggested location is, *The Den*. I wonder if Travis will be playing tonight. I doubt it though, considering he was only there last night.

The only other email that grabs my attention, is from someone internal named Cole Breyman. He informs me, that a group email has been sent to all the male cubies, who are placing dibs on me— apparently, I'm a 'hottie'. He politely asks me to refuse the advances of all other interested males in the office, and to let him buy me my first drink tonight—thus enabling him to win the bet.

I'll have to find out which cubie this Cole person is. Maybe I can have a bit of my own fun with this situation.

I decide to make a start on the cubie introductions and make my way around the floor. Winnie, the Receptionist, was right about there not being many women here. Out of the fifteen cubie staff, only three are women. Besides me, all the other senior staff are men. The ratios surprise me, as where I worked in Blackborough, the ratios between men and women were almost fifty-fifty. I wonder if there is a specific reason for it. I make a mental note to ask Jesse over lunch.

As I make my way around to all the cubies, I find them all to be equally as friendly as I did the senior staff. All are in their early twenties. Everyone seems casual and fun-loving, and nearly everyone makes a point of telling me to make sure I come along to as many staff social events as I can, as Jesse loves the sense of team building they provide. Besides official staff events, most of these guys seem to hang together, or even live together anyway. They're all like a big family. Just the kind of environment I need to become a part of. I'm so excited about this job.

I eventually introduce myself to Cole Breyman, who I learn is a twenty-year-old skateboarding enthusiast. He's ever the charmer and practically begs me to let him buy me my first drink tonight. Apparently, whoever manages to win over the new girl by buying her first drink, is given the honor of being the top dog cubie for a month. This role includes a lot of great perks and in his two years working here, he is yet to achieve the title. I ask him about some of the perks, and tell him I'm willing to offer a trade. I'll give him the honor, in return for some of his winnings. He also has to bring me coffee every morning for a month. He happily agrees and the deal is done. He also reminds me, that this is our secret. I'm happy to oblige—it should be a fun night. I'm certainly going to play it up and let him sweat a bit about it though.

After an interesting lunch with Jesse, where we talk about a few of the clients I will be working with, the rest of the day flies by in a blur. Before I leave for the day, I pop my head into Jesse's office and tell him I'm heading off. He reminds me about drinks at *The Den* at eight o'clock, and I assure him I'll be there.

"Excellent, I'll see you there then," he says with a huge smile.

⸺∞⸺

As soon as I get home, I search my wardrobe for something to wear to drinks. I want to make a good impression with my new colleagues, plus there's also the chance that Travis might be there. His bike wasn't in the drive when I got home, so there's a possibility that he's performing somewhere tonight.

I want something that's young and sexy and made for dancing the night away. I decide on my metallic silver, backless fitted mini dress with my silver dancing heels. I also have a silver clutch that will go with it perfectly.

I jump into the shower and wash my hair using my favorite fruity shampoo. Once I've dried off, I start blow-drying my hair and decide on wearing it down in soft curls. I throw on my dress and heels and call a cab so it will be here by the time I'm ready. For my makeup, I decide on soft smoky eyes and nude glossy lips. Just as I finish, I hear a car horn outside and run out to the cab. It's ten minutes after eight so I'm running a little late, but that's fine, I hate arriving at these sorts of things right on time.

As I walk into *The Den*, I notice our group in the back far corner, so I make my way over. As I get closer, Jesse spots me, and a huge smile lights up his face.

"Here she is everyone!" he announces happily.

Everyone cheers and claps and makes a giant fuss over me, and I feel myself turn beet red.

"You look amazing," Jesse gushes as he looks me up and down.

"Thank you," I reply shyly.

He places his hand on the small of my back and leads me to the bar.

"I believe there might be a bit of a fight amongst the men for your attention tonight," he declares with a smile.

"Is that so," I reply.

He gives me a soft shy nod.

As we reach the bar, one of the cubies, Denver, quickly rushes over and asks if he can buy me a drink.

"You know, I'm actually fine at the moment thanks," I smile.

"Okay, no worries," he says with his head dropped as he walks away.

I continue making small talk with Jesse, as a multitude of other guys approach and ask to buy me a drink. I give them all a similar answer, which in turn produces the same defeated look. If Cole doesn't approach very soon, he's going to lose this deal—I'm getting thirsty!

Just then, the DJ turns the music up, and Winnie comes over and asks me if I want to join the girls on the dance floor. I'm more than happy to oblige. Winnie, I and the only other female staff, Isla, Alice, and Colby, make our way to the floor. Gradually the space starts to fill up and we find ourselves in the middle of the pack having a great time. Some of the guys have decided to join us, and each of the girls has a partner to grind up against. I'm quite happy as I am, but then I feel a hand on my naked back.

"Can I join you?"

I turn around to see Jesse standing there.

"Absolutely," I reply. "Can you dance?"

"I'll give it a crack," he responds with a grin.

He puts his hands on my waist, and I place mine on his shoulders. Under his black dress shirt, he has broad shoulders that taper down to a trim waist. I can feel that he is extremely muscular—another man who obviously looks after himself. He isn't wearing a tie, and the top two buttons of his shirt are undone where I notice a small patch of chest hair poking through the gap.

"How am I doing?" Jesse asks after a little while.

"You're doing great," I say with a smile.

Just then, the song finishes and a slow ballad comes on.

"Are you okay to continue?" he asks me.

"Sure," I reply.

Jesse pulls me further into him and places one hand on the small of my back while keeping the other on my hip. I bring my hands up to rest behind his neck and my chest presses into his as he begins to sway me to the music. He's actually really good, and I feel myself relaxing into him.

"You've done this more than once before, haven't you?" I ask him.

"Maybe a few times," he smirks.

I give him a playful jab to the ribs and he laughs. We make a little more small talk as best we can over the music, and when the song comes to an end, I indicate that I need a drink. He leads me off the floor and toward the bar. As we get close, I see Cole approaching me—finally, I think!

"Darcy, do you think I might be able to buy you your first drink," he asks.

"I'm not sure that I'm ready for a drink yet. Thanks though," I reply.

I'm dying for a drink!

He looks at me with wide eyes, and I just smile sweetly at him. He walks off in shock and starts talking to one of the other cubies. They're all laughing at him and he looks dejected.

"Are you going to torture the poor guy?" Jesse asks me quietly.

"Just for a little bit," I reply with a smirk.

"You're going to fit right in here," he smiles.

I chuckle and turn to watch the rest of the girls tearing it up on the dance floor. They're having a great time, and I look forward to getting back out there with them again. After chatting more to some of my colleagues, I decide I should quench my thirst, and put Cole out of his misery.

I walk over to the group of guys he's talking with, and he catches my eye.

"How about that drink?" I ask him.

"Really?" he responds with a look of shock.

"Absolutely," I reply. "Dancing made me really thirsty, and what girl wouldn't want the cutest guy here to buy her a drink?"

He practically runs to the bar and orders me a strawberry mojito which he brings back to me, and I take a grateful sip.

"Thank you," I say with a kiss to his cheek.

He turns bright red, and our whole group starts whooping, cheering and slapping Cole on the back. He looks bloody pleased with himself.

"Three cheers for the new top dog," Jesse calls. "Hip, hip."

"Hooray, hooray, hooray," everyone replies in laughter.

I put my arm around Cole with a smile.

"I look forward to my daily morning coffee," I say quietly. "I take it white with one, thanks."

"Thank you," he whispers in my ear.

"You're welcome," I reply.

I notice that the girls have made their way off the dance floor for a rest, and are sitting in a corner booth. I grab my drink and head over to join them.

"Darcy!" they all chime.

"Hey, what's the gossip?" I ask.

"Alice was just mentioning that she has a thing for Patrick," Isla says.

"Which one's Patrick?" I ask looking over at the men.

Isla points to one of the guys standing in the group with Cole. He's definitely cute, and I notice him looking over regularly at Alice too.

"I think the feeling might be mutual," I say.

"I don't think so," Alice says. "He hardly says two words to me."

"He's probably just shy," I reply. "Why don't you ask him to dance? That'll break the ice."

Alice looks around the table at us all.

"Do you think so?" she asks.

"Go for it," we all say.

We watch as she nervously walks toward Patrick. She whispers in his ear and he nods at her with a smile. Success! They walk to the dance floor and soon become swallowed by the crowd.

"So, are you single?" Colby asks me.

"I am," I reply.

"I think Jesse's interested," she says.

"What? What makes you say that?"

"Well for starters, he never dances with the female staff, and secondly, he can't seem to take his eyes off you," Winnie says.

I look over in his direction and sure enough, he's looking right at me. I give him a quick smile and turn back to the girls.

"You're all imagining things. He's just being friendly on my first day," I say.

"Uh-huh," Winnie replies with a giggle.

In the background, I vaguely register the DJ introducing a live act, but it's impossible to understand him with the amount of noise in the bar. The girls and I finish off our drinks before they head back out onto the dance floor, and I make my way back to the bar to talk to some of the other guys. I don't want to stick to one group too much. I want to mingle as much as I can tonight, to show that I want to be a part of the team.

I join Ben, Dex and a cubie named Harley, for some small talk, before I recognize a familiar voice singing into the microphone. I look up, excited to see that Travis is standing behind the mic.

Before long, the three girls race up to me and beg me to join them on the dance floor.

"You have to come down to the front of the stage with us," they chirp. "The singer is a crazy-sexy cowboy."

Ben, Dex, and Harley all look at each other and roll their eyes. Then I see Jesse join the group.

"What is it about women and cowboys," he asks the others. They all shake their heads.

"They're hot," Winnie yells back as she pulls me away.

"I can't disagree," I call back as I'm dragged into the crush.

I follow the girls as we make our way to the front of the stage. When we get there, I notice that Travis is singing an upbeat number, but he has his eyes closed. All the women near the front, are going crazy over him—acting like love-sick teenagers and swooning all over the place. It's hilarious to watch. Winnie, Isla, and Colby are right amongst it, drooling all over him, so I decide to play along and join in the fun!

We're all screaming his name, trying to touch him, and begging for him to look in our direction. When he finally opens his eyes, it doesn't take long for him to recognize me right in front. He looks at me with a stunned expression, but hardly misses a beat. I reach up to try and touch him, and he reaches back and grabs my hand. The girls around me go crazy so I play along, throwing my arms in the air and jumping up and down screaming like a high schooler. Travis is doing his best to hold it together, but I can see he's struggling. I'm having a blast when Isla reaches over and yells in my ear.

"Oh my god, I can't believe he touched you. You're so lucky!"

I can't help but laugh.

When Travis finishes his song, he tells the crowd he's going to bring the tempo down a bit. The women scream again.

As Travis starts up a beautiful ballad, I feel a hand on my back, and Jesse leans into my ear.

"Do you think I could steal another dance?" he asks.

I nod and smile, then glance at Winnie who gives me an 'I-told-you-so' look. I shake my head and turn to Jesse.

Chapter Eight

• TRAVIS •

As I commence a slower ballad, I look up and notice a good-looking suit speaking in Darcy's ear. She gives him a nod and a smile and turns into him to dance. I watch him place his hands on the small of her exposed back—damn, that dress—and she wraps her arms around his neck.

As usual, she looks fucking beautiful. She's wearing a stunning silver backless dress, that shows off way too much skin; especially considering she's dancing with some random bloke and he has his slimy hands all over her. I suddenly feel the sharp pangs of jealousy, even though I know she isn't mine—though I want her to be. I thought we were getting somewhere last night. I thought she might have been feeling what I was, yet here she is dancing like that, with someone she met ten seconds ago. That doesn't really seem like *my* Darcy.

I try concentrating on my set, but find it hard to keep my eyes off her. I don't want to be too obvious, but I try to catch her eye as much as I can so she doesn't forget that I'm here. I find it hard watching her dance with someone else, to *my* songs. *She should be dancing with me!*

After another song, I notice another guy walk over and cut in. Now she's dancing with some surfy looking guy. Well, it doesn't look like she has a type—cowboy, businessman, surfer. I dread to think what will come next. I have to stop thinking like that though. She isn't mine—she's free to dance with whomever she wants to, even if I don't like it. I know she doesn't have any friends in Summerlake, so she's probably just trying to meet people—I still struggle to keep the jealousy at bay though. During the song, I see Darcy make a drinking gesture to surfer boy, and he leads her toward the back of the bar. After that, I lose sight of her.

After my next song, I announce that I'm taking a short break. I quickly jump from the stage and head toward the back in the direction that I last saw Darcy. I look around and see her talking with a group of about six men. She has her back to me, but I see that the first suit she was dancing with, has his hand on the small of her naked back again.

I walk towards her, call her name and she turns quickly at the sound of my voice.

"Trav!" she calls back, and runs over to me, throwing her arms around my neck, and reaching up to plant a kiss on my cheek.

"Hey beautiful, what are you doing here?"

"I'm here for 'welcome to the team' drinks with my new work colleagues," she replies.

"I see. How was your first day?"

"It was so good, Trav. Everyone is super friendly, and there's no one over thirty that works there, so it's a young, fun team."

"Wow, that's interesting," I reply. Now I feel old, even if I am only thirty-three.

"I'd love to introduce you to some of them if you don't mind?"

"Not at all," I reply.

She grabs my hand and pulls me in the direction of the group she was just talking with.

"Hey everyone, I want you to meet my only friend in Summerlake. This is Travis Gardel. He's an amazing singer, as you probably just heard. This is my boss, Jesse Scott, then there's Ben, Dex, Cole, Harley and Denver."

I reach out to shake the hand of her boss—the suit.

"Nice to meet y'all."

"You too," they all chime in.

"How did you meet Darcy?" Jesse asks.

"He's my neighbor," Darcy jumps in. She's holding onto my arm, and I see Jesse quickly glance down at it with a frown.

The next minute I know, we're surrounded by a group of four girls who are all jumping up and down, giggling.

"Darcy, do not tell us you seriously know the hot cowboy," they shriek.

Darcy laughs and puts her arm around my waist.

"Girls, this is my friend, Travis Gardel. Travis, this is Winnie, Isla, Alice, and Colby."

"Nice to meet y'all," I say.

All four girls continue to giggle and start touching my arms, as Darcy just stands there grinning. She's obviously enjoying this.

I turn back to Darcy, hoping to give her friends a hint. They seem to take it and head in the direction of a corner booth, but they don't take their eyes off us.

"Are you having fun?" I ask her.

"I am, thank you. It's been a great way for me to get to know everyone."

"I think your new boss might have the hots for you," I say.

"What? You're crazy. He does not. He's just friendly."

"He hasn't taken his eyes off you since I walked over here, and he was scowling at me when you put your arm around my waist. Plus, he was obviously enjoying dancing with you. You definitely have an admirer there."

"Well, he can admire all he likes. I don't mix business with pleasure. I've learned that lesson, remember. He's a lovely guy and I'll admit, very attractive, but getting involved with the boss is a super bad idea."

"I agree," I say.

"Good, that's settled then. Can I have one dance before you have to go back on?" she asks.

"I'd love to," I say as I grab her hand and lead her on to the dance floor.

As we walk into the mix, I'm certain I can feel more than one pair of eyes drilling angrily into my back.

When we get to the center of the floor, I put my arms around her waist and she wraps hers around my neck, and we start gently swaying to the music.

"You look beautiful again tonight," I say in her ear.

"Thank you," she smiles.

"I love this backless dress. It's sexy as hell," I say as I run my fingers over her bare spine.

She looks down and I see a huge grin spread across her face, along with that adorable blush.

"Darce?"

"Yeah," she replies looking up at me.

"Do you think I could take you home tonight?"

"I'm not sure if this dress and your bike would be a good mix," she says looking down at herself.

"I've got a jacket you can wear and I can cover your legs easily enough."

She looks at me and smiles her gorgeous beaming smile.

"Okay then."

Chapter Nine

• DARCY •

Following my dance with Travis, I head back toward my new colleagues. I notice the girls back in the booth, so I head over to join them.

"I can't believe you know Travis Gardel," Winnie says. "He's like a celebrity around here. Every girl wants him, and every man wants to be him."

I smile as I look toward the stage, and catch Trav's eye. He gives me a cheeky wink. He really is incredibly gorgeous.

"He is pretty special," I reply.

"He's more than special," Colby adds with stars in her eyes. "What I wouldn't do for a roll in the hay with him."

"Colby!" I shriek as I slap her arm playfully. She just laughs.

As the night wears on, more and more of my colleague's head home. I hear Travis mention that he has one more song for the night, which means we're probably not far from heading home too. As I wait at the bar for my last drink of the night, I feel a now-familiar hand on my lower back. I turn to see Jesse standing there with a friendly smile on his face.

"Hey, newbie."

"Hey, boss," I reply.

"Have you had a good night?" he asks.

"So good. Thank you, Jesse, it's been the perfect first day. I think I'm going to love working with you all. Everyone is so friendly. You've put together a great team."

"Thanks," he says. "We're like a big family."

"I can see that. It's really nice."

"Can I offer you a ride home?" Jesse asks. "I wouldn't want you taking a taxi."

"Thanks, but I've already got a ride home."

"Oh?" he enquires with a raised brow.

"Yeah, Travis is giving me a lift. He is my neighbor, after all," I smile.

"I see. I know you told me you were single, but you two seem pretty close. Have you started seeing each other since this morning?"

"Me and Travis? No, we're just friends. I've only been here a few days. He's just really taken me under his wing, that's all. He's a lovely guy."

Jesse gives me a nod and a small smile. I must admit; he is starting to act a little strange around me. Perhaps everyone's right. Maybe he is interested in me. That's ridiculous though. I haven't even known the guy for twenty-four hours. Besides, he has to know that a relationship with one of his staff could never happen.

As I'm finishing up my drink, I see Travis approach. Out the corner of my eye, I notice Jesse giving him a heated look, and he takes a step closer to me.

"Hey Darce. Are you ready to head off soon?" Travis asks me.

"Absolutely," I reply.

"Just let me say goodbye to the girls."

I run over to the corner booth, and let the girls know I'm leaving.

"Please tell me you're not leaving with Travis," Winnie says.

"He's just giving me a ride home," I huff with a smile.

"Lucky bitch," Alice smiles.

"I'll see you all tomorrow. Thanks for tonight girls, it's been awesome."

I turn and make my way back to Travis and Jesse, who seem deep in discussion. Although looking at their body language, it looks more like a pissing contest. *Oh boy!*

"You ready?" I ask Travis, with a hand to his shoulder. I see Jesse's eyes land on my hand. Perhaps this really is a thing. That can't be good. I don't want things to be awkward at work if that's really how he's feeling. I remove my hand from Travis' shoulder and reach out to shake Jesse's hand.

He takes my hand but pulls me in to plant a lingering kiss on my cheek. The kiss is definitely more than a boss/employee appropriate kiss, but I smile politely at him.

"Thanks again for tonight, Jesse. It's been a great night. I'll see you tomorrow."

"Will do," he says with a nod.

Travis grabs my hand and interlaces our fingers as we make our way to the door. Once we're outside and walking towards his bike, I ask him what he and Jesse had been speaking about.

"He wants you," he says matter-of-factly.

"Trav …"

"He does, Darcy. He told me flat out. He asked me if we were involved because he wants to take you out. He was very happy when I told him we were just friends."

"It's not going to happen," I say.

"Well, he didn't seem like the type who would give up something he wants very easily."

Travis slips his leather jacket over my shoulders and then turns me around so he can zip me up. I look up at him and he gives me a tentative smile.

"Are you okay?" I ask.

"Fine," he snaps.

"Is that a girl 'fine' or a boy 'fine'?"

"What's the difference?" he asks.

"A girl 'fine', means you're really not fine. A boy 'fine' means you are."

"Oh, sweetheart, I am definitely *fine*. Just ask any woman here!"

"Oh my goodness—you are so full of yourself," I laugh.

He laughs back as he passes me my helmet. He puts his own on, swings one leg over the bike, and holds his hand out to help me on the back. As I climb on, I notice the girls from work standing on the footpath watching us with mouths open. Jesse is also next to them, with his hands in his pockets watching us. I give them a smile and a small wave and then pull on my helmet. Travis starts the engine, and I wrap my arms around his waist tightly. I place my cheek against his back, and we take off down the road at a million miles an hour. I grip him with everything I have, and feel him chuckle against me. *Cheeky fucker is showing off!*

Winnie pounces on me the minute I walk through the door at work the next morning.

"Did you sleep with him?" she asks with excitement in her eyes.

"What? Who?" I ask.

"Travis Gardel, of course," she replies while bouncing on her seat.

"No," I answer. "I told you, he was just taking me home."

She looks at me with starry eyes.

"Watching you ride off into the night, wearing Travis' leather on the back of his bike, was hot," she says. "Jesse totally turned green. I think he nearly had a coronary. He's in a pretty foul mood this morning—that's not like him at all."

Oh man, this isn't what I need.

I make my way to my desk and pop my head into Dex's' office to say hi.

"Hey, biker chick," he says with a smirk.

"Hey, yourself," I reply with a smile.

I walk on, past Ben's office, noticing that he isn't in yet. As I pass my office, I turn to the group of cubies that are already here, and call out a collective "morning everyone".

"Morning, Darcy," comes back many replies. As I start walking towards Jesse's office, I hear a really strange sound. It's a sort of loud rumbling. I look around in confusion, trying to work out where it's coming from. All the cubies have their eyes on their screens. *Can no one else hear that?* It gradually gets louder and louder, when I realize it's coming from Cole Breyman's computer. He slowly looks up and gives me a sheepish grin, as it finally kicks in what it is. He's playing some kind of sound effect of a motorcycle revving its engine. Gradually, amused eyes start lifting from behind their screens, and all are directed at me.

"Nice guys, real nice," I say shaking my head with a smile.

Everyone absolutely cracks up, me included. I don't mind being the butt of a joke every now and then. I turn back in the direction of Jesse's office, and as I do, I call behind me.

"How's that coffee coming along, Cole?" I question with a smirk.

He quickly drops his head.

"Coming, boss."

Everyone laughs even harder now.

I quietly knock on Jesse's door and poke my head in.

"Morning, Jesse," I say.

"Hey, Darcy. They giving you grief out there?"

"Yeah, it's all a bit of good fun though," I smile.

"I'll let you settle in for a few minutes, then would you mind popping back in so we can have a chat?"

"No problem," I reply.

I make my way to my office, throw my bag in the bottom drawer, boot up my laptop and start checking my emails. It's much the same as yesterday; some junk and then a few emails from colleagues saying what a fun night they had. There is also a bit of talk about Travis too, which I expected. I know I'm going to hear about that for a little while, especially from the girls.

I grab a pencil and a notebook and make my way back to Jesse's office. I knock quietly again and he invites me in.

"Grab a seat," he says.

I pull up a comfy-looking bucket seat and sit myself down.

"Did you enjoy last night?" Jesse asks me.

"I really did. Thanks so much, Jesse, it was such a fun night. It was a great way to start to get to know everyone. You've put together a great team here."

"Thanks," he says. "They are a fun group. Should we get down to business?" he asks.

"Absolutely, hit me with it."

"Well, first off I wanted to go through some of the accounts I'll be handing over to you and then I'll run through how we work here, and how you can access assistance from the cubies. You've pretty much got fifteen personal assistants out there. Gradually you'll get to know them all better, and the style of work that best suits each of them. You can then pick and choose who you'd like helping you on each of your accounts."

"Okay, that sounds like a great way to work. I think I'll enjoy that."

"Good. Ben and Dex use the same system, and they find it works really well. Obviously, you can always go to them as well with any issues if I'm not available. We work on a massive range of accounts here, so there will always be something interesting happening. Once you get into the swing of things, certain clients will also start working with you directly, rather than going through me anymore. As I mentioned in the interview, there may occasionally be a little travel—sometimes to regional towns, sometimes interstate, but it doesn't happen that often."

We proceed to talk about the different accounts I'm going to be taking over, and what's involved for each of them. By the time we come up for air, we realize it's lunchtime.

"Wow, time flies. Can I take you out to lunch?" Jesse asks. "No work talk, I promise."

"Sounds great," I reply.

Jesse and I walk down to the local pub on the corner, and once inside he leads me to a corner booth.

"Can I get you a beer?" he asks.

"Yes please," I reply.

I watch him order at the bar and notice the attention he gets from the bartender. He really is very attractive, and he certainly turns heads everywhere he goes. I smile as I watch the bartender flutter her lashes at him, and push her inflated tits in his direction more than once. He doesn't seem to notice, or if he does, he doesn't give her the satisfaction of looking like he has.

He walks back to our booth with our drinks, and I glance at the bartender who proceeds to give me daggers.

"I think you've just ruined our friendship," I say to Jesse with a smirk.

"Whose friendship?" he asks curiously.

"That bartender and I. She's not happy that you're here with me. I'm currently getting stabbed in the face with her daggers."

Jesse turns around to look, and her expression instantly changes into a huge beaming smile. I just laugh.

"You either don't realize the effect you have on women, or you just ignore it. I'm not sure which it is."

"What?" he says with clear embarrassment all over his face.

"Okay, you don't realize it. I'll buy into that for now," I giggle.

He just shakes his head.

"Seriously, look around. Nearly every woman in here is eye-fucking you right now."

He looks down at his bottle and plays with the label.

"Perhaps, they're actually eye-fucking you," he says with a grin.

"I don't think so," I chuckle.

We grab the menus and place our order with the waitress—another of Jesse's admirers. Jesse orders a burger and I choose a Caesar salad. While we wait for our lunch, we make small talk, mainly about where I had worked in Blackborough, and the types of accounts I worked on. Then the topic of conversation turns to last night at *The Den*.

"Do you go out clubbing or to bars much?" Jesse asks.

"I did a bit in Blackborough, but that was usually with my

boyfriend. I do love going out dancing though. How about you?"

"Yeah, it's usually just with the guys from work. We probably spend most of our time at *The Den*. The music is always good and you get to know the regulars."

"Yeah, I've been to *The Den* twice now, and already I really like it. It has a great feel to it, and I have to agree about the music."

"So, Travis Gardel is your neighbor then?" he asks.

I was wondering how long it would take to get to this topic.

"Yeah. He actually rescued me on my first night here. I went out for a run and got lost. He was out riding his bike, recognized me and offered me a ride home. I invited him in for coffee, and we sort of hit it off. He's a great guy, and extremely talented."

"So, you're just friends then?"

"Well yeah, I've only known him for a few days. It's a bit early for anything else."

"But you're attracted to him?"

"I don't think there are many girls who wouldn't be attracted to a hot cowboy singer with a sexy American accent."

"It's always the accent, isn't it?"

"It helps," I giggle. "He's a lovely guy though."

"He wants you; you know."

I lean back abruptly in my seat in surprise.

"What makes you say that?" I frown.

"The way he was looking at you last night. Some of the things he said to me—warning me off."

"Is that right? He actually said the same about you," I reply with a smirk.

"He's right."

"Oh, okay then." I don't know where to look.

"You mentioned a boyfriend in Blackborough. That's not the case anymore?"

"No."

"Did you break up because you were moving here?" he asks.

"No, I moved here *because* we broke up. It's a long and messy story."

"I see," he replies.

Noticing my discomfort, he steers the conversation in a different direction.

"So, besides dancing, what do you do for fun?"

"Well, I'm a bit of a nerd, so I love curling up with a good book, I love exercising—although I have been a bit slack in that department the last few months, and I love the beach. It's one of the reasons I chose Summerlake. I really missed the beach living in Blackborough."

He nods. Looking at his watch, he raises his eyebrows.

"Wow, that hour went by quickly. We should probably head back. The others will be wondering what happened to us. Can I ask you a question before we go back though?" Jesse asks.

"Of course," I reply with a smile.

"I was wondering … perhaps if you might be interested … in maybe having dinner with me tomorrow night?"

"Oh! Um …"

"I know the whole boss, slash employee thing might concern you, but it won't be an issue, I promise."

"I don't know, Jesse. What will the others in the office think? Even if you weren't the boss, just the fact that we work together is an issue for me."

"We could keep it completely separate. And besides, it's just dinner."

"Things like this never stay completely separate. I know that for a fact."

"You and your boyfriend worked together?"

"Yeah, and that decision ruined my life."

"I'm sorry, I didn't know."

"It's fine. I just want to be very careful about getting involved like that again."

"Maybe I could fire you," he says with a laugh.

"You think I'd go out with someone who just fired me?" I ask with a raised eyebrow.

"Yeah, good point," he laughs. "Just friends, nothing more. It doesn't need to go any further than that. It's completely your call."

I look at him for a few seconds with narrowed eyes, mulling it over in my head.

"Just friends?" I ask.

"Just friends."

"Okay, dinner sounds nice."

Jesse beams.

"Awesome. I'll pick you up at seven."

"Sounds good."

"Great. We should go."

We stand, and Jesse makes his way over to the bar to pay the bill. I receive more daggers courtesy of the bartender, and we head towards the door with Jesse's hand on his favorite spot—the small of my back.

As we head back in through the reception area, Winnie gives me a discreet wink when we walk past. *What's that about?*

When I get back to my desk, I check my email and there's one from Winnie.

How did lunch with the boss go?
He asked you out, didn't he?
He's totally got it bad for you.

I send back a quick reply.

Lunch was 'friendly'.
Get back to work, you naughty gossip.

The rest of the day flies by again, as I start making phone calls to introduce myself to my new clients. I can't believe it when I look at the clock and see that it's six o'clock. I shut down my laptop and grab my bag. On my way out, I pop my head into Jesse's office to say goodbye.

"See you tomorrow, Darcy. Have a great night."

"You too, Jesse," I reply with a smile.

Chapter Ten

• TRAVIS •

"Hey, Brant. How's my favorite manager?"

"Good, buddy. You?"

"Yeah, well. What's been happening?"

"Not too much. Fielding lots of calls about where you are though. I've got so many talk shows chasing you for an interview. Can I give them any timeline yet?"

"No, sorry mate, not yet. I definitely won't be coming back until the divorce is final. I'm still waiting to hear back from Pete about that."

"Bloody lawyers, take forever and charge the earth."

"Yep, that sounds like Pete," I laugh. "I just want it sorted though. I've met someone actually."

There's silence on the end of the line.

"Brant? You there, mate?"

"Yeah, I'm here."

"Did you hear what I said?"

"I heard. Is it serious?"

"Well, I'm not actually seeing her as such. We're just friends. She just moved in next door, but she's amazing. If she's interested, I'd like to take her out."

"Does she know who you are?"

"She knows I'm a singer. She's heard me play at *The Den* a few times, but I've only told her the Gardel name. She's not let on at all that she recognizes me. She wasn't a country music fan until a few nights ago," I chuckle.

"Be careful, Travis. You know what women can be like. They pretend they don't know you, but they're just crazy stalkers who only want two things—celebrity dick and celebrity money."

"I know mate. I'm being careful. She's different though. She's genuine and super sweet."

"Just don't rush into anything too soon. We don't want another Laila on our hands."

"I'll be careful. Look, I better go."

"Alright, mate. Talk soon."

I hang up the phone and slump back into the couch. I know Brant is just looking out for me, but sometimes he can really put a dampener on things. Darcy is sweet, and I'm certain she has no idea who I really am. I love her company. She's fun, bright and extremely mischievous. It does look like I may have to fight for her attention though.

After speaking with her boss, Jesse, last night, he made it very clear he has every intention of pursuing her, and that I should back off. If I'm honest, I'm a little concerned. He's a good-looking guy and will be spending a lot of time with her from now on. My only saving grace is that Darcy said she wouldn't date anyone from work. She's been down that path and it ended badly for her. However, if he's persistent, there is every chance that she could crack. I have to let her know that I'm interested, and soon. I just don't want to scare her off.

The next night, I knock on Darcy's door to see if she wants to head out for a run together later on.

"Just a minute," she yells. Then I hear an almighty crash and a few curse words.

"Oh shit! Sorry, I'll be just a minute."

She eventually makes it to the door and swings it open with a huge smile; then her smile suddenly drops.

"Travis? Hi … I wasn't expecting you," she says as she looks out further towards the street.

"Yeah, sorry to disappoint. You were obviously expecting someone else."

"No, I'm not disappointed at all. But yes, I was expecting someone else. Come in," she says.

"Are you sure, I can come back another time."

"No, no, come in."

"Are you okay? I heard a big crash and then a few choice words."

She blushes and looks toward the kitchen.

"Yeah, I just knocked a saucepan off the kitchen bench, and now it's contents are all over the floor. You don't want to go back there, it's a car crash—I'll be cleaning that up for a week."

"You look beautiful," I say as I notice her all dressed up. "Are you heading out somewhere?"

She looks down and blushes again.

She's wearing a black fitted dress, that hugs her in all the right places, and falls just above the knee. The top has thin spaghetti straps, and the front is cut low, showing off her perfect cleavage. Her gorgeous silky hair is braided down one side and pulled across to the other side so that it hangs over the front of her shoulder. She looks sexy as hell.

"Um, yeah. I'm going out to dinner actually."

"Oh, a date?" I ask.

"No, not a date. Just dinner. It's actually with my boss, Jesse. Strictly a friend thing."

Damn, Jesse!

"You sure he knows that," I ask with concern.

"Yes. I made it very clear that if I was to go out with him, it was strictly as friends. I very briefly explained that I'd been in a similar situation before and it turned out bad. He said he understood, but he still wanted to take me out. I thought it couldn't hurt."

"You've got my number though, right? In case you need me for anything."

"I do, thank you. You're sweet," she says as she leans up and kisses me on the cheek.

"You've really made this move so much easier for me you know. I thought I'd be so lonely until I got to know people and made new friends and all that, but I haven't felt that at all. We've just kind of clicked, haven't we?"

"I feel that too. I've loved spending time with you. You're amazing."

"Thank you," she says with a shy smile. "You know, all the girls at work were completely jealous of me last night. They're calling me biker chick now. Apparently, it was hot—us riding off into the night together. They've been drooling over you all day."

I have to laugh at that.

"And what did you think?" I ask.

"Well, if I'm completely honest, I loved every minute. It was kind of nice knowing that they wanted you, but I was the one with my arms wrapped around you on the back of your *sexy* bike."

"Sexy bike?"

"Yeah … you know you look sexy riding that thing, otherwise you'd just drive a car like the rest of us."

I genuinely have to laugh now. She really is adorable.

"Winnie from Reception, looked at me like a crazy person when I told her I didn't fuck you. She's probably right."

Now it's her turn to laugh.

"Sorry, that was really inappropriate," she says shyly.

"No, not at all," I laugh. "I agree with her."

At this, her mouth drops open and she playfully slaps me on the arm. I just laugh as we hear a knock on the door.

Damn, Jesse!

"Excuse me," Darcy says as she walks over to open the door.

"Hi, Jesse," she says with a smile on her face. "Come in."

The look on Jesse's face when he sees me standing there is everything—I couldn't have asked for a better reaction. Once he recovers from seeing me, he gives me a quick nod then looks back at Darcy.

"You look amazing," he gushes.

"Thank you," she replies shyly.

"Are you ready to go?" he asks.

"I just need a few minutes if that's okay. I just dropped a pot of food all over the kitchen floor, and I need to clean it up."

Jesse looks toward the kitchen, and I see my chance to be the knight in shining armor.

"Darcy, honey, why don't you head off? I can stay back and clean up the mess. You can pick up your key from my place when you get home."

"Are you sure? You'd do that?"

"Of course, babe. Go, have fun."

She looks at me with wonder in her eyes and slowly walks toward me. She reaches up and cups my face with both her hands and leans in to plant a soft kiss right on my lips, lingering there for a few seconds. It's one of those perfect moments. The instant she pulls away, I miss the connection. I would have paid good money to see the look on Jesse's face again while he watched Darcy give me her thanks.

"You're a beautiful man. Thank you," she whispers.

"Of course, babe. Go, have a good night and I'll see you later."

She smiles at me then. She knows what I'm doing. Yes, I'm playing with Jesse, but I also want her to know that I'm her friend, and I'll do anything for her. She passes me her keys and makes her way out the door.

Jesse leads her to his car and turns back to look at me, just as he places his hand on the small of her back. *Game on, Scott!*

I go back inside and head toward the kitchen. Opening some cupboards, I locate the cleaning products and get to work. Darcy is right; it's everywhere! All over the floor, over the cupboard doors and up the wall. It takes a good half hour for me to finish and once I have,

I leave her place, lock up and walk back to my apartment to wait for her to come home.

After a short while, there's a knock at my door.

Chapter Eleven

• DARCY •

As we make our way to the restaurant, Jesse is pretty quiet. I can tell he is mulling over the fact that Travis was in my apartment when he arrived. When we're nearly at the restaurant, he finally speaks.

"So, does Travis spend a lot of time at your place?" he asks.

I look over at him, to see him staring straight ahead at the road.

"Um, he probably pops over once a day," I tell him.

He just nods at that.

"Jesse?"

"Yeah," he replies without looking in my direction.

"Is everything okay? You're very quiet."

"I'm fine," he says.

"You don't seem fine. Is this about Travis?"

He lets out a huge sigh and looks over at me, before returning his gaze to the road.

"I'd be lying if I told you that I was happy just being friends with you. I know we've only known each other a few days, but I really like you, Darcy. I find you completely captivating, and I want more than a friendship with you. I know you said that you wouldn't date someone you work with, and I respect that, but then I see Travis around you all the time, and I know that you obviously have some sort of feelings for him, and it makes me crazy. I know how stupid that sounds."

"It's not stupid at all, it's actually really sweet. I just … I'm not really sure what to say to that, Jesse."

"You don't have to say anything. We can talk more over dinner."

The waitress takes our order, after giving Jesse 'fuck-me' eyes, and of course, he is completely oblivious once again.

"You honestly have no idea how you affect women do you?" I ask him.

"What?" he says, looking at me like I've grown two heads.

"If you'd even looked in the direction of that waitress, she would have had her tongue down your throat so quick, you would have choked."

He nearly *does* choke at my suggestion.

"It's true," I say laughing.

"Are you jealous?" he asks with a cheeky smirk.

"No, not jealous. I genuinely like being with a man every other woman wants. It gives me a little confidence boost, and it makes things interesting. I get to play a little."

"Play?" he asks with narrowed eyes.

"Aha … play," I say with a smirk.

At that, the waitress is back with our drinks. She places mine in front of me, without taking her eyes off Jesse, and then walks around the table and positions Jesse's in front of him, while intentionally brushing her arm against his.

"Is there anything else I can get you, sir?" she says with a hand on Jesse's bicep and fluttering her lashes at him.

"Yeah, perhaps you could get your 'fuck-me' eyes off my boyfriend, and point them in another direction—that's what you can get for *me*. Oh, and while you're at it, remove your hand from his arm."

The waitress turns to me with wide eyes and stutters over her words.

"Oh … I'm so sorry … I, ah, meant nothing by it. I'm sorry."

"Your hand is still on his arm," I say with narrowed eyes.

"Yes, sorry."

She turns and practically runs back to the kitchen.

I glance at Jesse, who looks like he's about to explode into hysterics.

"I can't believe you just said that!"

"What? How was she to know you're not my boyfriend? She was completely inappropriate. I was just telling it like it is. I can be a very jealous fake girlfriend," I say with a smirk.

"Girlfriend, hey?"

"Just playing," I reply with a wink.

Jesse and I continue with a little small talk while we wait for our meals. When they finally arrive, Miss 'Fuck-Me' eyes places them in front of us without even a glance in Jesse's direction. This time I get all her attention. It makes me chuckle.

"Take a look around this restaurant, Jesse, and count how many women are looking at you. Seriously, it's ridiculous!"

"I'm not interested in them, I'm interested in you," he says with a resolved look on his face.

"Jesse, how are you thinking this will work?"

"I don't see how it can't? I'm not your ex, Darcy. Every situation is different."

"I know that, but being my boss makes it even trickier. I don't think it's appropriate. What will the others think?"

"I think they'll be happy that I'm happy!"

"I have to admit, it kind of feels like I might have been offered this job for all the wrong reasons, Jesse."

"I would never do that, Darcy. My business is important to me, and I want the right team around me for that. Your resumé earned you this job. I thoroughly researched your previous work, and you're very good. You earned this job."

I look at him and smile.

"My ex and I were together for four years. We met at work, and after being in a relationship for a few years we moved in together. Things were great for a while, but I started noticing things at work—lots of long lunch breaks, meetings off-site, that sort of thing. One day, I popped home early to get ready for a conference, to find him in bed with my sister. It had been going on for years. That day, I lost my boyfriend, my sister, my parents, most of my friends and my job. I can't go through that again, Jesse. I've hardly recovered from the first time; it would destroy me completely a second time."

"Shit, Darcy … I don't know what to say."

"It is what it is. I'm moving on."

"Can I ask you something?"

"Sure."

"I can understand losing your boyfriend, sister and perhaps your job, but why the other things?"

"My parents, for some crazy reason I am yet to understand, decided to side with my sister. It was something along the lines of 'I obviously wasn't satisfying him, so if Hannah could, then she should. I should just learn to live with it and be happy for them.' I obviously no longer speak to them, and have cut them out of my life. Our friend's kind of got scared about taking sides but didn't want to lose Hannah as a friend too, so again, I lost out. It's all good though. I made the decision to move here and start again; and so far, I'm pretty happy with how things have turned out. I really feel like myself again for the first time in a long time."

Jesse sits there looking at me, shaking his head.

"That's just messed up. I honestly think you are the strongest person I have ever met," he says.

"Thanks," I smile. "I'm getting there."

"I have to say it again, Darcy—I'm not Adam. I would never do something like that to you."

"Adam said the same thing to me once too. I'm just cautious, Jesse."

"I get that. Especially now I know your story."

"Can we just be friends for now? I've only been here a few days, and I'm still finding my feet. I just don't want to rush into anything, with you or anyone else for that matter. Can we just take things slow and see how they pan out? I genuinely like you, Jesse, so I don't want to be leading you on."

"What about Travis? Where does he fit into this story?"

"In about the same position as you. I like him, Jesse, I'm not going to lie about that, but if he is interested in me, then I'll tell him the same thing I've just told you. He already knows my story, but I need time to figure out what I want. Whether that's you or him or someone else entirely, I just need a little space to sit and be me for a bit. Do you think you can cope with that?" I ask him sincerely.

"Could I still take you out on 'friend dates'?" he asks.

"I'd love that."

"Then I can cope."

"Thanks, Jesse."

"Travis wants you though, and more than as a friend. That concerns me. He's a threat."

All I can do is smile at him. I don't know how Travis feels about me, but I will cross that bridge when I come to it.

As we pull into my driveway, Jesse asks me to wait. He runs around the front of the car and opens my door for me, while holding his hand out to help me out.

"Well, aren't you chivalrous," I chuckle.

"I try to be," he grins.

As he's walking me to my door, I remember that Travis still has my keys.

"Oh, I need to get my keys from Travis," I tell him.

"Before you do that, do you think I might be able to give you a kiss goodnight?"

"Do you think that's a good idea, Jesse?"

"Yes," he smiles mischievously.

I laugh at his confidence, and before I've had a chance to say anything else, he cups my face with his hands and covers my mouth with his. Before I realize what I'm doing, I reach my hands up and place them on his chest and lean into his kiss. His lips are warm and inviting—we start slow and soft, but soon I notice his tongue requesting entry. I open and let him explore my mouth; my tongue soon finding its way to his. *He sure is a good kisser.* All of a sudden, I feel extremely breathless and pull back quickly.

"I think that was a little more than a goodnight kiss, Jesse," I smile.

"I'm sorry, I couldn't help myself. You're just so damn beautiful," he says.

"You should go. I'll see you in the morning." I smile shyly.

"Will do."

"Thank you so much for dinner, Jesse, I had a great night. Sorry I went all crazy on that waitress."

"Don't be, I loved it!"

I walk towards Travis' door to collect my keys and knock quietly. To my surprise, it isn't Travis who answers.

Chapter Twelve

• TRAVIS •

I jump from the couch with Darcy's keys in my hand. She's back from her 'date' with Jesse. It isn't very late either, which is a good sign for me. I open the door with a smile, but it isn't Darcy standing in front of me.

"Laila?"

"Hi, baby," she says.

"What on earth are you doing here?" I ask in shock.

"I thought it was time we talked. Can I come in?"

"I don't think that's a good idea, Laila. You can talk to me through my lawyer. If you came all this way just to chat, then you've wasted your time and *my* money."

"Come on, Travis. We were married for six years; surely you can spare me a few minutes of your time. I won't take long."

I sigh and reluctantly open the door to let her in. She walks in and looks around the place for a bit.

"It's certainly different from our place in Nashville."

"*My* place. It suits me fine for while I'm here," I say. "What can I do for you, Laila?"

"I just wanted to talk about the divorce, Travis."

"What about it?"

"Are you sure that you want to go through with it? We were great together, Travis. Yes, I made a mistake, but that's over now and I want you back. You are the only one for me, and I know that now."

"Are you kidding me? Sleeping with my best mate for nearly a year is not a 'mistake', Laila. Sam get bored did he, or was it the other way around? I know exactly why you're here, Laila. It's the money. It was always the money with you, and I know that now. You were having your fun on the side, while still living the high life with my money. Now the money's gone, it's not so much fun anymore is it?"

"It's not like that, Travis … I miss you."

"Well, you can keep missing me—and my money. It's not going to happen, Laila. The divorce will go ahead, and you will get nothing more from me than you deserve. The prenup terms are ironclad. It's done. Your visit changes nothing. I've moved on, so should you. Go and find another rich sucker to leach off."

"Travis … please."

With that, there is another knock at the door. It must be Darcy this time. Before I even have time to react, Laila jumps from her spot on the couch and opens my front door.

"Yes, can I help you?" she asks in an abrupt tone.

"Oh, hi. Um is Travis home?"

It's Darcy. She sounds shocked by the situation in front of her.

"I'm his wife, can I help you with something?"

"His wife?" she asks.

"Yes, his wife. What do you need?"

"Oh, Trav has my house keys, that's all. I've just come to collect them. I live next door."

"Trav?" she says in disgust. "No one calls him, Trav. He hates being called that."

"Really? Hmm, he didn't seem to mind last night, when I was on my back and screaming it from under him."

I see Laila's jaw hit the carpet, and I jump from the couch as quick as I can and pull her back behind me.

"Hey, Darce. I'm sorry. Here are your keys. Can I pop by your place soon?"

"Sure," she says with a concerned look on her face.

She turns her back and heads toward her place, looking back at me once over her shoulder.

I shut the door and turn back to face Laila.

"You have the nerve to have a go at me about cheating on you, and here you are doing the same thing," she says furiously.

"Firstly, I'm not cheating because we are not together. Secondly, I'm not sleeping with Darcy, or anyone else for that matter, she was just playing with you. And I think she achieved the desired response, mind you." I chuckle. Darcy sure has spunk.

"You think this is funny?"

"Yeah, I do actually. I think it's funny, that you come in here and act all high and mighty, like I owe you something. I owe you nothing, Laila. I honored my marriage vows to you. I took care of you, I was always faithful and I loved you; but you made a mockery of yours, and I have nothing more to say to you, so you need to leave … now."

I walk over to the door and hold it open. Laila steps out and looks back at me.

"I did love you, Travis."

"Goodbye, Laila."

With that, I close the door on our marriage.

I knock on Darcy's door and wait a minute for her to answer. When she does, she almost knocks me over with a giant hug.

"I'm so sorry, Travis. I should never have said that to your wife. I'm such an idiot. Did I ruin things for you?"

I have to laugh. She really is adorable.

"No, everything's fine. You certainly gave her a shock, that's for sure. I'm sorry she spoke to you like that. I had no idea she was in the country, let alone planning on visiting me. I can't believe she flew all this way for a five-minute conversation."

"She's beautiful," she says solemnly.

"Yeah, maybe on the outside."

"Are you okay?" she asks me.

"Yeah, I'm fine. I could do with a coffee though, if that's alright?"

"Of course, coming right up."

I sit down on the couch in my usual spot.

"How did your dinner with Jesse go?" I ask.

"No way, you're going first."

She brings our coffees over, and instead of sitting in her usual spot at the other end of the couch, she sits right next to me.

"Spill," she says. "What did Laila want?"

"To get back together," I shrug.

"No! What did you say?"

"Have a nice life!"

"Wow. Are you sure that's what you really want?"

"Would you take Adam back?"

"Hell no, but we weren't married—you are," she says with concern.

"Unfaithfulness is not okay—whether it happens once or three hundred times. I am always honest in my relationships, and I expect my partner to be also. I can't overlook that."

Darcy looks at the carpet and nods gently.

"I kissed Jesse tonight," she suddenly blurts.

"You what?" I ask in shock.

"I kissed Jes …"

"Yeah, I heard you. I thought you weren't going there?"

"I'm not, I didn't. Well, I did but it wasn't like that."

"Then what was it like?" I ask.

"He asked if he could just give me a goodnight kiss, I said that was okay, but it was more than a goodnight kiss. I stopped it eventually, but I did let it happen."

Bloody Jesse. I swear I'll rip that fuckers' head off!

"We talked a lot at the restaurant, and I explained my situation—

he was very understanding. He still wants to date me, but I told him it couldn't happen, at least not for now."

"What did he say to that?"

"He accepted it, but still wants to be able to take me out on occasion as friends. I said I was okay with that. He also asked me where you fit into all of this too."

"He did? What did you say?"

"I told him that we're friends, that you also knew my situation and that I …"

Darcy suddenly turns bright red and looks at the carpet.

"That you what?" I ask intrigued.

"That I like you. That I'm attracted to you."

Darcy is shifting in her seat in obvious discomfort. I have to chuckle.

"You *liiike* me?" I ask drawing out the word with a super cheeky tone in my voice.

"Not anymore I don't," she says with a playful slap to my arm. I have to laugh now.

"Jesse seems very threatened by our friendship. He seems to think that there is more than a 'friendship' feeling from your side."

"He's right," I say, and I watch a blush creep across her face, as she bites into her soft bottom lip.

"I like you, Darcy. We've only known each other for such a short time, but I've not been able to stop thinking about you. You're amazing, beautiful, fun and gutsy. I'd be lying if I said I just wanted a friendship with you. I understand if that's all you want, and I'll accept that, but I think we'd be unbelievable together."

Darcy looks at the floor again, obviously not sure what to say to that. She slowly lifts her eyes to look at me, and just stares for what feels like hours. She eventually blinks and finally breaks the silence.

"I really want to kiss you," she whispers.

"I'm not going to stop you," I reply hopefully.

"I don't think that would be fair to you. I just don't know what I want yet—I don't want to lead you on, Travis."

"It's just a kiss. I won't read anything more into it than that."

She looks at me for a while longer, before she lifts herself and leans into me. She places one hand on my chest and wraps the other around my neck and slowly reaches up toward my lips. *Holy shit—she's actually going to kiss me!* She lingers there for a few seconds before she finally presses her soft lips against mine. It's true perfection. The way her lips feel against mine, I don't ever want to lose this feeling. We stay that way for a while, molding our lips together, until I run my tongue along her plump bottom lip hoping she'll open for me. She seems more than happy to let me in, and both our tongues begin exploring. I cannot contain a groan of pure pleasure.

All too soon, Darcy pulls back. I immediately want her back and reach up to cup her face.

"I think we should stop there, Travis, otherwise I don't think I'll be able to."

"I'm okay with that," I grin.

"Such a gentleman," she says and gives me a gentle shove to the chest.

"Hey, I forgot to thank you for cleaning up that mess in the kitchen tonight. Did it take you long?"

"Only an hour or so," I chuckle.

"Oh my god Travis, I'm so sorry! You should have just left it."

"It was fine, honestly."

She looks at me suddenly with narrowed eyes.

"Did you go snooping around my house while I wasn't here—looking through my underwear drawer and such?" she asks with amused curiosity.

"Maybe just a little bit," I grin.

"Travis!"

Chapter Thirteen

• DARCY •

I'm a little nervous about heading to work the next day, after I kissed Jesse the night before, but I needn't have worried. As promised, he keeps things strictly professional, which I appreciate. Again, Winnie the office gossip, wants to know what went down over our dinner, because apparently, Jesse can't wipe the smile from his face. I assure her that it was strictly two friends having dinner and she seems thoroughly disappointed with that. There is no way I'm going to tell her about our kiss. Who knows what she'll make of that?

Winnie is right though; Jesse is in a particularly good mood. I don't think he does any work all morning, instead just spends his time laughing with the cubies, and generally wandering around with a huge grin on his face. I'm glad that he's happy, but I'm also concerned that he might have read too much into that kiss.

When I ask him to have lunch with me, he couldn't look happier. I feel terrible, because I don't think he will be smiling much afterwards.

At one o'clock, Jesse collects me from my office, and we walk to the pub on the corner. Once we've ordered, I tell Jesse that we need to talk about last night.

"Did you not enjoy it?" he asks me with concern in his eyes.

"I did, I really did; but after thinking about it, I just don't think it should happen again, Jesse."

"What? Why?"

I watch as Jesse's smile completely drops from his face. He looks so forlorn and I feel terribly guilty.

"Because of that," I say, pointing at his sad face. "Look how sad you just got. I cannot drag you along, Jesse. I like you; I really do. And that kiss last night was … more than nice. But I like you too much to lead you on. Everyone in the office knows we went out last night, and you were in such a good mood this morning, so they all figured it went well—that it was more than a dinner between friends."

I take a deep breath and look up at him.

"Last night after you left, Travis came over."

At the mention of Travis' name, Jesse stiffens completely, and he seems to tune out of the conversation.

"Jesse?"

"Did you kiss him too?" he asks.

Instead of answering, I drop my gaze to the table, not wanting to look him in the eye.

"I see," he says.

"Jesse, I know how that sounds—kissing two different men within the space of a few hours, but it really wasn't like that. I'm not like that, and I don't like that it happened, and that's why I wanted to talk to you. I feel so guilty having kissed Travis just after you, but then I also felt guilty for Travis that I kissed you. Does that make sense?"

"Sure, I get it."

"Really?"

"Yeah, I can't say that I'm not disappointed, but I understand. Are you going to pursue things with Travis?" he asks with a sad look on his face.

"Honestly, I don't know, Jesse. I do like him; I've told you that. I'm just not sure how much I like him."

"Has he told you how he feels?"

"He has. He wants to be with me."

Jesse nods solemnly at that.

"I'm so sorry, Jesse. I hope this won't affect our friendship or working relationship. I respect you too much to screw things up in that regard."

I reach across the table and place my hand on his. He looks down at it again with that sad expression.

"Are we good?" I ask him.

"We're good."

"Thanks, Jesse, you really are amazing."

He looks back up at me with determination in his eyes.

"We should be heading back," he says.

I nod and we stand to leave.

"Can I give you one thing before we go?" I ask him.

"Sure, what is it?"

"This."

I lean up towards him, and with my hands on his chest, I give him a soft friendly kiss on his delicious lips.

"What was that for?" he asks with a groan.

"Just a thank you for being so understanding. Besides, a first kiss should never be a last kiss."

He smiles at me fondly, grabs my hand and leads me out of the pub.

I'm just about to settle on the couch with some popcorn and a movie when there's a knock at my door. Expecting that it's likely Travis, I'm surprised to find a beautiful, tall blond woman standing there instead.

"Laila?" I ask.

"Yes; do you think I might be able to come in and talk to you for a few minutes?" she asks.

"Um, I'm not sure why you would want to talk to me. Shouldn't you be speaking with Travis?"

"Travis doesn't want to speak with me."

"Then I'm not sure how I can help you, Laila."

"Just a few minutes. It won't take long." I let out a soft sigh and as I look her up and down, I open the door to let her in.

"Can I get you a coffee?" I ask her.

"No, I'm fine."

She pauses for a minute and then looks up at me with a frown on her face.

"I want you to stay away from Travis," she says with hostility.

"Excuse me?" I say in shock.

"You heard me. I said stay away from him."

"Yeah, I heard you, but are you delusional? Who do you think you are?"

"I'm his wife, and I don't need you screwing with our relationship."

"Well for starters, you won't be his wife for much longer. And as for screwing with your relationship, I think you did that all by yourself; or was it you screwing *outside* of your relationship that did it?"

With that comment, her jaw hits the floor.

"You bitch. How dare you speak to me like that. Who do you think you are? You're nothing but a little tramp that thinks she can weasel her way into my life. All you're after is Travis' money."

"Seriously? What planet do you live on? Firstly, Travis and I are neighbors and friends, that's it. Even if there was more going on, it has absolutely nothing to do with you. You treated him like shit, and there's no way you deserve a second chance. And from what Travis has told me, you're not getting one either. He's a good man, and you don't deserve him. As for his money, you really do have a few screws loose, don't you? I can look after myself just fine thanks. I don't need Travis, or any other man for that matter, to lean on financially. I do fine all on my own. Now you'll do fine to get the hell out of my house, and don't bother coming back."

"You're making a big mistake messing with me, lady," she says.

"Then I look forward to our future encounters," I bite back.

With that, she stands and makes her way to the door. As I open it to kick her butt into the street, I see Travis standing there about to knock.

"What the fuck!" he says looking between Laila and I.

"What the fuck indeed. I think this belongs to you," I snap.

"Not any more she doesn't! What are you doing here, Laila?"

"I just came to speak to your little friend, but now I'm leaving. Goodbye, Travis."

Travis watches her leave without saying anything.

"You coming in?" I ask him, as he just stands there dumbfounded.

"Huh? Ah yep, sorry."

"You okay?" I ask him.

"Yeah fine, are you? I can't believe she confronted you like that. You shouldn't have been put in that situation. I'm so sorry, Darcy."

"It's fine, Trav. Don't worry about it. That woman sure is unhinged though," I say with a laugh.

"Yeah, that's one way to describe her," he chuckles.

"Can I get you a coffee?" I ask him.

"Please. Popcorn?" he asks as he notices the bowl on the coffee table.

"Yeah, I was just about to sit down to a movie, when your wife knocked on my door."

"Ex-wife. What were you going to watch?" he asks.

"A bit of Nicholas Sparks," I say. "It's called *The Longest Ride*."

"Ugh," he says. "Chick flick?"

"Sit; you'll love it. It's right up your alley—it's got a hot cowboy," I giggle.

"And why would that be right up my alley?" he asks with a raised brow.

"Cause you're a hot cowboy," I reply with a smirk.

"Is that so?"

I bring our coffees over and place them on the coffee table, then fling myself on the couch right next to Travis. I throw my legs over his and snuggle in with the bowl of popcorn in my lap. He looks down at me and smirks.

"Comfy?" he asks.

"Perfectly," I nod with a smile.

As we watch the movie, I find myself relaxing into Travis' warm arms. Every now and then, he runs his fingers down the length of my arm and occasionally kisses the top of my head. It is such a nice feeling, and I imagine spending all my nights cuddled up on the couch with him like this. When the movie finishes, I stretch out and turn to look at him.

"Was that so bad?" I ask him.

"I'd watch any movie with you, if I could do it like that again," he says.

"You're sweet. That *was* nice though, I have to agree."

"How was your day today?" he asks me suddenly.

"It was … interesting. There was a bit of talk in the office this morning because Jesse was in such a good mood. I felt terrible about last night, so I asked him to lunch so we could talk."

"How did that go?"

"I told him that I didn't think it was a good idea to go on anymore 'friend dates', because I didn't want to lead him on. He was pretty upset. I think he was expecting the conversation to go in a very different direction. I also told him that I kissed you, and he looked shattered. I feel so guilty. But in the end, I think I did the right thing by keeping things professional between us."

"What are your thoughts in regards to us?" he asks cautiously.

I look up at him, smile and place one hand on his chest, and with the other, I wrap it around his neck. I pull myself into him and press my lips to his. He kisses me back eagerly, and we stay like that for ages. When I finally pull away, he looks at me with narrowed eyes.

"Does this mean you'll see me as more than a friend?"

"Is that what you want?" I ask with a grin.

"You know it is."

"Then okay. But I don't want to flaunt anything in front of Jesse if that's alright, especially not yet. I really respect him, Travis, and I don't want to hurt him. Are you okay with that?"

"Of course. Whatever it takes," he says as he grabs my hand and strokes my knuckles gently.

"I know everyone from work frequents *The Den* regularly, especially when you're playing, so I'll probably be there more often. How would you feel if Jesse were to ask me to dance?"

"Honestly, I probably wouldn't love it, but I can deal with it—as long as it's just a dance, and he keeps his hands to himself."

"Thank you for understanding."

"Anything for you, beautiful. You've made me very happy tonight."

With that, I lean up and give him another chaste kiss on the mouth.

Chapter Fourteen

• TRAVIS •

"Travis? It's Pete Gearin."

"Hey, Pete, how are things going?"

"Not bad mate, you?"

"Yeah, can't complain. Do you have any news for me yet? I just want this bloody thing to be over, so I can move on."

"Travis, you are officially a single man again. The paperwork finally came through today from Laila's lawyer. It's a done deal. Your marriage is over."

I breathe a huge sigh of relief. It's been three weeks since Laila's visit, and I was starting to wonder if she'd ever actually sign our divorce papers. I'm glad she's finally seen the light and made things official. Hopefully, now I've heard the last from her, and I can move on with Darcy.

My relationship with Darcy is going great. We've been spending a lot of time together over the past few weeks, and I'm loving every minute of it. Living next door makes seeing each other easy, but she is also working a lot which is keeping her at the office more than I'd like.

Considering the great news I've just received, I decide to call Darcy and see if she wants to catch up after my gig tonight. When I call her, I'm not surprised to hear that she's still at the office.

"Hey, Trav, I'm sorry, I'm snowed under here at the moment. Can I call you back?"

"I just wanted to quickly see if you want to catch up for drinks at *The Den* tonight after my gig, I have some news to share with you."

"Really? Okay, that sounds great. Some of the guys that are still here were planning on going for drinks anyway, so I'll see you then."

"Okay, don't work too hard."

"I won't, bye."

My set at *The Den* started at nine like usual, but by my first break, Darcy and her friends haven't arrived. In my second break, she still isn't here, so I decide to give her a call—it goes straight to voicemail. By the end of my set, she still hasn't turned up, so I head to the bar to wait. When she doesn't show up by one, I decide to give up and head home. How she can be expected to work that many hours, is beyond me. She told me that she's working on a particularly critical timeline for one of her clients, and there is no give whatsoever. It's for some television spot, and it has to be finished on time. Her deadline is just a few days away, and I hope once it's all over, she'll be able to come home at a decent hour for a change.

To say that I'm a little nervous with her spending so much time with Jesse, would be an understatement. Apparently, he's not supposed to be working on the account, but is always there 'helping out'. I can see what he's doing, but Darcy says he's just being a good boss, not letting her struggle through on her own.

By morning, I still haven't heard from her, and I never heard her car pull into the driveway overnight either. I try calling her again, and thankfully this time she picks up.

"Hey, Trav, what's up?"

"Seriously … what's up? Darcy, did you even come home last night?"

"I'm sorry, this account is kicking my butt. I'm coming home soon to take a shower and change, but then I'll need to come back. I can see you quickly then if you want?"

"No, I've got to head off to a brunch gig. Will you be coming home tonight?"

"I plan to," she says.

"You never showed at *The Den* last night. I waited till one o'clock and then gave up and went home. I had something I wanted to tell you."

"Trav, I'm so sorry, I got caught up, and then we had a few drinks here. You can quickly tell me now if you want."

"Don't worry about it. I'll talk to you later, okay."

"Trav …"

"Bye, Darcy."

With that, I hang up. It hurts that Darcy's just brushed me off so easily. I know this account is important to her, but it's really starting to affect our relationship.

"Travis, it's Brant. Do you have a minute to talk?"

"Yeah sure mate, what's up?"

"It's Lacey Wilde. I think we're losing her."

"What do you mean, losing her?"

"She's thinking it's all too hard, that this is not what she signed up for. She thought she would be working with you, and she's yet to meet you. She has a point, Travis. We promised her certain things, and none of that has come to fruition."

"Yeah, I realize that, but the situation changed. It was out of my control."

"Yeah maybe, but I think you need to come home. Lacey would be too big a loss for the label."

"I don't think I can yet, Brant. The divorce has gone through, but there's still a lot I need to sort out."

"I get it mate. I'm not asking you to come home for good yet, but I think you need to at least visit. Just for a week or two. Do you think you can manage that? I can have you on a flight tomorrow."

"Tomorrow? Jeez, that's a bit quick, mate."

"I wouldn't ask if I didn't think it was important. You know that."

"Yeah, I know. Can you give me a few hours to sort things out before you book any flights? I just need to notify venues that I've got gigs booked with."

"I can do that. Call me when you're done and I'll make the arrangements."

"Alright, thanks, Brant."

"Talk soon."

Shit, I'm heading home tomorrow! Calling all my venues, I plead my case, requesting two weeks leave. Thankfully, they're all okay with it, but not too happy with the short notice. I promise them I'll be back though, so they hold my usual time slots, which I appreciate.

I call Brant back and he informs me that he's managed to get me on a flight at nine the next morning. It doesn't leave much time to get sorted at all.

I decide to head to Darcy's office to give her the news, as it's unlikely I'll see her tonight, and I don't want to tell her this over the phone. We've already had one awkward phone conversation today.

I walk into Reception at Darcy's office, and I'm greeted by Winnie and her enormous smile. She stands up and reaches out to shake my hand.

"Travis Gardel! Oh my goodness," she squeaks.

I take her offered hand and give her a quick kiss, and she blushes from head to toe, unable to contain her giggle.

"Is Darcy in?" I ask her.

"Yeah. I'm pretty sure she's in a meeting with Jesse though. I'll let her know you're here."

"Thanks, Winnie."

Winnie calls through to Darcy, and I can hear the slightly uncomfortable one-sided conversation. She covers the speaker of the phone and looks at me.

"Can she call you later, she's a bit snowed under at the moment," she says apologetically.

"Can you tell her it's important please?"

"Sure."

I listen to a flustered Winnie pass the message onto Darcy, and then she hangs up the receiver.

"She's on her way down."

"Thanks, Winnie."

After a few minutes, I see Darcy walk around the corner.

"Hey, Trav," she smiles.

"Hey," I reply.

"Do you want to talk here, or come back to my office?"

"Perhaps your office might be a better idea," I reply.

She leads me back towards her office, and we pass Ben and Dex on the way. She then points out the staff she refers to as 'the cubies' and I give them a wave. I hear a few gasps here and there, and comments like "that's Travis Gardel". I have to stifle a chuckle.

As she directs me into her office, I take in my surroundings. She has a great office, with a large full-length window overlooking the street. Darcy sits behind her desk, and I take one of the bucket seats on the other side.

"I just thought I should pop in and let you know that I'm heading home to Nashville tomorrow morning," I say.

"What?" she asks surprised—quickly sitting taller in her chair. "You're … leaving?"

"There are some things I need to deal with, and I need to get back straight away."

"For good? Are you coming back?" she asks with worry in her

eyes.

"I'm not sure exactly how long yet, but it will likely be a few weeks."

"Is it something to do with your wife?" she asks hesitantly.

"No, that's all finalized. The divorce went through."

"Really? You never told me that!"

"I tried to, Darcy, but you've been a little pre-occupied."

She looks down at her desk.

"I know I have. I'm so sorry, Trav."

"It's fine, I know you've been busy."

"That's no excuse. Are you leaving because of me? Are you ending things with us?" she asks with tears in her eyes.

"Darce, I adore you, but I think this has come at the perfect time. It will give me time to think about where I want to be, whether that's here for a bit longer or whether it's back home sooner. Besides, it will give you the space you need to finish your work on this account."

"Trav, I don't want you to leave. I've taken you for granted, and I'm sorry. Please don't end things with us."

Tears are streaming down her face now.

"Don't cry. You're welcome to call me anytime you need. I want to be with you. I want a relationship with you, but I think you should use this time to think about whether you really want to be with me or not."

"I do, Trav, I do want to be with you. I'm sorry I've been so distracted."

"Just think about it, okay. I should head off; I have a lot of packing to do before I leave in the morning."

"Can I at least drop you off at the airport?" she asks.

"No, it's fine. I've already booked a taxi. We should just say goodbye now."

Darcy drops her head into her hands and tries unsuccessfully to hold in a sob. I get up from my chair, and walk around her desk and pull her into my arms. She wraps her arms tightly around my neck and cries softly into my shoulder. When her tears have subsided, I kiss the top of her head and pull back to look into her eyes.

"I'll call you when I land, okay?"

She just nods as more tears fall down her cheeks. I brush them aside with my thumbs and press a soft kiss to her lips. I pull away and head towards her office door.

"Trav!" she calls.

I turn around, and she holds my gaze for a few seconds.

"I love you," she says through a sob.

I drop my head and let out a soft sigh. I walk towards her and cup her face in my hands, giving her another kiss. As I break away, I press my forehead to hers, and we stay like that for a while, just enjoying the feel of each other.

"You don't need to say that," I whisper.

"I mean it," she says looking me straight in the eye.

"I don't want you to say anything back, but I wanted you to know how I feel about you before you leave. I love you, Travis. You're the most beautiful man I've ever met, and I don't want to lose you. I don't need time to think about it. I know what I want, and that's you."

I lean down to kiss her again.

"I'll call you okay?"

She nods again, and I turn and leave her office. As I pass Winnie on the way out, I ask her to look after Darcy for the next few weeks. She looks at me with concern in her eyes.

"Where are you going?" she asks.

"Home to Nashville."

Chapter Fifteen

• DARCY •

I'm in a meeting with Jesse when Travis pops into the office. The conversation is not what I am expecting at all, and once Travis leaves, I find myself alone and in a mess. I slump in my chair with my face in my hands and cry. After a minute or two, I hear a quiet knock at my door. I look up to see Winnie standing there with concern etched on her face.

"He's going home to Nashville," I sob.

She just looks at me sadly and nods.

"Can I get you anything?" she asks.

"No, I'm fine … thanks. Actually, can you ask Jesse to give me a few more minutes, and I'll be back in there shortly?"

"Will do," she smiles.

She heads into Jesse's office, and then I see her walk back towards Reception.

Having an office with glass walls is normally great, but at times like this, it really sucks. There is nowhere to hide when you just want to have a good cry. Everyone would have just seen that encounter between Travis and I, and knowing what I look like now, they'll know it didn't end well. Needing to get out of here for a minute, I start to make my way towards the bathroom. Before I make it out, Jesse is standing in my doorway.

"Pop into my office," he says.

Oh man, I just want to get out of here and sort myself out. I'm sure I look hideous—my face a mess.

I follow Jesse into his office, and he shuts the door behind me. As I sit down, I see him pull a privacy screen across the vast glass wall. Instead of sitting behind his desk, he pulls up another chair alongside me.

"I'm not going to ask if you're okay, because I can see that you're not," he says. "Can I do anything?"

To my humiliation, I burst into tears again. Jesse reaches across his desk to grab a box of tissues, and hands it to me.

"Thank you," I say.

He places his hand on my knee, and just watches me fall apart, and then eventually compose myself.

"Travis is leaving," I finally blurt out.

"Leaving?" he asks in confusion.

"He's heading back home to Nashville tomorrow morning."

"For good?" he questions again.

"He says it's probably only for a few weeks, but he doesn't know for sure. He says he suddenly has things he has to deal with at home. He also says he needs time to think about us, and that I should do the same. He seemed pissed that I've been working so much lately. I don't blame him. I've hardly spent any time with him at all over the past few weeks."

I feel another sob escape.

"You think he's ending things?"

"I don't know. He said he wasn't, but it kind of sounds like he is, doesn't it? He did say that he still wanted to be with me, but I should work out if I still want to be with him."

"What *do* you want?" he asks me.

I look at him sadly, then drop my head a little. I don't feel comfortable talking with Jesse about this, considering I know how strong his feelings still are for me.

"I told him I love him," I say.

"Wow," he says with a sad nod. "What did he say to that?"

"I asked him not to respond. I just wanted him to know how I feel before he left."

"Perhaps you're reading more into this than it actually is. Maybe he does just have some situation at home that he can't deal with from here, especially considering it's so sudden."

"I'm worried about his wife," I say.

"His wife? He's married?" he asks in shock. "You knew about him being married and you're still with him?"

"It's not like that. He's been separated for a while and has been going through a messy divorce. It's all just become official though, but it still concerns me."

"You think he's regretting getting divorced?"

"No, I don't think so. She'd been cheating on him for nearly a year with his best friend, and she seems pretty unhinged, but I'm still worried."

"That's understandable. What can I do?"

"Nothing … thank you, Jesse. I'm sorry for off-loading onto you."

"Of course. You know I care about you. I don't want to see you hurt."

"I just feel a bit awkward talking to you about this, knowing how you feel about Travis and me."

"Don't. You're welcome to come to me with anything, Darcy. My door will always be open to you, both as a boss and a friend. Yes, I wish the situation were different, but honestly, all I care about is your happiness. If you're happy then I'm okay with that."

"Thank you, Jesse, you're a good friend."

I lean forward and kiss him softly on the cheek. I see his eyes close, and he leaves them shut for a few seconds after I pull away. I hear him inhale a deep breath, and I really do feel sad for him.

"I should let you get back to it," I say as I stand.

"Are you spending the evening with Travis?" he asks suddenly.

"No, he said he needed to pack for tomorrow. He came here to say goodbye."

"How about I take you out for drinks tonight with some of the others? Drown your sorrows. I don't want you going home by yourself and moping all night."

"That sounds nice actually. Thank you, Jesse."

With that, I smile and leave his office.

Later that evening, a few of the staff head to *The Den* for drinks. We find a booth and settle in. Jesse buys the first round of drinks, much to the delight of the group of guys. None of the girls had been able to come out tonight, so it's just Jesse, Ben, Dex, Patrick, Cole and myself.

Once I finish my first drink, I start to relax a little. Tonight, a DJ is providing the music, so it's loud and hard to hear each other speaking. After a while, Jesse asks me to dance, and I happily oblige. I haven't been able to get out dancing for a little while due to my punishing schedule at work, so this is nice.

We make our way onto the dance floor, and Jesse places his hands on my waist, while I wrap my hands around his neck, and rest my head on his shoulder. He's a good dancer, and it's easy to relax into him. I remind myself of Travis' words on the night we got together, that he is uncomfortable with me dancing with Jesse, but okay with it. I have to make sure I keep things friendly with Jesse; I don't need to give Travis any other reason to question my feelings for him.

Throughout the night, I dance with most of the guys, but Jesse is never far from my side. I hope he isn't thinking about 'moving in' now that Travis is going to be out of the country. I need to keep my focus on Travis, and repairing whatever damage I have done in my recent absence.

As it gets late, I mention to Jesse that I'm getting tired, and plan to head home. Instead of letting me call a cab, he insists on driving me home, and I reluctantly agree. On the short drive, we make friendly small talk, mainly about work, although I do notice that he gets quieter the closer we get to my place.

When he pulls into my drive, I thank him for the lift and open my door to get out. He jumps out and runs around to help. He grabs my hand and starts leading me to my door, but before we get far, he gently pushes me against his car and leans in for a kiss. I quickly pull my arms up and push against his chest.

"Jesse! What are you doing?" I ask him in shock.

"I'm sorry, I just thought …"

"You thought what?" I ask him. "Jesse, after what I told you today, I thought you understood. This is not okay. I'm in love with Travis—I love him. The fact that he's leaving the country, does not give you permission to move in. I respect you, Jesse, but what you're doing goes against who I thought you were. I'll see you tomorrow."

I leave Jesse standing in front of his car with a look of humiliation. I feel bad for the guy, but I don't appreciate his behavior. I'm not about to cheat on Travis with any man. He does not deserve that again. I know what it feels like, and I would never put someone through that, especially someone I love.

Chapter Sixteen

• TRAVIS •

As I'm finishing up the last of my packing before heading to bed, I hear a car pull in the driveway. I peer out the window and notice a car I don't recognize. Just then, the passenger door opens, and Darcy hops out. The driver soon follows and races around to help her with her door. *Bloody Jesse, of course!*

I watch as he grabs Darcy's hand, and starts leading her towards her door, but stops at the hood of his car and pushes her against it. My heart stops as I watch the scene unfold in front of me. *The bastard is going to kiss her!* I'm about to rush through my front door to stop him, when I see Darcy push against his chest. I hold myself where I am to see how she handles this.

"Jesse! What are you doing?" she practically yells at him.

She's pissed—as she should be. The fucker is trying to take advantage of her when she's vulnerable.

After Darcy gives Jesse a piece of her mind, I hear her tell him that she loves me. *Fuck!* That means she meant it when she told me today in her office.

Seeing Darcy push Jesse off as she did, gives me a lot more faith in her, and confidence that she does want to be with me. I must admit, that makes leaving just that little bit easier.

As I disembark the plane in Nashville, I think of Darcy. As soon as I'm safely inside the terminal, I pull out my phone and dial her number. She picks up after two rings.

"Travis?" she asks with concern in her voice.

"Hey, Darce. Are you okay?"

"I suppose … no, not really. Have you arrived in Nashville?" she asks.

"Yeah, I just landed. I'm still in the terminal, about to go and collect my luggage. I miss you already."

Saying that, I hear a small sob escape her lips.

"Hey, no tears okay."

"I'm sorry, I'm trying. I just don't know where we stand, and I feel confused and upset."

"I know; I'm sorry, baby."

"Where *do* we stand, Trav? Are we still together?" she asks, her voice cracking on the last word.

"One of the last things you said to me was, 'I love you'. Do you still feel that way?" I ask her.

"Of course! I love you, Travis. I didn't just say that to make you stay. I meant it."

"Then we're all good baby. I know me being here scares you a bit, but I promise you it's all business, okay?"

"Okay," she replies.

"I saw Jesse drop you home the other night," I say.

"You did? He tried to kiss me, Travis, but I pushed him off and told him it wasn't okay. Things were a little weird at work yesterday, but it wasn't too bad today."

"I heard what you said to him—you told him that you love me," I say with a smile.

"You heard that?"

"Yep."

"He needed to know that he can't think he can just move in while you are out of the country, or any time for that matter. I would never cheat on you, Travis."

"I know that," I say.

"I would never cheat on you either. You know that, don't you?"

"Yeah, I know. Thank you for reminding me though."

"I better go and find my bags, baby, but I'll call you later, okay? Please don't be upset; we're all good. Hopefully, I can sort out this situation here quickly, and I can come home to you soon. Enjoy some time with your friends while I'm here, because once I'm back, you're all mine."

She giggles at that.

"Sounds good," she says.

"Bye, Travis."

"See ya, baby."

As I exit the terminal, I notice my manager, Brant, waiting next to the car in the pickup bay. I also notice something I haven't missed while living in Australia—paparazzi. Thankfully, there aren't too many here, but I do hear a few comments once people recognize me. I quickly make my way to the car, not wanting any added attention. This is a quick visit, and I don't want the press knowing I'm even back. The quieter my visit is kept, the better.

"Travis mate. Good to see you, my friend," Brant says as he slaps me on the back and grabs my bags. I jump in the car and wait for him to make his way into the driver's seat.

"Where to?" Brant asks me.

"I think I just need to go home and rest up for a bit before I head to Cumberland. Has Peggy been staying at my place while I've been gone?"

"Yeah, everything should be exactly as you left it."

"Great. I'm looking forward to Peggy's cooking. I sure have missed that woman."

Peggy Ramires is my housekeeper. She has worked for Laila and I since before we were married, and she's like one of the family. I pay her well, and she has a private wing in my house. She always seems happy to be working for me—and I'm glad—she takes good care of me.

When Brant pulls up to my place, I get out of the car and head up the front steps. *Gee, it feels weird being home.*

As I walk into the front foyer, Peggy comes to greet me with a giant bear hug.

"Oh, Mr Travis, Peggy has missed you so. Come, come, Peggy will cook for you."

How I have missed Peggy and her little quirks. She always refers to herself in the third person, something I find rather endearing.

Peggy is in her late fifties, with greying hair that she always wears in a low bun. She is quite rotund, and never without her apron. She is an amazing housekeeper; my home is always spotless, I am always well-fed, and she is a friendly ear to talk to. I have missed our chats. As I make my way into the kitchen, I take in the amazing aroma of something cooking on the stove. She was obviously expecting me for dinner. I thank Peggy for the welcome home and make my way to my bedroom to take a nap. I didn't manage much sleep on the plane, and I'm starting to feel it now.

Following my nap, I get up and make my way downstairs for dinner. Peggy has prepared her famous fried chicken, and it smells amazing. As we share the meal, Peggy asks about my time in Australia.

"What have you been doing, Mr Travis? Peggy worries for you."

"I've been fine, Peggy. I've mainly been playing at small venues, like bars and pubs. I've got a tiny little one-bedroom apartment, which is fine for me. It's a bit different from here though, that's for sure," I say with a laugh. "It's been so nice to be able to walk around outside and go places without being recognized or followed by paparazzi."

"Mr Gearin tells Peggy you and Mrs Danvers are married no more. I am happy for you, Mr Travis. That woman is no good for you."

"Yeah, the divorce went through very recently. It's all over … finally, and now I can move on with my life. I actually met someone in Australia, Peggy. You'd like her. She's beautiful, smart, funny, honest and a real sweetheart. Her name is Darcy. She's twenty-six, so she's a little younger than me."

"Mr Travis, Peggy thinks you are a cradle robber," she says with a laugh.

"Peggy! I can't believe you just called me that. It's only seven years. That's not too much of a difference is it?"

"If Miss Darcy makes you happy, age is no matter."

"Thanks, Peggy. She does make me happy. I'm just worried about what will happen when I come home for good though. Darcy has only just moved to Summerlake and started a new job, which she seems to love. I don't know how I could ask her to move across the world after only a few months, to start all over again."

"Does Miss Darcy say she loves you?" Peggy asks.

"She does. She told me the day before I left for the first time." I can't contain my smile, and Peggy notices.

"And Mr Travis loves Miss Darcy?" she asks with a smirk.

"I haven't told her, but yes, I think I do."

"Then you must tell her this, Mr Travis."

"I know. I just don't want to say something that important over the phone. I want to look into her eyes and say it."

"You are Mr Romance, no?"

"Yeah, something like that," I laugh.

Realizing that tomorrow is Saturday, I decide to call my parents and let them know that I'm home for a quick visit. I want to see if they might be able to get the family together for a bit of a reunion lunch. I have missed my family over the past few months, and I'm looking forward to seeing them all again.

After speaking with my very excited folks and having them assure me that everyone will be there tomorrow, I organize with Brant to meet me at Cumberland Records tomorrow morning. Cumberland Records is the record label that I started up with my best mate, Sam.

Since finding out about his relationship with my ex-wife, I bought out his share of the business, and have been running it myself. There is no way I could have continued working alongside him. I ask Brant to schedule a meeting with Lacey Wilde first thing in the morning, as she is the reason I'm back home anyway. Lacey is a new up-and-coming country music artist. She has only recently signed with my label, and she seems to be having issues settling in. I had promised her plenty of support, and to work with her on a few tracks, but my recent absence means that I haven't followed through on my part of the deal. I understand her issues. I just need to sit down with her, explain the situation, and reassure her that I will be back for good soon.

As I walk into my Cumberland Records office, I sit behind my desk and take it all in for a while. I didn't realize how much I'd missed this place. I've popped in early to get a few things in order before my meeting with Lacey Wilde.

When Lacey arrives, Brant brings her into my office, and we all sit around and chat for hours. Lacey leaves feeling much better about her decision to sign with us, and I don't feel so guilty about the way I left things with her. I promise to record one track with her before I go back to Australia, and she's thrilled with that.

The one thing that did come out of the meeting, is my commitment to be back in Nashville for good in two short months. This was a hard decision for me to make—two months is not long enough with Darcy. If I hadn't met her, I probably would have moved back home already, but now I have Darcy, I need to be with her. The thought of moving back to Nashville without her, terrifies me. I can't imagine that she'll want to move again, and I have to be okay with that somehow.

With lunchtime fast approaching, I pack up my things and head to our family home for lunch with the whole clan. When I arrive, everyone seems genuinely happy to see me. My nieces and nephews have grown so much in only a few short months. My brother, Wren's little girl, Evie, is the youngest of the kids, and she's my little mate.

I'm 'Unky Trabis' to Evie, and when she sees me, she throws her arms around my neck and climbs me like a tree. That's our thing; she would ride on top of my shoulders all day if she could. I love it—I am definitely her favorite, and secretly she's mine too.

My dear mama is thrilled to see me again too. I am still 'her baby' and she treats me like it. I can't do anything all day without her faffing all over me—I've kind of missed that too.

"So, what's been happening *down under*?" my brother, Kelly asks.

"Just playing lots of small gigs really—bars and pubs, that sort of thing. It's been nice. I hardly ever get recognized, and no paparazzi is chasing me around. It's been great."

"Now that your divorce is finally through, are there any special ladies in your life?" my sister, Quinn asks me with a smirk.

I look down at the table, suddenly feeling a little shy—all eyes of my huge family fixed firmly on me.

"Actually, I have met someone. Her name is Darcy, and she's my neighbor."

Quinn gives me a huge smile.

"I knew there must be someone! I haven't seen you look this happy in ages. You've got that sparkle back in your eyes again," she says. "So, spill—what's she like?"

"She's amazing," I gush. "She's beautiful, fun, smart, gutsy and sexy as hell."

"Travis!" mama chastises. "Don't say *sexy* in front of the children."

She whispers the word 'sexy', and we all crack up.

"Yeah? How sexy?" my brother, Leo asks waggling his eyebrows, and earning himself a slap on the arm from his wife, Ava.

"Sexy," I reply with a nod and a grin.

"Have you got a photo of her?" Quinn asks.

I whip out my phone and pull up a photo of Darcy and me together at *The Den*. I pass it to Quinn, and she gasps. She then passes the phone around to the rest of my siblings and their spouses.

"Geez, Travis, you're batting above your average with this one, aren't you?" my sister's husband, Ryan says.

"She's a total hottie," says my brother, Kelly. "She looks young though, you sure she's legal?" he laughs.

"Yeah, she's a bit younger than me; but that shouldn't matter if she makes me happy, right?"

"How much younger?" Quinn asks with narrowed eyes.

"She's twenty-six," I reply.

"That's not too bad," she says. "If she makes you happy, then I think it's great."

"Do you love her, son?" mama asks with a twinkle in her eye.

I can see right through her—she's thinking grandbabies already.

"Yeah, I do. I know it's quick, but she's something else, you know?"

"You can say that again," says Kelly, whose wife, Jade does not look happy with him.

"I don't know what's going to happen with us though. I mean, we live on opposite sides of the world. She's only just moved to Summerlake herself. She packed up her whole life following a bad situation, and she's only just started over. I don't think she'd do that again, especially for someone she's only known for a few months. I can't bear the thought of coming back home without her though," I say.

"Does she love *you*?" mama asks.

"Yeah," I reply with a smile.

"Then it will work out as it should," she says with a clap. Mama always knows the right thing to say.

After spending the day reconnecting with my family, I head home to ring my girl. She answers after one ring.

"Travis?"

"Hey baby, how are you?" I ask.

"I'm good, you?"

"I miss you."

"Me too—so much."

I smile at that. I'm glad she's missing me.

"How's everything going there? Are you sorting through your issues?" she asks me.

"Yeah, great actually. I had a business meeting this morning, and it went much better than expected. It means I should be home by the end of the week. I also had lunch today with my whole family, which was awesome. I've missed them, so it was good to catch up again."

"I'm glad, Travis. I can't wait to see you. I know it's only been a few days, but it feels like an eternity. You're never allowed to leave me like this again, okay?"

What do I say to that? I don't want to lie and say okay, because I know that more than likely in a few months, we will be separated for good. I don't want to think like that, but I just can't see Darcy packing up and moving overseas with a man she's only known a few months.

"I don't want to be apart from you either, baby," I reply—and I don't.

After spending the previous few days recording solidly in the studio with Lacey, I'm excited to finally be on my way home to Darcy. I'm so nervous, knowing I have to tell her who I really am, and that I'm heading home for good in just two months. Asking her to come back with me is going to be an interesting conversation. I have no idea how she will take the news.

Following the extremely long flight, I head into the airport terminal to collect my bags, then once outside, I hail a cab and start making my way home. It's early evening, and I'm dying to get home to see Darcy. I didn't tell her I was coming home tonight, as I want to surprise her. I just hope she's home.

As the cab pulls up on the street in front of my apartment, I notice that Darcy's car is in the driveway, and the lights in her apartment are on. I walk to her front door and knock gently.

After a few seconds, the door swings open, and instead of looking into Darcy's beautiful eyes, I'm looking at a man I've never met before. I stand there staring at him for a few seconds, not able to speak, as I take in the situation.

"Yeah, can I help you with something?" he asks me abruptly.

"Uh, yeah. Is Darcy home?" I ask.

He looks me up and down like he's trying to work out who I am, and I notice a hint of recognition in his eyes.

"Darcy!" he yells over his shoulder without taking his eyes off me.

I hear footsteps coming towards the door, and then she appears behind the guy in front of me. When she realizes it's me, she almost knocks the guy over as she pushes past him to get to me. She runs down the few front steps and launches herself into my arms, wrapping her legs around my waist.

"Travis! What are you doing here?" she asks, planting kisses all over my face.

"I wanted to surprise you," I smile.

"Oh my god, I'm so happy. I can't believe you're here," she says. The unknown guy in the doorway clears his throat, and Darcy turns her head towards him.

"Aren't you going to introduce us, baby?" the jerk asks with a smirk.

"Don't call me that you prick," Darcy responds angrily.

She climbs down from me, grabs my hand and leads me inside.

"Travis, this is Adam—my ex," Darcy says with hostility in her voice.

"Prick, this is Travis—my boyfriend," she smiles lovingly at me.

"Boyfriend?" Adam asks.

"Yes!" Darcy says. "I wasn't making him up, you jerk."

He looks at me suspiciously. I have a terrible feeling that he's recognized me and is just trying to piece it all together. If he asks me what I do for a living, it would be the nail in the coffin. I need to be the one to tell Darcy, not him.

"So, Travis, what do you do with yourself?" he asks.

Did this fucker just read my damn mind!

"He's a singer," Darcy blurts out. "And he's amazing!"

"Is that so?" Adam replies. "I thought I recognized you from somewhere."

Darcy looks at me with a funny expression on her face. I can't quite work out what she's thinking.

"Have you played in Blackborough before?" she asks me, looking confused.

I look at her and shake my head.

"Come on, Darcy, don't tell me you don't know who this guy is?" Adam says. "He's a big star in the States. Worth shit loads from what I hear. Don't tell me you've never heard of Travis Danvers?"

"I've heard of him … but," she looks over at me with hope in her eyes. "Your name is Gardel, right? Tell him Travis."

I can see Darcy doing her best to process this new information, as I drop my head sadly and look at the floor.

"Travis?" she whispers.

I can't even look her in the eye.

"Adam, you need to leave … now!" she says.

"Geez, who would have guessed; little Darcy Hastings hooks up with a big-time country music star and doesn't even know it. Typical, you never were very bright."

"Get the fuck out of here … now!" I bellow at him. "Before I rip your fucking head from your body."

Adam looks at me with surprise, but chuckles to himself as he walks to the door.

"Yeah alright, keep your shit together," he laughs. "Think about what I said, Darce. You owe me."

"I owe you nothing, you piece of shit. Get the hell out, and don't contact me again."

I walk over to the door so I can close it behind him.

"If you *ever* come near her again, I will make sure you regret it for the rest of your miserable life," I growl.

With that, he smirks and walks out the door.

Chapter Seventeen

• DARCY •

After Adam leaves, I walk over to the couch and slump down into it. My evening with Adam has not been pleasant, and when Travis unexpectedly showed up at my door, I was elated. Adam's news, however, that Travis is not who I thought he was, has hit hard, and bought me crashing back to earth.

"Darcy, baby?" Travis asks quietly.

I don't look at him, but instead, get up from the couch and make myself a cup of coffee, not offering him one. Trav's eyes follow me the whole time until I sit back down. He sits in his usual spot, and I keep to my end.

"Darcy, we need to talk about this. I need to explain some things to you."

I still can't look at him. I honestly don't know what to think of him at the moment.

"Darcy … please."

"Travis, I think you should just go home," I say sadly.

"I'm not leaving until you speak to me, baby."

"Don't call me that," I snap, looking him straight in the eye.

"Darce, come on. I'm the same person. Yes, I omitted a few details, but I need to explain to you why I did that."

"I can't believe how stupid I've been," I say angrily. "I'm dating a guy and I don't even know his name."

Travis stands up and moves towards me. He sits down next to me and grabs my hand, stroking my knuckles gently. It feels nice and familiar, so much so, that I don't want to pull away.

"Darcy, my real name is Travis Danvers. You know I'm a country music singer from Nashville, but I didn't tell you how successful I am in the States. You've heard of my name but didn't know enough about me to recognize me. Now and then I get recognized over here, but not very often. It's been great just being Travis for a while. I used the name 'Gardel', so it was harder for the American press to find me—it's my mama's maiden name. I just needed some space away from all that for a while. As I told you, I came here to get away from the whole divorce situation. I also needed a break from my business too. I own a record label, and I was in partnership with my best mate, Sam. After I found out he and Laila were together, I realized I couldn't work with him anymore, so I arranged to buy out his share of the company. My lawyers have been working through all that while I've been gone," he says.

He looks up at me, to see if I'm still listening. I'm looking at him intently, so he continues.

"Before I left to come to Australia, I signed a new artist to my label, Lacey Wilde. I made her promises, that before all this happened, I had every intention of keeping; however, being here made all that impossible. It was just things like recording a few tracks with her, and the like. She's felt abandoned and was threatening to leave the label—that's why I had to head home, to speak with her and explain my situation. She was understanding, and we recorded a track while I was there. In my meeting with her and my manager though, it was decided that I have to return to Nashville for good in two months."

"What!" I whisper, as my heart drops to the floor.

He nods sadly at me.

"You're leaving for good?" I ask, tears starting to roll down my cheeks.

"I have to, Darce. This was only ever temporary, and I have a career and business that I have to get back to, plus my family and friends," he says as he brushes the tears from my cheeks.

"What does this mean for us?" I ask through a sob.

"That's what we need to talk about," he says. "I want you to come back with me."

He looks at me again to gauge my reaction.

"You want me to move to Nashville with you?" I ask shocked.

"Yes. I know it's a lot to ask, and we haven't known each other for long but … I'm in love with you, Darcy. This past week without you has been hell. I don't want to be without you again. I realize you've just moved here, and you have your job and all that, but you'll have a job in Nashville … you can work at my label as our Graphic Designer. It'll be great, not having to outsource all that work, and I'll have my girl by my side."

I look at Travis in shock.

"You're in love with me?" I ask.

He laughs at my response.

"Yes, I love you. Do you still love me?" he questions hesitantly.

"Of course I do," I say. "It's just that this is a lot to take in."

"I realize that if you were to move to Nashville with me, your life would be very different from what it is here. I told my family about you and they were genuinely excited to see me happy again. They can't wait to meet you. I showed them a photo of us together, and my brothers think you're way out of my league, and Kelly even called you a hottie. My mama scolded me when I called you sexy."

I laugh at that, and it lightens the mood a little. I like that he told his family about me.

"Travis, I don't know what to think about this. It's huge. I'd be giving up a lot for something that may not work out, and then I'd be back at square one again—with no job and no friends. How can you be sure that this is the right thing to do?" I ask.

"All I know is that I can't bear to be without you. The thought makes me sick, and I can't imagine going back without you by my side."

"Where would I live? I don't know anything about Nashville—I wouldn't even know where to start."

"You'd live with me, baby," he says casually, as if any other option hasn't even crossed his mind.

"What? Travis, I can't move in with you!" I shriek.

"Why the hell not? I've got plenty of space. It's bigger than what I have here."

"That's not the point," I say.

"I'd be happy with you in a broom closet, but moving in together is a big step."

"I know it is, but I love you and I want to be with you, always. If you're really worried about it, you can always ask Jesse for six months of unpaid leave. At least then if you hate it, you can come back to your job and friends."

"How can I afford to move again? It costs so much and moving across the world will be so much worse. And then there are flights … I just don't know if I can manage something like that financially."

"Baby, I'll handle all that. It won't cost you a cent, I'll organize everything."

"I can't let you do that, Travis, I don't want to be reliant on a man. I want to make my own way in the world."

"I get that, I do, and it's one of the reasons I love you, but I need you with me, and I'll do anything to make sure that happens."

"Can I think about it?" I ask.

"Of course, but you can only say yes," he smiles.

The next day at work, I decide to speak with Jesse straight away about Travis' plans. Considering it's only two months away, I need to hear his thoughts on the situation, sooner rather than later. I haven't made up my mind either way, but I want to at least give Jesse a heads up and see if taking leave already is even a possibility.

I lightly knock on his door and he calls me in.

"Hey," he says. "What's up?"

"Not much," I reply with a straight smile. "Can I talk to you about something?"

"Of course, grab a seat."

I suddenly feel nervous. I don't have any idea how Jesse will handle this news. I can feel myself fidgeting, and I will my hands to stop shaking. Jesse looks at me with narrowed eyes when he notices how uncomfortable I am.

"Is everything okay?" he asks me with concern.

"Yeah, it is, but I have something to tell you, and I'm a little nervous as to how you'll respond," I admit.

"Okay," he says hesitantly.

I take a deep breath and fill him in on the situation.

"Travis has asked me to move to Nashville with him," I blurt out as quickly as I can.

"What!"

"Travis has asked …"

"Yeah, I heard, Darcy. Shit! You're leaving?"

"I don't know. I haven't made a decision yet, but I just wanted to give you a heads up. If I go, we'd be leaving within two months. I just wanted to know your thoughts about the possibility of taking six months of unpaid leave. As you can imagine, I'm a little nervous about the whole thing, and I know it's a lot to ask, but it would just be nice to know I had a safety net to fall back on if it didn't work out over there. I love working here, and this job is the biggest hurdle in my decision."

I watch as Jesse runs his hand through his hair.

"Two months? Wow, that's quick."

"Yeah, I know. He has business in Nashville he needs to get back to."

"It's a pretty big decision, Darcy. Are you sure you're ready for something like this? I mean you've only known the guy for a few months."

"I know; it's massive. I'm not trying to downplay it at all. I'd be moving in with him and I'd have a job in his company. It's a massive step. But I do love him, and he loves me, it just feels quick that's all."

Jesse nods in understanding.

"Can I think about the leave situation?" he asks me. "It's not something I would normally do, but as I've told you before, I care about you and want to see you happy. If you decide to go and this would help you feel a little safer, then I'd like to be able to give that to you."

"Thank you, Jesse. You have no idea what that means to me. I appreciate it. You're a good friend."

He smiles sadly at me.

"I'll miss you if you go. I don't want you to leave," he says.

"Thanks, Jesse, I'll miss you too. You've come to mean a lot to me."

Time seems to go so slowly, as I try to make my decision about whether to follow Travis to Nashville or not. I love him, but I'm still concerned about it all being too quick. Travis asks me constantly if I've made my decision yet. I know he's nervous about it, and I am too, but I have to make the right decision for me. I know time is running out—if I'm going to go, there will be so much for him to organize.

About a week after Travis arrived home, we're cuddling on the couch at my place watching a movie together, when I look over at him. He looks so handsome sitting there, watching yet another chick flick with me, not particularly enjoying it, but feigning interest just because I asked him to. Suddenly the answer to my dilemma becomes all too clear to me.

"Trav?"

"Yeah, baby?"

"You know I love you right?"

He chuckles softly.

"Yeah, I know."

"I can't come with you to Nashville," I whisper.

Travis shoots up from the couch like a rocket.

"What?" he whispers back. "No, please, Darcy."

He grabs my hand with a look of absolute agony on his face.

"I've got commitments here, Trav, and I can't just up and leave at a moment's notice. It's too soon. I'm worried that you've only asked me to follow you because you don't want to lose me, but I honestly don't think we're ready for that kind of commitment yet. What if we get there and you realize you've made a mistake? I'm stuck in a strange country, with no place to live, no job and no friends. That's scary for me, Trav. You have to see that. I feel like I'd be putting myself in a situation that I've already been in, and I don't want to go back there."

"Baby, I would never let that happen. Even if things didn't work out, I would always take care of you—get you back home safely, if that's what you wanted."

"It's just too soon, Trav. I don't want to lose you, but it's just too soon."

I look at Travis, just as a single tear escapes his eye. I cup his face in my hands and brush the tear away with my thumb.

"Please don't be upset with me. I'm just trying to do the right thing. You're the most amazing man I've ever met, and I don't want to throw your life into turmoil if I'm not the girl for you."

"How do you know you're not the girl for me? I love you, Darcy, and I want you in my life."

My head drops as I look at the carpet. Now it's my turn for the tears to fall. Not knowing what else to do; I climb onto his lap, my legs straddling his thighs, my arms wrapped around his shoulders and my head in the crook of his neck. I stay like that for ages, just crying softly into his skin.

He wraps his arms around my waist and holds me tight,

occasionally kissing the top of my head. When I've finally cried myself dry, I pull back and look into his beautiful chocolate brown eyes—they are just as glassy as mine are.

"What do we do from here?" I ask him. "Do we break up, or do we try long distance?"

"I don't know. What do you want to do?" he asks with sad eyes.

"I don't want to break up," I say quickly.

"Thank God, neither do I."

"Then why didn't you say that?" I say, shaking my head at him.

"I just wanted to make sure we're on the same page, that this isn't a one-sided thing."

"It's certainly not one-sided," I tell him. "I love you, Travis."

"I love you too, baby. Let me spend the night with you," he says stroking my face with the back of his knuckles.

I nod and he places his hands under my thighs. He lifts me a little and stands from the couch with ease. I keep my arms and legs wrapped around him as he carries me through to my bedroom.

Before I know what's hit me, it's time for Travis to head home. It's been the quickest two months of my life, and now that we're here standing at the departure gate, I can't imagine saying goodbye.

I beg him to stay and won't let him out of my hold. He is much the same, asking me to change my mind and come with him—keeping his arms firmly wrapped around my shoulders.

When the final call comes over the speakers for his flight, I just stand there looking at him and cry.

"Hey, no more tears, okay? We'll talk all the time on the phone— every day, I promise."

"It's not the same as actually being with you—having your arms around me," I say.

"I know, baby," he hugs me tighter. "I better go, otherwise they'll leave without me."

"I love you so much," I sob.

"I love you too, baby. Don't forget me, okay?"

"Never," I reply sadly.

He cups my face in his palms and gently kisses my lips. I never want him to pull away, but I know that he will eventually. When that time comes, I miss the feeling instantly. How long will it be until I feel those lips on me again? I don't want to think about that now.

Travis picks up his bag and makes his way to the door. He starts walking through the glass gangway and turns back to look at me about halfway down. With tears streaming down my face, I kiss my fingers and press them to the glass. He blows me a kiss in return, and then he's gone. I sit in the departure lounge watching his plane until it takes off and is completely out of sight.

When I've pulled myself together a little, I get up and make my way to my car, where I hop in and drive home to my very lonely and empty apartment.

Chapter Eighteen

• TRAVIS •

I've been home in Nashville now for over four months, and even though we speak every day, I miss Darcy like crazy. I'm keeping busy with my label and supporting Lacey Wilde with her new album, but I just can't shake the feeling of loss over not having Darcy with me.

My manager has been keeping me extremely busy to stop me from moping, but honestly, my heart just isn't in it anymore. I've done more interviews in the last few months than I think I've done in my whole career. Everyone wants to know why I silently slipped out of Nashville, and where I've been.

There are so many different stories floating around, but I decided right from the get-go, to just be honest. It's much easier that way, and the media will hopefully move onto something else soon.

I've spent lots of time with my family, who have been amazing, but are worried about me. They never say as much, but with their constant hovering, I'm sure they think I'm going to break at any minute. I try to stay as positive as possible, but I miss Darcy terribly.

Recently, I've started playing again at many of the larger venues around the state. Ticket sales are at an all-time high—it seems that my absence has my fans clambering for more. I've even performed a few times at the Grand Ole Opry, an experience that never fails to get my heart racing. I still get as much of a buzz out of it as the very first time I performed there. It's the home of American music after all, and a Nashville icon. I would love for Darcy to see me perform there. It's a bit of a step up from *The Den*—I wonder if she still goes there? She probably does, as it seemed to be the main watering hole for her workmates. I wonder if she ever thinks of me while she's there, imagining me singing to her?

During one of our recent label production meetings, my manager, Brant brings up the fact that Nashville's most popular entertainment show, *Nights in Nashville*, has been chasing me to appear on the show. After a lot of back-and-forth, Brant finally convinces me to take part. I'm to be interviewed by the host, Grace Sandell, and involved in some sort of fan game. I usually hate these sorts of things, but I actually like the show, and Grace is a good friend.

On the night of my appearance, Brant and I head backstage to the green room to wait until it's my turn to appear on stage. I've been through hair and makeup and have been dressed by the shows' stylist. We sit quietly sipping a few beers before the producer finally ducks his head in and tells me I'm up. As I make my way through the backstage corridors, I start to feel nervous. It's been a while since I've done one of these shows, and I'm hoping Grace won't prod too much into my divorce.

After a minute or two, I hear Grace introduce me, and the band starts playing to cue my entrance. I make my way towards the guest couch, while the audience—of mainly women—goes nuts. They're jumping and screaming and crying all over the place. I've never really understood that kind of reaction, but whatever floats your boat, I guess. I reach Grace on the couch and lean forward to give her a quick hug and a kiss on the cheek.

She gestures for me to sit down, and we wait a little for the crowd to calm before Grace starts with me. At first, she talks about some of the other radio interviews I've done recently, and how I told them I'd been in Australia for a few months break. She asks me a little about my divorce, but as usual, I play it out to be differences we couldn't get past. I don't need to bring up all the sordid details. That does nothing for anybody, and I'm not that kind of person.

I talk about my time in Australia, and how I'd been playing in small bars and pubs, and how nice it was not to be recognized all the time. Grace's next question has me floored though.

"Travis, I heard a little rumor, that while you were in Australia, you met a lovely lady. Is this true?"

I've not mentioned Darcy in any of my previous interviews, wanting to keep her to myself. *How on earth does she know about her?*

I know I can't lie to Grace. She knows me too well, and she'll call me out on it in front of a live TV audience if I did.

"Yes, I have met someone," I say. "She moved in next door to me a month or two after I arrived in Australia, and we became great friends. She's an amazing woman and I miss her a lot."

"So, she's still in Australia?" Grace asks.

"Yeah, it's a long story, but she's just started a great new job and was reluctant to leave it when we've only been together such a short time."

"What's the lucky lady's name?"

"Darcy," I reply with a smile.

"Is it serious? Grace asks.

"It's pretty hard living a million miles away from each other, but I love her, so yeah, it's serious. We speak every day on the phone, but it's hard."

Just then, the crowd starts oohing and aahing, and I notice a photo on the giant screen behind us. It's the photo of Darcy and me at *The Den*—the one I showed my family. I smile adoringly at Darcy's beautiful face.

"Your smile just intensified tenfold. How does it make you feel looking at that photo?" Grace asks me.

"Geez, it makes me miss her like crazy," I say as I rub my hands up and down my thighs. "How beautiful is my girl?" I ask the crowd.

Whistles and cheers lift the roof, and I can't contain my smile.

Grace soon moves onto other topics, such as my recent performance at the Grand Ole Opry, and some of my upcoming concerts. Before they cut to an ad break, Grace mentions that when we return, three fans will be selected from the audience to play a game, and the winner will score a lunch date with me. The crowd goes completely ballistic at this news.

What the hell! I haven't agreed to any lunch date with a crazy fan. I look to the wings of the stage and see Brant looking very guilty and avoiding my gaze. He will regret not telling me about this!

I smile at Grace and pretend to be excited. During the ad break, Grace and I make small talk, while the crew touch up our makeup. As the producer counts us back in, I look over to the side and notice some sort of screen set up—perhaps for the fan game.

Once we're back on the air, Grace reintroduces me and tells the audience that we're going to play a game to see who my biggest fan is. Three audience members were selected during the break and are waiting backstage for their chance to win a lunch date with me.

Grace invites me to stand on one side of the screen, and the contestants are bought out and placed on the other side.

Grace hands me a list of questions to ask the contestants—most are completely ridiculous, but the crowd loves it. The contestants are required to write their responses on a card, and then show the audience their answers. It's the crowd's job to select their favorite answer. Whoever has the most points at the end, is the winner. After a round of six questions, the winner is announced as contestant number two. The crowd goes crazy, clapping and cheering like nutters.

Grace announces that the runners up are allowed to walk around the screen and shake my hand. Contestant number one comes out first, and rather than shake my hand, she wraps her arms around me and gives me a giant hug. She's so excited—it's kind of sweet. Next, it's contestant number three's turn. Instead of the handshake, she pulls me in and kisses me square on the lips. I pull back in shock, and the crowd goes crazy. She turns around, jumping up and down, very pleased with herself. I have to laugh at her guts.

It's the winning contestant's turn—number two. Grace announces that I am to turn and face the screen, and she will pull it back so I can meet my lunch date. The crowd are clapping and cheering, and I suddenly do not want that screen to move. Before I know it though, Grace is walking backwards, and the screen is going with her. As it pulls back, I close my eyes to make it more of a dramatic unveiling, and when I open them, I am truly blown away by what I see.

My beautiful Darcy is standing there with a huge smile on her face, and a single tear rolling down her cheek. I am in such shock, that I drop to my knees on the spot, and put my head in my hands. I can't help the tears that flow then.

Darcy walks toward me and lifts my head in her hands. She wipes my tears away with her thumbs and pulls me up to her. I wrap my arms around her and lift her into the air, as I slam my lips onto hers. In the background, I can hear the crowd going berserk, but it's just Darcy and me on that stage. I can't believe she's here in my arms after all this time. I cannot stop kissing her, and I'm sure as hell not letting her go.

Grace eventually interrupts us and announces that we're heading to another ad break so I can get reacquainted with Darcy. She asks the crowd to thank me for joining them.

As I sweep Darcy backstage, I can't stop looking at her. I just can't believe that she's here; I have to make sure she's real.

"Baby, I can't believe you're here. How long are you staying for?"

"For good … if you'll have me," she says.

"Are you serious? Oh my god, you have no idea how happy I am right now."

I wrap her in a giant bear hug and crush my lips to hers. When I eventually manage to drag myself away from her, I grab her hand and lead her back to the green room where we meet up with Brant. As we walk in, Brant is casually lounging on the sofa with a huge grin on his face.

"Did you organize this?" I ask him.

"Yeah, maybe. I couldn't cope with you moping around any longer, so I contacted Darcy to see if she wanted to visit."

"I agreed to a visit right away, but after thinking about it, I decided to give living here with you a shot—with some conditions though," Darcy adds.

"What sort of conditions?" I ask.

"We can talk about that later," she says. "How about we talk about the fact that I just appeared on national television. I can't believe I just did that!"

I can't contain my laughter then. She is so excited. This is all so new to Darcy, and I love seeing the awe and thrill on her face.

"I can't believe how big you are over here. I mean, I'd heard of your name but didn't know much more about you. But here … you're like the golden boy of Nashville, aren't you? Your name is everywhere!" Darcy says.

"Your life won't ever be the same again after living in Nashville with Travis," Brant says to Darcy. "Are you prepared for the rollercoaster ride?"

"No," Darcy replies honestly. "But I'll give it a red hot go."

"Well then, let the fun begin," Brant says with his hands in the air.

With that, the green room door opens, and in walks Grace. We all stand up, and Grace approaches me first.

"Hey, Travis," she says with a kiss to both my cheeks. "Thanks so much for coming out today. I hope you had fun?"

"Are you kidding?" I reply. "I can't believe all that just happened. I was so pissed at first, because Brant didn't tell me about a fan lunch, but now I have my little winner with me, well I can't wait!"

Grace laughs.

"I'm glad I could be a part of your special reunion. When Brant told me of his idea, I jumped at the chance to bring some happiness into your life for a change."

"Thanks, Grace," I reply.

She then reaches over and pulls Darcy in for a hug. "It's so nice to meet you, Darcy. I've heard lots about you through Brent." Grace says.

"You have?" Darcy replies in astonishment.

"You're kind of all Travis talks about," Brant adds with a wink.

Darcy looks at me with the cutest grin.

"Is that so?" she giggles.

"Yeah well, we should get going," I say quickly, and everyone laughs.

Grace leaves us, and Brant directs us to our waiting car. Once we're on our way, I ask Brant about Darcy's luggage. He informs me that everything is in the boot of the car, as Darcy came straight from the airport. I'm shocked. I inform Brant that I need to quickly pop into the office to pick up a few things before we head home. So that's what we do.

When we arrive at Cumberland Records, I grab Darcy's hand and help her from the car. Media photographers and fans are already waiting on the pavement. Darcy is surprised by how many people there are.

"This is nothing," I say. "There will be at least double the number of people by the time we come out."

She looks shocked as she stares at me with wide eyes.

With a chuckle, I lead her through Reception and introduce her to my staff along the way. It makes me happy that everyone is so polite to her. It had never really been that way with Laila. I give her a quick tour of my company, and she seems impressed. As we near my office, I pop into the empty office that's next door to mine. I lead her through the door, and she looks around perplexed.

"Why are you showing me an empty office?" she asks.

"Well, it won't be empty for much longer. This will be your office. What do you think?" I ask her.

She looks over at me with a look that I'm not familiar with.

"Ah, it's nice," she says.

"But?" I reply.

"But … I'm not going to be working for you, Travis."

"Wait … what? What do you mean? I thought we talked about you working here with me, so you wouldn't need to look for another job. Plus, it would be great working together. Don't you want that anymore?" I ask.

"I think working together will become too much, Trav. I don't want you to get tired of me. I want you to miss me on occasion and look forward to seeing me at the end of the day."

"Are you kidding? I've done more than my fair share of missing you these past few agonizing months. I'm not going to be missing you anymore. I'm not letting you out of my sight!"

"I need to be able to do my own thing, Trav. I need to know that I made my own way in my career, not piggy-backed off my successful music star boyfriend. Jesse and I have been doing a lot of talking these past few months, and he has been looking at expanding his business overseas. He thought this was the perfect opportunity for both of us, and I agree. I will run Great Scott Design from here in Nashville. He will be here in a few weeks to start the ball rolling—finding an office and all that sort of thing. Don't be upset," she says.

I must admit her plan has knocked the wind from me a bit. Even though I didn't know that she was actually coming to Nashville, in the back of my mind, I had always hoped she would change her mind and join me here eventually. I also understand her concerns, and I want to support her—but does it have to be with Jesse? The guy just can't let her go—which I also understand.

"I'm not upset; disappointed maybe, but I also understand where you're coming from. Does it have to be with Jesse though? How long will he be staying here?"

"It makes sense, Trav. I know you're not Jesse's biggest fan, but it means I can continue with some of my clients, plus gain new ones without having to completely start all over again. I enjoy my job and working with Jesse, so I'm happy I can continue it. Jesse plans on sticking around for at least six months—after that, he's not sure. Depending on how things go, he might head back. He might even move here for good. Ben and Dex will be running the Summerlake office while he's gone."

It's even worse than I first thought. Here I am thinking Jesse might stay for a few weeks, not six months, or even for good! This is not part of the plan. I grab Darcy's hand and lead her out of the room and into my office next door.

"I just need to grab a few things and then we can head home. You're probably exhausted."

Darcy sits on the couch in the corner of my office and watches me like a hawk, while I grab a few things and send off a few emails. She has an amused look on her face.

"Enjoying the view?" I ask her.

"Absolutely," she replies with a smirk.

I have to chuckle.

"Good."

After a few minutes, I'm ready to go, so I grab Darcy from the couch and lead her to the car. As we get outside, I hear her gasp and feel her grip on my hand tighten considerably. As I thought it would, the crowd outside has more than doubled from when we came in. We have two bodyguards on either side of us making a path to the car. Fans are screaming my name, and asking for autographs, but I don't want to scare Darcy on her first day in Nashville, so I get her into the car as quickly as I can.

"Wow, that was intense," she says.

From the front, I hear my driver softly chuckle. Like me, he knows that was absolutely nothing.

"I don't want to scare you, but that was merely a few grains of sand in comparison to the beach I normally have to deal with."

She looks at me horrified.

"Really?"

"When we get home after you've rested, we can talk about how you want me to handle those situations with you. Laila always loved the limelight, but if you don't want that, we can talk about how we'll deal with the media. But I have to tell you—people are going to want to know about you. It's going to be crazy for a while, no matter what we do. I know this is not what you signed on for when we first got together, and I am so sorry about that, but I hope it's something that you'll learn to get used to."

Darcy snuggles into my side and puts one arm around my waist. I lean down and place a kiss on the top of her head.

"As long as I'm with you, I'm sure I can handle anything else that comes with loving you."

I cup Darcy's cheek with my hand and turn her face towards mine, placing a gentle slow kiss on her lips. She moans softly at the contact then pulls me in further, brushing her tongue over my bottom lip. I eagerly return her kiss, and our lips stay melded together until we arrive home.

As my driver, Chester nears the front of my place, the large metal gates at the end of my driveway slowly swing open. Darcy pulls away from me suddenly and looks out the window wide-eyed.

"I thought you said we were going home," she says with confusion in her eyes.

"We are," I reply.

"This is your house?" she asks in utter disbelief.

I look at her and gave her a small nod.

Chapter Nineteen

• DARCY •

Holy shit! This is not a house; it's a huge ass mansion.

"This is your house?" I ask Travis in disbelief. He actually looks embarrassed, the poor guy.

I look out the window, not quite sure what to say. I am completely stunned into silence. Not sure how I feel about living with Travis in a place like this, I keep my eyes looking out, not at Travis, in case he notices the shock in them.

We continue along the long driveway towards the house, where the driver stops just near the front double doors and then quickly jumps out. He is immediately at my door, holding it open for me, then reaches in for my hand and helps me out.

"Miss Hastings," he says with a polite nod.

"Please call me Darcy," I reply.

Travis lets himself out, walks around to my side and takes my hand from the driver—I'm pretty sure Travis called him Chester earlier.

"What are you thinking?" Travis asks me with trepidation.

"I'm thinking, what have I got myself into? This is really your house?" I ask him.

"It is," he replies. "I know it's a little different from my apartment in Summerlake."

"A little different?" I respond incredulously. "Travis, this is worlds apart. I feel like I don't know you at all. This is nothing at all like what I was expecting. To be honest, it scares me a bit."

"Please don't run. Give it some time. I understand it's a lot to take in, but you'll get used to it."

"I'm not sure I will, Travis. This is completely different from anything I'm used to."

"Let me show you around. Please just keep an open mind. If it's too much for you, we'll move. I'll do anything for you, just please don't run on me."

"What are you talking about? You can't move—this is your home!"

"It's not a home without you, it's just a house. It's not important … you're what's important to me. If you want a smaller place, I'll buy you a smaller place—if you want a bigger one, I'll buy you a bigger one."

"Travis, do they even make bigger houses than this?" I ask sarcastically.

He pulls me to him and cups my cheeks with his hands.

"I love you. I'll do anything to make you happy. Tell me what it is, and it's yours."

"Just you. I just want you. If I have you, I'll be happy."

"You've got me—I'm all yours."

"Good, then I'm happy. Now, show me this mansion of yours, Richie Rich."

As he leads me through the doors, I look around in wonder. The place is huge. Just his foyer is bigger than my whole apartment back in Summerlake.

"Shit, Trav," I mumble.

He just chuckles and continues leading me forward. We soon find ourselves in the largest and most stunning kitchen I have ever seen. An older woman is pulling something out of the oven and turns just as we walk in.

"Ah, Mr Travis … welcome home, my boy. I am preparing your dinner."

She looks at me and gives me a huge friendly smile.

"This beautiful woman must be your Miss Darcy."

Travis looks at me with pride. He wraps his arms around me and smiles at the woman.

"She is. Peggy, please meet Darcy Hastings. Darcy, this is Peggy Ramires … my housekeeper."

"It's so nice to meet you," I say.

"I am so glad to meet you too. Mr Travis can be happy again," she says.

I look at Travis and smile.

"It's true," he says. "I've been a miserable grump without you."

With that, he grabs my hand and leads me from the kitchen. We head towards an elaborate staircase and make our way upstairs. Along a wide corridor, I notice an abundance of closed doors. *Surely these can't all be bedrooms!* Towards the end of the hallway, is a room with double doors. Travis opens them wide and ushers me through.

Inside is the most amazing bedroom I have ever seen. It's enormous bigger than my whole apartment. In the center of the room is a huge king size bed, covered in gorgeous pillows and cushions. All the furnishings are beautiful. Despite the size, it is still very homey and comfortable looking.

"Is this your room?" I ask him.

"No, this is *our* room," he replies with a smile. All brand-new furnishings—free from ex-wife germs.

I drop his hand and walk over to a massive window to check out the view.

"Oh my god, Trav. This is amazing!" I say.

The window overlooks what I assume is Trav's backyard. Right below the window is an enormous tropical lagoon swimming pool with an attached spa. To the side of that, I can see a full-sized tennis court. The grounds surrounding it are immaculate … it's breathtaking. I turn to Travis with a smile.

"You want me to share your bedroom?" I ask him cheekily.

"Ah, yeah! There's more than enough space for you. In here is your closet."

He shows me to an open area behind the bed. Inside are wall-to-wall railings, shelving and baskets waiting to be filled. I look at him in shock.

"Is this all for me?" I ask with wide eyes.

"Yep," he replies with a smile.

"Trav, everything I own would fit on *one* of these racks. It's incredible—every girl's dream!"

"I'm glad." I look over at him, and he can't seem to wipe the smile from his beautiful face. I walk towards him and wrap my arms around his waist.

"Are you sure you're happy with me being here?"

"Baby, I've never felt happier. I can't wait for you to settle in and feel comfortable here. This is not *my* home; this is *our* home now. I do not want you to feel like you're a guest here. Whatever you need; let me know and it's yours. Peggy will also help with anything you require. She'll handle all the cleaning, cooking and laundry and any other general day-to-day chores."

"I knew you were wealthy, but you're *wealthy*, aren't you?"

Trav looks at me and just nods.

"I really do love you. I want you to know that. I'm not here for any other reason than you," I tell him.

He reaches down and places his lips against mine. As we move together, he walks me backwards towards the bed. I feel the backs of my knees hit the soft mattress as he lays me back against it. It has been so long since I've felt him like this, and I do not want to let him go.

As I slowly open my eyes, I take in my surroundings. *Where the hell am I?* I sit up quickly and soon remember … Trav's bed—*our* bed. I look beside me but realize I'm alone. I slowly get up from the bed and look around the room.

"Travis?" I call out.

There's no answer, so I decide to go in search of him. I make my way out into the vast hallway and head towards the stairs. As I descend, I can hear faint voices.

"Dinner will be ready in ten minutes, Mr Travis," I hear Peggy say.

"Thanks, Peggy. I should wake Darcy. She looked so peaceful though, I didn't want to disturb her."

"You are very in love with Miss Darcy, yes?"

"I really am, Peggy. I'm so happy she's here. I just hope she sticks it out with me. I know it'll be hard for her to adjust to my life—the house, the media attention, me touring. It's a lot to take on, but she's so strong—I'm sure she'll handle it easily. I hope she does anyway. I want her in my life, Peggy."

"I see that, Mr Travis. I have not seen you happier. You do not stop smiling."

I hear him chuckle and decide it's a good time for me to interrupt their conversation. Travis hears me approach and turns to look at me.

"Baby, you're awake. I was just coming up to get you for dinner. How are you feeling?"

"A little sleepy still, but I'll be okay. Something smells amazing!"

"Peggy is the world's best cook. You'll never go hungry when she's around," Travis says.

We eat our dinner in relative silence. I think it's a mixture of tiredness, and that the food is just that good. Travis is right—Peggy is an amazing cook. I sure could get used to this!

After dinner, Travis asks me what I want to do. I do want to see the rest of the house, but I know there'll be plenty of time for that. What I feel like, is a nice relaxing spa.

"What about a spa?" I ask him.

"Sounds great," he says with a smirk.

We head up to our room to change, but as we walk in, I notice that my bags are no longer just inside the door.

"Where are all my things?" I ask Travis.

"Check the closet, baby," he says. I walk around the bed and into the closet, and there arranged on the racks and shelves, are all my clothes and belongings. I gasp.

"Did you do this?" I ask Travis.

He shakes his head. "Peggy," he replies.

"Wow, when did she manage this?"

"Probably while we were eating dinner. The woman is amazing."

"You got that right," I reply.

I find my bikini, and get changed in the closet, while Travis waits for me in the bedroom. Grabbing a towel and my robe on the way out, I head towards Travis who grabs my hand and leads me downstairs. Rather than lead me towards the backyard, he takes me to a section of the house I haven't seen yet.

"Where are we going? I thought we were having a spa?" I ask him.

"We are."

"Isn't the backyard that way?" I point behind me.

"It is, but it's a bit cold out tonight, so I thought we'd use the indoor hot tub instead. I don't want you catching a cold and getting sick."

"You have two spas?" I ask in disbelief.

"Yeah," he replies, as if it's a completely normal thing.

I just shake my head as he leads me to the spa room. Once inside, I look around with wide eyes and my jaw on the floor. This is no normal spa room—it is nothing short of stunning. The giant spa sits in the middle of the room, and all around—on the floor, shelving and benchtops, are candles. I'm talking at least a hundred tealight candles. Scattered amongst the candles on the floor, are deep red rose petals. It looks spectacular and so romantic.

"Travis!" I gasp. "This is amazing. How did you manage this?"

"Peggy," he smiles. "I sent her a quick message just after dinner. I can't take the credit."

"You are incredible," I say. "You're spoiling me. I'm never going to want to leave after this."

"Good. That's the plan," he smiles.

I remove my robe and climb into the spa. It's heavenly. Travis follows me in and sits down opposite me. I quickly move over and climb onto him, straddling his lap and wrapping my arms around his neck. He lovingly smiles up at me, and I lean in to kiss him softly.

The next day, instead of heading into work, Travis organizes a get together so I can meet his family. I'm actually quite nervous—Travis has told me about his large family, and it's not something I'm used to. My family consists of mum and dad and my sister, Hannah. Travis having so many siblings, plus spouses and all their kids, is quite overwhelming.

As we walk through the front door of Trav's family home, he grabs my hand and holds on tight, which I appreciate.

"You ready for this?" he asks.

"Is it too late to say no?" I respond with a nervous smile.

"They'll love you—you have nothing to worry about."

He leans down and gives me a quick chaste kiss, before leading me further into the house. We pass through the kitchen and towards the back of the house. I can hear a lot of laughing and squealing coming from the backyard, as Travis leads me out the back door. As we walk out, he yells to his family.

"Hey y'all, we're here!"

Everyone stops and turns around with huge smiles on their faces.

"Travis!" they all call. One by one, I'm introduced to his family. It will take me a while to remember all their names though! Everyone is so lovely; I can see why Travis loves them so much. I am immediately treated as one of the family.

Following our gourmet picnic lunch, I'm sitting on the lawn watching the kids play, when one of Travis' brothers sits down next to me.

"Hey," he says.

"Hey, Kelly, right?"

"Yeah, good job. There are a lot of people to remember aren't there?"

"You could say that. I'm used to a family of three—mum, dad and my sister, Hannah."

He smiles a warm, friendly smile.

"So, he finally got you to move out here?" Kelly asks.

"Actually, he didn't know I was coming. I surprised him on *Nights in Nashville*. Brant set it all up. It was pretty crazy. I have never done anything like that before."

"Oh yeah, my wife did mention that. I don't watch that crap, but I guess I missed a good show."

"It was amazing. Travis cried when he saw me. It was super sweet."

"Travis cried? Big, manly, cowboy Travis cried? Shit, he *has* got it bad."

"Well, the feeling is mutual."

"So, you love him then?"

"I do. I've never met anyone like him. He's amazing. I know what people think though, so it does make things difficult."

"What do people think?"

"That I'm only here for the fame and money."

"Are you?" Kelly asks.

"Not at all. I fell in love with him when I had no idea any of this existed, when I thought he was Travis Gardel—bar singer. A guy living in a tiny one-bedroom apartment. There was no indication that he had any money at all. I kind of wish he was that guy. All this scares the shit out of me. His house is enormous, and all the photographers and press following him everywhere—it's pretty crazy."

"Yeah, he's not a man you're going to have a nice quiet life with."

"I realize that now. I had no idea before I got here though. I don't know what to make of it. It worries me that I won't be able to cope with it all, but at the same time, I don't want to lose him, you know?"

"I won't say it's going to be easy, because it's probably going to be hard, especially all the attention he gets from women ..."

"I didn't think of that! Shit! I don't handle jealousy very well."

"You just have to remember that Travis loves *you*—and he really does. We've never seen him this happy. Women will throw themselves at him, it's a given. You just have to learn to brush it off. It will be hard, but if you want your relationship to last, it's one thing that you will have to put up with. Just remember, he will always come home to you. Travis is as honest as they come. You won't have to worry about him straying."

"Yeah, I know that."

Just then, Kelly's little girl, Charli falls over and starts crying.

"Sorry, I better grab her," he says.

"Of course! Thanks for the chat."

"Any time," he winks.

Chapter Twenty

• TRAVIS •

"Your family is amazing," Darcy says as we're heading home. We spent most of the day with them, as I wanted her to get to know them as much as possible. They are such a big part of my life, and I want her to love them as much as I do. I plan on her being around for the rest of my life, so her getting along with them is important to me.

"They all loved you," I say. "Kelly said he had a really good chat with you. What did you talk about?"

"You," she says. "Mainly just about how I'm worried about what people will think of me. I know what they think I'm here for."

"What do you mean?" I ask.

"Travis, I'm not stupid. You're extremely famous with millions of adoring fans and very, very wealthy; everyone thinks I'm here for your money."

"It doesn't matter what they think. I know you're here for me. You loved me before you knew about all that."

"Yeah, but no one else knows that. I'd think the same thing if I was them."

"Baby, it honestly doesn't matter; but if it bothers you, I could talk about how we met in my next radio interview. I have one in a few days. I could tell our whole story—then everyone will know that you love me, not everything else that comes along with being with me."

"You don't have to do that," she says.

"If it will make you happy, I will. I don't want you thinking about that sort of thing. I want you to be happy and I will do anything to make sure that happens. I love you baby; you mean everything to me. I need to know that you are comfortable with how things are."

"You are the sweetest man I have ever met; do you know that?"

I place my hands on her beautiful cheeks and plant my lips on hers.

"I love kissing you, do *you* know that?"

She laughs and snuggles into me.

When Chester pulls up in front of my house, he jumps out and opens Darcy's door for her.

"Chester, you really don't need to open my door for me. I can honestly handle it myself."

"Of course, Miss Darcy," he nods at her. There is no way Chester isn't going to open her door for her every single time. Once we're inside, I ask Darcy if she wants to watch a movie like we used to.

"Are you talking chick flick?" she asks me with a grin.

"Yeah, if that's what you want to watch."

"Actually, I'd love to watch one of your concerts. Is that possible?"

"Really? You want to watch a concert?"

"Yeah. All I've seen are a few YouTube clips. I'd love to see you in action in real life sometime too."

"You've heard me in real life—at *The Den*."

"Yeah, but I'm sure that's very different from the big arena shows you're used to."

"True. Follow me."

I lead Darcy into my theatre room and direct her to sit in one of the recliners.

"I thought you said we'd watch it like we used to?"

"We are. What do you mean?"

"Sitting on a stuffy recliner by myself isn't what I had in mind. I want to snuggle with you on the couch—like we used to."

"Wait here," I say, quickly coming up with a new plan.

I have to remember that Darcy isn't a fan of my giant place. She's used to being with me when I had that tiny one-bedroom apartment. She likes the closeness. I'm not used to that, since being back in Nashville. Laila had never wanted to be close like that. All she cared about was the big house, where she could go off to her separate area and do her own thing. I make my way out of the theatre room and head to a sitting room next door. In here, I have a small comfy sofa that I can drag into the theatre. Hopefully, that will make Darcy feel more comfortable.

As I drag it in, Darcy looks up and asks me what I'm doing.

"You said you wanted to snuggle on the couch."

She gives me a beautiful smile and nods.

I position the sofa and get things ready to play one of my recent shows at the Grand Ole Opry. This is my favorite venue, so I want her to see that first before one of the arena shows.

We sit together on the sofa and Darcy snuggles right into me—just like old times. It's so nice; I forgot how good it feels to have her wrapped around me.

"Travis, I can't believe how amazing you are. Seriously, you are so incredibly talented. People love you!"

"I only care that you love me," I reply.

"I do love you; so much. I'm so glad I decided to come here. I couldn't handle being without you for any longer. It was the longest four months of my life, Trav."

"Me too. It was hell. I've never been more miserable. Even after I found out about Laila, being away from you hurt more than that."

Before I know what's happening, Darcy climbs onto my lap with her legs straddling my thighs. She wraps her arms around my neck and looks into my eyes. Her perfect greens are glassy and full of love.

"I want you to make love to me," she whispers.

"Here?" I ask.

"Here."

Heading into the office the next day is hard. I don't want to leave Darcy alone, but she seems more than happy to stay home and get to know the place a little better. There is still so much of my place that she hasn't seen, and I have given her free reign to explore. She seems uncomfortable with this, but I remind her that it's now her place too. I've also given her use of my driver, Chester, in case she wants to go out exploring. On my to-do list for today, is hiring Darcy a driver and bodyguard. I want to know that she is safe at all times and that she never has to worry about transportation.

I meet up with Brant in my office, and he informs me that we have four people coming in for interviews, starting in fifteen minutes. Besides being a driver, I need someone that has a strong personal security background. They need to be able to protect Darcy at all times, so there is more to the job description than just driving her around.

After interviewing the first three candidates, I feel a little concerned that I'm not going to find the right person for her. All three guys so far have families, and I want someone that can be at her beck and call whenever she needs them; someone that has no close ties and can live on-site.

The last guy that comes in certainly looks the part. He's tall, extremely well built, solid as a brick wall, has a military background and was also an FBI agent for a while. He's done a lot in his thirty-two years. The only thing that bothers me about him, is that he is a very good-looking bloke. I know it sounds stupid, but I don't want to put temptation in Darcy's path.

"Mr Danvers, I'm Reed Lewis." He reaches out to shake my hand.

"Nice to meet you, Reed. Please have a seat. As you know, the reason you are here today is a driving and security position within my team. You will be working for my girlfriend, Darcy Hastings. Darcy is twenty-six, Australian and has just moved here to Nashville to live with me. The position is live-in and your accommodation will be in the staff wing of my home so that you are available to her whenever she needs you. The main responsibilities will be driving her wherever she needs to be, and most importantly, keeping her safe as her bodyguard. As our relationship has only been announced recently, I'm not sure how she will be treated by either my fans or the paparazzi. She is to be protected by both at all costs."

"Of course," Reed nods at me.

"Darcy doesn't know anyone in Nashville besides my family, who you will meet, my manager, Brant and our housekeeper, Peggy. She will soon be starting work with the company she worked for in Australia—Great Scott Design. Her boss, Jesse Scott will be moving here in the next few days, so she will have a lot to do with him. He has a strong romantic interest in Darcy, so that's something you'll need to keep an eye on—more so that he keeps his hands to himself. You'll need to perform background checks on anyone that comes into regular contact with Darcy. Obviously, before you accept the position, there is a detailed contract that you will need to read and sign, plus a non-disclosure agreement. You'll be heavily involved in our day-to-day lives. Is this something you think will work for you?"

"Absolutely. It all sounds great, to be honest."

"I want to explain one of the things that you will notice in the contract. A lot of prospective employees find it strange at first, and it's often a deal-breaker for them. My security staff may have guests to the house; however, they must remain in the staff wing. They are never permitted in the main part of the house, unless invited by Darcy or myself. Any of your guests that make their way into the main house, will be the cause for your instant dismissal, and a substantial financial penalty. Those details are all in the contract. You may casually 'date', however, if you are wishing to pursue a more serious relationship, you will need to terminate your employment. We've found in the past, that people in committed relationships are unable to be fully committed to the job, which I completely understand, but when my girls' life is at stake, that doesn't sit well with me at all."

"I understand, sir. I'm single, so that won't be an issue."

"Great. Well, Reed, I think I've got a pretty good feel for you. If you're still interested, I'll grab a copy of the contract for you to read. If you're happy to accept all the terms, I'd be happy to offer you the position for a trial of one month. Obviously, Darcy will need to meet you, and if she feels comfortable with you after the month, then the job is yours."

"I'm definitely interested, thank you," Reed says.

"Fantastic. Here's a copy of the contract. Also, how soon can you start?"

"I can start tomorrow if you need me to."

"That would be great. It will be good for you to get to know Darcy before she starts work. You're welcome to move in as soon as you're able. I will organize movers for you."

"Sounds fantastic. Thank you so much."

"I'll leave you for a while to read through the contract. When you're finished, come out to reception and we can talk further."

"Okay, thank you."

I leave Reed with the contract and head off to sort out a few other things. I also call Darcy to let her know that I might be bringing her new security home to meet her. She's surprised to find out that she will have her own personal security and driver.

"Is that really necessary, babe?" she asks.

"Hopefully not, but I'd rather be safe than sorry when it comes to you. You still need a driver anyway."

"What about Chester?"

"I need him daily, so it will be too much for him to look after both of us. I would just feel happier knowing that you are safe and can get anywhere you need to go at any time."

"Okay, if you think it's best. I trust you. How old is he?"

"Thirty-two."

"Oh, so he's only young?"

"Yeah, he's ex-military and ex-FBI."

"Geez, that's a whole lot of training just to look after me!"

"You're worth it babe. This business can get a bit crazy sometimes and I want to make sure you're safe. I couldn't live with myself if something happened to you."

"You're a beautiful man, Trav."

"I better go, babe. I might see you soon if the guy accepts the contract and is free to come and meet you now."

"Okay. I love you."

"Love you too. See you soon."

I hang up from Darcy and notice Reed waiting in Reception.

"How did you go?" I ask him.

"Great. I'm happy with everything contained within the contract."

"Fantastic! The job's yours then if you want it."

"That's amazing. Thank you so much. I'm in."

"Awesome. If you've signed the contract and the non-disclosure, would you be interested in meeting Darcy now?"

"Definitely. I've left both the signed contract and non-disclosure on your desk."

I call Chester and ask him to bring the car around to the front.

"I'll have my driver take us home where you'll meet Darcy, then I can show you where you'll be staying. Chester can then bring you back here or take you anywhere else you need to go after that."

"Thank you so much. That sounds great," he says.

We make our way outside through a small group of fans and paparazzi, to the waiting car, and Chester drives us home. Firstly, I take Reed around to the staff entrance and show him his suite.

"The only other live-in staff member I have is my housekeeper, but you both have completely separate areas of this wing. In your suite, you have a bedroom, bathroom, living area, dining room and kitchen. Peggy will make all your evening meals and breakfast if that's what you prefer. You'll usually be out and about for lunch, so you can either grab your own, or Peggy will provide something that you can eat on the go. You can arrange that with her though. There is also a staff gym next door that you are welcome to use. I've never seen Peggy use it, so I'd pretty much say it's all yours."

"It's seriously amazing. I wasn't expecting anything like this,"

Reed says.

"I want to make sure my staff are taken care of. They usually become like part of the family, and if they're happy then they do their job better."

"Sounds like a good way to operate."

"If you'll follow me this way, I'll introduce you to Peggy my housekeeper, and then Darcy."

I lead Reed down the hallway toward the main house. In the kitchen I introduce Peggy and Reed, and she fawns all over him like a mother hen. She rubs his biceps up and down and kisses him on the cheek. She'll love having someone else to look after. Poor Reed looks rather embarrassed with all the fuss.

"Peggy, do you know where Darcy might be?" I ask her.

"Miss Darcy was swimming earlier in the indoor pool, Mr Travis."

"Thanks, Peggy." We make our way to the pool room, and I show Reed inside. Once there, I see Darcy swimming laps and wave to grab her attention. She sees me and gives me a huge smile while swimming to the side. I grab her towel for her, and she hops out. *Damn, why did she have to be wearing that skimpy white bikini today! She looks incredible, and no doubt Reed has also noticed—how could he not?*

"Hey baby," I say as I hand her the towel, and give her a soft kiss.

"Hey, Trav." She looks in the direction of Reed with interest.

"Darcy, this is Reed Lewis. He's your new driver and personal security."

Reed offers his hand to Darcy, and she takes it with a smile.

"It's a pleasure to meet you, Miss Hastings," he says with a polite nod.

"Darcy, please," she responds. "It's nice to meet you too, Reed. Sorry I'm not dressed."

"Not at all. Sorry to have interrupted your swim."

"I was done anyway," she smiles.

"Reed will be starting tomorrow and will be moving into the second suite in the staff wing," I say.

"Oh cool. I just checked that out today, pretty impressive actually.

I'm new here too," she says to Reed.

"Well, we can help each other out then," he replies with a smile.

"I should probably leave you to it," Reed says when he notices me giving him a look.

"Of course. Chester will be where we left him and will take you wherever you need to go."

"Thank you so much, Mr Danvers. I look forward to getting to work. Nice to meet you, Miss Hastings."

I lead Reed back towards the staff wing, and out to where Chester is waiting. I thank him for coming and ask him to be back by seven in the morning, before walking back to the pool room to check on Darcy.

"What did you think of Reed, babe?"

"Yeah, he seems really nice. Hopefully, we get on okay and it all works out."

"Well, he's on trial for a month, so if you feel that it's not working, or you don't feel one hundred percent comfortable, we can find someone else. You have to feel that you could trust him with your life. That's what he's there for after all."

"I'm sure it will be fine. Thank you, babe. I can't believe I have a personal driver. I feel like a movie star!"

"Anything for you, baby. You mean everything to me."

Chapter Twenty One

• REED •

The moment Darcy Hastings climbs out of the pool in that skimpy little white bikini, I have to use everything within me to hold back a gasp and keep my jaw from hitting the tiles. I've hit the fucking jackpot! I'm always extremely professional, and I'll continue to be so, but holy fuck, being around Darcy twenty-four-seven is going to be one hell of a challenge. The woman is a friggin' bombshell, and I'm not going to be able to touch her.

I have moved into the second suite in Danvers's mansion and have started my first day with Darcy. Because she hasn't started work yet, she's just hanging around at home for the day. When she's home, I keep to my suite unless she buzzes me for something. Apparently, her boss is arriving from Australia this afternoon, so I'll be taking her to pick him up from the airport. They are then heading to check out an office building where they plan to start up their business in Nashville. After that, we're to drop him at his hotel.

At three o'clock, I walk into the main house to find Darcy. We need to leave for the airport in fifteen minutes, and I want to check that she is nearly ready to go. I find her talking in the kitchen with Peggy, the housekeeper, so I stand in the doorway and quietly clear my throat to indicate my presence.

Darcy spins around and gives me a huge smile. *Fuck she's beautiful!*

"Hey Reed, is it nearly time to go?"

"Yes, Miss Hastings. I'll be waiting for you in the car when you're ready."

"Reed, this is not going to work if you don't call me Darcy."

"Of course. I apologize. Ready when you are … *Darcy*."

"Thanks, Reed. I'll be out in just a minute."

As I walk away from the kitchen, I hear Peggy and Darcy talking.

"Mr Reed is so handsome," Peggy giggles. "He has very big muscles, no?"

"Peggy, you have a thing for the hot young bodyguard?" Darcy asks laughing. "I'm a very lucky girl. Once Jesse arrives, I'll be surrounded by gorgeous men—in my bed, my car, my office."

"Miss Darcy," Peggy gasps.

Darcy laughs again and starts heading out of the kitchen. I race to the front door, so I don't get caught eavesdropping.

"Bye, Peggy," she calls back.

Darcy makes her way to the door, and I hold it open for her as she bounces down the front steps.

"How chivalrous," she giggles.

She heads towards the car, and again I open the back passenger door for her, and she climbs in.

"Thanks, Reed."

"You're most welcome, Miss … ah, Darcy."

She smiles up at me and pulls her seatbelt across her chest. I close her door, round the bonnet and climb into the front seat.

"Would you like me to engage the privacy screen, Darcy?" I ask her.

"What! No way. How am I supposed to talk to you if you put that thing up?"

"You want to talk to me?"

"Of course. Is that okay, or is it against the rules?"

"No, that's fine. I'm just not used to my employer wanting to talk to me."

"Well sorry, I'm a talker. Besides, how are we supposed to get to know each other if we don't talk?"

"You're right. I'd love to talk to you."

"Great. So, how old are you, *Mr Lewis?*"

"Reed. I'm thirty-two," I reply.

"Did you, or did you not know, that Peggy has the hots for you?"

I chuckle as I look back at her through the rearview mirror.

"She's a sweetheart," I reply.

"Yeah, she is. So, you were military and FBI before this?"

"That's correct."

"Sounds interesting."

"It was, but I wanted a new challenge."

"How can going from being in the military and the FBI, to driving me around be a challenge? Won't you get bored?"

"I doubt there will be a boring moment with you, Miss Hastings."

I again check the rearview mirror and notice her grinning back at me. We lock eyes for a moment before I turn mine back to the road.

"What do you think of the car, Reed?" she asks me. "Pretty fancy huh? I'm not used to this sort of thing. Back home, I drove a beat-up little hatchback."

"It's an amazing car. I can't complain when I get to drive an Audi S8."

She laughs at that.

"So, do you have a girlfriend, boyfriend, wife, husband, partner, significant other?" she asks me with a cheeky grin.

I chuckle.

"None of the above."

"Really? I would have thought a hot guy like you would have women, and men for that matter, falling all over themselves to get a shot at you."

"Is that right?" I laugh.

"Well, yeah. I mean … ummm," she stutters.

"Don't get shy now," I tease.

I peer into the mirror and notice a pink flush crawl up her neck and sweep across her face.

"Being in the type of work I've been, it's not conducive to building lasting relationships. Besides, if I'd been in a relationship, I couldn't have accepted this job."

Darcy looks at me in confusion.

"What do you mean?"

"Well, it's in my employment contract that I can't be involved in any committed relationship."

"What?" she shrieks. "Why?"

"It's fairly normal practice for this type of position. If I was just your driver, that might be different, but being your bodyguard, I need to have my mind one hundred percent on the job. If I were here worrying about getting home late to a wife or girlfriend, my mind wouldn't be fully on the job. Little mistakes can have serious consequences. Your life is in my hands, so I need to be fully committed to you, and I will be."

Darcy just looks at me in the mirror and shakes her head.

"Wow, it's all pretty full-on, isn't it? When Trav was in Australia with me, he was pretty much unknown, and we just went on with our lives as normal. I didn't even know he was famous until just before he moved back here. This is all so new to me. I'm actually going to have to think before I do things, aren't I?"

"Yeah, you probably will," I chuckle. "Are you usually an act first, think later kind of girl?"

"Yeah, you could say that," she laughs. "I like to play with people."

"Play with people?" I ask.

"Yeah," she chuckles. "I can be a bit naughty and tend to say exactly what's on my mind. I'm sure you'll see what I mean soon enough. I can't leave you out of the game. I'll need to get all my playfulness out of my system before people start recognizing me and connecting me to Travis. I wouldn't want to hurt his career because I can't keep my thoughts to myself."

I look in the mirror and smile back at her. This 'playfulness' she talks about sounds interesting. I'm looking forward to seeing her in action—I think!

We soon arrive at the airport, and I pull into the short-term parking lot.

"Will you be waiting here for me, Reed?" Darcy asks as I open her door for her.

"No, I'm sorry Darcy. I have to accompany you everywhere you go, especially somewhere like an airport."

"Oh, okay. Let's go then."

We walk into the terminal and with a hand on the small of her back, I direct her to the arrivals lounge.

"There's still about fifteen minutes until Jesse's plane lands," Darcy says. "Can I get you a coffee?"

"Uh, sure. That sounds great, thanks," I reply.

We sit down at a little coffee shop, and a waitress walks towards us.

"What can I get you both?" she asks looking directly at me with flirty eyes. I look at Darcy and see her roll her eyes. I narrow mine at her, wondering what that's all about.

"I'll grab a coffee, white with one and a chocolate muffin," Darcy says. She looks at me with a smile and I place my order.

"I'll be right back," says the waitress, who walks away before turning and looking back at me over her shoulder.

Darcy and I make small talk before the waitress brings our muffins over. She places Darcy's in front of her and then mine, again without taking her eyes off me once. She walks back to the counter to grab our coffees and brings them over with the same routine. The next minute, I feel her place her hand on my bicep.

"If there's anything else I can get you at all, please let me know," she smiles at me.

I look at Darcy who is giving the waitress dragon eyes, and I inwardly smile.

"There is something you could get actually," Darcy says to her.

"What's that?" the waitress asks, still with her eyes on me.

"Your hands *off* my boyfriend! What sort of woman feels up a customer, while his girlfriend is sitting opposite him? Why don't you just slip your tongue in while you're at it?" she asks.

My jaw hits the table. The poor waitress looks down at her hand on my arm, and quickly pulls away, before almost running back behind the counter. Darcy looks across at me with an enormous grin.

"I told you I like to play," she says.

I can do nothing but burst out laughing.

"Wow, you're mean," I say.

"Mean? No, I'm not. How does she know you're not my boyfriend? I've had to do the same thing while out with my boss, and also Travis. Now I'm going to have to do it with you too," she winks. "Although now that I think about it, perhaps you do want her tongue down your throat. I'm so sorry. I'll go apologize and get her number for you."

"I'm not interested in the waitress, Darcy," I smile. "I'm happy for you to step in and defend my honor."

"You realize then, that I'm going to have to at least give you a butt squeeze on our way out."

I look at her with wide eyes.

"Wow, you do like to play, don't you?"

"Yep. And considering the way you look, I'm pretty sure this won't be the last time. If you ever feel uncomfortable with something I do though, you have to let me know, okay? Sometimes I can get a bit carried away. Before Travis and I got together, I told a girl that Trav was mind-blowing in bed, and then I climbed into his lap and pashed him right in front of her."

"Oh my god, you're not serious?" I laugh.

"Absolutely. I can get very protective of my men—even if they're not technically my men."

"I think I'm going to enjoy working for you!" I say.

"I hope so," she replies with a smile. "We should go. Jesse will have landed by now. Get ready for your butt squeeze."

Darcy and I stand and head to the counter to settle the bill. The waitress who served us is at the till, and she turns bright red when she sees us approach. I feel Darcy place her hand on the top of my shoulder and slide her hand down the front of my chest. She stops her hand just above my abs and then snuggles into my side with her other arm around my waist. *And now I'm getting fucking hard.*

"That will be $22.50," the waitress says looking only at Darcy.

"I'll get this one, baby," Darcy says looking up at me.

She hands over her credit card, and as we turn to leave, her arm slips from my waist and lands firmly on my ass. She then looks over her shoulder at the waitress and gives my ass a squeeze at the same time.

"You really are bad," I say with a shake of my head.

"I know," she laughs.

"I see him," Darcy says, looking in the direction of the gangway doors. We walk towards the door and Darcy runs forward into the arms of a young guy, who must be her boss. They're a little friendly for a boss/employee relationship, I think to myself. *No wonder Mr Danvers is nervous about him.*

"Jesse!" Darcy shrieks. "It's so good to see you. I've missed you. How was your flight?"

"Hey, beautiful. It was good, thanks. I slept most of it which is unlike me."

I step forward to take Jesse's bag from him, and he looks at me strangely.

"Oh Jesse, this is Reed Lewis, my driver and bodyguard."

"Bodyguard?" Jesse asks in horror.

"Yeah, Trav is a bit overprotective. He's like Nashville's golden boy, so he's very well known around here. We can't go anywhere without fans or the paparazzi hounding us."

"Geez," says Jesse. "Are you sure you're okay with all this?"

"Well it's only Reed's first day, and he's already let me squeeze his butt, so yeah I think we'll get on fine."

Jesse looks at me then.

"She already started *playing*, has she?" he asks me.

"Yes sir, Miss Hastings is quite the character."

"Yeah, that's one way to put it."

"Hey," she says with a laugh.

As we make our way out of the airport and towards the new Great Scott Design office space, I watch Jesse and Darcy in the backseat. They're holding hands and acting like they're best friends, not boss and employee. *Geez, if she was my girl, there would be no way I'd want her working alongside this guy.* It's more than obvious that he is totally into her, and not afraid to show it either.

Once we arrive at the office, I open Darcy's door and hold my hand out to assist her. She grabs my hand but then strokes my knuckles as she does. *You are such a flirt, Darcy Hastings!* She smiles up at me, gives me a wink and then follows Jesse in.

Once inside, Jesse and Darcy look around the reception area, then he leads her back to where their offices are. There is a central communal area with a bunch of cubicles, and then three large offices, all with glass walls. Jesse takes the corner office, and Darcy's is next to his. The thing I find a little strange, is that Jesse's desk faces Darcy's office and vice versa. They will basically be sitting there looking at each other all day long. Mr Danvers is not going to like this. I wouldn't if I were him. I *don't* like it, and she isn't even my girl! After a little more of a tour, I see Darcy pull Jesse aside. She's talking quietly, and I can't hear anything, but every now and then, she looks back at me. *What is going on there?*

Once they've finished talking, Jesse leads Darcy out and towards the car. I follow behind but quickly jump in front so I can hold Darcy's door open.

"Thanks, handsome," she says with a smile as she climbs in.

Jesse looks at me with a frown, and then back at her.

"Should you be talking to your staff like that, Darce?"

"Really? Says you who *kissed* me—one of *your* staff!"

What the hell! He kissed her? Does Mr Danvers know about this?

"Okay, fair point."

"Jesse, you know me. I'm not a stuffy celebrity snob type. I'm just me. I'll treat Reed just like I would treat anyone else. I need to be able to trust him with my life, know that he's got my back in any situation. I'd rather have a friend in that position than just some guy who drives me around and never talks to me. Reed will probably end up being the one person who knows me better than anybody else. He'll hopefully become one of my closest friends."

I look at Jesse in the rearview mirror with the slightest grin. He doesn't look happy *at all*.

"I hope that's okay with you, Reed?" Darcy asks me.

"Whatever you need, Miss Hastings," I reply.

The remainder of the drive to Jesse's hotel is relatively uneventful. Jesse doesn't say much, and Darcy looks out the window most of the trip. When we arrive at the hotel, I jump out and grab Jesse's bags from the trunk. Jesse doesn't get out straight away, so I presume he wants to talk to Darcy without me listening in. After a few minutes, he finally emerges and takes his bags from me.

"It's been a pleasure to meet you, Mr Scott," I say.

He looks at me with a slight frown.

"You too, Reed. Take care of her, okay?"

"I'll protect her with my life, sir," I reply.

He nods and walks into the lobby.

As I get back into the driver's seat, I look back at Darcy.

"You okay back there?" I ask her.

"Yeah, I'm fine. I don't think Jesse is very happy about you though. He thinks you're too good looking to be my bodyguard."

"He said I was too good looking to take care of you?"

"Actually, his exact words were 'that guy is way too hot to be looking after you. You're gonna fall in love with him'."

"What!"

"I know, he's just pissed that you're always going to be around. I reminded him that I'm in love with Travis, and that I am perfectly capable of being around a gorgeous man without falling in love with him."

"Gorgeous, huh?" I ask smugly.

"You know you are," she huffs.

Chapter Twenty Two

• DARCY •

Reed Lewis is not at all what I'd been expecting when Travis told me I was getting my own security. My thoughts immediately went to an older gentleman type, much like Chester, but that's certainly not who Travis hired.

Reed is good looking, and I mean ridiculously good looking. His dark hair is short and neat at the back, and longer on top and I often see him running his fingers through it in a sexy way. He's tall, so very tall, and extremely well built, and definitely has that military vibe about him. I would guess that every moment that he isn't with me, he's spending in the gym. I have yet to view his naked chest, and I bet it's spectacular! I'm also certain he's the proud owner of a perfect eight pack which sits just above that glorious V that women go crazy over.

Although his face is male model perfect, he also has a very rugged look about him. He has just the right amount of sexy stubble that almost hides his gorgeous left dimple. His nose is perfect and straight, and he has the most perfectly chiseled square jaw and stunning hazel eyes, that make you believe you can see into his soul.

"Babe, can I ask you a question?" I ask Travis.

"Of course, anything."

"Why did you choose Reed for the job?"

"He's the most qualified. Why? Don't you like him?"

"Yeah, I do. I think he's great. I think we'll become really good friends. He's the type of guy I'd normally hang out with. He seems easy to talk to, friendly but also professional when he needs to be. I think he'll be very good at the job."

"So, what's the issue then?"

"I don't think there's an issue, it's just that …" I wonder if I should actually tell him the truth or not.

"That what?"

"Well … he's very good-looking, Trav. I'm surprised you chose someone like him. I thought I'd have someone like Chester, you know, older gentleman type, that would be more like a father figure, rather than a good-looking man my age."

"Do you think there's a chance you'd ever want to become more than friends with him?"

"No, of course not. I love you, but you know how I am, Trav. I'm a flirt, I like to play, and I don't want you to think things are there when they're not. I played with Reed the other day, and he was fine with it—I just told him before I did anything. I think he realizes already what a flirt I am. He says he can see that I'll be trouble."

"Yeah, I know what you're like, and I'm okay with it. As long as it doesn't go too far."

"What's too far in your eyes?" I ask him.

"Well, I don't like the fact that you would kiss someone else, that's for sure. But I know how you *play*, and I understand it doesn't mean anything to you when you do it."

"It doesn't, Trav. I appreciate that you're so understanding about that, I really am. Most guys wouldn't be. I would never cheat on you; you know that right?"

"Yeah, I know. Just tell me if you think you're falling for him though, okay?"

"Trav … I love you. There's no room for anyone else. I would never do anything to intentionally hurt you. You mean too much to me."

I reach out to wrap my arms around his waist.

"I know, baby. I love you too, so much."

With that, I lean into him and place my lips on his.

"How did I ever get so lucky to find a man as good as you?" I ask.

He throws me his gorgeous grin, and I melt in his arms.

"You heading off soon?" he asks me.

"Yeah, Reed should be here soon to take me. We're interviewing new staff today. We're already taking lots of calls, so we need to hire a receptionist as soon as possible. Jesse also wants to fill the three cubie positions straight away, otherwise, our individual workloads will get to be too much."

"Is there already enough work to keep you busy?" he asks me.

"Yeah, we're both working on Australian clients at the moment, but once we pick up clients here in Nashville, it will definitely be too much for just the two of us."

I turn at the sound of Reed clearing his throat in the doorway.

"Hi, Reed. Is it time to go?"

"Yes, Miss Hastings. I'll be in the car ready when you are."

"I'm ready. See you later, baby," I say as I kiss Travis goodbye.

"Okay, good luck with your interviews."

"Thanks. I love you."

"Love you too."

"How's your morning been, Reed?" I ask.

"Very good thanks, Miss Hastings. I spent it in the gym."

"Reed, you need to call me Darcy."

"I apologize. Can we please make a compromise though?"

"What is it?" I ask.

"I'm happy to call you Darcy when it's just the two of us, but if there are others around, such as Mr Danvers or Mr Scott, I would prefer calling you Miss Hastings. It would be unprofessional of me otherwise."

"Okay, I can work with that."

"Thank you, I appreciate it."

We pull up to the office parking lot, and Reed opens my door and helps me out. We make our way into the building, and I'm greeted by Jesse.

"Hey, gorgeous."

"Hey, Jesse. What time did you get in?"

"Only about fifteen minutes ago."

He looks over and acknowledges Reed, with that lift of the chin thing guys do.

"What time is the first interview?" I ask him.

"In half an hour."

"Okay, I'm going to do a few things in my office for a while. Reed, what are your plans while I'm working today?" I ask him.

"I'll just sit in the lunchroom perhaps, unless you need me for anything."

"Don't sit in there by yourself. At least join me in my office."

"You sure?"

"Yeah, of course."

The day flies by as we interview three people for the receptionist position, and three others for some of the cubie positions. Jesse and I agree on who we think might be good for the receptionist, and only one of the interviewees seems suitable for a cubie position. We're still holding more interviews tomorrow, so hopefully, we'll find someone else in that group.

All day I feel bad for Reed. I can't understand how he can just sit here all day, and not fall asleep. He always says he's perfectly fine though. I will have to find something entertaining for him to do during the day, even if it's just so that I can concentrate on what I'm doing, and not have to worry about him all the time.

Towards the end of the day, a courier delivers an envelope that's addressed to me. I open it immediately and gasp at what I read.

You can't have him, he'll never be yours.
I'll make sure of it—even if I have to get rid of you
in the process.

I look at Reed with concern, and he asks if I'm okay.

"Maybe you should look at this," I respond.

He walks over, takes the card from me and reads it quickly. In an instant, he's on the phone talking with someone and giving the details of the card.

"It's a threat and I need to know who sent it," he says. "I don't care about your policy. If you can't give me the details over the phone, I'll need to launch an official investigation which will get very messy for you," I hear him say.

He doesn't seem to get far with whoever he's talking to, so he hangs up and I hear him call Travis.

"Mr Danvers, It's Reed Lewis. I'm just informing you that Darcy received a threat today. Yes sir. Of course," I hear him say. "I will not let her out of my sight, sir. I'll fill you in further this evening. Of course, one minute."

Reed looks at me and hands me his phone.

"Mr Danvers would like to speak with you," he says.

I take the phone from Reed and bring it to my ear.

"Hey, Travis."

"Hey, baby. Are you okay love?"

"Yeah, I'm fine. It was just a strange message. You don't need to worry about me."

"Well, I am worried. If Reed thinks it's worth a phone call to me, then we need to treat it seriously."

"I'll be careful, baby. I'll make sure that I don't go anywhere without Reed. Do you think it could be Laila?" I ask carefully.

"I don't think she would do something like that, but who knows. I'll brief Reed tonight and he'll look into it. Don't worry though, we'll keep you safe."

"I know. I'm not worried. We'll be heading home soon anyway, so

I'll see you when you get home. Will you be late?"

"No, I'll come home early tonight. I just want to see you."

"Okay, see you then. I love you."

As Reed and I head home, we mostly make small talk, until he brings up the subject of my afternoon delivery.

"Are you concerned at all, Darcy?" he asks me.

"No, not really. I don't feel unsafe, if that's what you're asking."

"I'm glad. I will protect you. As long as you always stay close to me, I'll protect you."

"I know you will," I reply with a small smile. "Is there a reason you keep looking behind us though? Are you concerned?"

"I don't want to scare you, but I'm pretty sure we're being followed."

I spin around to look out the back window.

"Really? How can you tell?"

"There's a black vehicle a few cars back that has been weaving in and out and has been with us since we left the office. It could be nothing, but I'll run the plates just to see if it brings up anything of interest."

"Can you do that?"

"Yeah. Are you buckled in?"

"Yeah, I am."

"I want to do a few quick sharp turns to see if he continues to follow. I don't want to lead him back to your place. Let me know if I scare you, okay?"

"Okay."

Reed takes off suddenly from the lights and turns left quickly down a side street.

"Can you see who's driving?" I ask him.

"No, I haven't got a good look yet. He is following us though."

"Really. I don't get why anyone would be interested in me."

"Some fans can get very invested in their celebrity crushes. They become extremely obsessed and believe they are genuinely part of that persons' life. If someone is obsessed with Travis—and it's likely a woman—then she may believe that she is actually in a relationship with him, and you would be a threat to her. That could explain the card. It also sounds very much like a message from an ex."

"Well, his ex-wife is unhinged, so I believe she could be capable."

"I'll look into everything, okay? You don't need to worry about it. I'll take care of you."

"Thanks, Reed."

We make it home safely after Reed loses the car following us. He leads me into the house, and I ask him to stay with me until Travis gets home. He's reluctant, but agrees.

"Will you watch a movie with me?" I ask him.

"I don't think Mr Danvers would like that, do you?"

"He'll be fine with it, especially after what happened today. Do you have a movie preference?"

"No, you choose."

"You'll regret saying that," I laugh. "Travis always regrets letting me choose. I'm a chick flick kind of girl."

"I can cope with that for a bit, as long as it's not too mushy."

"So that would be a no to *The Notebook* then?" I giggle.

"Well, you are my boss, so I don't have much of a say, do I?"

"No," I laugh.

Thankfully, Travis has left the couch in the theatre, so I get Reed to sit, and I message Peggy to see if she can fix us some popcorn. I set the movie going and make myself comfortable next to Reed.

"Have you seen this before?" I ask him with a grin.

"Ah no, I can't say that I have."

I giggle and snuggle further into him, grabbing his hand and threading my fingers with his. After a few minutes, Peggy brings in the popcorn.

We settle into the movie, and I occasionally glance at Reed to see his reactions. I think he actually might be enjoying it, and now and then, I feel his thumb stroke my knuckles.

After about fifteen minutes, Reed suddenly grabs the remote and presses pause.

"What are you doing?" I ask him, sitting up.

He releases my hand and turns to face me on the couch.

"I can see why Travis fell in love with you," he says.

I look at him in confusion as he continues.

"Darcy, you're beautiful, fun, playful, cheeky, amazing. Being here holding your hand is one of the best feelings I've ever had. I've been sitting here this whole time imagining you're my girl—holding your hand, stroking your knuckles while we watch a chick flick. All I've wanted to do this whole time is bend down and kiss you, but then I remember I can't, because you're not mine. If Travis wasn't such a great guy, I probably would have tried something by now, but I respect him and I respect you. I think I just need to keep a little distance; otherwise, I'm going to give in to the temptation. If I don't keep things professional between us, I can see myself falling in love with you very quickly, and that wouldn't be good for anyone. I think you're fantastic, Darcy, and I don't want to ruin the great friendship we've already formed—I hope you understand."

I look at him shocked for a few seconds before I can respond.

"Wow, Reed, I'm sorry. I had no idea you felt that way. If I'm honest with you, I have to say that I'm very attracted to you—I think you're seriously hot, but at the same time, I'm completely in love with Travis and I would never, ever cheat on him. He knows what a flirt I am, I mean that's kind of how we got together, and he knows how I like to play, and how I build really strong connections with people and he's okay with that because he knows I would never cross the line. I'm so sorry I made you feel uncomfortable. I'll try my best to keep my distance. I don't want to ruin our friendship either, because even though we haven't known each other long, you've come to mean a lot to me already. Are we good?"

"Of course, we're good," he replies.

We soon resume the movie and settle back in. Before too long, I find myself getting extremely tired and can feel my eyelids getting heavier and heavier before I shut them for just a minute.

Chapter Twenty Three

• TRAVIS •

When I get home, I go straight to the kitchen in search of my beautiful girl, but only find Peggy.

"Do you know where Darcy is, Peggy?" I ask her.

"Yes, Mr Travis, she is watching a movie with Mr Reed in the theatre."

"Okay, thanks, Peggy."

I walk towards the theatre, and find Darcy and Reed on the couch together, watching what looks to be *The Notebook*, with Darcy asleep on Reed's shoulder. I quietly clear my throat as I walk in, and Reed turns to look at me.

"Evening, Mr Danvers," Reed whispers. "I apologize, Miss Hastings wanted me to watch a movie with her while she waited for you, but she fell asleep and I didn't want to wake her after the day she's had."

"Did she force you to watch some crappy chick flick?"

"Yeah, something like that," he replies.

"That sounds like her," I say with a smile. "I'll carry her up to bed now, but if you could meet me in my office in ten minutes, I'd like to run through today with you.

"Of course," he replies. I bend down and slip one arm under

Darcy's shoulder, and one behind her knees and pull her up into my chest. She stirs a little but doesn't open her eyes and snuggles further into my chest.

"Love you, Trav," she mumbles sleepily.

"I love you too, baby," I reply with a kiss to her forehead.

Reed gets up from the couch and holds the door open for me as I carry Darcy through. I take her up to our bedroom and place her gently in bed before covering her with the blankets.

I make my way back downstairs and head to my office to speak with Reed, where I find him waiting for me.

"Have a seat, Lewis," I say.

I take my seat behind my desk and ask Reed to fill me in on exactly what happened with the threat against Darcy today. He informs me that they'd been followed home, which concerns me more than the card delivery. The fact that someone knows where Darcy is working also worries me. I'm not sure how anybody could know that yet—they would have to be following her pretty closely for them to find out that information.

Reed says that he will follow up with the courier company, will look into Laila, and will also check out the vehicle that followed them. He also suggests that he'll take Darcy on a different route to and from work each day, just to make things a little harder for this person. I thank him for looking after her, and he retreats to his room for the night.

I make my way into the kitchen and chat with Peggy while she prepares our evening meal. I fill her in on the threat made against Darcy, reminding her to keep an eye out if she sees or hears anything suspicious around the house. When dinner is ready, I make my way upstairs to wake Darcy. She's still very sleepy on her walk downstairs, but she's hungry so she makes the effort.

"I'm doing a one night only show at the end of the week," I inform her after a few minutes of silence.

"Really? Where at?" she asks.

"Bridgestone Arena," I reply.

"Wow, that's a pretty big venue, isn't it?"

"Yeah, they can squeeze a few in it," I chuckle. "It's sold out, so it should have a great atmosphere. It's the first time I've performed a big event since I've been back, and I'd love you to come with me."

"Are you kidding? I wouldn't miss it!" she squeals.

Backstage at Bridgestone Arena, Darcy is jumping with excitement.

"Aren't you nervous?" she asks me.

"A little, but this is my job, it's what I do. I'm kind of used to it now," I reply.

"Oh my god, I'm about to pee my pants, I'm so nervous!" she responds.

I laugh and wrap her in my arms.

"Make sure you stay close to her tonight, Lewis," I say looking in his direction.

"Of course, sir. I won't let her out of my sight."

There's a knock at the door and Brant, my manager, walks in.

"Showtime in ten minutes, Travis. *Soulful Cargo* are just finishing up now."

"Great, thanks, Brant. Can you take Darcy and Lewis to the front VIP strip for me?"

"Of course, mate," he replies.

"I'll see you out there, baby," I say to Darcy as I kiss her forehead.

"Okay, have fun. You look fucking hot by the way," she whispers seductively in my ear.

I give her a quick slap on the ass as she walks past, and she lets out a little yelp. *How the hell did I get so lucky?*

I soon make my way towards the stage with my entourage of hair and makeup artists fussing over me. I'm pumped to be heading back on stage after so many months away, and I'm determined to put on a good show for my fans tonight.

Backstage, I catch up with the members of *Soulful Cargo* just as they come off and thank them for sharing the stage with me. I'm still in awe by the fact that bands like theirs would want to perform with me. The crowd is as much theirs as it is mine.

"Kill it, Travis," Dixie says.

I give her a wink and run towards the front of the stage, as the intro to my first song starts.

"Hey, what's up Nashviiiiiile!" I yell to the crowd. As usual, they go ballistic, and I get such a buzz. *I missed this feeling.*

Every now and then, I look down to the front of the stage where I see Darcy standing with Reed. She looks like she's having a blast, and I regularly throw a wink or blow a kiss in her direction. She throws them right back.

After a few upbeat tracks, I decide it's time to interact with the crowd a bit. I thank them for coming out to support me after my long break, and I talk a little about my time in Australia. Following this, I look to the band to start up our next song. I'm about to start one of my ballads when I look at Darcy.

"This is for my girl, Darcy," I say as I blow her a kiss.

The crowd goes crazy, and I see her eyes water a little, and I watch as she turns to Reed and says something with a laugh. He rolls his eyes with a grin.

Towards the end of the night, I see Brant lead Darcy and Reed backstage, and after addressing the crowd again, I soon follow. We eventually catch up in my dressing room, after I complete the usual fan meet and greet.

"What did you think?" I ask Darcy as I wrap her in my arms.

"It was amazing, Trav. Seriously, the best show I've ever seen. There was so much atmosphere, the crowd were eating out of your hand. You should have heard some of the comments I could hear from women behind me; they wanted in your pants," she winks.

"Is that so?" I ask.

"Yep, can't say I blame them though," she smiles with a mischievous look in her eye. "It's very nice in your pants."

"Darcy!" I groan, as I hear Reed practically choke in the corner.

"Hey, I was gonna ask you something," I say. "After I dedicated that song to you, you looked at Reed and said something, and you both laughed. What was it?"

"Oh, I said something like, *'He's so dreamy'*. Reed thinks I'm pathetic."

We both look at Reed, and he just shrugs his shoulders with the slightest hint of a grin. Darcy giggles and reaches up to kiss me.

"We good to head out now?" I ask both Brant and Reed.

"The car's waiting out back," Brant replies.

"Good from my end, sir," Reed responds.

I grab Darcy's hand and we make our way to the car surrounded by my security team. As we get to the limo, Chester opens the door for Darcy and I, and Reed climbs in the front.

"You were so hot tonight," Darcy drawls with a cute grin.

I laugh and pull her in for a kiss.

"It's the whole cowboy thing, isn't it?"

"It does things to me," she nods, rubbing her thighs together.

I grab her hand and intertwine her fingers with mine, just as I hear Reed clear his throat.

"Sorry to interrupt sir, but we received another communication tonight intended for Miss Hastings," Reed says.

"What sort of communication?" I ask.

"Chester was handed a note from someone who asked him to pass it onto her."

"What did the note say?" I ask.

Reed passes the note back, and I unfold it before reading it to myself. I look at Darcy and then pass it to her.

If you don't stay away from him, I will end you.
You are nothing to him.
You've been warned twice now—third time I won't be so nice.

"Geez, someone really doesn't like me, do they?" Darcy asks.

"I'm sure it's just some crazy fan baby. We'll take care of it. They're just notes."

"I know. I'm not worried when I have you amazing men looking after me."

"Thank you, Miss Hastings," Chester says.

Darcy, Reed and I immediately break into hysterics.

"Oh, Chester, you're a good sort, you know that?" I say through laughs.

"Yes, sir," he replies with the slightest grin.

Sitting in my office the next day, I can't take my mind off Darcy and the notes she's received. I know that a lot of this sort of thing happens to others in the industry, but it's never happened to me, or anyone close to me in all the years I've been in the business, and it's unsettling.

I've been dealing with my security team all day, about ways in which we can prevent further threats reaching Darcy, and I'm exhausted. I decide to head out for a bit and visit Darcy at work.

When I walk into the building of Great Scott Design, I notice that the new Receptionist has started. She's a pretty, young brunette woman, probably around twenty-five years old, with a slick short bob and giant emerald green eyes.

"Oh my god," she almost screams as I walk in. "You're Travis Danvers. Oh my god, I love you so much. I have all your albums. Can I get a picture with you … please?"

"Ah yeah, sure," I reply. She whips out her phone and takes a selfie of us. When she's finished, I tell her I'm here to see Darcy.

"Of course," she says. "I'll just ring you through."

"Darcy, you'll never believe who's waiting for you in Reception … Travis Danvers!" she half whispers, half shrieks. I have to stop myself from chuckling.

"She'll be out in just a minute, Travis Danvers."

"Thanks so much," I reply.

"I'm Amelia Clayton," the Receptionist says with a giggle. "I just started yesterday."

"It's nice to meet you, Amelia. I believe we'll be seeing a lot more of each other in the future," I say with a cheeky wink.

"Really? Oh my god," she giggles.

I can't help but chuckle a bit myself. *The poor girl is probably thinking I'm going to ask her out or something!*

Darcy suddenly walks around the corner, throws her arms around my neck and plants her beautiful lips on mine. I smile inwardly when I hear Amelia gasp.

"Hey, baby," Darcy says. "What are you doing here?"

"Just thought I'd come and see how my best girl is doing," I reply with a smile.

"Travis Danvers is your boyfriend?" Amelia asks Darcy in pure shock.

"Ah yeah, why?" Darcy asks.

"Well, when you said your boyfriend's name was Travis, I certainly wasn't expecting it to be Travis Danvers!"

Poor Amelia looks like she's about to faint.

"Don't you find it weird that everyone always uses your full name when speaking to or about you?" Darcy asks me.

"A little. but everyone does it," I reply.

"Yeah, I know. To me, you're just plain old Trav."

"Gee, thanks!"

"You know what I mean."

"I do," I reply as I kiss her on the forehead.

"We're just going to head back to my office, Amelia," Darcy says.

"Okay," she replies. "Bye, Travis Danvers."

I throw her a wink over my shoulder and follow Darcy back to her office. I'm surprised with how much they've done with the place already. As I sit in front of Darcy's desk, I look behind me and can see through the glass wall straight into Jesse's office. He's on the phone but gives me a polite nod.

"He still hate me?" I ask Darcy.

"He doesn't hate *you*, Trav, he just hates the fact that you're dating *me*," she replies with a smile.

"He should be grateful. If it wasn't for me dating you, he wouldn't be here in Nashville starting up another branch of his business."

"That's true," she replies. "Maybe you should mention that to him," she says with a giggle.

"You're a brat, aren't you?"

"Maybe a little," she replies with a wink.

I see Jesse finish up his phone call, and then walk into Darcy's office.

"Travis … good to see you again," he says extending his hand.

I reach out and shake it.

"You too, Jesse. Things are looking great around here."

"Yeah, I can't take any credit for it though. Our girl, Darcy here, is the one responsible for it all."

"*My* girl is pretty special," I respond with a sly grin.

Jesse just nods with narrowed eyes and makes his way out of the office.

"Oh, Darcy," he says as he turns his head back to her. "You and I have that meeting this afternoon at four with Fishers, don't forget."

"Nope, I won't. It's in my diary. Thanks, Jesse," she replies.

She looks seriously at me then, with narrowed eyes.

"You right over there?" she asks me. "You sure you don't want to come over here and piss a circle around me?"

"I just might if you don't watch that smart mouth of yours."

She rolls her eyes at me and shakes her head in exasperation.

"So how are things going here, with basically just you two working at the moment?" I ask, changing the subject.

"It's busy, but I like busy. Keeps my mind off other things," she smiles.

"Yeah, I get that," I reply. "Hey, I was thinking it might be nice to go out tonight. Just the two of us."

"Just the two of us?" she asks.

"Well, just the two of us plus the security detail," I reply.

She laughs.

"What were you thinking?" she asks.

"Have you ever heard of *The Bluebird Café?*"

"Yeah, isn't that kind of a Nashville icon?"

"Yeah, it is. It's a great place, and sometimes they even let me sing."

"Sounds great," she says.

"Cool. Did you want to go home to change, or should I just pick you up from here?"

"You might have to pick me up. I don't think I'll have enough time to change. Our four o'clock will probably go for at least an hour or so," she replies.

"Alright. We'll be waiting out front from six then."

"I look forward to it," she says.

I get up from my chair and walk around to Darcy to kiss her goodbye. She wraps her arms around my waist and pulls me in closer.

"Don't leave me!" she wails mockingly.

"Never!" I growl.

She gives me a sweet smile.

"I love you, Travis," she says and then plants another one on me.

Chapter Twenty Four

• REED •

I stand in the back corner of *The Bluebird Café*, while Darcy and Travis enjoy a bite to eat and the entertainment. Being Darcy's security, is a job I both love and hate in equal measure. I adore Darcy—too much. I love the fact that I get to spend almost every waking hour with her, but it also makes it so much harder to keep my feelings for her in check. She's previously admitted to me that she's attracted to me, which also makes things worse for me, knowing that if she wasn't with Travis, she could be mine. She's so close, yet so far. All I can enjoy is her friendship, yet I want to enjoy so much more.

I watch Darcy snuggle into Travis, and place both of her hands on his thigh. She pulls herself up and places her chin softly on his shoulder and whispers something in his ear with a smile, all the while looking behind at me! *What is she playing at?*

After a few moments, she stands from her seat, and I watch her as she makes her way over to me.

"Hey, sexy," she says as she places her hands on my chest.

"What are you doing, Darcy?" I ask with a warning tone in my voice.

"I just came over to see if I can get you something to drink?" she replies.

"I'm good, thanks," I say. "I don't drink on the job."

"Not even water? Surely I can get you something non-alcoholic?"

"I'm fine. I just need to concentrate on you."

"Is everything okay, Reed? I feel like you've become a little detached lately."

"I think that's probably a good thing, don't you?"

"No, I don't. I miss my friend. I've tried to take your advice on board and not be so flirtatious with you, and I'm trying, but it's hard to go against my nature, Reed."

"I just think we need to keep things strictly professional from here on out, okay?"

I feel my heart crack as I watch sadness sweep across Darcy's face.

"Of course, you're right, I'm sorry. I'll go."

She walks quickly back to Travis, and I'm left standing there, only able to watch her again. I have to seriously consider if this is a job I can continue to do. It's so difficult not being able to act on my feelings for Darcy, but at the same time, I also want her safe, and I know I'm the only person I trust to keep her that way.

Over the following fortnight, our routine is pretty much the usual—besides the fact I've noticed that Darcy has distanced herself from me quite a bit—until one night when I receive a concerning phone call from Travis on my night off.

"Mr Danvers, what can I do for you?" I ask.

"Where are you, Lewis?"

"Ah, I'm out with friends, sir, it's my night off."

"Shit!" he replies. "Sorry to have bothered you."

"It's no bother, is everything okay, sir?" I ask concerned.

"No, I don't think so. I'm at a restaurant with Brant, and we've just seen Darcy out with Jesse. I was just checking if you're with her too."

"No, sorry, sir. When I left Darcy this afternoon, she said she was staying in tonight."

"Thanks, Lewis. Can you meet me in my study first thing tomorrow morning?"

"Of course, sir. Are you sure there isn't something I can do now?"

"No, I'll deal with things tonight. You enjoy your night off."

Shit, what was Darcy doing going out without security?

I'm unable to enjoy the remainder of my night, as I can't take my mind off Darcy. How could she be so stupid? Firstly, going out without security, and then going out with Jesse? I wonder what Travis has seen. He sounded hurt, but pissed, so it can't have been good, especially considering he is so understanding in regards to her 'ways'. For some crazy reason, I have to admit that I also feel betrayed in a way.

The following morning, I meet Travis in his study. I knock on the door, and he calls me in. As soon as I walk in, I can tell things aren't good. He looks shocking. He obviously hasn't slept all night, and he has absolutely no color.

"Are you okay, sir?" I ask concerned.

"Can't say that I am, Lewis. Have a seat."

I sit on a seat in front of his desk and wait nervously for him to fill me in on the night before.

"As I mentioned last night, Brant and I were having a dinner meeting at a restaurant downtown. I happened to look out the window at one point and noticed Jesse across the street with a woman. He had her pressed up against a wall and they were kissing. Before long, Jesse picked her up and she wrapped her legs around his waist and things progressed from there."

"Geez," I respond in shock with my hand over my mouth. *What on earth was she thinking?*

"And you're positive it was Darcy?" I ask.

"I'm sure. They eventually turned around and headed off, and I couldn't have been more certain—it was Darcy. I took a photo on my phone as proof."

"Shit," I reply. "Can I see the photo?"

He passes me his phone and sure enough—there is no denying it's Darcy.

"When I got home last night, she was in bed reading and I confronted her. She completely denied it of course, even though I told her I had seen her with my own eyes. I asked her to pack and leave immediately."

"She's gone?" I ask in shock.

"Yeah. I called her a cab and she left. I don't know where she went."

"Fuck me," I respond.

"I just wanted to let you know, as you obviously won't be working with her any longer."

"I don't have a job anymore?" I ask.

"Yeah, you do, I'll just switch you over to my security team. Chester is getting on now and wants to cut back his hours a bit, besides he's happier just with the driving rather than providing security. If you're happy with that, so am I."

"Wow, okay then. I'm in a bit of shock to tell you the truth. I just can't believe all this. I mean, Darcy loves you—she tells me all the time. I just can't see how she could do this; you know?"

"Well, she obviously doesn't love me as I love her. It is what it is. You can have a few days off, as I won't be doing much over the next week. I'm going to be working from home, so I won't need the extra security. Take some time to make sure you want to continue working with me."

I look at the floor and give a small nod.

"I'll leave you to it then, sir—and I really am sorry."

"Thanks, Lewis," he replies.

I make my way back to my suite in a daze. I can't believe what I just heard, and I couldn't feel any worse for Travis—he looked absolutely gutted. I'm also really surprised that he asked her to leave immediately, especially considering she has nowhere else to go—and in the middle of the night! *Maybe she went to Jesse's—the thought makes me feel ill.*

I know I can't leave things as they are; I have to find Darcy and make sure she's okay. I decide to head to her office first and try to speak with her there.

"Hi Reed, how is Darcy feeling?" asks Amelia, the Receptionist at Darcy's office.

"Ah, I'm not sure, to be honest, I'm not working with her at the moment. I've been moved to Mr Danvers's detail," I reply.

"Oh, I see," she replies. "That's a shame, we sure will miss you around here."

"Thanks, Amelia. Darcy called in sick then?"

"Yes, sir. I can leave her a message if you like, for when she returns."

"No that's fine. Is Jesse in?"

"He is. You can just head back if you like. He doesn't have anyone with him."

"Okay, thanks," I reply.

I head back to Jesse's office and knock on the door.

"Come in," he calls.

"Jesse," I say with a nod. The prick leans back in his chair and crosses his arms over his chest.

"I'm surprised to see you here today, considering Darcy is out sick," he says. "Shouldn't you be off following her around like a lost puppy?"

"Well, considering I no longer work for Miss Hastings, I have a little extra time on my hands," I reply.

He looks at me with confusion.

"What? You think Travis would want to keep Darcy around after what you two got up to last night, you prick?"

"I have no idea what you're talking about," he replies with a smug grin.

"I'm talking about you having your way with Darcy up against a wall last night. Travis was across the street in a restaurant and saw the whole thing, you bastard. Did you sleep with her too?"

The asshole doesn't even have to answer; I can see it on his face.

"Did she stay at your place last night after she left Travis?"

"No, she didn't," he replies with concern. "Why, don't you know where she is?"

"No, she left in a cab around 3.00am and we haven't heard from her since."

"Have you tried calling her?" he asks.

"Gee, I didn't think to try that," I reply sarcastically. "Of course I fucking did, asshole, don't you think that's the first thing I tried?"

"Should I try?"

"Can't hurt I suppose," I grumble.

I watch him dial Darcy's number, but as it had with me, it goes straight to voicemail.

"I'm going to go look for her," I say.

"Is there anything I can do?" he asks me.

"Yeah … stay the fuck away from her. Oh, and I imagine you should expect a visit from Travis too. I'm sure he wants to mess that pretty face of yours up real good."

Following my visit with Jesse, I make enquiries with every hotel in Nashville, until I'm finally able to locate Darcy. Being in the security business gives me a few extra perks in being able to obtain the information I need. I make my way to the Baymont Inn and sweet-talk my way to a room key for Darcy's suite. I walk to her room and knock on the door.

"Darcy, it's Reed. Can I come in?" I call.

"Go away, Reed," she replies in a hoarse monotone voice.

"I'm coming in, Darcy," I respond.

I push my keycard into the slot and hear the click before I push the door open. Darcy is sitting in a tub chair staring out the window. She doesn't even turn to look at me.

"Darce, what happened?" I ask her.

She doesn't answer, so I walk over, squat in front of her and grab her hands in mine.

"Darcy; Darcy, look at me, sweetheart. What happened?"

She slowly turns her head to face me. Her eyes are red, and her face is swollen and puffy, but she's still stunning.

"How did you find me?" she asks in a small voice.

"I have my ways," I smile.

She doesn't even blink but instead turns back to look out the window. I cup my hands around Darcy's cheeks and turn her head to face me.

"Talk to me," I say.

"What's there to say? Travis left me and I have no idea why. He wouldn't even let me speak. He just kicked me out at three in the morning with nowhere to go," she says with tears rolling down her face. "All he kept saying was 'how could you, how could you?' How could I what? I have no idea what I did wrong!"

"Darcy, he saw you last night."

"Saw me where? I never left the house, Reed."

"He saw you with Jesse, Darce. He was in a restaurant with Brant across the road. Didn't he tell you any of this?"

"No, he just came home, freaked out and told me to pack up and leave immediately. He said he couldn't even look at me—and he didn't, the entire time I was there—not once! Reed, I swear to you, I never left the house. I was in my room all night reading. Obviously, he saw someone who looks like me with Jesse, but it wasn't me! I would never do that to him."

"Darcy, I went to your office earlier to check on you, and I spoke to Jesse. He admitted it. He admitted to what Travis saw you two doing, and he also admitted to sleeping with you."

"What!" she cries suddenly standing up. "Reed, it did not happen. You have to believe me!"

"Darcy, it's a bit hard when two people saw you, and then Jesse admitted to it. If you honestly can say it didn't happen, is there any chance that Jesse could have drugged you somehow?"

"I don't think so," she replies. "The last time I saw him was at work yesterday when I left for the day. I did have a drink on my desk, but I can't imagine him doing something like that. Besides, you took me home, Reed. Are you suggesting he came to the house and kidnapped me without me even knowing it? I don't know what the hell is going on, but I wasn't with Jesse last night. You have to help me, Reed. You have to make Travis understand that it wasn't me."

"He has a photo of you two together, and it's very convincing, Darcy. I'll look into it, okay, but I can't promise you anything."

She nods as the tears continue to roll down her beautiful face.

Chapter Twenty Five

• DARCY •

I look at Reed with tears streaming down my face, as he kneels in front of me. I can tell he doesn't believe a thing I'm saying. I don't blame him though. I don't think I would either if the situation were reversed. I'm so confused. I know that I was not with Jesse last night though, so what the hell is going on?

"Have you lost your job now?" I ask Reed.

"No, Travis has added me to his detail, although he has given me a few days off to consider if that's what I really want to do."

"Will you stay with him?" I ask.

"Yeah, I will. Besides, I'm sure we can work this all out and you'll be back before you know it."

"I'm not so sure, Reed. He was really pissed. I don't think he'll ever forgive me, and if he believes what he thinks he saw, then I don't blame him. Besides, if he actually thinks that I would do that to him, then perhaps we don't belong together after all. I miss him like crazy though. I want to be with him. I love him, Reed. I don't think I can cope without him."

"Have you tried talking to him?" he asks me.

"He won't take my calls. Earlier this morning, he texted me and told me not to contact him ever again or he'll take out a restraining order against me. How can we go from being head over heels with each other, to this? I just don't understand why he won't even let me speak with him."

"He's hurt, Darcy. You should have seen him this morning. He looked fucking awful, completely gutted. There was no life in his eyes—he was barely functioning."

Hearing how Travis is also struggling, starts the tears again, and I just can't stop them. Before I know it, I've fallen into Reed's arms, and I sob uncontrollably into his shoulder. I don't know how long we stay like that, with Reed stroking my back trying to soothe me, but I'm so glad to have him here.

Eventually, I realize he's lifted me from the chair I was sitting on and is carrying me towards the bed. He lays me down gently and sits on the side.

"Hop in," he says quietly. "You need some sleep. You obviously didn't get any last night."

"I can't sleep," I say.

"I'll stay with you, if that will help," he replies.

"Really?" I sob.

"Of course."

I snuggle into the bed and pull the sheet over me.

"Could you do me a favor?" I ask Reed.

"Of course, what is it?"

"Can you call Jesse and tell him I'm taking two weeks leave effective immediately. I can't work for him when there's obviously something going on here. I don't know what he's done but until we work it out, I can't be near him."

"No worries. I'll sort it out. You just sleep."

"Will you hold my hand until I fall asleep?" I sniff.

Reed looks at me with sadness in his eyes and grabs my hand. He places a kiss to my forehead, and I shut my eyes.

When I wake, Reed is still here but is lying next to me on top of the sheets looking at me.

"Hey," he says. "Feel better?"

"A little," I lie. "What time is it?"

"Nearly seven."

"Really! Wow, I must have been tired. Did you sleep at all?"

"No, I just laid here so you weren't alone. I tried to get up to get a drink of water once, but you got upset in your sleep and asked me not to leave you, so I stayed."

"I'm so sorry, Reed. You can go. I'm fine."

"Do you have anything here to eat?" he asks.

"No, but I can order in."

"How about I run to the store, then come back and cook you something. It can't be any worse than takeout."

"You don't have to do that, Reed, you've done more than enough for me, and more than I obviously deserve."

"It's fine, Darcy, I want to. I'm sure there's more to this story than what we can see at the moment, and I promise I will find out what it is, okay?"

"Okay, thank you. You're a good friend, Reed."

"I'll be back soon."

"Okay, I'm just going to take a shower while you're out."

"Alright. See you in a bit."

With that, he turns and heads out the door. I make my way to the bathroom, where I take a shower. While I'm drying my hair, I hear the suite door open, and I stick my head out.

"I'm just in here," I call.

"Okay, I'll start dinner," Reed replies.

While we eat, we make small talk, and I mention how I've been thinking that I might head home to Australia.

"Really?" Reed asks. "I think you should give it some time, Darce. It's only been twenty-four hours. Give him some time to settle. He loves you; he'll come around eventually. He's still in shock. Take the time off and do a few things for yourself. I'll look into everything that I can. Just don't leave."

I smile at him warmly.

"You're a good guy aren't you, the whole package—a great friend, sexy as hell *and* you can cook!"

He laughs at my comments, then stands to clear our plates.

"You sure know how to boost a guys' ego, don't you?"

"I'm not trying to boost your ego; I'm just being honest. You'll make some lucky girl very happy one day, Reed."

"Honestly, I wish that girl could be you," he says looking at the floor. "I know you're in a bad place at the moment, but if things don't work out with Travis, I'd like you to give me a chance to make you happy. I know what a prick I sound like saying this to you now, but god, Darcy—I've fallen in love with you and there's nothing I can do about it."

I look at him in shock.

"You're in love with me?" I whisper.

"Yeah, and I'm so sorry because I know how inappropriate that is, but I couldn't help it, Darcy. You're just so damn beautiful, with enough personality to fill three people and you're so bloody fun to be around."

I can't believe what I'm hearing, and before I know what I'm doing, my legs walk me over towards him. I look him in the eye before wrapping my hands around his neck and pulling him towards me. As I press my lips against his deliciously soft mouth, I hear him groan and it spurs me on even more.

After a few seconds, Reed quickly pulls back.

"Stop … I'm sorry, Darcy. I can't do this. I can't take advantage of you when you're in this place. As much as I want your lips on me more than anything else, I just can't do it, to you or to Travis."

What is wrong with me?

Before I know what's happening, my legs buckle, and I fall to my knees in a sobbing mess.

"I'm so sorry, Reed," I cry with my head in my hands.

"It's okay, sweetheart—I understand. I shouldn't have said what I did. I confused you; it's my fault. Please don't be upset."

He gets down on his knees in front of me and wraps his strong arms around my heaving shoulders. I press my face into his chest and

I can't stop the tears. I feel like I've been kneeling here with him for hours, before I finally have nothing left.

"You should go," I eventually say. "I'll be okay."

"Are you sure?' he asks.

"I'm sure. Thank you, Reed."

"I'll pop back tomorrow sometime to see how you are, okay?"

"Alright," I reply.

Reed stands up, walks to the door and leaves. I get up and make my way to bed. I'm still so tired, even after my big nap that afternoon.

Over the following weeks, I spend a lot of time in my hotel room reading. I find there isn't much else to do. Occasionally, I go for walks and do a little sightseeing, plus I spend quite a bit of time in the hotel gym and pool. Reed visits me every couple of days, but I never hear a thing from Travis, and I miss him desperately. I avoid all contact with Jesse, and if I'm ever needed for anything work-related, I only ever respond to Amelia. I had Amelia tell Jesse that I'm not able to return to work until the situation has been sorted out, and for some reason, he seems to accept that. So far, I've been off work for just over two months, and I'm going crazy. If Reed doesn't find out anything soon though, I'll have to find other work. My savings are running dangerously low—living in a hotel is expensive business.

One afternoon, I decide that I have to make some enquiries of my own, so I make my way into the office to speak with Jesse.

As I walk through Reception, Amelia greets me cheerfully, and I ask if Jesse is in. She informs me that he is, so I head back towards his office. I knock on his door, and he calls me in. As I open the door and walk in, Jesse gasps and stands quickly.

"Darcy!" he exclaims in shock. "I thought I was never going to see you back here again. What's going on?"

"That's what I was going to ask you," I say as I sit down. "Why did you tell Reed that we went out that night and that I slept with you?"

"Because you did, Darcy," he says in confusion.

"Jesse. I don't know what drugs you were on, but I spent the whole night at home in bed reading. I don't understand any of this at all."

"Darcy, I don't know what to tell you. You saw me at that bar, and *you* approached *me*. You know how I've always felt about you, so when you told me how you felt about me, I found it very hard to say no to you. You begged me to take you back to my place."

"Don't you find it strange that I have absolutely no recollection of this,' Jesse?" I ask.

"Well yeah, of course I do. You didn't seem drunk at all, but I'll admit, you were behaving slightly out of character. I just thought you had changed your mind and were perhaps feeling a little guilty."

All I can do is nod at Jesse. He's given me no new information to work with, and he's certainly positive that it was me that was with him.

"You realize that I'm going to have to look for a new job, Jesse. I just can't see how I can come back here now."

"Darcy, it doesn't have to come to this."

"I think it does, Jesse. I'll let you know if I find anything okay. I'll see you around."

With that, I stand and walk out of his office. When I get back to my hotel, I call Reed. I suddenly have a great desire to see the photo that Travis took of me and Jesse—I don't know why I didn't think to ask to see it earlier.

"Hey, Darcy, how are you?"

"I'm okay, thanks, how are you?"

"Yeah, I'm good. What can I do for you?"

"I was wondering if you could ask Travis for a copy of the photo he took of Jesse and me. I think I have a right to see it."

"Okay. I'll ask him, but I won't retrieve it without him knowing."

"No, that's fine. I wouldn't ask you to do that. If you could just ask him, please."

"Sure thing."

"How is he, Reed? Is he seeing anyone?" I ask barely holding it together.

"He's not great, Darce, and no, he's not seeing anyone. He's still pining for you."

"Does he know you still speak to me?" I ask him.

"Yeah, I told him after that first time I visited you."

"And he was okay with that?"

"He wasn't thrilled at first, but I think he likes the fact now. He asks about you after every visit. He misses you, Darcy, the man's a wreck."

"Then why won't he speak to me?"

"I think he knows that if he saw you, he wouldn't be able to hold himself together. He's still hurting, Darce."

"I spoke with Jesse today," I tell him.

"Really? How did that go?"

"Not that well. He didn't tell me anything more than what I already know. He's convinced that he was with me, and he didn't seem to think that I was drunk – just acting out of character a little."

"Yeah, that's what he told me when I questioned him. I have to go, Darce, but if Travis is okay with showing you the photo, I'll bring it over tomorrow, okay?"

"Alright, thanks, Reed."

The following day, Reed comes over with an enlarged copy of the photo from Travis. When Reed hands it over, I'm shocked—it sure looks like me, I can't argue with that. The fact that the image couldn't have been altered as Travis took it himself, makes me feel ill. I honestly don't know what to think of it.

"It's pretty convincing, isn't it?" I ask Reed.

"Yeah, it is, sweetheart," he replies sadly.

I place my hand over my forehead and rub it gently as I study the image some more.

After a while, something catches my attention, and I narrow my eyes to try and get a better look. I suddenly freeze in shock.

"Holy shit!" I cry. "Reed, I need you to take me to Travis, now!"

Chapter Twenty Six

• TRAVIS •

I'm sitting at my desk in my study when there's a knock at my door.

"Come in," I call.

"Mr Danvers, I have someone here who I think you should speak with."

I look at Reed with narrowed eyes.

"Okay," I say suspiciously.

In a second, Darcy walks into the room with tears streaming down her cheeks, and my breath catches in my throat. *My girl!*

"Hi, Travis," she sobs. "Can I please have a minute of your time?"

I look at Reed and he turns to Darcy.

"You okay if I leave?" he asks her.

She nods and gives him a small smile, so he turns and walks out of the room.

I look at Darcy and have no idea what to say to her. I'm finding it really hard to hold myself together. All I want is to jump over the desk and wrap her in my arms.

"How are you?" I finally manage to ask.

"Honestly … not great. It's been a very hard two and a half months," she replies.

"Yes, it has," I agree.

"I want to thank you for letting me see the photo you took that night. I wish I'd asked to see it sooner—it might have saved a lot of heartache."

"How's that?" I ask confused.

Darcy reaches over with the enlarged print of the photo I took and places it on the desk.

"I've seen the image, Darcy—I took it. I'm not sure what you want me to say."

"Have a look at the woman's neck," she says with a sob.

"What?" I ask confused.

"Look at her neck," she says a little more forcefully.

I look down at the image.

"Okay, I'm not sure what I'm looking for, Darcy," I reply.

"Now, look at my neck," she says. I look at Darcy's beautiful neck and hear an involuntary sigh leave my lips.

"Tell me what I'm looking for, Darcy?" I say a little panicked.

"The woman in the photo has a large freckle at the base of her neck. I don't have a freckle at the base of mine. The woman in that photo, and the woman you saw that night is not me, Travis. The woman you saw is my sister, Hannah—my identical twin. Hannah has a large freckle at the base of her neck. She tricked Jesse into thinking that she was me. The only way people have ever been able to distinguish between the two of us is that freckle. Even our voices are near identical."

I look at Darcy in absolute shock. She'd been honest with me, and I didn't believe her. I didn't even give her a chance to talk to me. I feel sick. I think I sit here in silence for a good five minutes.

"God, Darce, I don't know what to say. I never even considered Hannah. Why did you never tell me she was your identical twin? Why would she do something like that?"

"Why does Hannah do any of the things she does? She's a conniving and deceitful person who wants whatever I have. As far as telling you we're identical—I don't know, it just never came up. Now that I've worked it out, it doesn't surprise me. I'm just sad that it took so long to realize, and now it's ruined our relationship."

"Darcy, I'm so sorry I didn't believe you. But it was pretty hard with the evidence I had. I saw who I thought was you with my own eyes. Then with Jesse backing up the story … what else was I supposed to think?"

"You were supposed to believe me," she sobs. "You were supposed to trust me. You didn't even give me a chance to speak or respond, Travis. You just kicked me out in the middle of the night with nowhere else to go. Who does that? Who does that to someone they're supposed to love?"

I can't hold myself together any longer, and I let the tears fall down my cheeks.

"I am so sorry, baby. I was so hurt; I just didn't know what to do."

"Two and a half months, Travis. You haven't spoken to me in two and a half months!"

"I know and I am so sorry. I wanted to call you so many times, but I just didn't know what to say." I stand up and walk around my desk, wanting to pull her into my arms. Darcy stands too but backs away from me.

"I need to go," she says quickly.

"No, don't go—please stay. We need to talk more," I beg.

"I can't stay, Travis. I'm going to go and see Jesse and fill him in. I think he has a right to know too. I just wanted to come and tell you myself what I found, and to say goodbye. I've decided to go home. There's nothing here for me now, and I'm sure I can go back to work in the Summerlake office. Things with Jesse are too weird."

"Darcy, please no … don't do that. Don't leave. We can work this thing out. I love you and I know you still love me too. We'll get through it, baby. I made a mistake; you have to give me another chance. I can't live without you—I need you in my life!"

"You've managed fine the last few months," she replies with a sob.

"I've not managed at all, Darcy. I've not been able to function normally at all. I've been a shell of a man. You have to take me back,

Darce … please," I beg.

"I have to go," she says again, with tears rolling down her face as she walks towards the door.

"Bye, Trav. I'll always love you."

And with that, she turns and walks out of my life.

The following day, I'm in no shape to go to work, so I decide to go and visit my folks. When I get there, I find that my sister, Quinn is there with her husband, Ryan and their two girls. Out of all my siblings, Quinn and I are the closest, and the moment she speaks to me I break down. She immediately grabs my arm and leads me outside.

"Darcy?" she asks with a look of concern in her eyes.

"I screwed up big time, Quinny. It wasn't Darcy I saw that night with Jesse."

"What do you mean? I saw the picture, Travis, it was Darcy."

"No," I shake my head.

"Darcy has a sister, Hannah. They're identical twins. The only way people can differentiate between the two of them is by a large freckle that Hannah has at the base of her neck. Apparently, even their voices sound the same. The woman in the photo was Hannah. Darcy noticed it yesterday when I showed her the image."

"Holy shit," says Quinn.

"Yeah, you could say that. Darcy has decided to move back home," I choke out.

"Why? Now that it's all sorted, and you both know the truth, why doesn't she go back to you?"

"I hurt her. That night, I kicked her out at three in the morning, Quinn. Who seriously does that? I haven't spoken to her at all, until yesterday."

"What? You didn't contact her to see if she was okay that whole time?"

"No. I texted her that first night after she'd been calling me, and told her if she contacted me again, I'd take out a restraining order against her."

"Oh, Travis. Why did you do that? You love her!"

"I know; I was an idiot. I was so hurt; I didn't know what else to do at the time."

"Well, you can't let her go, Travis. It will kill you if she leaves, you know that."

"I know, but what can I do? I can't physically stop her from leaving. She came over yesterday to say goodbye. I thought I was in pain before, but I'm broken, Quinn—I want her back so bad."

"You have to go to her, Travis. Plead your case. Don't give up. Prove to her how much you love her; that you can't live without her. She's the woman for you, Travis. We all know it, you know it—you'll never find another Darcy."

"God, are you trying to kill me here. I feel shitty enough!"

"You need to go now, Travis. Don't let her think on it any longer. The longer you leave it, the harder it will be."

I look at Quinn and wrap her in my arms. Thanks, big sister; you always know what to say. I stand up and make my way towards the back door.

"Go get her, little brother," she calls after me.

When I get inside, Mama asks if I'm staying for dinner.

"No," Quinn replies. "He's gotta go win back his girl."

"What?" Mama questions. "What's going on?"

"I'll explain later, Mama," Quinn replies. "Go," she says to me, shooing me out the door.

I run to my car and jump in the back.

"Where to, sir?" Chester asks. "First stop, Union Street please, Chester. Then onto the Baymont Inn."

"Very good, sir," he replies.

I'm going to get my girl back, and I'm not taking no for an answer!

I stand outside Darcy's door for a few minutes before I work up the nerve to knock. When I finally do, I can hardly keep my heartbeat under control. Darcy eventually opens the door and looks surprised to see me.

"What are you doing here?" she asks.

"Can I come in?" I reply.

"I'm not sure that's a good idea, Travis."

"Please, Darcy. I really need to speak with you."

She looks at me for a little while, then lets out a long soft sigh, but stands back and opens the door wider, indicating for me to enter.

"Thank you," I say as I walk inside.

"Have a seat," she says while pointing to the only sofa in the room.

She sits down beside me and mutes the TV that's on in the background.

"What can I do for you, Travis?" she asks sadly.

I look into her beautiful blue eyes and ask if I can hold her hand. She struggles to hold in a quiet sob but gives me a small quick nod. I pick up her small hand in mine, and gently stroke her knuckles with my thumb.

"I need you back in my life, Darcy. I cannot go on, knowing that you are out there and you're not with me. You are the only woman for me; there will never be anyone that I could ever love as much as I love you. I'm human, Darce. I screwed up, but I promise I'll spend the rest of my life making it up to you. I thought I was in pain these last few months, but after you said goodbye and walked out yesterday, I've never felt so broken. You are everything to me, baby, and I need you back," I sob as I cup her cheek with my other hand. "Please say you'll come back to me."

She looks at me with tears pouring down her face.

"Trav, you have no idea how much I want to be with you. I've missed you more than I've ever missed another person in my life, but I just can't see how we can repair what's been so badly broken," she cries.

"Baby, we can only repair it if we're together, we can't do that apart. We are not irreparable. We're too good together to give up that easily. I can't give you up, Darcy—I need you to breathe," I say as I wipe away her tears.

She looks at me with such a sad look in her eyes, that my heart nearly stops. I stand from my seat and kneel in front of her, so I can look straight into her eyes.

"Please Darcy, I need you baby. I love you so much and I can't live my life without you."

She looks down at me, then slowly leans forward and gently places her arms around my shoulders, presses her face into my chest, and just sobs. I wrap my arms around her back and pull her close. She hugs me tighter, and I feel my own tears wetting my cheeks. After she can cry no more, she pulls back slightly and looks into my eyes.

"I love you, Trav, I want to be with you. I want to spend my life with you too."

"Really?" I sob. "Can we make it official then?"

"What do you mean?" she asks confused.

I reach into my jeans pocket and pull out a small velvet box. Darcy looks at me with wide eyes as I open the box containing a platinum diamond ring.

"Darcy Hastings, I love you. I want to spend the rest of my life showing you how much I adore you. Please make me the happiest man alive and be my wife."

She looks at me, then at the ring before placing her hand over her mouth to stifle another sob.

"Oh my god, Trav. Are you serious?"

"I've never been more serious about anything else in my life, baby. I am never letting you go again. Please say yes … marry me."

Before I know what's happening, she throws her arms around me and pulls me in for the most amazing kiss of my life.

"Is that a yes?" I ask with a smile.

"That's a hell yes," she replies with a huge laugh. I pull the ring out of the box and gently place it on her finger.

"Beautiful," I say as I kiss her lips.

"It's stunning, Trav, thank you. You have amazing taste. I love it, and I love you."

"We're going to be happy, Darcy, you and I."

"I know we will."

I can't describe the joy I feel at that moment. All the heartache of the past few months has suddenly vanished, and I have my girl back, forever.

"Have you eaten?" I ask her.

"No, not recently," she replies.

"Okay, I'll call Peggy and tell her there'll be two of us for dinner tonight. While we're eating, I'll get Chester to drive her back here so she can pack all your stuff."

"What do you mean?" she asks me.

"Baby, if you think you're spending another single night away from me, you are very much mistaken."

"You want me to come back to your place tonight?"

"Of course! Don't you want that?"

She looks me straight in the eye and then promptly bursts into tears again.

"Yes, I do. I've missed falling asleep with you, and I've really missed waking up next to you. I just can't believe this is all happening."

"I have to fix up my account here though," she says concerned.

"No, you don't, I've sorted it. I'm sure you've probably run through all your savings by now, and you wouldn't be here if it wasn't for me, so I've taken care of it—all of it. You will be reimbursed what you have already paid before now."

"Travis, no, you can't do that. This is not your fault—it's Hannah's and she's my family. I'm covering the costs."

"It's not going to happen, baby. I want to look after my girl, and this is one way I can do it."

"Have I ever told you how much I love you?" she asks with glassy eyes.

"Just a few times," I reply with a smile.

"I mean it, Travis. I love you so much. You are the most amazing man I have ever met. You are beautiful inside and out. There is nothing I wouldn't do for you."

"Just love me. That's all I need you to do."

"Done," she replies with a glowing smile.

On our way back home, I sit with Darcy in the back seat, linking her fingers with mine and just watching her. I can't take my eyes off her. Having not seen her for two and a half months, I feel starved—starved of her gorgeous face.

"There's one thing we do need to talk about, baby," I say to her.

"What's that?" she asks.

"What do you want to do about Hannah? Have you had any threats made against you since we broke up?"

"No, I haven't. I don't get it, though. If the threats were her, why trick Jesse into thinking he's with me, rather than you?"

"That's if it was Hannah. We still don't know that for sure, but it does seem likely."

"She needs to be punished, Trav. If she's not, she's going to keep doing things like this and she needs to understand that it's not okay to mess with people's lives."

"It's fraud, so she'll likely be arrested once found. Are you sure you're okay with that?"

"I'm fine. Hannah has never been anything but horrid to me. We've never had that twin connection that people talk about. It's more like we're strangers than twin sisters. Our looks are where our similarities end."

"Okay, then first thing tomorrow morning, I'll get Reed onto finding out where she is and speaking to the police. You'll likely have to make a statement, as will I."

"Okay, thanks, Trav. Speaking of Reed," she continues. "I have to tell you something. I want to make sure I'm honest and upfront with you before you take me back. The day after we broke up, Reed came to see me. I was upset and looking for comfort, and I ended up kissing him. He stopped it almost immediately, but I still did it. I was so confused and I'm so sorry, Trav."

"It's okay baby. Reed told me about it. He was also upfront about why it happened, so I understand. He also told me how he feels about you."

"He did? Wow."

"Yeah. I get it; you're easy to love. It does concern me whether he's able to do his job properly though."

"Reed is a professional, Trav. In a way, I think his feelings will make him more intent on protecting me, don't you think? Besides, now that we're engaged, those feelings might change. He'll see that I'm no longer going to be an option for him."

"Yeah, maybe. Let's worry about that later. I want to get home and have dinner with my fiancée," I say.

"I like the sound of that, fiancé," she replies.

Chapter Twenty Seven

• REED •

If I said I wasn't a little heartbroken over Darcy and Travis reuniting—and getting engaged—I would be lying. Of course, I want them both to be happy, but at the same time, I want to be happy … with Darcy. I know that pushing my feelings aside for good is going to be one of the hardest challenges I'll have to face.

Since their reunion, things have slowly started to get back to normal. Darcy has decided to go back to work for Jesse, and Travis is back in the recording studio and running Cumberland Records. We've all settled back into a good routine. Darcy's sister, Hannah, still hasn't been found, however, we know that she's at least still in the country. Darcy has also started receiving threats again, so Travis has assigned more security for her.

Spending a quiet Friday morning in my gym as I do every day, I'm surprised to turn around and see Darcy watching me in the doorway.

"Sorry, I didn't mean to disturb you," she says. "I just came to see if you want to hang out tonight. I know it's your night off, but if you're interested, all the staff from Great Scott are heading out to *Bar Melee* for dancing and drinks. Travis is recording with Lacey Wilde all night, so if you're not doing anything more exciting, I'd love you to come. Trav is fine with it too, in case you're worried about that."

"Oh, is this something you usually do?" I ask.

"I haven't been out since I got to Nashville, and this is the first time we've been out together as a staff. We used to do it all the time with the Summerlake team, and it was always so fun. I really miss it."

"I'm not sure that dancing is my thing, and I wouldn't feel right drinking in front of you considering I work for you."

"Well, you don't have to dance, although it would be a shame, and you can drink in front of me—in fact, I'll insist on it. You'd be just out with friends tonight; I'll have other security there. You're just there to have a good night. What do you say?"

"Sure. I don't have any other plans. I was just going to head back in here."

"You're ripped enough," she smiles. "I'll have security ready with a car at nine."

With that, she turns on her heel and walks out. Going out with Darcy and her friends could be fun. I've never seen her in an atmosphere like that before. I'm really looking forward to it. This will be the first time we've done anything together just as friends—besides the time I spent with her during her breakup with Travis, and that couldn't be described as fun, although I did enjoy every second I spent with her.

As I wait for Darcy to come downstairs, I can't help but feel a little nervous. Although I know all the staff at Great Scott Design pretty well now, I don't know how they will feel about me crashing their party. Darcy assures me I'm practically one of them anyway; it's just not Jesse paying my salary.

"Hey, you!" I hear Darcy call, as she bounds down the stairs. "All ready to go?"

I turn my head and can't keep my mouth from falling open. She looks incredible!

"Wow, Darcy!" is all I can manage to get out.

"Do I look okay?" she asks seriously, looking down at her dress.

"Are you kidding me, woman? You look absolutely beautiful! How the hell am I supposed to keep my hands off you when you wear a dress like that? How is *any* man supposed to keep his hands off you? You kill me, Darcy."

I hold my hand to my chest feigning anguish.

She continues toward me giggling, and then grabs my hand and leads me to the door.

Once inside the club, we notice our group near a back corner and make our way over. Darcy is turning heads from every direction. I have to admit, I love the feeling I get knowing that every man in here wants to be the one holding her hand, just as I am at that moment.

"Hey, Jesse," Darcy says as she reaches in and gives him an awkward kiss on the cheek. She still finds it quite difficult being around Jesse after everything that's happened, but she's determined to put it all behind her, and not let Hannah win. She wants to repair the relationship, and Jesse is certainly on the same page.

"Hey, gorgeous. You look stunning as usual."

"Thank you," she says.

"Reed," Jesse nods at me.

"Jesse."

I release Darcy's hand and place my palm on the small of her back.

"Can I get you a drink, sweetheart?" I ask her.

"I'd love one," she gushes.

As I make my way to the bar, I watch Darcy interact with the members of our group. As usual, Jesse can't take his eyes off her. He's practically devouring her, yet Darcy is completely oblivious.

I pass Darcy her drink and join a conversation with a couple of the new cubies, Miller, Christian and Raif. All three men are great guys, and I get along with each of them, but of course, all three of them have a thing for their gorgeous boss. Everyone who meets Darcy has a thing for her. They're all talking about who's going to be the lucky guy to get the first dance with her.

"You're the luckiest son of a bitch I know," Miller says to me. "You get to spend practically every waking minute with her—just being able to watch her constantly and not be considered a fucking perv."

"True, but it also sucks at the same time. Do you know how hard it is being with someone like her, and not being able to do a damn thing about it—watching her with Travis all the time, wishing it were me instead. It's fucking torture, trust me!"

"Yeah, you've got a point there," he says laughing.

We all turn and watch as Darcy and the only other two female cubies make their way to the dance floor.

"You got to admit; Jesse sure knows how to pick 'em. Beth and Aisha are hot too," Christian says.

"Yeah, but they're no Darcy," Raif responds.

I have to agree. Both girls are beautiful, but standing next to Darcy, they're never going to get a second look. Every eye on that dance floor is firmly directed at her. She looks incredible, dancing around having fun in a gorgeous silver halter neck dress that clings in all the right places. Her back is completely bare, and the dress shows off those two delicious dimples just above her ass. The length of the dress, combined with the height of her heels, makes it look like her legs go on forever. She's a siren, and I wish more than anything that she was mine.

As the song finishes, the girls make their way back to a booth and sit, chatting with their drinks. All three look at our group, which now includes Jesse, then over to Darcy's backup security guy, Charlie and back again. Obviously, something is extremely funny because the three of them can't stop laughing and fanning themselves. I decide to make my way over to see what they're up to.

"What sort of trouble are you ladies causing over here?" I ask with narrowed eyes.

"Nothing at all," Darcy replies with the most fake innocent look she can muster.

"Yeah, we weren't all just deciding which one of you gorgeous men each of us would like to take home for the night," responds Aisha with a giggle.

"Is that so?" I reply with raised brows. "So, who are the lucky gentlemen?"

"Well, we all decided that we'd each be happy with any one of you, but the final call came down to one vote for Miller and two votes for you," Beth says with a wink.

"So, which one of you didn't choose me?" I ask in mock displeasure.

"Aisha chose Miller," Darcy replies with a smile.

"Aisha! I'm wounded," I say with my hand to my heart.

"Baby, I'll take you home any day of the week, but I figure that I have a better shot with Miller tonight if these two are fighting over you."

"You ladies are a treat," I say shaking my head. "I'll leave you to count your votes."

I make my way over to the bar to grab another drink, before heading back to the guys.

"What's going on over there?" Christian asks.

"You don't want to know," I say shaking my head. "The girls are placing votes on which of us they'd like to take home for the night."

"Well, that sucks," says Raif. "There's only three of them and five of us. Who did they choose?"

"Aisha chose Miller."

"Oh yeah!" Miller responds with a satisfied smirk and a little jig.

"And Darcy and Beth chose me," I reply smugly.

"Fuck off," says Christian with a look of disgust. I look at Raif who looks much the same, but Jesse looks downright pissed.

"You right there, Jesse?" I ask.

"Fine," he replies and then storms off towards the girls.

"Geez, I hope I didn't just get them all in trouble," I say.

"Nah, Jesse will just be pissed that Darcy didn't pick him. He's got it pretty bad for her you know," says Raif.

"Yeah, I know."

I watch as Jesse speaks to Darcy and holds out his hand to her.

She nods and then takes his hand as Jesse leads her to the dance floor, where he wraps his arms around her waist, and she places her hands around his neck. I watch them move together, as a twinge of jealousy hits me in the chest. They're looking right into each other's eyes, deep in conversation and Darcy has her head tilted to the side just a little. What I wouldn't do to hear that conversation.

I decide to get a little closer to the action, so I make my way over to Beth and ask her to dance. Thankfully she is more than happy to oblige.

I lead Beth onto the dance floor and position us near Darcy and Jesse. Darcy catches my eye and gives me a small smile and I return the gesture.

"You're dancing?" she mouths to me.

I respond with a small shrug, and with my arms around Beth, I slowly start moving to the music. Dancing isn't on the top of my list of favorite things, but I give my best effort, even if I am a little stiff.

"You're not a big dancer?" Beth asks me.

"Is it that obvious?" I reply.

"No, you're doing fine, but you need to loosen up a little," she giggles.

"I'm not really sure where to put my hands, to be honest," I say.

"As long as they're around me, you're good," she smiles.

Beth and I chat for the remainder of the song, while I try my best to keep my eyes off Darcy. Now and then I catch her looking at me, and it gives me a little thrill, but she soon turns back to Jesse and engages him in conversation.

When the song is through, I see Darcy and Jesse break apart and make their way off the dance floor. I thank Beth for the dance, and quickly head over to intercept Darcy before she leaves the floor.

"Where are you running off to?" I ask.

"Oh nowhere, I was just going to head back to the booth."

"Can I get a dance before you do?" I ask.

"You want to dance with me?" she asks in surprise.

"Of course I do. That's the only reason I came out tonight—even if I'm not much of a dancer."

"You looked like you were doing pretty well with Beth," she replies with a raised brow and a twinkle in her eye.

"I wasn't. She told me I needed to loosen up."

Darcy laughs and then wraps her arms around my neck as she'd done with Jesse. I place my hands on her waist and start to move a bit.

"Beth's right," Darcy giggles. "You do need to loosen up."

"I'm sorry, I'm just not very good at this sort of thing," I frown.

"For starters, you need to pull me in closer. Holding me at arm's length makes things a little awkward—relax into it. Don't think. If you think about what you're doing, you'll just stiffen up. Just think of it as a moving cuddle."

"A moving cuddle?"

"Yeah," she smiles.

After a little while, Darcy moves one of her hands to my chest and places her cheek just next to it. I move my arms further around her back and really pull her into me.

"See how much better this is?" she says.

"It's pretty fucking amazing," I reply with an enormous grin. I could stay like this all night. "We'll have to do this more often; I obviously need the practice."

"Mmmm," she hums into my chest.

"You smell so good," I say as I inhale her fruity scent.

"So do you," she replies. "Being this close to you makes me feel a little giddy—you smell good enough to eat."

Fucking hell!

I'm somewhat relieved when the song comes to an end. I don't know how much longer I can stand here with her like this, without doing something I'll likely regret.

"Thanks for that," Darcy says. "It was really nice. Perhaps we can have another one a little later?"

"Love to," I reply.

We make our way back over to the group, and I head in the direction of the guys. Darcy makes her way back over to the booth where the girls are still sitting.

"You are one lucky bastard," Miller says as he slaps me on the back.

"What did you do to have her nuzzling into your chest like that?"

"Told her I couldn't dance, so she had to 'teach me'," I reply.

"You sly dog," he laughs. "Smart, but sly."

After a little while, I notice Darcy get up from her seat and head across to the other side of the bar. She turns down a hallway, towards what I presume is the ladies room. I look over towards her security guy, Charlie, and give him a nod to follow her. I don't want her anywhere by herself, especially in a crowded place like this.

Chapter Twenty Eight

• DARCY •

"I'm just heading to the bathroom," I say to the girls as I stand from the booth.

"Do you want a buddy?" Aisha asks me.

"Nah, I'm good. I'll be back in a sec."

As I walk out of the restrooms, I have my head in my phone sending a text to Travis and don't see the large body on the other side of the door—slamming straight into a hard chest.

"I'm so sorry," I mumble. "I wasn't paying attention."

"No, you weren't," replies a very familiar voice. I look up at the owner and freeze in position.

"Adam?" I ask in complete shock. "What on earth are you doing here? Is Hannah with you?"

"What? No, I'm here for you."

"What do you mean you're here for me, Adam?"

"I want you back, Darcy. You and I were good together, you know we were."

I look at him in absolute bewilderment. He looks completely genuine.

"You're serious, aren't you?"

"Of course. You think I would travel all the way over here if I wasn't serious? I need you back, Darcy. I can't believe I was so stupid to get with your sister; she's crazy. I was happy with you, but I didn't realize how happy until you were gone. I know you still love me; you have to still love me."

"Adam, if you're really here for me, then why is my sister here also?"

"She's not. I came alone. We're done, and I only want you."

"Adam, Travis has seen her. She's been here causing trouble."

"What? She's here in Nashville?"

"Yes! You didn't know?"

"I had no idea. I swear, Darcy, I came here for you. Why the hell would I bring your crazy sister with me?"

What the hell is going on here? Hannah and Adam both in Nashville, but he doesn't seem to know about it?

"Did you end things with Hannah, or did she?" I ask.

"I did, Darce. She's not you, and I realize that now. She went crazy on me when I ended it though. I told her I was still in love with you and wanted you back. She didn't take it well."

Things suddenly start to fall into place. That first note I was sent—

You can't have him; he'll never be yours.
I'll make sure of it—even if I have to get rid of you
in the process.

I'd thought the note was talking about Travis, but perhaps it's actually talking about Adam!

"Adam, I think Hannah's been making threats against me, I thought they were about Travis, but it all makes sense now. Travis and I actually broke up over this."

"You did?"

"Yeah. Things were really messed up for a while, but we've sorted it all out now, and I'm happy for the first time in a long time."

"You're back with him?" he asks in a heated tone.

"Yeah, we're engaged. I'm marrying him, Adam."

"Fuck!" he almost yells at me aggressively.

"Adam, even if I wasn't with Travis, there is no way I would go back to you. You cheated on me with my sister and took everything from me! You honestly thought I would just run back to you because you asked? You're as delusional as she is."

Before I know what's happening, Adam has his hand around my throat and is pushing me up against the wall. His face is full of rage as he yells and hits me across the cheek. I'm in so much shock, I can hardly fight back. I try to speak but can't—I can't catch a breath! Adam's holding my whole body by the throat, so my feet are dangling off the ground. I'm desperate, but unable to push up to get a little air. As I frantically try to pry his hands away from my throat, I look at him pleadingly. An evil grin forms on his face and he glares at me.

"If I can't have you, neither can he," he says in a slow lazy drawl before his fist lands suddenly on the side of my head.

I'm instantly thrown sideways, and I feel a searing pain pass through my skull. I continue to kick my legs frantically, but quickly find myself running out of air and strength, as I feel the darkness looming. Over the sound of the loud hum in my ears, I just barely make out someone calling my name.

"Darcy! God, Darcy!"

Then … blackness.

Chapter Twenty Nine

• REED •

"Darcy! God, Darcy!" I yell as I turn the corner and notice some guy with his hand around her throat. He turns to look at me and releases his grip as he steps away. I watch as Darcy's lifeless body slips to the floor in a heap. Charlie has the guy in a chokehold within seconds, as I run towards her. I watch as Charlie slaps cuffs on the guy, then drags him out of the bar. I bend down to Darcy and call to her.

"Darcy, sweetheart can you hear me? Darcy?"

Panic starts to set in, but I know I have to keep calm for her. I check her breathing, which is slow and shallow and notice a dark bruise already starting to form on her cheek. I carefully pick her up, cradling her in my arms and walk back down the hallway towards the entrance of the bar. As I wade through the crowd, Jesse catches my eye and runs over.

"What the hell happened?" he asks in horror.

"She was just attacked in the hallway by some creep. I'm taking her to the hospital now."

"Shit!" he replies.

I don't stop to chat any further, but instead, run outside to our waiting car and gently place her in the back seat. I slide in beside her and prop her against my shoulder.

"Darcy, honey, Darcy can you hear me?" I say as I stroke her cheek.

She's still not responding, so I pull out my phone as Charlie pulls away from the curb en route to the hospital.

"Mr Danvers, it's Lewis," I say quickly.

"What can I do for you, Lewis? I'm in the middle of recording at the moment, so you'll need to make it quick."

"Get to the hospital. Darcy's been attacked," is all I say before ending the call.

I place my cell back in my pocket before again trying to rouse Darcy.

"Come on sweetheart, you need to open your eyes for me," I say again without any response.

I frantically pace the hallway as I wait for any news on Darcy. As soon as we arrived, the emergency team sprang into action, and she was whisked away immediately. I'm still waiting to hear any news on her condition, and Travis hasn't arrived yet either.

After what feels like hours, a doctor comes out of the room and heads in my direction.

"Are you family?" he asks me.

"I'm her security," I respond. "Is she okay?"

"I'm sorry, I can only talk about her condition with a family member."

"She doesn't have any family," I reply. "She does have a fiancé though who should be here any minute."

"Then I think it's best if we wait for him," he replies.

"Can you just tell me if she's woken up yet?"

"No, she hasn't I'm sorry."

"Fuck!" I mutter under my breath.

In the next second, I turn my head to see Travis running full pelt down the corridor towards me.

"Here's her fiancé," I call to the doctor before he goes back into Darcy.

"Travis Danvers?" the doctor asks in stunned surprise. "You're Miss Hastings' fiancé?"

"Yes, is she okay? Can I see her?"

"She's still unconscious, but stable. I can take you to see her now if you like."

I watch as the doctor leads Travis through the door. Before he goes through, Travis turns back to me.

"You coming?" he asks.

"Yeah, of course, if that's okay?" I reply.

The doctor looks back at me with a frown.

"We're the only family she's got," Travis responds annoyed. "She'll want him there."

"Very well, but not too long. She needs to rest."

We all walk into Darcy's room where she's lying there as white as a sheet, propped against a few pillows.

"As you can see, Miss Hastings has received a bruised cheek, and also severe bruising around her neck. We believe she's also received a punch to the head, but the scan didn't show any worrying signs, however, we'll keep an eye on that. She'll likely have a shocking headache when she does wake. The fact that she hasn't regained consciousness yet is concerning, considering the time she's been out. We would have hoped by now that she would at least be showing signs of rousing, but she is yet to do so."

"Is she going to be okay?" Travis asks with a horrified look on his face.

"That all depends on how long she was without oxygen. It's all up to her now. Her body may still just be recovering from shock too. I would suggest talking to her softly and trying to wake her that way. Avoid moving anything but her hand though. I'll leave you to it."

I watch as Travis pulls up a chair next to Darcy and sits down. He grabs her hand and rubs his thumb over her knuckles gently.

"Hey, baby. I'm here. You're going to be okay, you have to be okay. I need you to open your eyes for me, sweetheart. I need you to show me your beautiful eyes, baby. Come on."

I watch as Travis stares at her, willing her to open her eyes. The guilt that washes over me is tremendous.

If I'd been with her, I could have stopped this.

"What happened?" Travis asks as if reading my mind.

"She went to the ladies' room, and I signaled for Charlie to follow her to the hallway, which he did. After a bit, I realized she'd been gone for a while, so I went to check on her, and found some guy pinning her up against a wall with his hand around her throat. I called out her name and he immediately dropped her, but she just slumped to the floor. Her eyes were still open when I called her name. I should have checked her sooner," I gasp.

"Where was Charlie?"

"He was right there behind me. He didn't go down the hallway with her, but stood waiting just around the corner. Geez, Travis, I'm so sorry."

"You weren't on duty. It's fine. I'm just glad you got there when you did. Who the hell was the guy anyway, and where is he now?"

"I don't know who he was. I've never seen him before, but Charlie cuffed him and he's with the cops now. I'm sure we'll find out soon enough, unless you'd like me to go find out now and give my statement."

"Maybe that's a good idea. I want to know who the bastard is, and make sure he's never able to hurt her again. I'll call you as soon as she wakes up. She'll want to see you too."

"Okay," I reply.

I walk around the other side of the bed to Travis and pick up Darcy's hand to give it a kiss. Then I lean in and press my lips to her forehead.

"Get better soon, sweetheart. You have two men here who love you and want to see your happy, beautiful eyes again."

"Look after her," I say to Travis as I walk from the room.

"Mr Danvers, It's Lewis."

"What can you tell me, Lewis?"

"It's Adam Clarkson sir … the ex."

"What the fuck?"

"Apparently he's been in the country for about two weeks, trying to track her down."

"What does he want?"

"The bastard wants her back. Darcy told him that you're engaged, and he lost his shit. He didn't know about Hannah being here though. He broke up with her so he could get Darcy back. It seems Darcy also told him that she thinks it was Hannah who sent those threats to her, but it was over Adam, not you as we first thought."

"What a bloody mess."

"Yeah. The cops are charging him now, but it also depends on how Darcy is as to what he'll be charged with. How is she doing? Has she woken yet?"

"No, there's still no change."

"Bloody bastard. What I wouldn't do to be left alone in a room with him for five minutes. Can I get you anything before I turn in for the night, sir?"

"Perhaps contact Chester and see if he can bring in a change of clothes for tomorrow morning for me, and also get him to contact Brant for me and explain the situation. He'll have to clear my schedule for at least the next two days at this stage."

"Will do. Try and get some rest yourself."

"I don't think I can. I need to know she's going to be okay. I want to make sure I'm awake when she wakes up."

"I understand. We'll talk tomorrow."

Chapter Thirty

• TRAVIS •

I've been sitting here in the same chair alongside Darcy for two days now, and there's still been no change in her condition. As every hour passes, the doctors seem to worry more and more, and I'm ruined. Never in my life have I felt such utter helplessness. All I can do is sit here and will my girl to open her beautiful eyes, but she just sleeps on.

"Hey, how's she doing?"

I turn my head towards the door and see my sister, Quinn and her two girls, Everly and Haven.

"There's been no change. She still hasn't moved or opened her eyes. I'm so scared, Quinn. What if she doesn't wake up?"

"She will, Travis. She's been through a lot and her body is in shock. She just needs rest and then she'll come back to you. She's tough, just give her time."

I watch as Everly and Haven climb up onto the foot of the bed and start poking Darcy's legs.

"Wake up Aunty Darcy, wake up!" Everly calls.

"Yeah, wake Un Darce," replies little Haven.

Having my family here with me, makes me smile for the first time in two days.

"Have you moved from that chair since Friday night?" Quinn asks me.

"No, and I won't be either, so don't even try."

"Surely you need some fresh air, Travis. Go get yourself a coffee or something … but at least get up and move—I'll stay with Darcy."

"I'm not leaving her side. I don't need anything; I just need her to wake up."

"Okay. We're not staying long, I just wanted to make sure that you were also looking after yourself, and I see that you're just as you should be, so I'll leave you to it. She'll come good, Travis, there's no way she'll give you up."

"Thanks, Quinny." I stand and hug her, then give both my nieces a high five while Quinn kisses Darcy on the forehead.

"Make sure you wake up soon, okay," she says to Darcy. "My brother here looks like hell, and he needs you back."

She gives me a wink, grabs the girls' hands and walks from the room.

The following afternoon, I'm napping with my head on Darcy's hand, when I feel the slightest twitch of her finger. I sit bolt upright and look at her face.

"Darcy, sweetheart. Can you hear me, baby? Open your eyes, honey. Let me see your eyes."

I rub her hand encouragingly and wait patiently. After a few minutes talking to her, I eventually see her eyes flutter just the slightest bit.

"Darcy, Darcy … open your eyes, baby."

After another minute or so, a single tear rolls from the corner of her eye and I move to wipe it away with my thumb, as I try to contain the lump in my throat.

"Darcy, baby, I'm here. I'm here, beautiful. Open your eyes," I cry with tears now falling down my cheeks.

"Trav?" Darcy croaks in a small hoarse whisper.

"I'm here, baby. Open your eyes, I'm here."

I watch as Darcy slowly blinks her eyes open, and then gingerly turns her head towards me.

"Hey there, beautiful girl," I sob.

"Hey, Trav," she whispers. "Why are you crying?"

"I've been so worried about you. You've been unconscious for nearly four days, baby."

"I have? I'm sorry for worrying you."

"It's fine, baby, just as long as you're okay."

"I need some water," she states quietly.

"Let me just call for the nurse, okay. I just want to make sure you're allowed to."

I press the button to call the nurse and place a kiss on Darcy's forehead in the process. A few moments later a nurse walks into the room.

"Welcome back, Miss Hastings. How are you feeling?"

"Thirsty and a bit stiff and tired."

"That's to be expected. You can sip some water slowly. Would you like to sit up a bit?"

"Yes please," Darcy replies.

"You're a very lucky girl, you know. This lovely man has not left your side for a second the whole time you've been here. All the nurses have been fighting to be assigned to you, just to get a glimpse of your big-time music star fiancé."

"He's a good egg," Darcy smiles at me.

"He sure is," the nurse agrees.

"I'm the lucky one here," I reply. "Look at this beautiful, amazingly brave woman I get to marry."

"I'll leave ya'll to get reacquainted."

The nurse leaves us, and I stand up to sit on the side of Darcy's bed.

"You gave me such a fright," I say. "Could you hear me talking to you at all these past few days?"

"I could hear bits and pieces, but I just couldn't seem to open my eyes or move. Then I would lose consciousness again, so I didn't hear everything. It was nice to know you were here though."

"Of course, baby, where else would I be?"

As I reach across and press a kiss to her forehead, I hear a noise near the door and turn to find Reed standing there.

"Come on in, Lewis," I say.

"Hey, Reed," Darcy smiles. "Sorry I ruined our night out."

Reed walks over to the bed and looks to me for permission to hold her hand, and I give a small nod.

"Are you kidding, girl. I'm so sorry I wasn't there when you needed me, Darcy. If I'd just gotten to you sooner, you wouldn't be in this condition."

"Reed, you weren't working. You were there to have fun, not look after me. The fact that it was you that got to me anyway, says a lot about the kind of man you are."

Reed gives her a small smile and then looks at me guiltily.

"Lewis, I'll be forever grateful for what you did. You'll be working for me as long as you want to," I say.

"Thank you, sir," he replies.

"When can I get out of here?" Darcy asks.

Reed snorts and I just look at her in shock.

"Baby, you just woke up after four days, I don't think they're going to let you out of here just yet!"

She looks at me with a sad smile.

"I just want to cuddle up in my own bed," she says.

"I know baby, trust me, I want nothing more than that too, but we need to make sure you're okay before you go anywhere."

She looks at me with her beautiful blues and pleads.

"It won't be long baby, and you'll be back in my bed where you belong, and trust me, I won't be letting you out of there for days!"

I look up and notice Reed looking away uncomfortably, and I immediately feel bad for the guy. It must be hard watching someone you love with someone else. I kind of know what that feels like, and I don't envy his position. For some reason, I decide it might be nice to give the two of them a few minutes to themselves, so I excuse myself and step out of the room for a bit. I don't want to head too far away, so I just wait in the hallway near her door—not very private I suppose, but I just can't bear the thought of being any further away from her.

"I'm so glad you're okay," I hear Reed say. "I would never have forgiven myself if you were hurt any worse than you already are."

"I'm fine, Reed, honestly. I was just a little over-tired and needed to catch up," she teases.

"Over-tired? Geez, Darcy, you scared the shit out of me—and poor Travis has not left that chair since you got here."

"I know. He's a good man. He really loves me."

"Yeah, he does. I hate to admit it because I want you for myself, but he's a good man and he treats you right. If I have to give up on the thought of ever being with the woman I love, then I can deal with the fact that you're with him. I can't fault the guy—and believe me, I've tried! He's the luckiest son of a bitch on the planet and I just hope he realizes it."

"He does," I hear Darcy say. "I understand how you feel about me, Reed, and if things were different, I'd be with you in a heartbeat. But I have Travis and I love him so much. I would never do anything that could hurt him. He makes me happy, Reed."

I feel my heart stop for a moment as I continue listening.

"I know, beautiful. I see that you're happy, and honestly that's all I care about. But I swear, the moment you're not, I'm swooping in—got it?"

"Got it," she laughs. "Reed, can I ask you something?" she says with a serious tone.

"Of course, anything," he replies.

"Will you be my man of honor at our wedding?"

"Your what?" I hear him gasp. "Is that even a thing?"

"Sure it is," she replies. "I haven't asked Travis, but I'm sure he won't mind."

"I think it's a brilliant idea," I say as I walk back into the room with a smile.

"Looks like it's a done deal then," Reed replies.

Darcy grabs both our hands in each one of hers.

"I'm so happy," she says. "My two amazing men."

Chapter Thirty One

• DARCY •

Sleeping in my own bed after a week in the hospital has never felt so good. Having Trav's arms wrapped around me feels even better. He seems to be having a hard time coming to terms with what happened to me, and he won't let me out of his sight—I can't even walk into the bathroom without him following to see if I'm okay.

Reed is much the same. He seems to be struggling with guilt. Even though he wasn't on duty to protect me that night, he still feels responsible.

As Adam's now out on bail, it's making Trav really nervous, and he's upped our security. The fact that we don't even know what's happened to Hannah, worries Trav even more—we just don't know what her story is and whether she's still even in the country.

While I let the men worry about security, I just want to get back to normal. Even though I've been told to have a few more days off work, I hate the thought of sitting around at home doing nothing. Trav is working from home, although I know he desperately needs to get back into the studio to record with Lacey Wilde.

As I head into the kitchen for breakfast, I notice Travis talking with Peggy—they're working on this week's menu.

"Morning, Miss Darcy," Peggy says. "How are you feeling today."

"I'm good thanks, Peggy. Really good. I'm actually going to head into work today, so I just might grab something quick if that's okay?"

"What?" Travis says. "Baby, you can't go into work. You need to rest!"

"Trav, I've been resting for a week now. I need to get back into things. I promise you I'm feeling fine. And besides, I know you need to head back into the studio. I don't want you falling behind because of me."

"I'm worried though, baby. We don't know where either Adam or Hannah are, and I can't protect you in your office. At least here, no one can get to you."

I walk over to him and wrap my arms around his waist, looking up into his eyes.

"I love that you're so protective of me, Trav, but I'll have Reed with me. I'll be fine. I can't stay locked up here all the time, I'll go mad!"

"Promise you'll be careful," he says.

"I promise. Will Charlie be coming along as well?" I ask him.

"Absolutely. Until we know the whereabouts of Adam and Hannah, you'll have at least two bodyguards on you at all times—one of them will always be Reed."

I pull up on my tippy toes and lean into him to press my mouth against his.

"I love you; you know that?"

"I love you too baby."

It is so good to be back in the office. Business has really started to pick up and I'm loving the challenge and extra responsibility Jesse has given me. I now oversee all the cubies, while Jesse focuses just on the clients.

As I sit behind my desk and start going through the enormous number of emails, Jesse pops his head into the doorway.

"Hey! How are you feeling?" he asks as he walks further into the room. "Should you be back yet?"

"I'm good thanks, Jesse. I can't sit at home any longer—I'll go mad. I may just do a few half days if you're okay with that to start though?"

"Of course, sweetheart. Anything that helps, I'm good with."

"Thanks. You're a good boss and a great friend."

"Do you think you'll be free to catch up over lunch today?" he asks.

"Yeah, that sounds great. I'm sure there's heaps to go over."

"Yeah, there's quite a bit coming up that I'd like your input on. Twelve thirty work for you?"

"Done," I reply. "I think it'll take me that long just to get through all these emails!"

Sitting at a booth in the corner of a small, dimly lit, quiet bar around the corner from our office, I wait as Jesse orders drinks from the bar. As usual, the cute female bartender is flirting with him, and once again, Jesse is oblivious to it—the poor girl is working hard too, and he's giving her nothing.

"Jesse, you can't tell me you didn't notice that girl pulling out all her best moves over there?" I ask as he returns to our table.

"What?" he replies turning to look at her.

"She was all over you, and you gave her nothing!" I respond.

"Darce, in case you've forgotten, I'm not interested in other women. You know how I feel about you—that hasn't changed. It's not likely to either."

"But Jesse, I'm engaged. You can't sit around waiting for something that's not going to happen."

"You're not married yet," he replies. "And even if you were, there's always hope for me that things don't work out."

"Jesse, you can't be serious. Are you telling me you're not going to date other women and risk the fact of spending your life alone, just on the off chance that things with Travis might not work out and you'll be able to swoop in?"

I look at him in astonishment and he just gives me a small shrug.

"Hmmm mmmm," he replies.

"Jesse, please listen to me," I plead as I grab his hand in mine. "Who's to say that if Travis and I don't work out for some reason, that I would even fall to you anyway? What you're saying is crazy—it doesn't make sense. You're a good friend, Jesse, and I care about you. I don't want to see you alone and sitting to the side waiting for me. You deserve to be happy, and I know there's a beautiful woman out there who is just waiting to love you the way you deserve to be loved. Maybe if things were different and I hadn't found Travis, we might be together, but that's not the case and I hate seeing you waiting like this."

"I appreciate what you're saying, I do. But the fact is, I'm in love with you, Darcy. How can I be with another woman, when I'm in love with you? It wouldn't be fair to her, or me."

I look at Jesse and my shoulders sag with a heavy sigh. I really do care about him, and I care about our friendship and our working relationship. He really is a good boss and a great friend, and I don't want to lose that.

"You're a bloody decent guy, Jesse, you know that?"

"You reckon?" he replies as he looks over to the opposite corner of the room where Reed is keeping watch. "I don't think he thinks so."

I follow Jesse's gaze and smile at Reed.

"He's in the same boat as you, Jesse. Reed's in love with me, and it has to be hard for him too, having to shadow me practically twenty-four-seven, watching me interact with others, the way he's not able to. Reed doesn't have anything against you as such, he's just wary of you—especially after the whole Hannah thing. Reed is a fantastic guy. I wish the two of you would get along better."

"If it will make you happy, I'll make more of an effort."

"I'd appreciate that … thank you. Speaking of Reed—I asked him to be my Man of Honor at our wedding."

Jesse looks at me as though I've grown two heads.

"What? Is that even a thing?" he asks with a raised brow.

"Yeah, of course it is. I was actually hoping you would be my bridesman," I say with a wary look.

"Your what now?" he asks with horror splashed across his face.

"My bridesman!" I reply with a giggle. "I can't help it if my two best friends are men. I'm not going to let that stop me from having you both by my side at my wedding. Please say you'll do it," I beg.

"God, Darcy, the things I do for you. You better not tell me that I have to wear a dress or anything girly, cause that's where I draw the line."

"Of course not, you'll look just as sexy as you always do in a stunning suit."

Sitting on a stool in our kitchen, I watch Peggy prepare our evening meal.

"Are you sure there isn't something I can help you with, Peggy? I feel really useless just sitting here watching you work."

"Oh no, Miss Darcy. Peggy likes to cook for you."

I give her a soft smile as I hear my phone ringing from my purse. I pull it out and see Trav's face looking back at me on the screen.

"Hey, Trav," I say.

"Hey, babe. Listen, I'm sorry but I'm going to have to miss dinner tonight. We really need to keep working on this track."

"Seriously, Trav? That's like the third time this week!"

"I know, I'm sorry. But the sooner Lacey and I get this finished, the sooner I can spend more time with you."

"Okay," I sigh with resignation. "What time will you be home then?"

"Not sure, but don't wait up."

"So, late then?"

"Yeah late. I'm sorry, baby."

"Okay, I'll see you tomorrow then … maybe," and with that I hang up the phone and slump on the stool.

"It's just me again tonight, Peggy," I sigh.

"That's a shame, Miss Darcy. I will put the leftovers in the fridge for Mr Travis."

"Thanks," I reply sadly.

This recording with Lacey Wilde is really starting to bug me. Besides the three very late nights he's had this week, Travis has also been receiving a constant string of texts and phone calls from her—and they always have to be answered then and there, whereas my calls are starting to go unanswered more and more frequently. I don't think there's anything going on other than work, but the *amount* of work sucks, and I now understand how Travis must have felt when I worked so much back in Summerlake.

Deciding not to sit at home alone for another night, I go and see where Reed is and if he's interested in catching a movie. I walk down the corridor, knock on his door and I'm surprised when a gorgeous tall brunette opens the door.

"Ah hi," I say with a shocked look across my face. "Is Reed here?"

"Yeah, come in, Miss Hastings, he's just getting out of the shower. I'm Jocelyn, by the way."

"Hi Jocelyn. I'm Darcy," I reply.

"I know. You're Travis Danvers' fiancée. You're so lucky; Travis is totally hot. Every woman in Nashville is so wishing they were you right now."

"Is that right?" I laugh.

"Are you kidding? He's the golden boy of Nashville. Everyone wants a piece of him."

"Yeah, I'm getting that." I reply. Just then, the bathroom door opens, and Reed walks out in nothing but a towel. *Damn he has a great body!*

"Hey, beautiful," he says looking at me. "I thought I heard voices. Whatcha doing here?"

"Oh hey," I reply trying to hide the blush I feel creeping up my neck. "I just popped in to see if you wanted to catch a movie, but I didn't realize you had company, so I'll leave you to it."

"Actually, a movie sounds great—would you mind if Joss tagged along though?"

I don't like that a quick twinge hits me in the chest, but it does. Why am I jealous that Reed has a date? I know he has feelings for me—loves me in fact—but I can't expect him to sit and pine for me for the rest of his life. But it still hurts a little, that he's possibly trying to move on. It's good for him though, he should move on.

"Oh no, honestly I don't want to intrude. I'll leave you two to your night." I say heading towards the door.

"Seriously, it's fine. You don't mind do you, Joss?"

"Not at all," she says. "Will Travis be coming? I'd love to meet him. Do you think he'd sign something for me?"

"I'm sure he would … but no, he's not coming. He has to work late tonight."

"Again?" Reed asks.

"Yeah," I reply a little deflated.

"Then that settles it. We're all heading to the movies."

"Reed, honestly I don't want to intrude on your time with your date."

"Date! Ewwww," Jocelyn cries as she pretends to gag.

"Jocelyn's not my date, she's my little sister!" Reed replies in horror.

I look between them both and try not to let my relief show.

"Your sister? Reed, you never told me you had a sister. I thought you were my best friend! Seriously … men!" I scold.

"Sorry," he replies. "It just never came up."

I walk over to Jocelyn and pull her into a hug.

"I'm so sorry about the awkwardness before," I say to Jocelyn.

"I just felt bad thinking I'd walked in on something between you two."

Jocelyn shudders and I laugh.

"I get that women think he's hot and all that, but he's my brother. It kind of grosses me out to think of him like that!"

"That's probably a good thing," I laugh.

"Besides, it would make him a bit of an asshat if he'd had a date here when he's in love with you, wouldn't it?"

I look at Reed and he drops his head to the floor. *He's told his sister he's in love with me!* I can't help but feel a warm buzz run through me.

"How about you both have dinner with me, rather than here in your room? Considering Travis isn't here, I was going to be eating alone anyway."

"I can't have guests in the main house," Reed reminds me.

"Well, she's not your guest, she's mine, so it's fine. Now go and put some clothes on. I may be engaged, but I'm only human, Reed."

He chuckles and makes his way to his bedroom as I turn for the door.

"I'll see you out there in about ten minutes," I say to Jocelyn.

"Can't wait," she replies.

Following our dinner, we head to the cinema—all five of us. Reed, Jocelyn, my two security guys and me. Even though it's Reed's night on, I made him get two other guys to act as my security for the night. He seems a little worried by that and thinks Travis will have an issue with it, but I tell him that I'll handle Travis.

Following the movie, the three of us decide to go for coffee at a little hole in the wall place around the corner. Jocelyn and I sit on one side of the table while Reed sits opposite me.

"Hi, what can I get you?" the waitress asks us; but of course only has eyes for Reed.

We each give our orders and the waitress turns and heads back to the kitchen.

"So, Reed, can I play tonight, or should I just keep my mouth shut for a change?"

"What do you mean, *play*?" Joss asks me curiously.

"Well, whenever I go out with either Reed or my boss Jesse, women always hit on them—when I'm right there. How do they know we're not together? I just find it rude. It used to happen in Australia with Travis too, where he wasn't well known."

"So how do you *play*?"

"Can I show her, or will it make you uncomfortable?" I ask Reed.

"Sweetheart, I love it when you play. It's the closest I get to having you … so play away. Do with me as you wish," he laughs.

"Okay, I'll just head to the bathroom and wait till the waitress comes back. If she flirts with you, I'll move in."

Joss looks at me and laughs.

"I can't wait to see this," she says with a smile.

I watch for a few minutes as Joss and Reed chat together. He's sweet with her and it's nice to see another side of him. After a few more moments, I see the waitress make her way back to our table. She places our coffees down with a huge flirtatious smile aimed at Reed, and then goes back to the kitchen to retrieve the rest of our order.

After she returns with Jocelyn's blueberry muffin and Reed's slice of chocolate cake, she fluttered her eyes at Reed again and places her hand on his shoulder.

Every time!

"Is there anything else I can get you—my number perhaps?" she asks Reed seductively as I approach our table.

"I think he's good," I reply as I lift her hand from Reed's shoulder.

"Excuse me?" she responds with a look of indignance.

"I said, he's good," I reply as I sidle in beside him and wrap my hand around his neck.

"Hey, baby, there you are," he smiles while looking right into my eyes.

Oooh, Reed is playing too!

I pull him towards me and place my lips on his. I'm just planning on a quick soft peck, but he goes in for the full-on pash. *God he's such a good kisser!*

After a few moments, I hear Jocelyn clear her throat.

"Ahh guys, she's gone and has been for a while!" she giggles.

I pull back and look at Reed.

"Well, that was unexpected," I say breathlessly.

"I had to make the best of the opportunity placed before me," he replies with a smirk.

"Can you blame him?" Joss asks me. "The man is in love with you!"

"Maybe I shouldn't have done that after all. I'm sorry, Reed," I say as I look down at the table.

He grabs my chin and turns my head to look at him.

"Sweetheart, I know the situation. It's good; I kissed you. You don't need to feel bad. It was all in good fun."

"Are you sure you're in love with Travis?" Jocelyn asks me. "You two look made for each other."

"Joss," Reed chastises her sternly.

"I love your brother, Joss, I really do, but I'm with Travis who is an amazing man. If I hadn't met Travis, I could easily be with Reed. He's incredible," I say looking at him then turning back to Jocelyn. "But that's not what happened. He's my best friend and I don't want to lose that."

I look at Reed.

"I do love you; you know that right?"

"I know beautiful," he smiles flashing those gorgeous dimples.

Chapter Thirty Two

• REED •

"You know she's in love with you, don't you?" Jocelyn says back in my suite.

"Joss. She's engaged to Travis. She loves me like a friend, that's it."

"Nope, I don't believe that for a second. You can see it in her eyes when she looks at you, how she acts around you—she's in love with you, Reed. I'm not saying she doesn't love Travis, but I'm sure you can be in love with two people at the same time, and I'm certain she is. She wants you bad, and I can see that it's killing her not to be able to act on that."

"Look, as much as I'd love to be with her, I know she's happy with Travis, and all I want is for her to be happy. Of course, I wish the circumstances were different, but they're not, so I have to live with that. If for some reason things go south with her and Travis, I'll be here. In the meantime, I'll just be her friend."

"Doesn't it bother you though, being second best if it comes to that?" Joss asks.

"Honestly, I've thought about it, and it does bother me, but I love her, Joss, and I'll take her any way I can get her."

"I just want you to be happy, big brother. I worry you'll spend your life pining over a woman you can't have."

"I'm good … trust me. I have a great job, awesome family and brilliant friends. I'm happy, Joss."

Driving Darcy to work the next morning, we got talking about our plans for the weekend.

"I'm not sure what my plans are yet," Darcy says. "I just never know if Trav's going to be home or not. Usually lately, he's not."

"He is working a lot of hours at the moment," I reply.

"More than a lot. And it's not just the long hours. If he is at home, he's always on the phone with Lacey. I know they're trying to finish this album, but it's seriously starting to get to me. Honestly, I don't think he'd even notice if I moved out, Reed."

"Of course he would, sweetheart."

"No, I'm serious, Reed. I don't think he would. He's not even sleeping in our bed at the moment—he says he doesn't want to wake me up when he gets home so late. Some nights he doesn't even come home. I know I shouldn't think it, and I trust Trav, but it's screaming 'affair' to me. I've been there, I know the signs."

"There's no way Travis is cheating on you, Darce. The man worships the ground you walk on. He's just busy. It'll all be over soon, and everything will be back to normal, you'll see."

"I hope so," she replies with a sad smile.

On our drive home from the office that day, Darcy receives a text from Travis informing her that he'll be late home again, and not to wait up.

"Reed, do you think we could swing by the studio before we head home. I haven't seen him in two days, so maybe I can take some food in for him."

"Of course, sweetheart. I'll pull over just up here to get some food then we'll head round."

"Thanks, Reed."

After we collect some Chinese takeout, we pull into the carpark of the recording studio. I grab the food and follow Darcy in. We make our way to Reception where Darcy asks which studio Travis is in.

"Hey, Darcy. Travis and Lacey are in Studio 3. Do you know your way back there?" the receptionist asks.

"Yeah, we know the way; thanks, Heidi," Darcy responds with a smile.

Darcy and I weave our way through the corridors and back towards Studio 3. I push the first door open and let Darcy through before she heads on into the control room which is currently empty. I watch as she makes her way towards the glass before she completely freezes.

"Darcy?"

I move further into the room and look through the glass to see what Darcy is looking at.

"Shit!" I mutter under my breath. "Come on, sweetheart, let me get you home," I say as I wrap my arm around her and pull her towards the door.

Darcy isn't moving and seems frozen to the spot. I drop the bag of takeout onto the table, bend to scoop her into my arms and carry her through the door. On our way past reception, Heidi catches my attention.

"Did you find Travis?" she asks. "Yeah, we did, thanks."

"Are you okay?" she asks looking at Darcy concerned.

"She's fine," I reply. "She's just not feeling well all of a sudden."

"Okay, hope you feel better soon. Enjoy your night," she says cheerfully.

We leave the building, and I carefully place Darcy into the back seat of the car and buckle her in. I get in the driver's seat and start the journey home. As I look back at Darcy, I see a single tear roll down her cheek and my heart breaks for her.

"What can I do, sweetheart?" I ask. She looks at me as though her whole world just caved in—I suppose it has.

"Just take me home, Reed. I need to pack," she replies through sobs.

"Darce, don't worry about things like that tonight. You can do that anytime."

"I'm not staying in that room another night, Reed. I'll be out before he gets home. Do you think you could make me a hotel reservation for tonight at least?"

"You are not staying in another hotel, Darcy. You can stay in my suite tonight. At least then I know you're safe. We'll work out what to do from there in the morning, okay?"

"I can't stay in your room, Reed, you only have one bed."

"It's fine, honey. I'll sleep on the couch, and you'll take my bed."

"Reed, I'm not kicking you out of your own bed. A hotel is perfectly fine."

"Darcy, it's not open for discussion," I reply sternly.

I watch as she slumps back into the seat looking defeated. She continues to sob quietly while looking blankly out the window. All I want to do is climb back there and wrap her in my arms, and that's exactly what I plan to do as soon as we get home.

Watching Darcy sleeping peacefully in my bed is a sight I've longed to see, just not under these circumstances. Walking into the studio and seeing Lacey and Travis making out, was not something I ever expected to see—certainly not from Travis, and especially after all they've been through.

When we arrive home, Darcy goes straight to her room and packs all her belongings into suitcases. I watch as she removes her engagement ring and places it on Travis' bedside table. She then turns and walks out of the room with tears streaming down her face, looking completely devastated. I could kill Travis for making her look like that. I bring her suitcases down to my suite and put them to the side.

We sit together on the couch for a while, and I hold her as she cries. We don't talk, we don't do anything. I just let her cry until she falls asleep in my arms.

When I'm sure she won't wake, I lift her from the couch and carry her into my bedroom and gently lie her in my bed. I pull the covers over her and place a soft kiss on her forehead.

"I love you," she whispers softly as I pull away.

"Go back to sleep, sweetheart," I reply quietly.

Back in the living area, I pull a blanket and spare pillow from the linen closet and place them on the couch before climbing underneath. It isn't the most comfortable couch to sleep on, but one night certainly isn't going to kill me.

I soon find myself drifting off to sleep, but well before I'm ready to wake, I hear pounding on my front door.

"Lewis! Wake up, wake up."

I look at the clock on the wall and notice that it's only four thirty in the morning, which can only mean one thing.

I get off the couch and walk over to the door, opening it slightly.

"Travis," I say quietly.

Chapter Thirty Three

• TRAVIS •

The long days and also nights are killing me. I'm so over recording this album, and Lacey is draining the life right out of me. I know it's starting to get to Darcy too, and I really don't want her upset, or to feel that I've abandoned her. I miss her like crazy, but I just have to get through the next two days, and I'll be done with this thing for good. Lacey is a talented woman, but fuck is she high maintenance!

Once again, I apologize to Chester profusely for the extremely late night, or rather early morning, as he drives me home. It's just after four in the morning, and I'm beat. Although I haven't been sleeping in our bed on the night's I come home late—not wanting to wake Darcy—I'm desperate this morning just to cuddle up to her soft, warm body.

As I climb the stairs to our bedroom, I quietly push open the door so as not to wake Darcy. I creep over to her side of the bed, before I notice that she's not actually in there.

What the hell?

"Darcy!" I call as I head to the bathroom. "Are you in there, baby?"

There's no reply, so I head downstairs to check the kitchen, but she's not there either. Next stop is the theatre room, but that also comes up empty, and now I'm starting to panic. I pull my cell from my pocket and bring up her number, but as I expect, it goes straight to voicemail. I run back upstairs to our room and into our walk-in robe and … freeze. All of Darcy's things are gone, everything! *What the actual fuck is going on?*

I walk out in a daze back towards the bed, and out of the corner of my eye I see something that makes my stomach drop—Darcy's engagement ring is sitting on my bedside table. I feel as if I'm going to be sick.

I bolt from our room and run down the stairs and along the corridor towards Reed's suite. As I get to the door, I pound hard with my fist.

"Lewis! Wake up, wake up." I wait a few agonizing moments, before Reed finally opens the door.

"Travis," he says quietly.

"Darcy's not in our room, I can't find her, and all her stuff is gone. Do you know where she is?" I ask in a panic.

Reed quickly steps outside the door, and quietly closes it behind him.

"She's fine, she's safe."

"Where the hell is she?" I ask in confusion.

Reed looks at me heatedly.

"She's in my bed."

"What the fuck!" I rage. "You better start talking fast, Lewis."

"It's not what you're thinking—I've been sleeping on the couch. After the evening she's had, it's the least I could do."

"What are you talking about? What's happened?"

Reed snorts.

"Really? You have no idea?" he asks in disgust.

"You fucking better start talking, Lewis, before I lose my shit."

"Darcy was missing you, so she asked if we could stop off for some Chinese takeout and deliver it to the studio on her way home from work."

"So that's where that came from?" I ask. "Why didn't she bring it in herself and say hello?"

"She did," he says with fury in his eyes. "When she walked in and saw you and Lacey sucking face, she froze up and I had to carry her out of there."

"Oh fuck!" I say as I feel my stomach drop to the floor. "It's not what she thinks. She misinterpreted what she saw."

"I was there with her, Travis, there was nothing to misinterpret."

"Fuck! Let me in, I need to speak to her."

"That's not going to happen, Travis. Not now anyway. She's asleep and she's not in a good place. You need to give her time and space to come to terms with things, and then see what she wants to do after that."

"She needs to give me a chance to explain!"

"What, like you gave her?" he seethes. "Go to bed, Travis—get some rest, then we can look at things at a more reasonable hour."

"This is my fucking house!" I roar.

"Keep your bloody voice down. This is my suite—if you don't like it, you can kick me out, but I'm taking Darcy with me."

"Like hell you are! You must be loving this, aren't you?"

"Travis, this isn't you," he says calmly. "There's nothing I like about this situation. That gorgeous girl in there is crushed, and you did that. Get some rest. Darcy's here, she's safe. We won't do anything until I speak with you again in the morning."

I look at Reed and admit defeat. He's right; I've crushed her. She's so hurt that she's obviously broken off our engagement. I've hurt her. I've hurt Darcy. I've let her down … again.

The next morning, I decide to wait for Reed to come to me. I don't want to force myself on Darcy and push her away for good, but by the time noon rolls around, I can't wait any longer.

I stroll down the corridor towards Reed's suite, feeling extremely nervous as I knock on his door.

He opens quickly and looks at me with a scowl.

"How's Darcy?" I ask quietly.

"She's still asleep," he replies.

"Still?"

"She's emotionally exhausted, Travis. As soon as she wakes and I talk to her to see what her plans are, I'll come and talk to you, okay?"

"Please don't let her make any decisions before speaking with me, Lewis … please. I need to explain the situation. I understand it must have looked bad, but it was nothing like the way it seemed."

"I'll let her know you want to speak to her, but I can't promise you anything," he replies.

Just then, I see movement behind Reed, and notice Darcy standing there looking extremely tired. Her shoulders are slumped, and she has red puffy eyes.

"Darcy, baby, please let me speak with you," I call.

"Just go Travis. I don't want to speak with you. I know you don't have a twin, so I know exactly what I saw."

"Darcy, I made the biggest mistake of my life when I didn't give you a chance to explain about you and Jesse. Please give me the opportunity to fix this. If you still don't want me after I explain the situation, I won't bother you anymore. But please don't give up on us without hearing me out. You are my life, Darcy, and I can't go on without you. Nothing is right without you. Please," I beg.

Darcy looks at Reed and he gives her a sad smile.

"You don't have to if you don't want to, Darce, but remember how you felt when Travis wouldn't give you the chance to explain. Don't live with regrets," Reed says.

Darcy thinks for a minute, then looks at me.

"Fine," she says as she walks towards the door.

"You'll be here?" she asks Reed.

"Of course, sweetheart."

Darcy nods at him, then turns to follow me to our sitting room. When we get to the room, Darcy sits at the far end of the couch. I place myself next to her, but I can see how uncomfortable she looks—almost like she's scared of me.

"Can I hold your hand, please?" I ask quietly.

"No," she replies abruptly.

I drop my head sadly.

"Okay," I say. "I understand."

For some reason, I really feel that I need to have Darcy's engagement ring with me. I have no idea how this chat is going to go, but I'm determined to have that ring back on her finger by the end of it.

"I'm really sorry, baby, but can you just give me one second? I'll be right back—it's important."

She looks at me with narrowed eyes but doesn't say anything.

I jump from the couch, and quickly run upstairs to grab her ring from my bedside table.

When I sit back on the couch, I pick up Darcy's hand. She looks at me and tries to pull away, but I hold tight.

"Baby, I need to hold you. Please."

She gives me a defeated look without saying anything, so I decide it's best to start on my explanation.

"Firstly, I want to say how sorry I am for what you walked in on yesterday. I honestly know how hard that was for you to see," I say as I remember how I had thought I'd seen her kissing Jesse.

"But, baby, you have to believe me—I did not want it at all. Lacey has been making subtle passes at me for a few weeks now, but I've always brushed her off and not really thought much of it. Yesterday, completely out of the blue, she jumped me. You must have walked in at just that moment. I was so shocked, I literally froze. But as soon as I realized what was happening, I pushed her off me. I did not kiss her back. You have to believe that! I told her that we will not be recording together ever again, and that we will be recording the remainder of the album separately. I have also dropped her from my label. You are the most important thing in my life, Darcy. You know I would never cheat on you. That's not me. I would do anything for you, baby. I will not give you up."

I reach into my pocket and pull out her ring.

"Darcy, I understand you're hurting, and I get that, but you are my fiancée, and I will stop at nothing to have my ring back on your finger. Please tell me you believe me, and you forgive me for those few seconds I froze. You're it for me, baby. There will never be anyone else."

Darcy looks at me with tears running down her cheeks. I reach up and cup her face in my hands. I brush at her tears with my thumb and press my forehead against hers.

"Please tell me you'll take me back," I say shaking my head slightly. "I need you in my life, Darcy."

I hear Darcy stifle a sob as she pulls back and looks at me.

"Trav, that was the hardest thing to see. It was worse than when I walked in on Hannah and Adam in bed together. I couldn't even walk out of there. Reed had to pick me up and carry me out. I've never felt so hurt."

"God, baby I know—you'll never know how sorry I am, but I will do anything to regain your trust. I didn't cheat on you though, Darcy. I was just caught unawares and didn't respond quick enough."

"Would you have told me if I hadn't walked in and seen it?" she asks me.

"Absolutely! I had every intention of telling you as soon as I got home, but then I found you gone."

"Why didn't you leave as soon as it happened then? Why would you continue to work with her after that?"

"I need to get this recording done, Darce. I want it finished. But I sent her home … she wasn't there for the rest of the evening. I recorded alone. You can check with the guys in the booth if you don't believe me."

"I do believe you," she replies sadly.

Still holding onto her ring, I lift it up to where she can see it.

"Please tell me you'll wear my ring again. I love you, Darcy and I'm hoping you still love me too."

Darcy looks at the ring and another sob breaks free.

"Please, baby. I would never betray you; you are my life. Take me back," I plead.

Darcy lifts her arms and wraps them around me, hugging me close as she breaks into tears again.

"Please tell me this is a yes hug. Please don't tell me you're saying goodbye," I say with tears in my eyes.

"I love you, Travis," is all she says.

Chapter Thirty Four

• DARCY •

I love him. There's no doubt about that. I know I want to spend my life with him, but I have to know for sure if he wants only me. After sobbing into his chest for what seems like an eternity, I pull back and look up into his glassy eyes, wiping some of the moisture from his cheek with my thumb.

"Do you have any feelings for Lacey at all; even the slightest bit?" I ask him.

"Baby, not even a hint of anything! You're it for me. If I can't have you, I will spend my life alone—and I mean that. I don't want anyone else, I never will. I adore you, Darcy. It's not just a matter of wanting you; I *need* you. Please believe how much I love you, and how much I need to have you in my life."

I know what he means. I need him too. Not just want; but *need*. I look up at Travis, lift my left hand, and present it to him.

"You're it for me too, Trav," I say. "I'll have my ring back now, please."

Travis looks at me in astonishment and then promptly bursts into tears.

"Hey, ya big softy," I say as I stroke his cheek.

"Baby, you have no idea. I thought I'd lost you for good."

"I love you, Travis. I was hurt, but I'm here for you. I should have known I could trust you. I know women are going to throw themselves at you, and I have to remember that and try not to be too jealous. Just promise me, that if any woman ever tries to kiss you—or succeeds for that fact, that you'll tell me … just like I always tell you if I kiss Jesse or Reed when I'm playing with them.

"Deal," he replies with a soft smile.

Travis has decided that he wants to finally make our engagement public. It could mean a few things—possibly more security for me due to his fans, other threats, less sales for him, more sales for him—we have no idea how the public will take the fact that their golden boy is off the market again.

Trav's manager, Brant; has arranged for us both to appear on *Nights in Nashville* again with Grace Sandell. I'm super nervous as we wait backstage. Travis is doing the first half of the interview alone, and then they'll call me out. First up, Grace and Travis talk about his up-coming tour around the country. It's only for four and a half months and I'll be joining him for a few weeks of it, but I'm still anxious about him being away. I know this is what I've signed on for though—this is his job, and he's good at it, and his fans love him.

Grace then mentions the new album he's just finished recording with Lacey, and I prickle. I hate that the release has gone ahead, and I hate it even more that Lacey is joining him on this tour. Travis seems really angry about it too. Even though he's the boss and could have said no, he *and I* both know it would seriously sabotage his career if she weren't to tour with him. I know Travis is concerned, but I try to ease his stress by telling him that I understand it has to be done, as long as she keeps her paws off him. I also know there will be lots of publicity shots of the two of them together, which will be hard to see, but as Trav tells me—that's just the business.

I think this is why Travis wants our engagement to go public before the tour, so the media don't see images of him and Lacey together and run with a story that isn't true. He wants them to know that I'm it for him—I'm going to be his wife.

Before long, I hear Grace calling my name, and with as much confidence as I can muster, I make my way out onto the stage. Grace comes over and hugs me and then directs me to sit next to Travis, who gives me a sweet kiss. Grace gets straight to it—telling me how good it is to have me back after my last visit when I surprised Travis as one of his 'fans'.

We talk a little about how I'm enjoying Nashville, and my favorite things about the city, and then she asks about our relationship. Travis looks at me sweetly and takes my hand in his.

"I've never met anyone in my life that makes me as happy as this woman right here," he says to Grace. "I have an amazing family, great friends, brilliant colleagues—but this woman here—she makes me whole. She is everything, and I love her more than I've ever loved another person before."

He looks at me again and presses another soft kiss to my lips. Then Grace directs her next statement at me.

"And you obviously feel the same way, Darcy, considering you agreed to marry him," she says.

"Of course I do—look at him!" I burst out.

The crowd screams, whistles and hollers and I laugh at their response.

"I snagged myself a hot, sexy, singing cowboy, and let me tell you ladies, what's underneath all this," I say as I wave my hands along Trav's body, "is nothing *close* to what you are all imagining—it's a million times better, and he's all mine!"

The crowd goes nuts then, and I laugh as I watch Travis shake his head with an embarrassed smile.

Sitting in a corner booth at *Bar Melee*, I think back to the last time I was here. My awful encounter with Adam is something I never expected from him, but I wanted to come back with my friends to a place we'd previously enjoyed—drinking, dancing and having a few laughs together.

I've given Reed the night off so he can join in the fun, but I can see he's anxious. He's still carrying a lot of guilt over what happened to me here, but I want to show him that I'm fine. I want him to let go of his guilt and enjoy the night.

All the staff from Great Scott are here: Jesse, Amelia, Beth, Aisha, Christian, Miller and Raif, plus Reed, Travis and myself. Jocelyn—Reed's sister—had also joined us.

It's not quite the same with Travis here, as it was in Summerlake—here everyone knows him and everyone wants a piece. It's really hard just to get some time alone with him for a simple dance, but we manage it a few times. It makes me so proud seeing the way people react to Travis. I know it bothers him sometimes, not being able to get away from his fans, but at the same time he's always great with them—understanding that if it weren't for them, he wouldn't be where he is.

While Travis is busy getting phones shoved in his face and signing autographs, I take the opportunity to ask Jesse to dance.

"Hey Jesse," I say. "Fancy a dance?"

"Sure! I'd love too. Will Travis mind though?"

"I think he's a little preoccupied, don't you?" I reply with a laugh as we both look over in his direction.

"Yeah, I guess so," he chuckles.

Jesse takes my hand and leads me onto the dance floor. I place my arms around his neck, and he wraps his around my waist and pulls me close as we start to move together.

"How are you?" he asks sincerely.

"I'm good, thanks," I reply with a smile. "Why do you ask?"

"I just wondered, you know, being back here."

"I'm fine, honestly … thanks Jesse. If it had just been some random attack, that might have been different, but it was Adam so, I don't know, it just makes it a bit easier somehow. Reed's struggling with it more than I am."

"He really cares about you, doesn't he?"

"Yeah, he really does," I say as I look in Reed's direction. "He would give up his life for me in a heartbeat, I have no doubt about that."

Reed catches my eye, and I mouth the words "you're next". He gives me a shy smile and nods.

"So, who's the girl that came with you, Travis and Reed tonight?" he asks me.

"Oh, that's Jocelyn, Reed's sister," I reply with a smirk. "Are you interested?"

"Well, she's no Darcy Hastings, but she is cute."

"I don't know her that well yet, but she seems really lovely, Jesse, you should ask her to dance."

"What, and walk out of here with a black eye? Reed won't let me get within two meters of her, I can assure you."

"I'll talk to Reed," I say.

"I don't know, Darce. My feelings for you haven't changed."

"I know, but maybe she's just what you need to help you move on from me. Go, she'd be crazy to turn you down."

He nervously looks in Jocelyn's direction, and I reach up and give him a kiss on the cheek.

"Jesse, you're a god damn confident, successful, gorgeous looking man—she's going to *fall* into your arms. Go!"

He drops my hand and walks off in Jocelyn's direction. I follow him off the floor and made my way towards Reed. I come up behind him as he's talking to Miller and wrap my arms around his waist, placing my hands on his firm abs. *God, they're good!*

"Hey sexy, am I interrupting?" I ask.

"Not at all, *gorgeous*," Miller replies with a cheeky grin.

"I was actually talking to my hot bodyguard and best friend here," I say with a smile.

"Of course you were," Miller replies hanging his head in mock disappointment.

"Will you dance with me?" I ask Reed.

"Of course, sweetheart. When do I ever say no to you?"

"You never do," I reply looking straight into his eyes. "That's one of the reasons I love you so much."

He looks at me with the sweetest smile I've ever seen, flashing his gorgeous dimple. I grab his hand and drag him towards the dance floor. As we move together, I press my cheek against his chest and hold him close, taking in his glorious scent.

"God Reed, why do you always smell so damn good? You make it nearly impossible for a girl not to want to jump your bones."

He pushes me back a little and looks at me as he bursts out laughing.

"You want to *jump my bones*?" he asks incredulously.

"Yes, I do! God, you're standing there looking all hot and sexy, and you smell so damn good, and I seriously just want to climb up your body and dry hump you."

"Oh my God, Darcy, stop; you're killing me," he laughs.

"Reed, it's not funny. I'm serious!" I say trying to hold in a smile.

"Hey baby, I'm not stopping you," he says holding his arms out to the side. "Hump away!"

"Don't tempt me. If Travis wasn't here, I probably would."

"Come here," he says chuckling, as he pulls me back into his hard chest.

"I love you so much, you know that?"

"Yeah, I know. I love you too," I say as I reach up and give him a quick chaste kiss on the mouth.

We stay like that—moving together—for a few more minutes before I hear Travis' voice behind Reed.

"Mind if I dance with my beautiful fiancée?"

"Not at all," Reed replies as he lets me go.

"Thanks, Reed," I say as he leaves the floor with a flirtatious wink.

"So, how's the future Mrs Danvers enjoying her night?" Travis asks me.

"I'm having a great time. What about you, Mr Danvers?"

"Not too bad. I love my fans but sometimes it would just be nice to go somewhere where nobody knows me."

"Yeah, I get it. It's your own fault though for being so damn gorgeous and so damn talented!" I reply.

"As long as you're my number one fan, that's all I care about."

"Always baby … always," I say as I snuggle into his warm, strong arms.

"God, I can't wait until you're my wife," he says quietly into my ear. "I can't wait for you to be mine."

"Trav, I've always been yours."

Chapter Thirty Five

• DARCY •

There are so many things I have to be thankful for in my life. A great job with fantastic colleagues, brilliant friends, an amazing home; and I have one man to thank for it all—Travis Danvers, my fiancé.

My only complaint in life would probably be that I hardly get to see said fiancé. Since the launch of his latest album with Lacey Wilde, Trav's schedule has been nothing but hectic. Before he left on tour, his days were filled with interviews and appearances, and he's been on tour now for the past two and a half months, with only a few quick visits home in that time. I miss him. I miss him a lot.

Although we speak most days on the phone, not having him here is starting to weigh heavily on me. I'm worried about all the time he's spending with Lacey, especially after what happened between them. But I also feel like we're starting to drift apart. I know Travis feels it too. I'm unsure if we'll get through the next two months unscathed. When he does fly home for a few days, we always feel detached from each other. Conversation doesn't come easily, and he wants to spend a lot of time with his family. I'm certainly feeling like a second priority. As much as I love Travis, I'm worried that we're losing what previously held us together. We've had our fair share of issues, but we've always managed to find our way back to each other. I feel the bonds are becoming weaker as the weeks go by.

My saving grace in my loneliness is Reed. Reed is my life. I adore him and he adores me. He knows me better than anyone, and I trust him with my life. With Travis away all the time, Reed and I spend a lot of our free time together, and we've grown extremely close. I could not imagine my life without him in it.

"Hey beautiful, what're your plans for this weekend?"

I look up to see Jesse standing in the doorway of my office. Jesse and I have a great friendship. We've been through some hiccups along the way, but he's a great boss and an even better friend.

"No plans yet, I don't think. What about you?" I ask.

"Jocelyn and I are probably going to head to Club Melee tonight if you guys want to come with?"

I hear a low growl coming from the corner of my office and look up with a grin at Reed, who is sitting at his desk giving Jesse the evil eye. Reed is not too happy about Joss and Jesse dating. I think it's great! For the past few months, he's been seeing Jocelyn and things seem to be going well. She's great and becoming one of my closest friends; and I'm stoked for Jesse that he was able to move on from me and be happy with someone who can return his feelings.

Reed, however, doesn't quite share the same thoughts as me. He's glad Jocelyn's happy, but I think he wishes she'd chosen someone other than Jesse. Although we've pretty much moved on from what happened between Jesse and my sister, I know it still bothers Reed a little. He just can't fully trust Jesse.

"We'd love to come, wouldn't we, Reed?" I ask him with a smirk.

"Yeah sure, whatever you say, baby," he replies with narrowed eyes.

I let out a chuckle as I make my way over to Reed's desk and sit on his lap with my arms around his neck.

"You love me. You know you do," I laugh.

"You're just damn lucky I do, woman, otherwise I sure wouldn't put up with half the shit you put me through."

I wrap both my palms around his cheeks and place a soft chaste kiss on his lips.

"How did I ever survive without you in my life?" I ask him.

"Honestly babe, I have no idea."

As usual, Jesse, Joss, Reed and I spend a lot of our time on the dance floor at Club Melee. I love my time dancing with Reed; it gives us a chance to really talk without other things interrupting.

"Have you spoken to Travis today?" Reed asks.

"No," I reply sadly. "I tried calling him, but he didn't pick up. He hardly ever picks up anymore."

"You know how busy he must be, right?"

"Yeah, I know, but it's not just that, Reed. Even when he does ring, he's usually only got a few minutes to talk, and then the conversation is always so awkward—not like us at all. I don't know what's going on, but I don't like it. I feel like I hardly know him all of a sudden, and as the weeks pass it just gets worse."

"Have you mentioned this to him?"

"Yeah, and he agrees, but at the same time he kind of brushes me off. He doesn't seem to want to talk about it and says that we'll just deal with it when he gets home. With the way things are going, I don't think we'll still be engaged by the time he gets home. I knew things would be hard with him gone so much, but I never thought he'd close himself off like he is. I already feel liked he's checked out of our relationship. How can I marry someone who shuts me out the minute he's not around me?"

"Geez, Darce, I don't know what to say. It doesn't sound like Travis at all."

"I know, right? I know I'm not imagining it. I just wish I knew what he was thinking. If he wants out, then he should damn well tell me and not just drag me along pretending to still love me."

"Darce, he still loves you."

"You sure about that?" I ask. Reed looks at me with concern in his eyes.

"I hate seeing you this unhappy," he says.

"I'll be okay," I reply as I snuggle my face into his neck. We continue to dance a little while longer until my feet start to ache. Reed leads me over to a booth where Jesse and Joss are talking, and we sit down with them.

"You two looked cozy," Joss says with a smirk.

"I love this man," I say with my hand on Reed's shoulder.

"I can see that," Joss replies with a smile. "I still don't see why you two aren't together."

"Joss," Reed growls in a warning tone.

"What? You love her, she loves you—what's the problem?"

"The problem is that she's engaged to another man, Joss. She doesn't love me like that. Drop it, okay?"

I look at Reed lovingly. He sure will make some woman very, very happy one day.

"He's too good for me," I say to Joss, but not taking my eyes off Reed.

And he is. Reed is one of the most amazing men I have ever met. He is devoted to me in every way, and puts me before everything else. He is kind, funny and protective in a way that certainly goes above and beyond his role as my bodyguard.

"You wanna head out?" Reed asks me.

"Sure," I reply.

Back home, Reed and I decide to cuddle up on the couch and watch a movie before bed. These days, most of my time at home is spent in Reed's suite. Trav's mansion is just too big, especially when it's just me and our housekeeper, Peggy home.

"What do you want to watch?" Reed asks me.

"Something romantic," I reply dreamily.

Reed snorts.

"Babe, that's all we ever watch. I feel my balls shriveling just at the thought."

"I can massage them for you if you think that'll help," I reply with a smirk.

I watch with delight as Reed chokes on my response.

"You're a filthy minx, you know that?"

"I really do," I smile.

We settle in on the couch together, me with my legs over Reed's lap, and enjoy a romantic comedy together.

"Reed?"

"Yeah, sweetheart?"

"What do you think I should do about Travis?"

"What do you mean?" he asks.

"I mean, do I stick it out for another two months and continue my somewhat miserable existence, or do I confront Trav and see what the hell is going on?"

"I can't answer that, Darce. You need to decide what you want. If you want Travis no matter what, then you might have to fight to keep him. Confront him and see if he wants the same thing. I know his lifestyle must be hard for you and that you miss him, but that's his career and there's always going to be times when he's gone for months at a time. If you feel that his touring is going to be an issue in your marriage, then you need to do something about it now. You should date the handsome bodyguard instead," he says with a grin.

I look over at him and gave him a whack across the chest.

"I'm serious, Reed. I don't know what to do."

"I know; I was just messing with you, I'm sorry. It's a huge decision, but either way, you need to speak to Travis."

"I know. I just wish I knew what he was thinking. I feel like he's given up on us."

"Call him, Darce, and don't give up until you get an answer."

"Hey, guys," I call out to the cubies as I enter my office the next morning.

"Hey, Darcy," comes back the mumbled response. I make my way to my desk, as Reed heads to his. I turn on my laptop and start plowing through my emails. Mid-way through, I look over at Reed—also on his laptop—and stare at his handsome face, as butterflies fill my stomach. *God, he is so beautiful.*

"Reed?"

"Yeah?"

"I love you," I say.

"I know, sweetheart. I love you too," he says with a smile, and without lifting his eyes from his screen.

"No, Reed. I love you. I'm in love with you."

Reed stops what he's doing, and looks up at me.

"Darce—you're engaged to Travis. You love Travis. You're just feeling a little lost at the moment."

"That's not it," I reply looking down. "I think I've known it for a while, and I've tried to tell myself that it's just a friend love, but it's more than that, Reed."

Reed looks down at his desk with a frown.

"Darcy, you've known how I've felt about you for a while now, and that hasn't changed …"

"But?" I interject.

"But I know you love Travis, and as much as I love you, I don't want to be your second option because Travis isn't around. I thought I could deal with being your second choice, but I can't. I want to be your first choice, Darcy. I want to be someone's first choice. I need to realize that I can't have you and move on, as much as I hate that thought."

"I don't want you to move on," I say in a panic. "I know how selfish that is and you deserve the absolute best, but I can't bear the thought of you being with someone else."

"Darce, it's going to happen at some point. Maybe not right away, but at some stage. I want to fall in love with someone who loves me in return, marry and have a family. Do I want that with you—hell yeah, I do, but I'm also realistic and realize that's not going to happen. We'll always be friends, we can never let that go, but as far as anything else, we both know that can't happen."

I stare into Reed's eyes and feel a knot forming in my throat. *Oh god, I'm going to cry. I can't let Reed see me cry over this.*

I excuse myself and start to make my way to the bathroom.

"Darcy!" Reed calls after me worriedly.

"I'm okay. I'll be right back," I reply without turning around.

As I push open the door of the bathroom, I feel a strong arm quickly pull me in and another hand wrap hard across my mouth. My eyes widen in terror as I look into the mirror to see my ex, Adam.

"You make a sound and you won't get out of the hospital this time—got it?"

I nod my head in agreement as I listen to him give me directions about how we were going to walk out of here.

Chapter Thirty Six

• REED •

I'm sitting at my desk in silence, waiting for Darcy to return from the bathroom. I knew she loved me but having her admit that she's *in love* with me is another thing. Have I been dying to hear those words from her lips? Absolutely, but not like this. Not when she's in this situation with Travis.

We have grown closer in the last few months, but again, I know she wouldn't have been spending so much time with me if Travis had been here. Although I've felt that our relationship has changed somehow, I also know that I need to start distancing myself from Darcy, not as a friend, but as a romantic interest. As much as I want her, as much as I want her in every part of my life, she's off limits. She belongs to Travis. She isn't mine.

Looking through the glass wall of Darcy's office, I notice Amelia, the Receptionist, coming out of the staff break room.

"Amelia!" I call out. "Would you mind checking on Darcy in the bathroom please? She's been in there for a little while and she was upset."

"Sure thing, Reed. I'll be back in a sec."

I watch as Amelia makes her way to the bathroom and then sit back in my chair, hands clasped behind my head. I don't want things to be awkward between Darcy and me. I know I've hurt her feelings by saying what I did, but surely she understands. We'll chat, as we always do, and I'll help her understand.

"She's not in there, Reed," Amelia says as she pokes her head in the doorway of Darcy's office.

"What? Where did she go then?"

"I'm not sure. I haven't seen her recently," Amelia replies.

I jump from my desk and make my way out to the cubies area and whistle to grab the attention of all staff.

"Did anyone see Darcy come out of the bathroom recently?" I yell.

"No," comes back the mass of confused mumbled responses.

I make my way into the women's bathroom to check myself, and then back out into the reception area when I find no sign of Darcy. Starting to panic now, I decide to check into the security system I had set up. There are cameras set up both inside and outside the building, and if Darcy has left, at least I'll know which way she's headed.

I run back to my desk, jump onto my laptop and log in. I pull up the surveillance footage of the last 30 minutes and focus first on the reception area. If Darcy's left the building; through the reception area is the only way out.

I fast-forward the footage until I see two figures on screen. Backing up a little, I press play and watch the scene unfold in front of me.

I see Darcy walk past Amelia's desk heading for the door, with a man right behind her. He has one hand around the back of her neck, and with the other hand he's holding something under his jacket. A weapon, I presume.

"Fuck!" I curse.

Pausing the footage, I zoom into the guys' face.

"Fuck, fuuuck!!!" I yell, slamming my fist on the table.

"What the hell's going on in here?" Jesse asks as he pokes his head into the doorway and looks at me in anger.

"Darcy's been taken," I yell as I slam my laptop shut.

"What do you mean, taken?" Jesse asks with fear in his eyes.

"I mean, her fucking ex was obviously hiding in the bathroom, and just walked out with her. He was holding a weapon to her side—I have to go."

"I'm coming with you," Jesse replies.

"No, you stay here. I don't need any liabilities. My team will handle this. I'll let you know if I hear anything."

I quickly message Charlie, Darcy's other bodyguard and driver, as I grab her phone and bag from her desk and all my gear, then quickly make my way out of the building.

Charlie's brought the car around as requested, and I jump in the back seat.

"Where's Miss Hastings?" Charlie asks concerned. "Her fucking ex got her again," I reply in disgust. I can't believe I've let her down again.

"How the hell does this guy keep getting past us?" he asks.

"I don't bloody know, but I swear when I get my hands on him, he'll be sorry he ever stepped foot in this country."

"What are your plans? Where am I headed?"

"I need to call it in first, then call Travis. Perhaps head to the station and we'll take it from there."

I call the officer who worked on Darcy's case when Adam last attacked her. He's pissed. Adam had skipped bail after he'd attacked Darcy the first time, and there was a warrant out for his arrest, but they had no idea where he was. I let him know we're on our way in.

As we make our way through traffic, I punch in Travis' number.

"Lewis, what can I do for you?" he answers.

"Travis, it's Darcy."

"What about her, Lewis?"

"She's been kidnapped sir. Adam Clarkson has her."

"What the absolute fuck!" he screams down the line.

"Look, I don't have time to explain things now, I need to concentrate on finding her, but I wanted to let you know. I presume you'll be making your way home straight away?"

"I can't just up and cancel the tour, Lewis. I hired you to take care of her. Find her before that fucker hurts her again and keep me updated."

"You're seriously not coming home?" I ask incredulously.

"I have a tour to finish, Lewis. I can't just drop everything and run home."

"She's your goddamn fiancée, Travis. What the fuck? Darcy deserves better than this."

"Oh what, and you think you know everything now?"

"I know she deserves better than you being unavailable to her these last four months, and I don't just mean physically. And now when she needs you the most, you're too fucking busy to be there for her? Fuck that, Travis, you don't deserve her."

I end the call and throw the phone onto the seat next to me.

God, what a jackass!

I've always liked Travis and had a lot of respect for him, but in that one phone call he'd just erased it all.

It was obviously now just up to me to be there for Darcy. But first I had to find her.

"Do you have anything I can work with?" I ask Officer John Covington.

"Not much," he replies. "We've got the security footage from her office that you gave us and also the footage from the street outside the building."

"Does that show anything?" I ask in anticipation.

"We see them cross the street together, him very close behind her, and he helps her into the passenger side of a car. We can see him fumbling around, leaning into the car for a bit, so we are presuming he might have handcuffed her, perhaps so she can't run as he walks around to the driver's side. He gets in and they drive off. We've got the plates but it's a rental car and he's used a different name from the one you gave us."

"What's the name of the rental company? I'm going over there now to see what I can find out."

"Maybe you should leave this to us, Lewis. I know you have a personal relationship with the victim, so your good judgement is going to be compromised."

"I've already let Darcy down by allowing that bastard to grab her in the first place. I'm sure as hell not stopping until I catch the asshole and bring her home safe. Now, the company name?" I ask him.

He lets out a heavy sigh and passes me a card with all the details on it.

"Just don't do anything stupid, or illegal, we need to do this by the book if we're gonna put him behind bars."

"Got it," I reply as I make my way to the door. "Keep me informed if you get any further information."

I run down to the street, jump in the passenger side of the car and give Charlie directions to the hire car company.

"You think they're gonna give you the information you need?" he asks me.

"Doubtful," I reply. "But I have to try—we've got nothing else to go on."

"Let's just hope you'll be dealing with a woman."

"Why's that?" I ask.

"Come on, Lewis. We all know how women react to you. As soon as you walk into a room, women practically throw their panties at you."

I snort as I shake my head at Charlie.

"What? Don't say you don't notice it. You love the way women respond to you."

"The only woman I care about at this moment is Darcy, so I'll do whatever it takes to get her back. If that means flirting with a female employee to get my own way, then that's what I'll do."

We eventually pull into the parking lot in front of the car rental company, and I jump out.

"Wait here," I call back to Charlie.

I make my way inside to the reception area, and thankfully there's a pretty brunette behind the desk. She looks up and flashes me a huge smile.

"Hi there, how can I help you today?" she asks as she flutters her eyelashes at me. Perfect!

"Hi, beautiful," I say. "I was hoping you might be able to help me with some information I'm after."

"Sure, if I can," she replies with a blush.

"Great," I smile. "I'm after the name of someone who recently hired one of your cars and also the location of that car at the moment."

Knowing giving out this kind of information would be against company policy; I gave the woman my most charming smile.

"I'm so sorry, sir, but we're not allowed to give out that kind of information. It's against company policy."

"Of course it is. I'm sorry to ask, but it's really important. The man who hired this car, did so under a false name. He's extremely dangerous and he has now kidnapped a woman. The cops are on their way over here with a warrant to obtain the information anyway, but this woman's life is in danger, and I'm not willing to risk her life for the sake of some paperwork. If you could help me out here, I would make it worth your while."

"I don't know," she responds. "I really need this job, and if I give you that information, I'll get fired."

"I promise you; I'll see to it that you don't. Please, I'm running out of time here."

She looks at me trying to decide whether she should help me.

"Please," I beg.

She lets out a long sigh and looks around nervously.

"Do you have any details on the car?" she asks.

I give her the plate number and wait for her to do her thing.

"The car was hired out to a Jacob Thompson. Let me just see what the GPS tracker is telling me."

I pace anxiously as I wait for the location of the vehicle.

"Shit," she says after a few minutes. "It looks like the GPS has been disabled."

"Damn it," I say as I run my hand through my hair.

"We do have a back-up tracker on the vehicles though, in case something like this happens. Most people don't realize that. Let me just bring that up. It'll just take a few minutes."

"Whatever you can do," I reply.

After what feels like an eternity, I finally walk out of there with an address.

"Where're we headed boss?" Charlie asks me.

"I have an address for a house over near Vanderbilt University, so head in that direction."

We travel in relative silence until we're on the street of the house we're looking for.

"What's your plan boss?" Charlie asks me.

"Pull over here," I tell him. "I don't want to draw any attention."

Charlie pulls over to the side of the road and I open my door to get out. Charlie also goes to get out.

"What are you doing?" I ask him.

"You think I'm letting you go in there alone without backup? You're fucking crazy, dude."

"Are you packing?" I ask him.

"Of course," he replies.

"Shit! Alright but we need some sort of plan. I doubt he'll be holding her out in the open. There's likely to be some kind of basement; there usually is in these older houses."

"Agreed," Charlie responds.

"Let's check all the windows on the ground level and see what we come up with first."

"Are you going to call this in at all?" Charlie asks.

"Not yet. I don't want all their bloody sirens spooking him so that he does something stupid. We need the element of surprise here."

"Alright, but if I even get a whiff of anything going south, I'm calling it."

"Done," I reply.

We slowly start walking towards the house, checking our surroundings as we go.

"I can't see the car," Charlie says. "You sure this is the right house?"

"This is the last place it was located, so we'll start here."

Charlie and I eventually search the entire property and come up with nothing. There are no signs that either Adam or Darcy have been here. I feel completely deflated, but terrified for Darcy. There are no other leads to follow. Nothing to give me any indication of where she might be and whether she's hurt.

"I'm gonna call the rental company back, see if I can't get another location," I say to Charlie.

He nods his agreement and waits for me to make the call.

After speaking with the same woman from earlier, I'm able to get another location, although it seems the car is on the move. She tells me that the vehicle had been stationery for some time at an address just outside of Nashville across the other side of town but was now moving again. I take the address from her, but we decide to try and eventually catch up to the car. Either way, it has to eventually lead us to Darcy. She's either been stashed at the first address or she's now with Adam in the moving car.

Charlie and I make our way through traffic across town following regular text updates from Sally, the woman at the hire company. The car seems to have stopped again, so it gives us more of a chance to catch up a bit.

When we finally catch up, we find ourselves at another house where we see the car parked in the driveway. Charlie parks down the street a little, then we both jump out and make our way toward the house. As we near, we see the front door of the house swing open, and both Charlie and I jump back behind a hedge to watch.

We watch as Adam and three other men make their way out, laughing and talking amongst themselves. There's no sign of Darcy though.

All four men jump into the car, reverse out of the driveway and drive off in the direction we just came from.

"Are we following them?" Charlie asks concerned.

"I just want to check out this place first, in case Darcy is here," I reply.

Charlie and I quickly force our way into the house and complete a sweep, but again come up with nothing. Perhaps Adam and his mates are heading back to Darcy at that other address now, I think.

Adam with three mates on their way to Darcy terrifies me. I have a pretty good idea what his plans might be, and I will do anything to stop him.

Charlie and I run back to our car and make our way as fast as we can to the first address Sally gave us. When we arrive on the street, we can see the car ahead of us parked in another driveway. It's empty, the four men obviously already inside.

Charlie parks down the street again, and we both jump out and run towards the house.

"You take the front and I'll jump the fence and check the back," I say to Charlie.

"Got it," he replies.

I quickly swing myself over the dilapidated wooden side fence, making as little noise as possible, and head towards a small window located low to the ground. I listen carefully for any sound before I edge my head across the glass to get a look in. The glass is filthy and it's dark inside, but I can just make out a few things. I quickly message Charlie to direct him round to the back, telling him that I think I've found the basement.

I very carefully rub the side of my fist over the corner of the glass to get a better look, and what I see knocks the wind right out of me.

Darcy.

Chapter Thirty Seven

• DARCY •

I'm sitting here blindfolded and handcuffed to a chair in a cold, dark basement and all I can think about is my last conversation with Reed. Does he think I just left the office without him because I was embarrassed about what was said? God, I hope not. Surely he realizes I wouldn't be that stupid. Has he realized what's happened? Is he looking for me? Does Travis know? All these thoughts are running through my mind as I listen to Adam moving about the room.

"Adam?" I ask hesitantly.

"Quiet bitch," he replies gruffly.

"Adam, please. Why am I here? What do you want?"

"I want you to suffer, just like you've made me suffer over these past few months."

"Adam, I've done *nothing* to you. I left because *you* cheated on *me*. You were the one who didn't want me anymore; you wanted my sister, so I left you to it. I thought you would be happy about that. Then just as I'm moving on, you come here and try to stake a claim again."

"You belong to *me*, Darcy," he growls. "You are mine."

"Adam, I stopped being yours the moment you climbed into bed with Hannah."

The moment I say my sister's name, I feel a powerful hand strike against my left cheek. The force so great, the chair I'm sitting on almost tips over. Tears burn under my eyelids beneath my blindfold as I try to hold them at bay. I do not want to give Adam the satisfaction of seeing me cry.

"You speak again, and I'll put the end of my gun in that pretty little mouth of yours. Got it bitch?" he grows.

I quickly nod, not wanting to make a sound.

"I need to head out and pick up a few mates. We're going to have a fun night with you; that's for sure. You sit tight, baby," he laughs.

I hear Adam's footsteps retreat, and a door open and close. In the distance, I faintly hear a car engine start up and the vehicle drive off. I feel my shoulders slump as I finally relax a little. My blindfold suddenly becoming damp as I let the tears fall that I've been holding onto. I can only imagine what he and his mates have in store for me.

After a little while, I feel myself getting sleepy, but I fight it as best I can. I cannot let myself fall asleep knowing that Adam will be back at any moment with his mates. God only knows what he's planning, but I have a pretty good idea.

After what feels like hours, I faintly hear a car pull up and then a bunch of car doors banging closed.

I wriggle on my chair, but there is absolutely no give with the metal handcuffs Adam has used on me. I can feel them painfully cutting into my wrists.

After a few minutes, I hear the door of the room I'm in open, and a bunch of heavy footsteps make their way over to me.

"She sure does look pretty, restrained like that," one of the men says with a throaty laugh.

"Hey, baby. I thought I'd bring the guys over to have a bit of fun. What do you think?" Adam asks me with a smug sounding chuckle.

"Go to hell," I reply bravely.

I suddenly feel another whack across the cheek; the shock making my eyes water again.

"Now that wasn't very nice, was it?" he asks. "If you don't use your manners, baby, I'll have to teach you a lesson in front of the boys here. Are you going to be nice now?" he asks patronizingly.

I nod my head slowly.

"Answer me," he snaps.

"Yes," I reply quickly.

"Good girl. Now are you going to behave if I take off your blindfold?" he asks.

"Yes," I reply again softly.

I feel him reach behind me and untie the blindfold, dropping it to the floor. I blink rapidly, my eyes trying to adjust to the dim light in the room. I look around quickly and gasp at what I see—Adam with three of his mates from back home. Mates that I know well. Guys I had been friends with too.

"What are you guys doing here?" I ask in disbelief.

"We came to see you, sweetheart," Brad replies with a smile.

I look around at the others. James has a sly grin on his face, while Brandon looks at me hesitantly.

"Why are you doing this?" I ask them with sadness in my eyes. "You guys were my friends. Why would you listen to Adam? He's obviously lost his mind."

"You promised you would be nice," Adam says as he drops to his knees in front of me. "Now, how about we shut that smart mouth of yours?"

He grabs my cheeks between his palms, and I wince at the pain I feel, thanks his previous slaps. Before I know what's happening, he plants his mouth over mine in a possessive kiss.

He pulls away quickly and then gestures over his shoulder to Brad with a smirk. I watch as Brad walks slowly towards me with an arrogant swagger and starts unzipping his fly. *Oh god!*

"Open up," Brad says as he pulls out his cock.

"There's no way I'm putting that ugly thing in my mouth," I reply flatly.

"You don't have a choice, little lady," he says smugly.

"You put that thing anywhere near me, and I'll bite it off," I say with feigned confidence. "And you really can't afford to lose any length; you're even smaller than Adam."

I hear Brandon snort just before I feel Adam's hand suddenly grip my hair at the nape of my neck and pull back sharply. With my head back pointing at the ceiling, he looks over me with rage burning in his eyes.

"You're going to pay for that comment, you little whore," he says angrily.

Before he can do anything, I hear an almighty bang and I see Reed burst through the door. I immediately slump in my chair with relief as tears pour down my cheeks. Reed has found me. How he managed it so quickly, I don't know, but I'm so grateful to see him.

"Reed!" I gasp.

"Get the fuck away from her," Reed yells at Brad noticing his unzipped jeans. "Before I shoot that fucking twig from your body."

Brad quickly pulls himself together and steps back, looking to Adam for direction. I feel Adam quickly step behind me and grab me around the throat. Within seconds I also feel the butt of his gun at my temple.

I look to Reed with terror filling my body as I begin to shake uncontrollably. I plead him with my eyes to help me. In the next second, I see Charlie enter the room behind Reed with his gun drawn.

"You three, out!" he yells at Brad, James and Brandon.

I watch as the three men stumble out quickly, with Charlie following close behind. That just leaves me, Reed and Adam.

"Put your gun down, Adam," Reed says in a calm tone. "There's no way out for you. You either leave here in cuffs or a body bag. It's your choice."

"No," I sob looking at Reed.

As much as I hate Adam right now, the thought of him being carried out in a body bag horrifies me.

"Please, Adam, do as he says. I don't want you hurt."

"Shut up, bitch. If anyone's going out in a body bag, it's Romeo over there."

"If you don't put your gun down, Adam, I *will* shoot you," Reed warns.

"Please, Adam," I sob.

In that second, I feel Adam lift the gun from my temple, and I hear the shot a split second before I see Reed collapse to the floor.

"No!" I scream. "Reed!"

Before I know what's happening, Charlie bursts through the door and Adam also drops to the floor. Charlie runs over and kicks the gun from Adam's reach, and then the room is filled with half a dozen police officers.

"Charlie, help Reed!" I yell. "Call an ambulance!"

I look over at Reed who hasn't moved—a pool of blood forming around him. *Please let him be okay!*

I look at Charlie, who's kneeling beside Reed.

"Is he breathing?" I ask Charlie with absolute terror in my voice.

"Just, but his pulse is weak. We need to get him to the hospital, quick."

Just then, two paramedics run into the room and I watch helplessly as they start working on Reed.

"Please help him," I call. "Don't let him die!"

Two more paramedics come through the door, and they make their way to Adam. This is all a horrible nightmare. After a few moments I feel someone behind me undoing my handcuffs and helping me from my chair. I immediately run over and slump over Reed.

"Don't you dare give up, Reed," I sob. "I love you and you cannot leave me; do you hear me?"

"Come on, sweetheart, let them work on him," Charlie says quietly.

"I'll take you home and I'll let you know as soon as we hear anything."

"Charlie, I'm not leaving him. I'm going with him to the hospital."

"That's not a good idea, Darcy."

"I'm not leaving him!" I yell back.

The paramedics carefully place Reed onto a gurney, and start to wheel him out. I grab Reed's hand and hold on tight as we make our way to the ambulance. I look down at Reed's body, and notice the bullet wound on his abdomen. There is so much blood, and the sight of it terrifies me.

Reed is pushed into the ambulance, and I climb in beside him. Before long, I hear the sirens wailing as we make our way to the hospital.

Sitting in the waiting room while Reed is in surgery is the worst torture I have ever experienced. So far, he's been in there for four hours and I've had no word.

Charlie's waiting with me and trying to do anything he can to take my mind off things. I appreciate the effort, but it isn't working—at all.

All I can think of is Reed. If he dies because of me, I could never live with myself. I could not live my life without him in it. No matter what happens between Travis and me, Reed is a truly important part of my life.

After another two hours of pointless pacing and endless cups of revolting instant coffee, a doctor dressed in scrubs enters the waiting room and calls Reed's name.

I jump from my seat and quickly make my way over to him. Charlie follows behind.

"How is he?" I ask scared out of my mind.

"He made it through surgery, but he's still got a long way to go. We lost him a few times but managed to bring him back. He's a very lucky man. He's in recovery now and will be taken up to the ICU soon. As soon as they move him up, someone will come and get you and you should be able to see him."

"But he's going to be okay?" I ask.

"I can't promise you anything, but he's doing well considering the injury he received."

"Thank you so much," I cry.

The doctor leaves and I make my way back to my seat and slump down. Charlie sits next to me, and I immediately burst into tears.

"It's all good, Miss Hastings. Reed's strong, he'll pull through."

"I love him, Charlie. What will I do if he doesn't make it?"

"Let's not talk like that, okay. Reed will be fine. He wouldn't let Adam have one up on him like that. You two have become very close recently, haven't you?"

I look at Charlie and nod.

"I've fallen in love with him," I say sadly.

"Oh dear," Charlie replies.

"Yeah," I laugh. "Oh dear, indeed."

"What does that mean for you and Travis?"

"I'm really not sure. Travis and I have drifted apart over these past few months. I'm not sure he wants to marry me anymore, and to be honest, I'm not sure I want to marry him either. It's just all so confusing. All I can think about now though is Reed recovering."

After another half an hour of waiting, a nurse finally comes into the room and tells us we can make our way up to the ICU.

Walking into Reed's room, I get quite a shock seeing him hooked up to an array of machines, with tubes sticking out everywhere.

"Can I touch him?" I ask a nurse who's looking over his chart.

"Sure. Perhaps just hold his hand, okay? And be gentle; he's been through a lot."

"Thank you," I reply.

I pull up a chair close to Reed's bed and take hold of his hand.

"Hey, Reed, it's Darcy. You're going to be okay. Thank you for what you did for me, for finding me. I love you, Reed. Please don't give up."

I bend down and gently kiss his forehead.

After sitting with him and talking to him for about an hour, a nurse comes in and says it's time to leave.

"I'm not leaving," I tell her. "This man saved my life today. There's no way I'm leaving him. I want to be here when he wakes up."

"I'm sorry but the ICU has strict visiting hours."

I look at her with determination.

"I'm not leaving him," I reiterate.

The nurse looks at me with a frown and turns on her heel with a huff and leaves the room.

"I'm not leaving you, Reed," I say as I stroke his forehead with my fingers. "Rest for now, but wake up soon okay. I miss you so much."

"Are you staying here the night?" Charlie asks me.

"I'm not leaving, Charlie. Not until Reed kicks me out himself."

"Can I bring you anything in the morning?"

"Maybe just a few changes of clothes and some toiletries if possible. Peggy can help put a few things together. Thank you, Charlie," I say as I give him a hug. "Thank you for what you did today too. If it wasn't for you, things could have been a lot worse, and I probably wouldn't be here."

"Of course, Miss, any time. Is there anything else I can do for you?"

"Actually, would you be able to contact Reed's sister, Jocelyn? I've been so worried, I completely forgot to call her earlier. She should know what's happened."

"Of course, Miss Hastings. I'll call her on my way out."

"Thank you," I reply.

"Try to get some sleep, okay?"

"I will. Goodnight, Charlie."

I spent a very uncomfortable night sleeping in the chair alongside Reed, but I don't care. All I care about is the fact that I'm with him, holding his hand. He still hasn't woken up, but his doctor says he's showing signs of improvement.

"Morning, Reed," I say as I lean over and kiss his forehead. "Are you going to wake up for me this morning?"

I re-adjust his blankets a little, and try to make him as comfortable as I can without moving him too much. After a little while, I hear a knock at the door and look up to see Jocelyn standing there.

"Hey, Joss, come in," I say.

"How's he doing?" she asks with a worried look on her face.

"He hasn't woken yet, but he's doing well considering. The doctor said his vitals have really improved overnight."

She walks over towards the bed, and I stand up and give her a hug. She reaches down and takes Reed's hand.

"Hey, big brother. Wake up soon—we need to know that you're going to be okay."

"I'm so sorry, Joss," I say. "This is all my fault. He's in here because he was protecting me."

"Don't be silly," she replies. "He was doing his job. I know he would give his life for you in a heartbeat, Darcy."

"I know he would too, but I don't want that. I couldn't live without him. I would rather go than him. He's become so important to me. I adore him, Joss."

"I can see that. You're in love with him, aren't you?"

"Yeah, I am," I say quietly as I grab his hand again. "I can't help it. He's always been amazing, but these last few months, he's been everything to me. I don't know what I would have done without him."

"What does this mean for you and Travis?" she asks.

"Honestly, I don't know. We've definitely grown apart since he's been away on tour, and Reed and I have grown closer. I've not heard from Travis either yesterday or today, and I'm certain Reed would have called him and told him what happened. That pretty much tells me what I need to know."

"Reed truly loves you; you know that don't you?"

"Yeah, I do," I say as I look at him lovingly, and brush my hand across his forehead.

"Does Jesse know what's going on?" I ask.

"Yeah, I filled him in when Charlie called me last night. He was really worried about you."

"He's sweet. Could you tell him that I won't be in the office until

Reed has recovered? I just don't want to leave him."

"Of course," Joss replies with a smile. "He understands."

"I might get Charlie to pick up my laptop for me, and I can work from here. At least it will give me something to do."

"Okay. Look I might head off, but you'll call me when he wakes?"

"Of course," I reply.

Joss reaches over and places a soft kiss on Reed's forehead.

"Get better soon big brother, you have two girls here who love you very much."

Joss leaves the room with a smile, and I turn back to look at Reed. I want him to wake up so badly.

After a little while, Charlie pops in with a bag of my things. I ask a nurse if there's somewhere I might be able to take a shower. Although it's against the rules, she kindly lets me into the nurses change room. I ask Charlie to stay with Reed until I get back. I don't think I've ever showered and dressed as fast as I just did. All I care about is getting back to Reed.

When I walk back into his room, his doctor is with him and looking over his chart.

"How's he doing?" I ask.

"He's doing really well. All his stats are improving as we'd like them to, and his wound is looking pretty good also. I think once he wakes up, we'll be able to move him to a ward."

"So that's good, right?"

"That's very good. To be on a ward the day after the surgery he went through, is truly a miracle. Mr Lewis sure is fighting to be here."

"He's the strongest man I know," I say as I stroke his head. "Should he be awake by now though?"

"Everyone's different and I'm not too concerned yet, but I would like him to wake by tomorrow."

"You and me both," I reply with a smile.

"I'll leave you to it," he says as he makes his way out the door.

"I might head off too," Charlie says. "Let me know if there's any change though."

"Will do. Thanks for the clothes, Charlie."

"Any time, Miss," he replies.

"Oh, before you go, Charlie, I was going to ask if you know how Adam is?"

"It was just a flesh wound. I only shot so he'd drop the gun. I didn't want to injure him badly. He's been stitched up and he's now in custody along with his mates."

I shake my head, not believing what's taken place.

"Thanks, Charlie."

I sit back down alongside Reed and take his hand back in mine. I stroke my thumb over his knuckles as I watch his chest slowly rise and fall.

After a few quiet hours talking to him softly, I suddenly feel Reed start to stir. I quickly press the call button for the nurse and stand up to brush my hand over his forehead.

"Reed, can you hear me?" I ask. "It's Darcy, open your eyes, Reed."

He stirs a little more, just as the nurse walks through the door.

"I think he's waking up," I say quickly.

She walks to the other side of the bed, and gently taps on Reed's shoulder as she tries to rouse him. Eventually his eyes start to flutter open, and he groans a little as if in pain.

Reed looks around the room slowly, trying to work out where he is. I squeeze his hand and he turns his head to look at me.

"Darcy?" he asks with a croaky voice.

"Hey, you," I say as tears roll down my cheeks.

"What's the matter, Darce? Are you alright?"

I laugh as I bend down and kiss him softly on the forehead.

"You scared the hell out of me, do you know that? God, Reed, I thought I'd lost you. I nearly did!"

"I'm okay, sweetheart."

"Reed, you were shot. You are not okay," I say as more tears fall down my cheeks.

I lean down and place my cheek against his, and hold his other in the palm of my hand.

"I love you," I whisper into his ear. "Thank you for finding me, Reed. I was so scared, and I can only imagine what would have happened if you didn't show up when you did."

"I'm so sorry, Darce. Adam should never have been able to get to you in the first place. I let you down."

"Shh, no you didn't. You've never let me down, Reed. You are the most incredible person I've ever known, and I don't know what I'd do without you in my life."

A few minutes later, Reed's doctor enters the room.

"Welcome back, Mr Lewis, I'm glad to see you're awake. How do you feel?"

"Like I've been shot," he smiles.

"Well, everything's looking really good. You're a very lucky man, Mr Lewis. The surgery took around six hours and we lost you twice, but you fought like hell, and we obviously managed to get you back."

Hearing this again, I can't control the sob that escapes my lips.

"Hey," Reed says as he squeezes my hand. "Enough with the tears, okay? I'm fine, sweetheart."

"You have one dedicated woman here," the doctor says. "We have strict visiting hours in the ICU, but we have not managed to kick her out since you arrived. She's very stubborn."

"Yep, that sounds like Darcy," Reed says with a smile.

"Perhaps now you've seen that Mr Lewis is going to be fine, you can pop home and get some rest," the doctor suggests.

"I told you, I'm not leaving until Reed does."

"Darce, you can't sleep here, baby. I'm fine. Go home and get some rest—you can come back later if you really want to."

"You men really seem to be having a lot of trouble understanding me, don't you? I'll say it slowly for you—I'm. Not. Leaving. I'll sleep on the floor if I have to, but I'm not leaving without Reed."

Reed looks at me and lets out a long sigh.

"Well then, I'll leave you to it," the doctor says. "If you need any pain meds, Mr Lewis, just press this button here and it will administer automatically through your IV."

"Thanks, doc," Reed replies.

Once the doctor leaves the room, I sit back down in my chair and squeeze Reed's hand.

"Sweetheart, you really don't need to …"

"Reed," I cut him off. "I'm staying. Deal with it."

He chuckles softly, and I can see it hurt him. I watch as he presses the button for pain relief.

"Does it hurt a lot?" I ask concerned.

"It doesn't tickle, but it's not too bad," he smiles.

"Do you mind if I borrow your phone, Reed? I just need to ring your sister and Charlie to let them know that you've woken up. They've both been in to see you."

"Yeah of course, that's fine."

"I should also ring Travis and let him know what's going on."

"He hasn't contacted you?" Reed asks incredulously.

"No, I haven't spoken with him for a few days."

"Bastard!" Reed spits.

"It's okay, Reed," I try to placate him.

"No, it's fucking not, Darcy. He should be here. After what you've just gone through—he should be here for you."

"It's okay, I have you. You were there for me," I say quietly.

"It's not good enough, Darcy. You deserve better than that. He's your bloody fiancé and he should be here."

"I don't think he's going to be my fiancé for much longer," I say sadly.

"What? What do you mean?"

"As you said, Reed … he should be here. If you love someone, you drop everything to be with them when they really need you. I really needed him these last few days and he wasn't here. He didn't even try to contact me. What does that tell you? I knew we were growing apart but that pretty much gives me my answer. He doesn't want me anymore."

"If that's true, Darce, he's an idiot."

I stand up and place a kiss on his cheek.

"I better go and make these calls," I say. "Don't you go anywhere. I won't be long."

"Take your time, sweetheart."

I duck out of Reed's room, and quickly place calls to both Jocelyn and Charlie who are stoked to hear that Reed has woken and is doing fine. Next, it's time to speak with Travis.

Travis answers my call after a few rings.

"Lewis, what can I do for you?" he asks abruptly.

"Travis, it's Darcy. I borrowed Reed's phone."

"Hey, baby. How are you?" he asks as if nothing is out of the ordinary.

"Well, I was kidnapped at gunpoint, handcuffed to a chair in a dark room, slapped across the face multiple times, had Adams' mate's cock shoved in my face, watched Reed get shot in front of me, sat in a waiting room for six hours while he underwent surgery, heard that he died on the table twice, and then sat by his bedside until he just woke recently. Other than that, I'm fucking fine. How about you?" I ask sarcastically.

"God, Darcy, I'm so sorry," he says.

"Look, I need to get back to Reed, but I wanted to tell you that if you're not home by tomorrow at the latest to talk about our situation, our engagement is off."

"Come on, Darcy. I can't just call off my shows at such short notice."

"Then I'll call off our engagement. Tomorrow, Travis," I say and then hang up.

I suddenly feel sick. I have no idea whether Travis will show up or not. The way he sounded on the phone, I don't expect to see him tomorrow—but at least I'll have my answer. I still love Travis, but I don't know if I love him enough anymore to marry him. I suppose I'll find out soon enough.

I make my way back to Reed's room and sit down next to him as he dozes. I take his hand in mine and bring it to my lips.

"I love you," I whisper softly in his ear.

Chapter Thirty Eight

• TRAVIS •

Walking into the hospital ward, I have to admit, I feel nervous for the first time in a long time. I can perform in front of thousands of people, but this, this is going to be a life changing moment, and I know it. There was no point heading home first—I know that Darcy will be spending all her time at the hospital with Reed, so I came straight here after my flight landed. I've been told that Reed's condition has improved, so he was moved to a general ward the night before.

As I stand in the doorway of Reed's room, I look at the sight before me, and my heart drops just a little. Reed is in bed asleep, with Darcy asleep beside him, her head resting on his shoulder, and her arm sprawled across his chest.

I walk in slowly and gently tap Darcy on the shoulder. She sleepily looks up at me in shock.

"Travis?" she asks.

"Hey, Darce."

"I wasn't expecting you," she says quietly, looking at Reed.

"You told me to come home."

"Yeah, but I didn't actually expect you to," she replies with a frown.

"I'm not a complete asshole, Darcy."

"I know you're not, Trav, you've just been acting like one lately."

"Fair enough, I suppose I deserved that. You said you wanted to talk."

"I do, but not here. There's a family room down the corridor we can use."

I watch as Darcy leans over and whispers in Reed's ear, while rubbing her hand across his chest. Then she walks towards me, grabs my hand and leads me out of the room.

We sit in the family room and look at each other for a few seconds before either of us says anything.

"I missed you," she says with a small smile.

"I missed you too, sweetheart," I reply as I grab her hand.

"Why did you stop calling, Trav? Are you with Lacey now?"

"What! No, of course not, babe. I'm not interested in Lacey, okay? But I know I've neglected you this tour. Things have been extremely busy, but that's not an excuse for the way I've treated you. Have you noticed how even when we do speak, we don't actually really speak much? There's lots of awkward silence and we never talk about anything of any substance."

She laughs a little at this.

"Of course I've noticed, Trav. It's almost all I've thought about. We've grown apart," she says with a small shrug.

"Yeah, we have" I say sadly. "What do you want to do about it? Do you still want to marry me?"

"Honestly, I don't know," she responds, and my heart sinks a little. "I don't know that I can live your lifestyle, Trav. I love you—have no doubt about that—but these past few months were hard. That much time away from the man I love was hard. I thought I'd be okay with it—I knew it would be difficult—but I wasn't coping, Trav. I was lonely, and I was starting to resent you. I don't want to do that. I don't want to grow to resent you. Going into a marriage knowing that this is going to be my life scares me."

"I get it, baby," I say. "I really do. There are not many people that could cope with my lifestyle and all the touring that's involved. It's always so much harder for the person left behind."

Darcy looks at me with tears in her eyes and nods sadly.

"Our relationship is over, isn't it?" she says as the tears start to roll down her cheeks.

"Is that what you want?" I ask as I feel my own cheeks dampen. "All I want is for you to be happy, sweetheart, and suddenly I don't feel like I'm the man that can make you as happy as you deserve."

Darcy starts sobbing now, and I can do nothing but wrap her in my arms.

"You know I'll always love you though, right? It doesn't matter if we're not in a romantic relationship anymore, you'll always be in my life—that's a non-negotiable, do you understand?"

Darcy looks at me and nods.

"I want that too. You are my best friend, Trav, and I don't want that to change. I want you in my life … forever."

"Good, then that's where I'll be."

I look down at Darcy as she studies her left hand, then slowly removes her engagement ring.

"I have loved wearing this, but you should have it back," she says with tears in her eyes, as she passes the ring to me.

"God, this sucks!" I say.

"Yeah, it really does," she laughs sadly. "I should probably move out too. I'll get that organized soon, okay!"

"No, please. I don't want you to move out, Darcy. For starters, I'm hardly ever there, so there's no point. Plus, Peggy loves having you there. Even when I do come home, I don't see any issue with us living together, do you?"

"No, I'd love that. But I at least have to move out of your bedroom."

"No, I want you to keep the room. Again, I'm hardly there and you need the closet space more than I do. I'll take one of the other rooms."

"Trav, I can't do that. It's your house. And I'll be paying rent from now on."

"Darcy, I'm serious. The room is yours, and stop being ridiculous.

You are not paying bloody rent for goodness sake."

Darcy looks at me and shakes her head.

"My life has been nothing but amazing since I met you. Do you realize that? You've made me so happy, Travis. I'm so thankful to have you in my life, and I'll never be able to repay you for everything you have done for me. You deserve so much happiness and I wish for nothing more than for that to be true."

"Thank you, babe. The same goes for you too. Even though this didn't work out between the two of us, I'll be forever grateful for every minute I've had with you, and will continue to have."

Darcy reaches up and places both her hands on my cheeks and presses her lips against mine. It's the perfect goodbye kiss. We just look at each other for a few more minutes, both feeling content with our decision.

"Now," I say as I pull back a little. "There's something else we need to talk about before I head off."

"What's that?" she asks in confusion.

"You and Reed."

"Oh right. I suppose he doesn't really have a job anymore, does he?"

"Of course he does. None of that changes, unless you want it to, Darcy?"

"You still want to provide security for me?" she asks incredulously.

"Yeah, sweetheart. You'll still be very much associated with me and a part of my life, and I'd like you to keep the security."

"Okay," she agrees. "Thank you, Trav. So then what about Reed and me?"

"I know he loves you, Darce, and I'm pretty sure you have serious feelings for him too. I want nothing but for you to be genuinely happy, and if Reed makes you happy, I want you to pursue a relationship with him. I respect Reed and I know he'll treat you right and take good care of you."

"Trav, we *just* ended our engagement minutes ago, and you're already telling me to pursue another relationship?"

"Sweetheart, I just want you happy. Honestly, I'll be happy if I know you're happy and being looked after, and I think Reed will do that for you."

"I don't believe you, I honestly don't. You are more than amazing, Travis, but Reed doesn't want to be with me. He doesn't want to feel like he's my second choice."

"He'd be crazy not to want you, beautiful. Just give him some time, yeah?"

Darcy looks at me with wonder in her eyes, then leans in and hugs me tight.

"I love you so much," she whispers in my ear.

"I love you too, and I always will—*always*."

Darcy pulls back and grabs my hand.

"I should let you get back to Reed, he'll be wondering where you got to."

We stand up together, hand in hand, and make our way back to Reed's room.

"Would you mind if I had a quick word privately with Reed?" I ask Darcy.

"Of course not," she replies.

"I need to freshen up a bit anyway, so I'll just head to the bathroom. I'll see you back here in a minute. Don't leave without saying goodbye though, okay?"

"Wouldn't dream of it, sweetheart."

She smiles at me and then turns in the direction of the bathroom. Making my way into Reed's room, I notice that he's woken.

"Travis!" he says surprised.

"Hey, Reed. How are you feeling?"

"I'm doing okay, thanks. I'm not sure where Darcy is. I woke up and she was gone."

"It's all good", I say. "We were just down the hall talking. She's in the bathroom freshening up. I wanted to thank you, Reed, for what you did for Darcy. I can only imagine what would have happened if you hadn't found her."

"Of course. Just doing my job."

"You've never just *done your job*, Reed. You've always done more than is required, and I can't tell you how much I appreciate it. You put your life on the line for her, and you very nearly lost it, and I can never repay you for that. You'll always have my utmost respect."

"Thanks, Travis. I appreciate that."

"I wanted to let you know that Darcy and I have ended our relationship."

"Oh god, Travis, I'm so sorry. Are you okay? Is Darcy okay?"

"We're both fine. Obviously, this is not how we wanted things to end up, but it's the right decision for both of us. She deserves so much better than what I can give her. She deserves you, Reed."

"Travis …"

"No listen, Reed. I know you love Darcy, and I know you'd do anything to protect her—you've just proven that, but she loves you too. She's in love with you; I can see it in her eyes. She deserves to be happy, Reed, and I know she'll be happy with you. I want her to be happy. Don't ever think of yourself as her second choice either, because that's not the case at all. Things change, feelings change, and you've been nothing but a constant support to her and she's fallen in love with you."

"God, Travis, I don't know what to say to that."

"You don't need to say anything. Just know that you both have my blessing if you want to be together."

A moment later, Darcy walks back into the room, and wraps her arm around my waist.

"I need to head off, so Darcy can fill you in on some of the other details. I'll leave you to it though. Thanks again, Reed for everything you've done for Darcy, and I hope you feel better really soon."

I walk over to Reed's bed and shake his hand with a huge smile. Turning back to Darcy, she wraps her arms around me again and pulls me in tight.

"I love you so much, Trav. Have a safe flight, okay, and call me when you land so I know you've arrived safely."

"Will do," I reply.

I pull her in again, and place a soft kiss on her lips, and when I pull back a little, I notice tears in her eyes.

"Hey, no more tears, okay? We're good," I say as I brush the moisture from her face with my thumbs.

"Look after her," I say, as I look to Reed.

He gives me a nod of acknowledgement, and I start to make my way towards the door.

"I love you, Trav," Darcy calls after me.

"I love you too, sweetheart."

I exit the room, closing the door softly behind me.

Chapter Thirty Nine

• REED •

I wake to find Darcy holding my hand and resting her head on my shoulder asleep. I know she's exhausted, but she refuses to leave my bedside. I adore her for that, but I also know she needs a decent night's sleep and a home cooked meal, not the revolting cafeteria food she's lived on this past week.

Travis has been gone a few days now, and I worry how Darcy is coping with their broken engagement. It seems that because she'll still be living with him, and they've decided to remain close friends, it's helped ease the pain of their lost relationship. She doesn't feel as though she's lost him altogether.

I look up as my doctor walks in the room, and I quickly press the side of my index finger to my lips. I don't want Darcy to wake—she needs her rest.

"You've got quite a woman there," the doctor whispers nodding his head in Darcy's direction. "I don't think I've seen her leave this room all week."

I reach up and stroke her hair gently.

"Yeah, she's pretty special. Just a damn shame she's not my girl," I reply.

"You're kidding me?"

"Nope. We're just friends. I actually work for her. I wish we were more, but up until a few days ago, she was engaged to another man, so she's off limits."

"I've worked in hospitals for a long time, my friend, and I've seen a lot, but I'll tell you this … I've never seen a woman sit beside the bed of a *friend* for their entire stay. You're more than a friend to that girl."

I look down at Darcy's beautiful face. She looks so peaceful in her sleep—angelic—and she's my angel.

"So, I have some good news," the doctor says in a cheerful whisper. "I reckon we're happy to kick you out today. How does that sound?"

"Yeah?" I ask. "That would be bloody awesome."

"Do you have someone who can stay with you for at least the coming week? You'll need to take things really easy—lots of bed rest."

"Yeah, we have a live-in housekeeper, and Darcy here also lives in the house."

"Great. You'll be well taken care of then," the doctor replies.

"I think so," I smile.

"I'll get the nurse to pop in and remove your IV, check your dressing and she'll also give you tips on wound care. We'll also get you to sign your discharge papers. Then you can be on your way."

"Sounds amazing," I say.

"Are you comfortable?" Darcy asks me.

"Yes angel, I'm fine. Please stop fussing."

She grabs another one of my pillows and fluffs it some more before re-arranging it behind my head.

"I just want to make sure you're alright. Can I get you anything? Something to eat, drink, read, watch?"

"Darcy, you've done more than enough. I'm fine. Honestly, I'd actually just like to lay here and have a nap for a while—the drive home from the hospital took it out of me a bit."

"Of course, I'm so sorry, Reed. I'll turn off the light for you."

"Thanks, angel."

"Do you mind if I sit here in this chair though? I just want to be near you in case you need anything."

"Darcy, I'm not going to die in my sleep. It's just a bullet wound, honey. I'm okay."

She looks at me and I reach for her hand as she bursts into tears.

"I was so scared I'd lost you," she sobs.

"Hey, hey, I'm fine, Darce. I'm here. I'm not going anywhere. It will take a lot more than a bullet to the stomach to get rid of me. Come here," I say.

She gingerly climbs onto my bed and sits next to me.

"Nope, under the covers with me," I say.

"I can't, Reed. I don't want to hurt you."

"Darcy—under, now!"

She slowly raises the covers, slides underneath and curls up next to me. I pull her into me further and wrap one arm underneath her, so her head is lying on my shoulder.

"Are you sure I'm not hurting you?" she asks.

"Not a bit," I reply. "Rest, angel. You've been sleeping in a chair for a week. You need to look after yourself before you can look after me."

"Mmmm," she replies quietly. I stroke her hair gently as I listen to her breathing slow and grow shallow. Within a few minutes she's sound asleep, and I follow closely behind.

Waking up with Darcy in my arms, is the best feeling I've had in a long time. We'd slept for a few hours, and now it's late afternoon. Darcy is still asleep, but she's a little restless, so I expect her to wake any minute.

I softly stroke her head and place my nose in her hair, breathing in her delicious fruity scent. *What I wouldn't do to wake up like this every morning.*

Darcy eventually stirs and looks up at me.

"Did you have a nice nap?" I ask her.

"I did. What about you?"

"Just what I needed," I reply. "What are your plans for the rest of the day?"

"I plan to stay right here and take care of you!"

"Angel, you need to get out and take a break from me. I'm fine here alone. Why don't you call my sister and go out for the night? Have some girl time."

"No, Reed. I'm not leaving you alone. What if you needed something, or fell over?"

"Darcy, I'm perfectly capable of walking without being assisted. I don't plan to go out jogging or anything like that. I'm just going to sit out on the couch and watch a movie or something."

"But I'm worried about you," she replies with a furrowed brow.

"I know, and I truly appreciate your concern, but I don't want you re-arranging your life around me. You've already taken a week off work to stay with me. You need to do things for yourself now, okay?"

She looks at me unconvinced and grabs my hand.

"Do I need to call Jocelyn myself?" I ask.

"She's probably busy."

"Call her!"

"Geez, you're bossy when you're injured," she replies with a smirk.

I watch as she reaches over and grabs her phone from the bedside table and calls my sister, making plans to go out clubbing tonight. As much as I would have loved for her to stay in with me for the night, I can't have her dropping everything for me. She also needs time away from me to sort through her feelings and to deal with her breakup properly.

Chapter Forty

• DARCY •

I'm excited to be back at our favorite bar. I haven't been out in a while, and as much as I really didn't want to leave Reed alone, I'm happy to be spending some time with Jocelyn.

I made sure that Peggy would check in on Reed throughout the night. He didn't seem too thrilled about the idea, but I told him it was the only way he would get rid of me, so he reluctantly agreed.

Joss and I make our way to our favorite corner booth and sit down with our drinks.

"How are you?" she asks me.

"I'm good. You?"

"I'm fine, but how are you really?"

"Honestly, Joss, I'm fine. Yeah, it's been a rough week, but I'm just glad Reed's going to be okay. I don't know what I would have done if he'd been more seriously injured or even killed. God, the thought terrifies me!"

"It would take a lot to knock my brother down," she says.

"Yeah, I can see that. He's pretty amazing."

"So, he told me that you and Travis broke off your engagement. That's pretty big on top of everything else. I'm just worried about you."

"I think I'm okay with the Travis thing, because I kind of knew it was coming, you know? Things hadn't been great for a few months, and I knew that I couldn't continue to be in a relationship where I was never with him. I don't do long distance well."

"Yeah, I understand that. It would be pretty hard."

"I love Travis, I think I always will, but I don't think our relationship could withstand the constant travelling that he has to do. I feel bad that I kind of piked out during his first tour while he's been with me, but this is going to be our lives. It'll always be like this, and I know that I'd probably end up resenting him for being away so often, and I don't want to do that. I'm going to remain living with him for now and we'll keep our close friendship, so I'm not losing him completely."

"What does this mean for you and Reed?" she asks.

"I want him," I say with a small smile. "The day Adam took me, I told him that I was in love with him."

"Really? How did he respond? He must have been over the moon."

"Not exactly," I reply. "He pretty much said that we couldn't be together. He wants to be someone's first choice, and he feels that he would never be mine."

"How do you feel about that?"

"Devastated, but what can I do? I want him to be happy, and whether that's with me or someone else, I just have to accept it— although seeing him with someone else would kill me."

"Just give him time. I know he wants you more than anything, but I'm sure he'd also like to make sure that you're definitely over Travis before starting anything with him."

"It's so damn hard. Even when I was with Travis, I wanted him. And now that I'm single, I just want to throw myself at him. Today we had a nap in his bed together all snuggled up, and waking up with him was the best feeling ever—it just felt right, you know?"

"Well, he's my brother, so ewww, but yeah I get what you're saying. Just take it a day at a time and see what happens."

"Thanks, Joss. Thanks for coming out with me tonight."

"Anytime, babe. Now I think we should dance. There are a lot of fine looking men out on that dance floor and you're single now and able to grind up against as many as you like!"

"Gross!" I laugh.

We both jump up and make our way out onto the floor. Joss is right. There did seem to be an awful lot of hotties out tonight. Before long, a very good-looking guy in a suit that looks like it's literally spray-painted on approaches Joss. I watch as he flirts with her, but she's very polite in telling him that she isn't available. I often forget that she's with Jesse now.

"How is Jesse?" I ask, as the music thumps around us. "I feel like I haven't seen him in forever."

"He's good. Things are going good. I really like him, and he treats me well."

"I'm glad. He deserves someone great like you. He's always been such a good friend to me, so I'm stoked to see him happy."

As we laugh and dance to the music, I suddenly feel someone rubbing up against me from behind. I look to Joss in front of me, her eyes wide, as she tries to hide a huge grin while looking over my shoulder.

"I've been watching you all night," comes a deep voice from behind me. "I had to come over and see if you taste as good as you look."

Before I have a chance to turn around, I feel a warm wet tongue trace up the side of my neck. I spin around in an instant, and I'm faced with an overweight man, probably in his late forties, balding, and basically not my type at all.

"You seriously did not just lick my neck," I gasp.

"Come on, sweetheart, I know I'm not the fittest guy in the place, but I've got plenty of money and I could make you really happy."

"Thanks for the offer, but I'm not interested," I reply with a fake smile plastered across my face.

I turn back to Joss with wide eyes, and she bursts out laughing.

"Did that seriously just happen?" I ask incredulously.

"Wow, Darce, I can't believe you just turned that poor guy down—

especially after he licked you!" she says still giggling.

"You're welcome to him," I reply. "I'm just going to run to the ladies, and wash his tongue juice from my neck."

"Make sure you take Charlie or Nash with you," she calls after me.

Nash is my second backup bodyguard while Reed is out of action. Travis had insisted that I continue with a security detail. I appreciated it but didn't really feel like it was necessary now that Adam was in custody. But Travis was resolute—especially considering our broken engagement had not been made public yet. I wave in Nash's direction to let him know where I'm going, and he quickly follows behind.

Once I make my way back to Joss, she's ready to sit and have a drink. We head back to our booth and slump in our seats. After a few minutes of some girl talk, a waitress brings over a couple of drinks for us.

"We didn't order these," Joss says quickly.

"No," the waitress replies. "They're from the two gentlemen at the end of the bar."

She nods towards two men sitting together at the bar. Both are extremely handsome and very well dressed—businessmen by the looks of them.

I raise my glass in a gesture of thanks, and Joss smiles and does the same. I'm sure it won't be long before they both make their way over, but we're surprised when neither guy moves from his spot at the bar.

Finishing our drinks, we decide to head back out to the dance floor. I keep my eye out for my mysterious neck licker, but he seems to have disappeared, thank god!

Joss and I enjoy the music together, until I notice one of the bar guys sidle up behind her. I gave her a small grin and turn a little away from her, but right into the other guy from the bar.

"Hi," he says cheerfully.

"Hi, yourself," I reply with a smile.

"I'm Finn."

"Darcy," I respond as he reaches out to shake my hand.

"Beautiful name."

"Thanks," I say.

"So, what do you do for a living, Darcy?" he asks as we continue to move around the floor. I notice both Charlie and Nash hovering close by. I give them both a brief smile to let them know I'm fine and not feeling threatened.

"I'm a graphic designer," I reply.

"And Australian from the sounds of that accent."

"Spot on," I say.

"Are you just here on holiday or do you live here?"

"I moved here to be with my boyfriend about ten months ago."

"Boyfriend?"

"Ah, ex-boyfriend, or rather ex-fiancé to be exact—as of a few days ago."

"So, you're here nursing a broken heart then?"

"A little, but he and I are still best friends. He just travels constantly for work and it's really hard to continue a relationship like that."

"So, you're single?"

"Yeah, I suppose I am," I reply.

"What about your friend?" he asks me.

"No, Joss is dating my boss actually, so she's off the market."

"Oh, poor Jax," he laughs.

"Jax is your friend?" I ask looking towards him.

"Yeah, he and I both actually wanted to dance with you, so we had to flip a coin to see who the lucky one was."

"So, I guess you won the toss?"

"That I did."

"Jax is going to be pissed if he's got no chance of scoring tonight," he sniggers.

"Unfortunately, you have no chance either—with me anyway."

"Oh, come on, Darcy. You're single; I'm single—what's the problem?

"The problem, *Finnigan*, is that I just broke off my engagement a few days ago; I'm in love with another man—who was very recently shot when he rescued me from another ex who kidnapped me at gunpoint—basically my life is a little messy right now. You don't want to get involved in that kind of crazy, even for a night, trust me!"

"Geez girl, you've had a rough week!"

"Yes, I have. So, you can see why I just wanted to come out dancing tonight with my friend to take my mind off things for a few hours, before I head back home to take care of my gun-shot victim."

"So just a dance then?" Finn asks with a grin.

"Just a dance," I respond.

"I can deal with that."

"Have fun ladies?" Reed asks us as we walk in his front door. He'd been sitting on his couch watching TV.

"We did," replies Joss. "Darcy even got her neck licked by some hottie."

"What?" Reed says, sitting up quickly.

"Joss! Really?"

"What? You did. Don't worry though, big brother, she washed. This one was quite popular," she says as she points her thumb in my direction.

"It was a smorgasbord of delicious men tonight, and it was like they all knew Darcy was suddenly single."

Reed gives me a disapproving look, as I start taking off my coat.

"What?" I ask. "I was just dancing. Besides, I am single now, so I can dance with who I like!"

"Yeah, and if you're not quick, big brother, this one's gonna be snapped up before you can blink twice."

"Joss, seriously," I respond. "We had fun. That's it. Now I'm home to look after you again," I say to a grumpy looking Reed.

"Well, I'm going to head off and leave you two love birds to it," Joss says.

"Joss stop, please," Reed responds annoyed.

"What, Reed? You're both single. She loves you; you love her, what's the problem? Life's too short for wasting time—you of all people should understand that after this last week."

Reed and I watch as Joss walks to the door and opens it.

"See you guys. I love you both you know, and I just want to see you happy," and with that she walks out the door and closes it behind her.

"Well, I think I might head off to my room," I say with an air of melancholy. "Are you okay getting into bed yourself?"

Reed looks at me with a sad expression on his face.

"Yeah, I'm okay."

"All right then. I'll see you tomorrow," I reply as I leave his room.

Chapter Forty One

• REED •

It was nearing noon and I still hadn't seen Darcy, which surprised me. Since I'd been shot, she'd pretty much not left my side, and I missed her this morning. I knew she'd be back at work tomorrow, so I was hoping to spend the day with her, being lazy. When Peggy brings me my lunch, I ask her if she's seen Darcy.

"Miss Darcy left early this morning with Charlie and Nash, and she has not been home since," Peggy replies.

Although I'm glad she took security, it also worries me for two reasons—the fact that she didn't even come and say hello, which is unusual for her, and the new bodyguard worries me a little.

I know she's just friendly with Charlie, and he's not her type anyway; but Nash is a fit, young, good-looking guy who is definitely her type. Darcy being Darcy, means she's likely being super friendly, and would be trying to build a strong rapport with him, which he might take the wrong way. This worries me. I know that's not fair considering I've told her we can't be together, at least not yet anyway. She needs time to get over Travis, and decide if I'm who she really wants.

Later in the evening, Darcy knocks on my door, but comes straight in.

"Hey," she says. "I just wanted to check that you were okay, and to see if you needed anything."

"No, I'm good thanks. You been out all day?"

"Ah yeah, I was just running some errands and then caught up with friends … that sort of thing," she says with a small smile.

"Oh okay, that's good. I'm glad you could go out and do some things for yourself."

"Yeah; well, I better get back to it. I might not see you tomorrow as I'm heading back to work and I'm pretty sure it will be a long day, so I'll just see you around, okay?"

"Yeah okay," I reply concerned. "Hey, Darce?"

"Yeah."

"Are you okay?"

"Of course, why?"

"You just seem a little … off."

"No, I'm fine. I'll see you later."

She walks over and gives me a chaste kiss on the cheek, and then leaves my room. I'm sure I'm not imagining it. She definitely seems like she's avoiding me. Maybe she's just sick of me after all the time we've spent together recently. It seems like more than that though. I miss her, and I want to speak to her, so I decide to head into the main house to find her.

Walking too much still causes me a great deal of pain, but I really want to speak with her. I don't want to leave it a few days.

As I slowly shuffle along the corridor holding my abdomen, I make my way to the kitchen. As I get closer, I hear Darcy laughing, but it isn't with Peggy, it's a male voice. I stop for a bit and listen. There is definite flirting going on, mainly by him. *Who is this guy anyway? Surely she hadn't moved on already!*

I make my way into the kitchen, and Darcy swings around when she hears me enter.

"Reed, what are you doing in here?" she asks looking like she's been caught with her hand in the cookie jar. "You shouldn't be up and walking around."

"I'm fine," I tell her.

"No, you're not. You've been shot and I can see that you're in pain. You need to get back to bed."

I look over at the guy she's with. *A fancy looking suit.* He gives me a knowing smirk. What the hell is going on?

"Reed this is Finn—we met last night at the bar. Finn this is my bodyguard, Reed."

So, I'm just the bodyguard now. Nice. The suit reaches out to shake my hand, and I take it with narrowed eyes.

"Have you got a sec, Darce?" I ask her.

"Can it wait?" she asks me seemingly annoyed.

"No, it can't sorry."

She looks at me with a challenging look in her eyes, and I respond with a raised brow.

"I'll be right back," she says to Finn.

"No worries, take your time."

"Peggy!" Darcy calls.

"Yes, Miss Darcy?"

"Would you mind fixing Finn a drink for me please? I'll be back in just a sec."

"Of course, Miss Darcy."

Darcy turns and follows me down the corridor towards my room. We step inside and I carefully sit on the couch, exhausted from my little excursion.

"Are you okay?" Darcy asks.

"Just a bit worn out from my walk," I say still holding my abdomen.

"Reed, you should not be walking around like that yet. You need to let your body recover."

"Darce, what's going on?"

"What do you mean?" she asks.

"You know what I mean. You were out all day, without even popping in to say hi before you left. Then you bring some random guy home after meeting him the night before in a bar. That's not you!"

She looks at me sadly.

"I just can't be around you right now, okay!"

"What? Why the hell not? You're my best friend, Darcy—talk to me."

"I can't. Look, I'll check on you each day until you're well again, but I just need to stay away from you for a little while. Can you understand that?"

"No, I can't!" I respond dumbfounded. "What's going on, angel?"

I take her hand and stroke her knuckles, as she looks at me with a sadness I haven't seen from her in a while. I can see the tears welling in her eyes.

"Angel?"

The tears start rolling down her cheeks, and I grab her and pull her into my arms.

"I feel lost, Reed," she sobs into my chest. "I knew everything with Travis was coming to an end, but it still threw me a little, you know?"

"Of course, sweetheart. You were engaged. It's going to hurt for a bit."

"Yeah, but it's not even that really. I've loved you for a while now, and I suppose I just thought we could be together now that I'm no longer with Travis, and I think that threw me a bit too."

"Angel, we will be together—don't doubt that. I just want to give you time to get over Travis. You need to take the time, not just for yourself, but also out of respect for Travis."

"But I want to be with you so much," she cries.

"I know, Darce. Believe me, I've wanted nothing but to be with you since the moment we met; but I want us to start out right. I don't want to screw things up with you. It's too important. You're it for me. Do you understand that? You're it!"

Darcy pulls back from me a little and looks into my eyes. She gently places her hands on my cheeks and pulls my face towards hers. I look at her as she slowly places her lips on mine. I close my eyes and enjoy every second of her mouth on mine. Every part of it feeling so incredibly right. Eventually she slowly pulls away.

"I love you," she whispers.

"I love you too, angel."

She looks at me and smiles sweetly.

"I should go and see to Finn," she says. "Can I pop back later and have dinner with you?"

"Of course, you're welcome here any time."

"Okay, see you soon," she smiles.

She gets up from the couch and makes her way to the door. Before walking out, she turns to look at me and places her index and middle fingers to her lips. I smile back, and do the same.

Six weeks later, and I'm finally back working as Darcy's bodyguard. My recovery took so much longer than I'd hoped or planned, but at least I'm back. Travis has officially announced to the public that he and Darcy have broken off their engagement, but clearly stated that they are remaining the best of friends. However, Darcy has received a bit of backlash from a few die-hard fans. I'm just glad that I'm back on her security team. I trust Charlie and Nash with her safety, but it's not the same as being with her myself.

Our friendship has continued much as it has in the past. We aren't together as such, but we're spending a lot of time with each other outside of work. There is always a little tension, but we keep it to ourselves, and go about our business.

After being with her in the office all day, we head home to have dinner together as we often do. Rather than eating alone in the main house, Darcy often joins me in my suite where it's a little more intimate. After Peggy has come by to collect our dishes and clean up, we settle on the couch together to watch a movie.

It's my turn to pick, so we're watching some action flick, which I can see Darcy isn't totally into, but she doesn't complain. After a little restlessness, she moves from the couch and heads to the fridge, asking me if I want a beer. She brings back two bottles and places them on the coffee table.

Instead of returning to her spot on the couch next to me, Darcy makes her way straight to me—sitting on my lap facing me, with her legs on either side of my thighs.

"Hey," she says with a cheeky smirk.

"Hey," I reply in a questioning tone.

"You're pretty hot—did you know that?"

I snort and smile at her. "You're pretty sexy—did you know that?"

She laughs at me, then wraps her arms around my neck.

"I'm pretty much done waiting for you to be mine," she says matter-of-factly.

"Is that so?"

"It is."

"So, what are you going to do about it?" I ask.

"I'm going to take you back to your bedroom and make love to you … slowly," she replies.

"Fuck, Darcy," I almost choke.

"That's the plan," she grins seductively.

She stands from my lap, grabs my hand and starts leading me towards my room.

"Are you sure about this?" I whisper.

"So sure," she replies.

Chapter Forty Two

• DARCY •

Waking up wrapped around Reed is one of the best feelings I'd had in a long time. I think back to the previous night with a huge smile—I can't wipe it from my face in fact. Reed stirs a little and opens his eyes slowly to look at me.

"Good morning, angel. What are you smiling about?" he asks.

"Just thinking about last night," I reply, caressing his beautifully toned and muscled chest.

"Yeah? You hoping for a repeat?"

"Do you even need to ask?"

"Obviously not," he says, before rolling over me and having his way with me again.

***

"So, I've been thinking about something," Reed says as we lie in bed together snuggling.

"What's that?" I ask.

"Well as you know, I'm not going to be able to work for you for much longer. Travis has his rules about being in a relationship, and I'll choose you over my job any day."

"But what will you do? I don't want you protecting some other woman. You're too easy to fall in love with."

"I was actually thinking about starting my own security firm. I've been thinking about it for a while now, and it just seems like the perfect time. I think I'm over the bodyguarding. Being shot like I was, makes you look at things a little differently. I would never want to put you through that again."

"That sounds like an awesome idea, you'll be amazing at that. I have to admit, the bodyguarding really worries me, even if you are looking after someone boring like me."

"Babe, you're never boring … trust me."

"Yeah, but it's not anything exciting like protecting the President, is it?"

"You, angel, are the most exciting person I have ever met."

"God, I love you," I say as I press a soft kiss to his mouth.

Reed and I decide to call Travis together about our new relationship. I know Reed is really nervous about telling him, but I'm confident he'll be fine with it. We also need to know his thoughts on whether he wants Reed to continue working or not.

"Hello, sweetheart."

"Hey, Trav. How are you?"

"I'm good, hun. How about you?"

"Yeah, good too."

"How's Reed's recovery going?"

"He's really good. Getting back to normal. He's here with me actually."

"Hi, Travis," Reed says.

"Nice to hear you're doing well, Lewis."

"Thanks. Took longer than I would have liked, but at least I feel a little more human now."

"Trav, we want to talk to you about a few things if you have a minute."

"Of course, sweetheart, shoot."

"Well, I wanted to let you know that Reed and I are seeing each other now."

"About bloody time," Travis responds cheerfully. "I really am happy for the two of you."

"You are?" I ask nervously.

"Of course. I knew it was a sure thing between you two. I'm just surprised it took you so long."

"Thank you, Trav. You have no idea what it means to me that you are so understanding."

"Just let me say this though, Lewis. If you hurt her, I will personally rip your arms from their sockets. Got me?"

"Got you," Reed laughs.

I laugh too, and Travis sounds highly offended.

"What are you laughing at?" Travis asks.

"Nothing," I reply with a giggle. "It's just that Reed is ex-military, Trav and you're … well you're a musician."

"You think I can't take him?"

"I'm sure you could, Trav. I've seen you, you're more than ripped."

"And don't you forget it—you either, Lewis."

"Wouldn't dream of it, sir," Reed responds with a chuckle.

"Trav, we also wanted to speak to you about Reed's job. We know you have your rule about being in a relationship, so do you need Reed's resignation or how do you want to handle it?"

"What are your thoughts on the situation, Lewis?" Travis asks.

"Well to be honest, I was actually looking at starting up my own security business, but obviously that will take a little bit of time to get up and running. I'd be happy to continue working for Darcy alongside Charlie and Nash if that's what you'd like, but I also understand if you don't want that to happen anymore."

"Actually, I'd prefer that. I know she'll be looked after by the best, and I know you'll only have her best interests at heart. It'd be different if you were in a relationship with someone else that you wanted to get home to, but you're with Darcy, so I'm good with it. Even if you just work part time while you start up your business, I'm happy with that too. I can always give Nash more hours. Are you happy with Nash, sweetheart?"

"Yeah, he's good," I reply.

"Okay then, if you and Nash sort things out between yourselves, Lewis, I'm happy with that. As long as Darcy always has two guys on her at all times, I don't mind who it is."

"Thank you, Trav. So, how's your tour going anyway?"

"It's good. I'm pretty over it now though. Only another two weeks and I'll be home."

"Really!! I'm so excited. I can't wait to see you. I've really missed you."

"Me too, sweetheart."

"Well, we better let you go, and thanks again, Trav. I love you; you know that?"

"Love you too, sweetheart. Bye, Lewis."

"See ya, Travis."

Chapter Forty Three

• REED •

6 Months Later

After Travis had returned home from his tour, I thought things might get a little awkward between him, Darcy and I, but they just didn't. All three of us got along great, and Travis didn't seem to show signs of jealously at all. He genuinely seemed to be happy for Darcy and me.

One Monday morning, after Darcy had already left for work, I walked into the main house to try and catch Travis before he headed into the studio for the day.

As I approach the kitchen, I notice Peggy cleaning up after preparing breakfast for everyone.

"Hey, Peggy, have you seen Travis recently?" I ask.

"Mr Reed, yes Mr Travis should be down soon. He was just getting ready for work."

"Thanks, Peggy. Do you mind if I wait here for him?"

"Not at all, Mr Reed. It's nice to see a pretty face while I work," she smiles at me.

"You are such a charmer, Peggy," I laugh.

"If only I was thirty years younger, you would be in a lot of trouble, young man."

"Are you flirting with my staff again, Peggy?" Travis asks with a chuckle as he walks into the room.

"Mr Reed is a very handsome man, Mr Travis," Peggy replies with a blush.

"You can't blame an old woman for trying."

"If you say so, Peggy," Travis replies with a grin.

"Travis, do you have a minute to chat before you head off?" I ask quickly, as I try to calm my nerves.

"Ah yeah, I've got a few minutes. What can I do for you?"

"Peggy, would you mind giving us a few moments?" I ask politely.

Peggy gives me a quick nod and a smile before she shuffles quickly from the kitchen.

"What's up, Lewis?" Travis asks.

"Ah, I wanted to ask you a question if I could?"

Slowly I reach into my pocket and pull out a small black velvet box. As I open it, Travis looks down and a slow grin forms on his face.

"You know I like you, Lewis, but I'm gonna need you down on one knee if you're going to propose to me," he chuckles.

"Huh? Ah no. I mean … I want to ask for your blessing. I want to ask Darcy to marry me. I know it's quick, and I know you two were only together about eight months ago, but I love her, Travis and that's not going to change. I want to spend my life with her, and I just hope …"

"Lewis, breathe. You've got my blessing."

"What? Really?"

"Of course, mate. I know you love her, and I know she loves you too. You guys are great together. If there's anyone I'd like to see Darcy with, it's you. I know you'll protect her with your life, and I know you'll make her happy."

"Thanks, man. You don't know what that means to me. You've been nothing but amazing about our whole relationship. There aren't many guys that could take things as well as you have."

"I love Darcy. I think I always will, but I couldn't give her what she needs. I couldn't make her happy the way she deserves. And she does deserve that. She deserves to be so happy, and you make her happy, Lewis. As long as I can hold onto her as my best friend, I happily give my blessing for her to be your wife."

I look at Travis and shake my head, not quite believing that he's being so great about this.

"Go and put that ring on her finger, yeah," Travis says. "I've gotta get to the studio. Good luck mate—not that you'll need it."

Chapter Forty Four

• DARCY •

It's been a little while since Reed and I have been out to dinner like this—all dressed up and enjoying an amazing meal at a gorgeous intimate restaurant. Reed looks hot in a deep charcoal three-piece suit and a baby blue tie that matches his beautiful eyes perfectly.

"How's your dinner, angel?" Reed asks me.

"Amazing. Yours?" I respond.

"So good!"

After we've finished our main meals and are waiting on dessert, Reed reaches forward and grabs my hand, stroking his thumb across my knuckles.

"Are you happy?" he asks suddenly, looking serious.

"Of course, baby. Why are you asking that? How could I not be happy? I'm sitting here with the most amazingly sexy man who I adore, and who looks at me like you are now, getting me all hot and bothered."

"I love you so much, Darcy. I ache when I'm not with you. I never want to imagine my life without you in it."

"Then don't," I reply. "I love my life with you, Reed. I'm not going anywhere."

"Good," he replies as he reaches inside the breast pocket of his jacket. "Because I don't plan on letting you get away."

I watch as he rises from his seat, comes around the side of our table and then drops to one knee. I hear myself gasp, and my hand lifts to my lips as I watch him open a small black velvet box containing the most gorgeous diamond ring I have ever seen.

"Angel, I love you with everything that I have, and I want nothing more than to take care of you and protect you for the rest of my life. You make me happier than I thought was possible, and there's nothing I want more than to be your husband and to make you just as happy in return. Darcy Hastings, will you marry me?"

I can feel the tears running down my cheeks but there is nothing I can do to stop them. I haven't felt the pure joy that I was feeling in this moment in a long time.

"Oh my god, Reed. Yes, yes of course I'll marry you!" I say as he stands and takes me in his arms.

I reach up and wrap my hands around his neck and cover his mouth with mine. Around us, I'm faintly aware of the other patrons clapping and congratulating us, but I'm focused on Reed, my new fiancé.

"Here," Reed says as he grabs my left hand.

I watch as he gently places the ring onto my finger, and I lift my hand to look at the diamond sparkling in the dim restaurant lights. I reach up and kiss him again before we take our seats.

"I'm so happy!" I say as Reed grabs both my hands and runs his thumb over my new ring.

"Me too, angel. I've never been happier. I also wanted you to know that I asked Travis for his blessing, which he was very happy to give. I figured that was the next best thing to asking your father."

"Really? I can't believe you did that. It was such a sweet thing to do. He was really okay with it?"

"Yeah, he was great. He said as long as he can still be your best friend, he was glad we were happy together."

"That sounds like Trav."

"He's a pretty decent guy."

"Yeah, he really is," I say with a smile.

After a few moments, the waitress brings over our desserts and congratulates us on our engagement. We both thank her and then quickly finished off our meal.

Reed again reaches for my hand across the table and asks if I want to go home, or if I want to head out somewhere else to continue the celebrations. Just as I'm about to respond, he suddenly pulls back from me, taking the ring box with him and placing it slowly back in his pocket.

"Reed?" I ask as his gaze focuses over my shoulder. He doesn't respond and seems to have frozen, as I turn my head to follow his gaze.

My eyes lock on a beautiful, tall, blond woman who is walking towards our table with a megawatt smile directed at Reed. I don't think she even notices me sitting here.

"Reed Lewis; I thought that was you sitting there. How have you been, Darling?"

"Stacey," he replies. "It's good to see you again."

I watch as *Stacey* places her hand on Reed's forearm and strokes him as she leans into him.

"You have to tell me what you've been doing with yourself."

"Just working in security," Reed replies quickly, not taking his eyes off her and still not introducing me.

I'm starting to feel very uncomfortable, and very much like the third wheel, so I decide to quietly excuse myself. I quickly pick up my purse and make my way to the bathroom. Reed doesn't even acknowledge that I've spoken, and still doesn't look away from Stacey.

When I look back before heading into the hallway leading to the bathrooms, I notice that the woman has made herself comfortable in my seat and is holding Reed's hand across the table. I have a horrible feeling of dread come over me suddenly, and I rush into the bathroom.

After composing myself a little, I make my way back out to the dining room but stop once again in the hallway to take in the sight in front of me. Stacey's hand is caressing Reed's face, and he's smiling at her. He no longer looks shocked by the woman's presence, but quite comfortable sitting there with her in my place. I start to feel really unwell, and quickly pull out my phone to send a text to Chester to bring the car around to the front.

Holding myself together as best I can, I slowly make my way to the front door of the restaurant, passing by our table slowly. Reed is completely oblivious to my presence, so I continue on out the door, straight into the waiting car.

"Is Mr Lewis on his way out, Miss Darcy?" Chester asks looking confused.

"Ah no, Chester. Reed met up with a friend inside. It's just me. Can you take me home please?"

"Of course, Miss."

As we drive home in silence, I try to get my head around what the hell just happened. One minute I'd been enjoying the greatest night of my life, the next I'm going home alone, having been engaged just five short minutes.

As I walk inside the front door of Trav's house in a daze, he appears in the front entrance.

"Hey, Sweetheart," he calls excitedly. "How was your night?"

I look up at him and can't help the tear that slips down my cheek.

"Darce? What's wrong, honey? Where's Reed?"

"At the restaurant," I reply softly.

"Okay … why isn't he here with you?"

"I don't know?" I respond numbly.

Travis grabs me around the waist and walks me into the kitchen, sitting me down on a barstool. He cups my cheeks with his hands and looks straight into my eyes.

"What happened, Darcy? Why didn't Reed come home with you?"

"He asked me to marry him. I said yes!"

"That's great, sweetheart. I'm so happy for you. Congratulations."

"Thanks," I reply. "But something happened, and I don't know what to make of it."

"Okay," Travis responds.

I give Trav the details of what occurred after Reed proposed, and he listens quietly.

"What do I do, Trav? I'm so confused."

"Yeah, that's a strange one. I'm not sure, Darce."

"Can I sleep in my old room tonight?" I ask him. "I just feel a bit weird going into our suite when I'm not sure what's going on with him and that woman."

"Of course, honey, whatever you need. Do you want me to tell him where you are if he's looking for you?"

"Yeah, that's fine. Though, by the way he was acting, I doubt he even remembers I exist."

"I'm sure that's not true, sweetheart. He's probably going out of his mind wondering where the hell you went."

"It's more likely that he hasn't even noticed I'm gone yet. I think I'll head up to bed now. Thanks, Trav."

I reach up and press a kiss to his cheek.

"Night, baby girl. Everything will work out. You'll see."

I smile as I turn towards the stairs.

"I hope so."

The next morning, I wake disoriented. Sitting up quickly, I look around the room and realize I'm back in my old suite, and everything from the previous night comes flooding back. Reed's obviously not come looking for me. The feeling I get once that realization sets in makes me feel sick. I need to know what's going on, so I get up and quickly dress.

I slowly make my way towards Reed's suite, and I'm about to knock, when I hear his muffled voice through the door. Freezing at the sound, I press my ear against the wood.

"Did you want some coffee, Stacey?" I hear him call out.

"That would be great, baby, I'll just jump in the shower first though."

I'm going to be sick—physically sick. I turn from Reed's door and run as fast as I can up the stairs towards my room. On the landing, I bump into Travis but push my way past without saying a word.

"Darcy … Darce! Sweetheart, what's wrong. Are you okay?" Travis calls after me.

I can't stop; I have to get to the bathroom. I make it just in time before emptying my stomach into the toilet bowl. Travis follows me in and pulls my hair back from my face while rubbing my back.

"Sweetheart, are you okay?"

I collapse back against the bathroom tiles, with my hand covering my mouth. I look up at Trav's concerned face and shake my head.

"Are you not well? Do you need me to call a doctor?"

Again, all I can do is shake my head.

"Talk to me, Darcy. I can't help if I don't know what's going on."

I go to stand up, but Trav bends down and scoops me up into his arms and carries me towards my bed. Once I'm sitting on the edge, he looks at me with worried eyes.

"Talk," he says.

I look at his concerned face and can't stop the tears from falling. Trav reaches up and gently brushes them away with his thumb.

"Reed never came looking for me last night."

"What? Are you sure? Perhaps he found you in here sleeping and didn't want to disturb you."

I shake my head and continue.

"No, as soon as I woke, I went down to his room, our room, to speak to him, but I heard him talking to the woman from the restaurant. She'd obviously spent the night, Trav. He was asking her if she wanted coffee before her shower. If she had just popped over this morning, she wouldn't be needing to use his shower now, would she?"

Travis wraps his arm around my shoulder and pulls me into his warm body.

"God, Darcy, I don't know what to say. It just doesn't sound like

Reed at all. He adores you; has since the day you climbed out of my pool in that skimpy bikini. I knew it then ,and I know it now. He loves you. It has to be some kind of misunderstanding."

"Then why hasn't he even come to find me, Trav?"

"I don't know, baby, I don't know."

The next few days pass in a blur. I haven't seen or spoken to Reed, although Travis told me that he'd asked for a week's leave to deal with some personal issues.

I keep myself busy with work, and instead of having Reed as my bodyguard, Travis organizes for Nash to be my permanent shadow.

Late one night while sitting on the couch with Travis watching TV, he asks me how I'm doing.

"I'm just so confused, Trav. One minute I'm being proposed to, and the next I'm being ignored. It's been four days now and I've not heard a word from him. Obviously, my engagement is over. I've worked that much out at least."

"Are you sure?" Trav asks me.

"Yeah, I'm sure. How can we go forward after this?"

Trav just looks at me and shakes his head.

"I don't know, sweetheart."

"When do you leave for the next leg of your tour?" I ask.

"In two days," he replies sadly.

"Shit," I respond. "Then I'll really be alone. I don't want to stay here by myself knowing Reed's just downstairs with that woman in his bed. Argh, I hate this, Trav. I don't even have my things—everything's in his room."

"Come with me," Travis suddenly blurts out quickly.

"What? Come where?"

"On tour with me. It'll be a blast. It's only four months this time, but you can come home whenever you've had enough. I've got plenty of room on my bus, and you know Jesse will let you work on the road."

"I don't know, Trav. How am I supposed to organize everything before then … when will I pack? I'll have to sort things out with Jesse and then go purchase a whole new wardrobe."

"Let me handle everything. You deal with Jesse; I'll sort everything else. Do you trust Peggy and I with your wardrobe and everything else you'll need?"

"Yeah of course, but are you sure about this, Trav. I don't want to cramp your style."

"Sweetheart, you could never cramp my style. You are my style," he laughs.

Chapter Forty Five

• REED •

It takes me about eight days to sort out the issue with Stacey. Eight horribly long days without my girl, but now that the situation is handled, I need to speak to Darcy and explain everything. Getting her involved before now would have caused more problems for everyone and I didn't want Darcy to have to deal with that.

Making my way upstairs to her room where I knew she would have been sleeping, I softly knock on the door. It's early and I don't want to scare her. I know Travis left on his tour the previous day, so it's just Peggy, Darcy and I in the house. Not hearing any response, I knock again and call out her name before slowly pushing her door open.

As a small amount of light filters into the room, I notice that Darcy is not in her bed and it's already made. I look around and then make my way towards her bathroom. I call out a second time, but again get no response. Looking around the room, I notice that there are no personal items anywhere. There is nothing in her closet, although I expect that, as all her things are in our suite.

Looking back towards her bed, a sheet of notepaper sitting on top of her nightstand, catches my eye. I walk towards it but stop short when all the breath leaves my body in an instant, as I notice what's sitting on top of the note.

I bend down and pick up Darcy's engagement ring before reaching for the note and reading her soft girlish handwriting.

Reed

I'm returning your ring, as it's very clear our
short engagement and relationship is over.
I have gone on tour with Travis, so I hope you will give
me the space I need to get over you by not contacting me.
I hope you find happiness in your life, Reed.
I will always love you in some way.

Darcy xx

"Fuuuck!" I yell as I drop the note to the floor. What the hell have I done? I should have spoken with her. Asked her to give me some time to sort this thing out with Stacey.

"Fuck!" I scream again as I smash my fist through the drywall in her bedroom. "Dammit!"

Racing back to my room, I grab my phone and try Darcy's number. There is no way I'm going to let her go that easily. I need to explain things. As I expect, my call goes straight to voicemail, so I try Trav's number. After a few rings he picks up.

"Lewis, what can I do for you?"

"Travis, I need to speak to Darcy, please."

"Sorry mate, she doesn't want to talk to you."

"Please, Travis. I need to explain. I know things probably look bad from her side."

"Mate, they look fucking awful. Darce is crushed. She hasn't left her bed since we got here, and she can't stop crying. She needs time to sort herself out and you're going to give it to her. She'll contact you when she's ready."

"And if she never does?"

"Then you'll just have to learn to live with that."

"Fuck!" I say as I run my hand through my hair.

"I can't live without her, Travis."

"I understand, honestly I do, but this is her decision now. Give her some time, and when we get back, I'm sure she'll be ready to speak with you."

"Four months! You expect me to wait four months to speak with her?"

"I expect you to wait for as long as she needs you to."

"I'm not giving up."

"I'd be disappointed if you did."

"So, I shouldn't try calling her again later on?"

"I'd leave it. I'll let her know that you've called though, okay?"

"Fuuuck! Can you tell her that I'm sorry, and that I love her."

"Will do. She'll come around, Lewis. I know she loves you. She's just really hurting right now."

"Look after her, okay?"

"Always. Bye, Lewis."

Chapter Forty Six

• DARCY •

2 Months Later

"Hey, sweetheart. Whatcha doing?" Travis asks me.

"Just working on a campaign for Jesse," I reply.

"That's still working out okay?"

"Yeah, it's good. How was sound-check?"

"Good. No issues. You coming to the show tonight or you gonna stay in?"

"I was thinking of going tonight. Is that okay?"

"Yeah, of course it is. You know you're always welcome. Do you want a front of house seat, or a backstage/wings pass?"

"Just a backstage, I think. I like hanging with the guys while you're on."

"Done. I know they like having you back there too. I'm actually trying a new song tonight … see what kind of reaction it gets before I consider it for a single. Would love your opinion."

"You know I love all your stuff. I don't see how this one would be any different."

"It's just a bit of a different sound for me, that's all."

"What's it about?" I ask him.

"You'll hear it tonight."

"You're not going to tell me?"

"Nope."

Later that night, I'm backstage watching Travis perform from the wings, when one of his roadies, Ryker, sidles up next to me.

"Hey, sweet cheeks, you looking forward to hearing the new song?"

"Yeah, Trav mentioned he has a new one. Said it was a little different to his usual stuff."

"Yeah, you could say that," Ryker replies. "I'm pretty sure it's the next song up."

"Oh cool. I'll hang here for a bit longer then. Thanks!"

I watch as the crowd screams and yells for Trav as he finishes his song. The lights go down and I can just make out Trav moving to a stool in the center of the stage. He starts playing the intro to a soft ballad on his acoustic guitar, as a lone spotlight draws all the attention straight to him.

"This is a new song I recently wrote for the most amazing person in my life. This one's for you, Darcy girl," he says as he turns to me in the wings and gives me a wink.

The crowd goes nuts again, whistling and hollering as Trav starts to sing. Me—I stand there in shock.

The song is beautiful. A romantic love song to anyone else listening, but from Trav to me, I know it has another meaning.

He sings of the deep love between two friends, rather than between two lovers. Him spilling his guts to me about how he feels about me, and how all he wants for my life is happiness with the man I love. There are hints throughout, that only I would be aware of. He's talking about Reed, not about himself. I can't help but let the tears fall as I listen to him sing. I notice Ryker appear at my side again with a box of tissues.

"That man sure does love you," he says with a soft smile.

"Yeah, I know. The feeling's mutual," I reply with a sniff.

"Lucky son-of-a-bitch," he mutters as he walks off.

I giggle to myself as I watch Trav finish up the song.

Back on the bus, I pull my laptop out and get back to work while I waited for Trav to return from the arena. After about twenty minutes, I hear my phone ringing from the back of the bus and run to grab it. Looking at the screen, I notice it's Reed's sister, Jocelyn. Taking a deep breath, I answer the call.

"Joss, hi," I say.

"Darcy, how are you?"

"I'm okay, thanks. You?"

"Yeah good. I'm here with Jesse."

"Hey, Darce!" I hear Jesse call out.

"Hey, Jesse," I reply with a giggle.

"So, you guys are all good then."

"Yeah, we're all good," Joss replies with a smile in her voice.

"Are you guys in luuurve?" I tease.

"Moving along," Joss replies. "So, when are you coming home? We miss you."

"Not entirely sure yet, but it's likely I'll stay with Travis for the length of the tour."

"That's another two months, Darcy!"

"Yeah, I know but I'm not sure I'm ready to come home yet."

There's an awkward silence on the other end of the line.

"Joss, you there?" I ask.

"Yeah, I'm here."

"How is he?" I practically whisper.

I listen as Joss lets out a long breath.

"I'd be lying if I said he was doing okay, Darce. He's a wreck, a shadow of himself. He doesn't leave his suite; I think he'd be lucky if he showered once a week. He's hurting—a lot."

"I get it, I feel much the same—except for the showering part. The showering happens daily here. I miss him."

"Then call him, Darcy. I don't understand. If you're both miserable without each other, why can't you be together and be happy. Talk to him. He deserves at least that."

"I can't talk to him over the phone. What we have to talk about needs to be done face-to-face."

"Then come home, Darcy. You need each other—that much is obvious."

"I miss you guys. Talk soon?"

"Okay," she exhales heavily. "Bye, Darce."

"Bye, Joss".

A little while later, Travis returns to the bus.

"There you are. I was wondering where you ran off to."

"The song was amazing, Trav. Honestly, beautiful. Thank you so much … for everything; but I think I need to go home."

He looks at me with a mischievous grin.

"Good, it worked then. Go get your man, sweetheart."

Chapter Forty Seven

• REED •

Picking up my iPad, I settle on the couch for my daily torture session. I've set up a google alert with Darcy's name, and because she's traveling with Travis, there's been at least one mention of her each day since she'd left in some sort of online report.

It's not like I'm stalking her or anything; I just need to see that she's okay. The pain of seeing that she's obviously back with Travis, is just the price I have to pay. But I love her, and I want to see her happy. If that's with Travis again, then that's where she should be, as much as it's killing me. I've watched her with him once before, and I will just have to do it again. Yeah, this time will be a hell of a lot harder, and it will tear my already shattered heart to shreds, but I'll do it for her.

The first article I come across is a report about Trav's concert two nights earlier. Apparently, he sung a new song—a love song—a new style for him, and he'd dedicated it to Darcy. Just to add to the crushing feeling my heart is already experiencing, there is also a photo of Darcy standing in the wings watching him, with tears in her eyes. She looks absolutely beautiful, but her tears are for Travis, not me, and that hurts. Even after two months, it still hurts like hell.

I throw the iPad onto the coffee table and lean back into the couch with my hands behind my head and close my eyes. After a few moments of peace, there's a knock at my door.

"Thanks, Peggy, but I don't feel like lunch today."

There's another knock.

"Go away, Joss," I call out.

Another knock.

"For God's sake, let me wallow in peace," I call out as I get up to answer the door.

I quickly pull the door open in a huff and I'm utterly shocked by who's standing there.

"Darcy?" I whisper.

"Hi, Reed."

Chapter Forty Eight

• DARCY •

I stand at Reed's door with my heart hammering in my chest. Looking into his beautiful blue eyes, everything I feel for him comes rushing back in an instant. No matter what's happened between him and Stacey, I know I love him and need him back in my life.

"Can I come in?" I ask him as he just stares at me. "Reed?"

"Of course, yeah … sorry. Come in. Sorry … sorry about the mess. Let me just clean this shit up."

"Leave it, Reed, it doesn't matter."

"I'll just be a minute. Have a seat."

"Reed … leave it, it doesn't matter to me."

"Can I at least get you a drink?"

"No, I'm good thanks. Just come and sit with me."

"When did you get back?" he asks me.

"Just this morning."

He nods at me as he nervously plays with his fingers in his lap.

"You look beautiful … but then I suppose you always do," he says with a sad smile.

"Thanks," I reply. "You look good too. Different, but good."

"Yeah, right. I haven't really got out much. I've kind of let things go a bit."

"You'll always be handsome to me, Reed."

I watch as he winces a little, but I have to agree, he has let himself go a bit. His body is still in amazing shape, probably even better shape than before, but he looks tired; really tired. His hair is a lot longer and shaggier all over, and it looks like he hasn't shaved since I left.

"How have you been?" I ask him.

"Do you want an honest answer to that question?" he replies with a raised brow.

"Yes, I do. I want an honest answer."

I watch as he closes his eyes and rubs his forehead with his hand.

"Honestly, Darcy, it's been bloody hell. Two months of this continuous pain in my chest, that I just can't fucking get rid of."

I look at him and all I see is pain—obviously more than I'm experiencing too. I'd had Travis to help me deal with things; he'd had no one.

"I'm so sorry that I left without giving you the chance to explain, Reed."

"Why did you?"

"I was so hurt. You'd just proposed, and then suddenly it was like I didn't exist to you anymore."

Reed looks down at the floor.

"I'm so sorry for everything that happened that night, Darce. I handled everything so badly. I would give anything for a do-over."

"Can I ask you a question?"

"Of course, anything."

"Do you still love me?"

Reed looks at me like I'm speaking a foreign language. He grabs my hand and looks straight into my eyes.

"Of course, I still love you."

"Do you still want me?"

"More than anything," he whispers with his eyes closed. "But I know that you're back with Travis again."

"Travis and I aren't together, Reed. He's been nothing but a good friend the past two months."

"But I read about that love song he wrote you, Darcy. I saw the photo of your reaction to it."

"Travis wrote that song for us, Reed. That song was what made me realize that I needed to come home to you."

"I don't know what to think anymore, Darcy," Reed says as he shakes his head.

"I feel like I really need to hold you while we talk. Would that be okay?" I ask him.

"More than okay, angel," he whispers again.

Reed sits towards the front of the couch, so I stand from my spot on the opposite sofa and place my hands on his shoulders. He shuts his eyes again as I straddle my legs over his lap.

"Would it be okay if I wrap my legs around you?" I whisper. "I just want to feel close to you."

"God yes," he replies with his eyes still closed.

I wrap my legs around Reed's back and hook my ankles together. I then place both my hands on his cheeks, feeling his overgrown beard underneath my palms.

"Open your eyes and look at me, Reed."

He does so and I stroke his face again.

"I need you to explain to me what happened that night. But before you do, I need you to know something."

"Okay," he replies hesitantly.

"I need you to know that I love you; that I never stopped loving you, and that I missed you so damn much I thought I was going to suffocate from the pain."

"Angel," he groans. "I never stopped loving you either. You're all I thought about for two long months."

"Do you still want to be with me, Reed?"

"Of course I do, baby. I want nothing more."

"Okay, then let's talk about things, so we can get back to what matters—being together. What happened that night, Reed?"

I watch as Reed takes a deep breath and starts his story.

"The woman that came up to our table that night is Stacey

Rivers—my ex-fiancée."

"You've been engaged before?" I ask shocked.

"Yeah, about twelve years ago when I was twenty-one."

"Why did you never tell me that, Reed?"

"Honestly, it wasn't a good time in my life, I was young, and I've tried to forget about it. I haven't seen Stacey in about ten years."

"What happened between you two?" I ask.

"Stacey and I were high school sweethearts. We were each other's first. However, she soon became very clingy, and when we graduated, I broke up with her as we were going away to different colleges. Stacey wasn't happy about it and continued to call me every day. I started seeing other girls, but whenever she found out about it, she would threaten the girls with all sorts of horrible things. She also made me out to be some sort of monster, saying that I had repeatedly sexually assaulted her during our relationship. Pretty soon no one wanted to have anything to do with me, and I had to move away."

"God, Reed," I say as I run my fingers over his beard.

"I changed my number when I moved, and never told her where I was going, but after searching for me for about a year, she found me again. She was relentless, and soon after I had to get a restraining order against her. It didn't make much difference though. The cops never did anything because she hadn't physically hurt me in any way; she was just a nuisance. A little while after this, I had a very bad lapse in judgement, and I slept with her … just the once, but unfortunately she fell pregnant."

"Oh god, Reed, no."

"I thought I was doing the right thing by asking her to marry me, even though I didn't love her. She started planning the wedding straight away, and also planning for the birth of our baby, but at around sixteen weeks, she miscarried. She was obviously devastated. I however am ashamed to admit that I was relieved. Stacey went into a deep depression and was eventually admitted to a hospital for treatment. She never fully recovered and has had mental health issues ever since. She's been in and out of treatment facilities her whole life. After we lost the baby, her parents told me that she had been unstable even before she met me. After a few months of her receiving treatment, I finally had the guts to call off the wedding. She was surprisingly okay with it, and we went our separate ways. That was the last time I saw her up until that night when she approached our table."

"Wow, Reed, I don't know what to say. I'm so sorry you went through all that, baby."

"When I joined the military, it was easy to forget about her and move on, you know? My whole life changed after that. While I was deployed, I heard that she had gotten married, so I was really happy for her. Towards the beginning of this year though, I sadly heard through an old friend, that she had lost her husband in a car accident, and understandably her mental health suffered again also. Running into her at the restaurant that night was a total coincidence. When I looked up and saw her, I was frozen with shock. I didn't really know how to react, except that I didn't want her to know that I was engaged, because I didn't know how she would react. I didn't want to introduce you to her because if she knew your name, I knew you could become a target for her. After you left the table, I quickly worked out that she was extremely unstable. It seemed like for her; no time had passed at all. She was talking about our upcoming wedding and the baby. She was picking out names and then talking about floral arrangements—it was really sad actually. I knew from previous experience though, that it was better to play along until I could get her somewhere safe. I knew that you had left the restaurant, and I was so thankful for that, but also terrified of what you must have been thinking. While we were still at the restaurant, I managed to escape to the bathroom for a few minutes and I was able to contact her parents. They live a few hours away and weren't able to get there until the following morning. They begged me to take her home and look after her until they were able to pick her up. I reluctantly agreed and took her home. I tried so many times to pop out to speak to you but she was so erratic that I just didn't trust her. I promise you, Darcy; we never shared a bed. I let her sleep in my bed and I slept on the couch. I never touched her in any way, and I didn't let her touch me, apart from a few times where she grabbed my hand in the restaurant."

"I believe you, Reed."

"Anyway, the next day, her parents eventually arrived around lunch time, but she refused to go with them. She wanted me to stay with her because in her mind, I was her fiancé. We decided that I would go with them back home and we had her admitted to a mental health facility straight away. Her parents thanked me and then I made my way back home but by the time I got back, you were gone. Seeing your ring sitting on your nightstand gutted me, baby."

"Was it you who put a hole in my wall?" I ask.

"Sorry, it couldn't be helped."

"I'm so, so sorry, Reed. When I went to confront you that morning and I heard you two talking in our suite, I got physically sick. I couldn't believe that you would bring another woman back to our apartment on the night of our engagement. I was so hurt and angry that I didn't stop to think clearly about it. If I had, I would have realized that you would have never done anything like that to me—that there was a very good explanation. I'm so sorry, baby. I'm sorry that I stole those two months from us, and I'm sorry that I hurt you so badly. Do you think you will ever be able to forgive me?"

"It's done."

"I'm serious, Reed."

"So am I, angel. I could have tried harder to get a message to you and that's on me."

I can't stop the tears from flowing then. I wrap my arms tight around Reed's neck and pull myself further into his warm body.

"God, I missed you, baby," he whispers in my ear.

"I'm so sorry, Reed. Please take me back," I cry into his neck.

"Darcy, you were never not mine. From the moment I laid eyes on you, you were mine. You will always be mine. I will never let you go—do you understand me?"

I pull back to look into his beautiful blue eyes.

"Yes, I'm yours."

"Good, now come here."

Reed pulls me in close and covers my mouth with his in the most passionate and drugging kiss I have ever received. When we break apart, we are both panting.

"I need to take care of a few things this afternoon, baby, but tonight I'm taking you out and we are finally going to celebrate. How does that sound?"

"Sounds perfect."

I unwrap my legs from around Reed's waist, stand up and start to make my way to the door.

"Nash will be ready for you at seven, okay, angel?"

"Okay," I reply with a smile.

"I love you."

"I love you too."

"See you soon, baby."

I blow him a kiss and make my way back to my room feeling the happiest I have in two months.

Chapter Forty Nine

• REED •

I have my girl back, but I need to make tonight a night she will never forget—for all the right reasons this time.

My first stop is Travis. I have an idea that I need his help for, but I want to know if it'll be possible with his schedule. I give him a call and he answers after a few rings.

"Lewis, what can I do for you?"

"Travis … I need to thank you for sending Darcy back to me."

"I didn't send her anywhere, mate. She just needed a little nudge to help her realize where she really wanted to be."

"Well thanks anyway. She told me about the song. Where are you at the moment?"

"I'm actually in Charlotte, so not that far away. Why's that?"

"Do you have a show tonight?"

"No, we have the next two nights off. What do you need, Lewis?"

"I have an idea and was wondering if you'd be able to help me with it."

"I'll see what I can do. What's your plan?"

After sorting things with Travis, my next call is to my sister, Joss.

"Hey, big brother, what's up?"

"Darcy's back."

"What? Oh my god, Reed. Have you seen her?"

"Yeah, she came to our suite today. We had a huge talk and everything's good. We're all good. We're back together."

"Oh, Reed, I'm so happy for you. How do you feel?"

"I can't remember the last time I felt this happy. Well actually I can, but then that night didn't turn out how I'd planned, so I'm having a do-over tonight, and I need your help."

"Whatever you need, big brother. What can I do?"

Next stop for me is to purchase a new suit. Since Darcy left, I'd spent all my time either at home or in the gym, and I'd bulked up quite a bit in the last two months—the suits I currently owned no longer fit. Following my purchase, I spent some time in the barber's chair, getting a haircut and removing the two months worth of growth that had overtaken my face. Once I'd made it home, I made a few final preparations before I got ready for the most important night of my life.

Heading into *Bar Melee*, I notice that Joss has definitely come through for me. All the team from Great Scott Design is here, along with most of Trav's family, as I know Darcy has become quite close with them.

"Hey, big brother. How are you feeling?"

"Hey. Yeah, a bit nervous, but I'm good. Thanks for organizing everyone."

"Of course! You look great by the way. I'm so glad you got a haircut and got rid of that caveman beard. So much better. I can see my handsome brother again."

"Haha, thanks! Is Travis here yet?"

"Yeah, he's out the back getting ready with the band. I told him it's probably better for him to stay back there until it's time anyway. Keeps the surprise that way."

"Great, thanks."

I can feel my heart beating a million miles an hour. I don't know why I'm so nervous. She already said yes to my last proposal, so I'm just hoping she'll say yes again. I guess the past few months may make her reconsider marrying me, at least for a while anyway. Suddenly I'm starting to second-guess my decision. Feeling a vibration in my pocket, I reach in to fish out my phone, finding a text from Nash stating he's ten minutes away with Darcy. No time for second-guessing.

Chapter Fifty

• DARCY •

I'm really looking forward to a night out dancing with Reed. My favorite club; my favorite man and some good music—nothing better to get our relationship back on track. I knew I had missed him; but seeing Reed again this morning brought back so many crazy feelings, I can't wait to wrap my arms around his body again.

Nash helps me from the car and quietly closes the door behind me.

"Reed will be waiting for you inside, Miss Hastings," Nash says with a smile.

"Thanks, Nash. You coming in too?"

"Of course, Miss. Always two," he replies.

"Always two," I respond with a smile.

I head towards the front of the club, where Nash gives the bouncer a nod, before the doors are opened for us.

Once inside, I look around for Reed, but actually catch sight of Joss. I hurry over to her with a smile.

"Hey, girl, I didn't know you were going to be here tonight!"

"Darcy! It's so good to see you. We've missed you so much!" Joss replies with a giant bear hug.

Jesse is by Joss's side, and I reach over and pull him in for a hug too.

"Hey, you," I say as I kiss him on the cheek.

"Hey, sweetheart. It's so good to have you back. I've missed having my partner around the place."

"I know. I'm so sorry I took off like that. I have no idea why you keep me around, Jesse. You're too good."

"I could never get rid of you, sweetheart, I love you too darn much."

"I love you too, Jesse. So, you guys are good?" I ask looking between the two of them.

"Yeah, we're good," Jesse replies as he wraps his arm around Joss's waist.

I smile happily at the two of them. I really do love Jesse, and I'm so glad that he's finally found happiness with Joss. They are perfect together.

"So, have you seen your handsome brother anywhere around here?" I ask Joss as I look around the club.

"I suppose that would be me," comes a super sexy voice from over my shoulder.

I quickly turn around to find Reed standing there with a huge grin on his face.

"Holy shit, babe! You look sexy as hell," I gasp as I stand back and admire my man. I can't help but let my eyes devour his delicious body and take their fill. "Seriously, Reed, you look hot! What gives?"

"What? I can't try and look nice for my girl on our first night back together in over two months?"

"Well yeah, but I'm going to seriously have to hold onto you tight tonight—the women in here are going to be throwing themselves at you from every angle. I actually think it might be best if you just take me home now, and have your filthy way with me," I say with a wicked grin.

"Woah gross, seriously TMI, Darcy," Joss says with a disgusted look on her face.

"What? I can't help it! He seriously looks so good. I just want to run my tongue over every inch of his perfection."

"Ewww, right that's it—I'm out. Dance with me, babe before I throw up," Joss says as she pulls Jesse to the dance floor.

I can't take my eyes off Reed. He always looks good—too good, but tonight he was mouth-watering.

"I need to get my body as close to yours as I can right now," I say to Reed in a soft whisper. "Dance with me?"

"I'd love to," he replies with a chuckle, as he grabs my hand and leads me to the dance floor.

As I wrap my arms around his neck, Reed pulls me in close at the waist.

"I love this dress on you," he whispers in my ear. "So damn sexy, angel."

"I knew you liked this one, that's why I wore it." Even before we started dating, I always saw how he watched me heatedly whenever I wore it.

"You make me weak in the knees, you know that? Every time I look at you, my heart does backflips. You are the most beautiful woman I have ever met, and I have to pinch myself to make sure that you're real and not just some goddess-like creature that I have created in my mind. I have to continually remind myself that you are actually mine."

"I'll always be yours, Reed—always," I reply softly.

"Really?" he asks hopefully.

"Always."

"Then I want to ask you a question."

"What is it?" I ask as I notice the music suddenly go quiet, and Reed slowly dropping to one knee while taking my hand in his.

"Reed?" I gasp as it kicks in what he's actually doing.

"Angel, the last time I did this, I made a complete mess of things. Darcy … you are everything in my life that is good. You are the most compassionate and courageous woman I have ever known and being without you these past two months was the most painful experience of my life. I am nothing without you, baby, and I never want to live another day without you in my life. Darcy Hastings, angel—will you make me the happiest man alive and become my wife? Marry me."

"Reed," I whisper as I look into his eyes—completely enamored with him. "Nothing would make me happier, baby. Of course, I'll marry you," I reply as I place my palms on his cheeks and bend down to kiss him passionately on the mouth.

We eventually break apart, and Reed places my beautiful ring back on my finger, just before I pull him up and wrap my arms around him. This time, his hands are on my face as we seal our commitment with another kiss.

All around us, I hear applause, cheers and whistles as I stare into Reed's eyes. The music is just starting up again when Reed grabs me around the waist.

"Dance with me, angel."

"Okay," I reply with a loving smile.

As the music starts to take hold, I wrap my arms around Reed's neck, and we sway into each other with our foreheads pressed together.

Soon after, the singer begins the first verse of the song, and I suddenly stop moving. I know that voice almost better than any other. I swing my head around to look at the stage, and there stands Travis, microphone in hand, singing the song he wrote for Reed and me.

I quickly look back to Reed with wide eyes.

"Did you organize this?" I ask him with tears in my eyes.

"Yeah angel, I did. Are you happy?"

"You are the most beautiful man, Reed. I'm so happy. Thank you," I whisper.

I turn my head back to watch Travis perform, and place my cheek against Reed's chest, feeling every beat of his heart as we continued to dance and listen to our song.

As the song comes to a finish, I watch as Travis jumps down from the stage and heads towards us. When he's within hugging distance, I pull him close and wrap my arms tightly around his shoulders.

"Thank you, Travis," I sob into his chest. "That was beautiful. I don't know what I would have done these past few months without you. You have changed my life in so many ways, and I have no way of showing you how much I truly do appreciate and love you."

"I have a request," he says with that beautiful, dimpled smile.

"Anything," I reply. Travis leans in and whispers in my ear.

"Save a tiny piece of that beautiful heart of yours just for me, okay?"

"You got it," I reply as I pull him back in for a giant cuddle and a kiss on the cheek.

As we separate, Travis reaches over and takes Reed's hand in a handshake.

"Congrats, mate. She deserves nothing but the best, and I know you'll be that for her."

"Thanks, Travis. You don't know how much I appreciate all this."

"It's no trouble at all. I reckon it's time to celebrate, yeah?"

"Sounds good," we both reply as Trav races back onto the stage.

"What's up y'all?" Travis calls over the microphone as the crowd goes crazy around us. "I'm Travis Danvers, and I'm here tonight to celebrate the engagement of two of my closest friends—Darcy and Reed. I wish you both a lifetime of love and happiness. I love you both. This night is yours."

With that, the band starts up and the crowd pours onto the dance floor. Reed and I stay on the floor dancing for one song, before he pulls me off to grab us a drink. Standing at the bar, I look around the room and for the first time notice all my work colleagues from Great Scott Design, and all of Trav's family. I am so surprised; I burst into tears again!

"Angel, what's wrong?" Reed asks me worriedly.

"Nothing … I just love you so damn much. I was so enthralled in you earlier; I didn't even notice all our friends and family are here too. I can't believe you did all this in just one afternoon. You are incredible, Reed!"

"Anything for you, angel."

Epilogue

• REED •

"Angel? I need to head off, babe," I call into our bedroom, as Darcy is getting ready for work.

"Okay. Kiss me goodbye?" she yells back.

I sneak in behind her and wrap my arms around her waist as she fixes her makeup in the bathroom mirror.

"Have I ever not kissed you goodbye?"

"No, but maybe you're getting tired of the goodbye kiss."

"Angel, I will never tire of kissing you; ever. Besides, what sort of husband would I be if I didn't kiss my wife goodbye on our one-and-a-half-year anniversary."

"Really? One and a half?" she giggles.

"Yeah. What's funny about that?"

"You're so adorable, celebrating half year anniversaries."

"Babe, I celebrate every day that I get to spend with you."

"I know you do. You're so corny—but I love you more than I know how to say."

I take the mascara from Darcy's hand, place it on the vanity and spin her to face me.

"You are everything that is good in my life."

"I know that too," she smiles at me. "Have a good day."

"You too, angel. Nash is out front, ready when you are. I'll let him know you're not too far away."

"Okay, thanks. Be safe—I love you, Mr Lewis!"

"Love you too, Mrs Lewis," I grin. Damn, calling her that, never gets old.

I make my way out the door, jump in my truck and head to work. A few months after Darcy and I married, I finally started up the security business I'd been planning for a while. Lewis Security is located in a hip, converted warehouse in an upcoming commercial area. Darcy has been instrumental in setting the place up for me, with her key eye for design. The place is modern and edgy, but also really comfortable to work in. The actual building had been a wedding gift from Travis—totally over the top and way too generous, but hey, that's Travis.

The past one-and-a-half years of married life with Darcy, has been a crazy whirlwind. Between Darcy continuing to work with Jesse, and me starting my own business, life has been hectic. Throw being close friends of Travis on top of that, and things couldn't get crazier.

Six months ago, Darcy and I decided to get our own place, after living with Travis for the first year of our marriage. Although we both miss hanging out with Trav when he's not touring, it's been nice to have our own space too.

Trav insists on continuing to pay for personal security for Darcy (even though my company provides it) as she is still hounded daily by the paparazzi—she has become a celebrity in her own right really—which in turn throws me into that category too, I suppose. The people of Nashville love her. They can't get enough, and she loves playing up to the cameras.

Her main security detail, Nash, has been great. He moved over to Lewis Security when I first started up, and has been with Darcy ever since. I must admit, I get a little nervous every time I think about the two of them together—I mean, she fell for her bodyguard once before, so you can't blame me for that. I trust them both though. I know Nash well enough to know he'd never cross that line, and since being married, Darcy has really cut back on 'playing'—except with me. Feisty doesn't even cover it if she catches a woman flirting or hitting on me. She's protective as hell, and I love it.

Every day, I'm thankful that Travis hired me. It certainly wasn't the most conventional way of meeting my wife, and I often still feel guilty about how it all went down, but Travis has never held anything against either of us. He knew he couldn't give Darcy the stable life she was after, so he gave her up for her happiness. He is a hero in my eyes, and after the last few years, my best mate. I know that if anything were to ever happen to me, Darcy would be taken care of, and I feel completely comfortable with that thought. He loves her just as much now as he ever did, even though he's recently started a relationship with a great girl, who also works in the industry. Darcy and Lake have become good friends too. She's an amazing woman and makes Travis happy. She fits in with our little group perfectly.

• DARCY •

A year-and-a-half of marriage. It's crazy how fast that time has gone by. It doesn't feel that long ago that Travis walked me down the aisle toward my stunningly handsome husband. Reed has been everything and more than I could have hoped for in a husband—I love my crazy, hectic life with him—and it's only going to get more so.

I've waited three long weeks to give Reed our good news, but I know how much he loves celebrating milestones, so I thought I would wait until today—even though I pretended this morning that I didn't realize it was our one-and-a-half-year anniversary.

Tonight, we are spending the night in, just the two of us, and I'm counting down the minutes until he walks through the front door.

I have borrowed Peggy for the night, who has prepared an amazing meal, and I have set the table with candles and have placed tealights all around the room. It looks intimate and romantic.

Just as I hear Reed's keys jiggle in the door, I grab the gift box off the counter, and place it in the center of the table. Sitting down in my chair, I wait for Reed to make his way into the dining room.

"Darce, you home, baby?" he calls out.

"In here."

As Reed walks through the door, he stops suddenly with a hitch in his breathe when he notices the room.

"Baby, what's all this?"

"Well, I know how much you love celebrating milestones, and you're always the one to plan surprises, so I thought I'd try and do something nice for you this time."

Reed looks at me with that sexy, cheeky grin I have always loved, and runs his eyes up and down my body taking me in slowly.

"Angel, you honestly don't expect me to sit here and eat a meal with you looking like that, do you?"

"What?" I ask innocently. "You don't like it?"

Reed drops his bag on the floor and walks slowly toward me. He places his hands on my waist and quickly lifts me into his arms. I wrap my legs around his waist as he slams his mouth over mine.

"Do you have any clue what you do to me, Mrs Lewis?"

"I have an idea," I reply with a smile. "It's the same thing you do to me. Now sit, I have a gift for you."

"A gift?" he asks as he sits at the table.

"Mmm hmm."

"You didn't need to get me a gift. It's not even a real anniversary."

"I know, but I've wanted to give it to you for three weeks now and I can't wait any longer, so I thought tonight would be the perfect excuse."

"Okay, what is it—because looking at you right now wearing all that lace, I'd say I already have my gift."

"Well, this is part of your gift, but the rest is in that box on the table."

As Reed turns his head to locate the box on the table, I feel the butterflies in my stomach take full flight. I know he is going to be stoked. We've been waiting for this for a little over a year now, but I'm still nervous about his reaction.

"Should I open it now?" he asks.

I sit down on a chair next to him and nod my head slowly, as he gently pulls the silver satin ribbon from the box. He removes the lid and places it on the table, then pulls back the white tissue paper inside.

"What is it?" he asks with a furrowed brow.

"Pull it out and see."

Reed lifts the fabric from the box and slowly unfolds it, as realization hits and his head suddenly snaps to look at me.

"No!" he says in a disbelieving whisper and his eyebrows nearly hit his hairline.

"Yeah. You're going to be a daddy, Reed," I reply with tears in my eyes.

"I'm going to be a dad?" he asks in shock.

"Aha."

I watch him as he stares at the tiny outfit with disbelief in his watery eyes.

"I'm going to be a dad?" he asks again, still not quite believing it.

"Yeah, baby, you're going to be an amazing dad."

He suddenly grabs me and drags me across his lap and then places a hand gently on my belly.

"My baby is in here?" he asks with tears streaming down his face.

I nod my head at him as I place my hands on his cheeks.

"Yeah. Your nine-week-old beautiful baby is sitting in here waiting to meet their amazing daddy."

"I'm going to be a dad," he whispers again to himself shaking his head. "Thank you, angel," he says looking into my eyes. "Thank you for everything. You make me so happy, and I can't wait to meet our beautiful baby—a part of me and a part of you. Nothing could be better. I love you."

"And I love you."

~ The End ~

Acknowledgements

Firstly, thank you to my husband and daughter who have allowed me to do something that I love. We're a good team who have a lot of fun together. I love you both. Your Rummiking champion!

To Kimberley, who spent hours reading and re-reading, editing and offering suggestions—your help has been appreciated.

To Jirrico, who encouraged me through this process more than anyone. I don't think either of us could have imagined where we would end up after I responded to that first letter. I have loved every moment of our story. You have changed my perspective on so many things, and I have learned so much from you. I look forward to many amazing journey's in the future. I love you.

About The Author

Jane Rhyan has lived in Australia her whole life.
She is married with a daughter and has two maltese chihuahua's.

She has a special kind of love for Henry Cavill, Farmers Union
Iced Coffee and Haigh's Peppermint Frogs.

She loves reading and her favourite authors are Meghan March,
Jodi Ellen Malpas and Sylvia Day.

Falling for Nashville is her first novel, however she plans to write
more in the future—even if no-one reads them!

You can contact her via her Facebook page:
www.facebook.com/janerhyan